Annie Rose

Also by Gary E. Eddey, *The Weather House*

Annie Rose

A novel inspired by more than one true story

Gary E. Eddey

DICKENS POINT PUBLISHING

Library of Congress Control Number: 2026911402

ISBN – HARDBACK: 978-0-9855386-7-5
ISBN – QUALITY SOFTCOVER: 978-0-9855386-8-2
EISBN – E-BOOK: 978-0-9855386-9-9

Typeset: Calibri.
Printed by Lightning Source; Distributed by Ingram and Amazon.

DICKENS POINT PUBLISHING
212-706-4287
115 WEST 227TH STREET
NEW YORK, NY 10463-6701
GARYEDDEY@GMAIL.COM
EDDEY.COM

For My Seven Grandchildren

Block Island, Rhode Island

and

Washington, DC

1912–17

Prologue

Manuscripts, fiction or nonfiction, that explore intelligence missions face numerous challenges. The better the intelligence and the more sophisticated the organization behind it, the more difficult it is to accurately tell the story. Understanding clandestine operations from 100 years ago, when other historical truths become clear, remain almost impossible to figure out. The 1917 Zimmermann Telegrams and the range of "activities" of the British Secret Intelligence Service (SIS), the best intelligence organization in the world at that time, are a prime example. By their very nature these preplanned espionage events are complicated and as resistant to the telling now as the day they were executed.

The story of *Annie Rose* begins before the United States enters the Great European War. In October of 1916, Annie wonders if three mystery men who appear suddenly on Block Island are German spies. Enter the Office of Naval Intelligence (ONI), the only operational United States intelligence agency at the time. Her performance impressed Naval Officers in the ONI and she is offered a position in early 1917. President Wilson clings to his belief that neutrality is the right course of action, despite British Intelligence, the NYPD Bomb Squad, and the Secret Service aware of German sabotage and their well-funded misinformation campaign in the Americas — Mexico, the United States, and Canada. What will it take to change Wilson's perspective?

The action starts on Block Island, Rhode Island, the island home of Annie Rose and her younger sister, Emma. It is the story of Annie's perseverance in the face of her acquired complicated disability, and the love between the sisters as they adapt to the disability that changed their lives. It is the story of how they embrace every difficulty that confronts them, as they strive for a better future, including a multitude of people's attitudes that thwart their dream of leaving Block Island *together*. Those are but a few of the issues faced on their journey to, and on, the mainland.

As the Great War raged in Europe the number of troops in the U.S. Army was fewer than 200,000. The Navy only had 200 ships, in addition to 44 submarines. When Admiral Sims, disguised in plainclothes, sailed to England on a fact-finding mission, he found a Royal Navy overwhelmed, essentially frozen by German U-Boats. He found demoralized British citizens believing Britain would soon lose the war. Alarmed, Sims wired Wilson: Send destroyers and build more. Send cruisers. Build ships for transporting troops.[1] Shortly after in May 1917, with pomp and circumstance, General Pershing leaves New York Harbor for France, to observe for himself the reality of the Western Front. The great General Pershing wires President Wilson: I need 1,000,000 troops. Eventually 2,000,000 sail to Europe.

The intelligence community, except the ONI, was in no better shape, in fact it was non-existent. To be kind, it was in its infancy. In early 1917, Major Ralph Van Deman held meetings at the Army War College in Washington, DC to plan for a Military Intelligence Service (MIS). During this novel, the MIS is born and administratively housed at the Army War College under the direction of Brigadier-General Kuhn. General Kuhn and General Pershing are converts to the need for comprehensive intelligence services. Astonishingly, few other generals in the Army see it that way, a significant obstacle Major Van Deman must confront. Whereas France's military and intelligence branch welcome General Pershing and provide him with near-real-time data, on the home front Major Van Deman struggles to organize a comprehensive, integrated intelligence agency. How does he do it? He starts by holding secret meetings and trainings at the Army War College. It was into this situation that our twenty-two-year-old intelligent flâneur, an astute observer of everything, found herself.

It was anticipated that Annie would fill a role in ONI's Code section.[2] But with her interest in negative intelligence, Van Deman considers her for a section of the MIS that became known as MI 3C. Major Dansey, an important visiting attaché from the British Embassy, contributes significantly to the organizational structure of the MIS. The meetings progress with Dansey's lectures having armed guards at the doors. Annie learns everything possible, and at the same time completes her secret mission assigned by the director of the ONI. As the course progresses, she becomes distracted by inconsistencies in the story of the Zimmermann Telegrams[3] as told by the head of SIS's Room 40. Dansey, the British Naval Attaché, pays close attention to Annie's ideas and reasoning ability. In the second week of training, he realizes Annie is close to figuring out the truth of an important British Intelligence secret, if she has not done so already. Without explanation, he pressures Van Deman to deny her a position, to thwart further scrutiny. After completing her secret mission, they find an excuse to send the sisters back to Block Island, under the pretense of a "much-needed" vacation. Annie understood the repercussions for her career but is fully aware that exposing the Admiralty's secret was not an option.[4] How does she confront this difficulty?

Annie Rose introduces disability culture primarily through the behaviors and actions of Annie, Emma, and the men at the Army War College. While a few officers feel comfortable with her, most do not. Will working with Annie and learning to communicate with her, help? Annie's self-advocacy skills are well developed, and through interactions with the men, demonstrates rugged individualism, yet at the same time stresses the importance of the value of *interdependence,* an essential component of Disability Culture.[5]

The novel is inspired by several true stories of America's fledgling WWI intelligence agencies, that set the stage for a permanent intelligence community decades later.[6 7 8] It is well known that navigating the intrigues of espionage is difficult, but the challenges faced by a significantly disabled, nonverbal young woman in 1917 are as formidable, if not more so.

1

EMMA

A twelve-minute walk from the Old Harbor on Block Island up High Street leads to our home. Before our accident at sea, Annie and I would race up the street and cut that time to a few minutes. Our house is hidden behind the Union House Hotel at the end of a long dirt lane barely wide enough for a car. It holds many memories, both the good and the sorrowful ones, as our mother Lillie says.

To take advantage of Block Island's growing prosperity among hotel owners, in 1883, Lillie's father built the Union House Hotel — but only after he had moved his home 30 yards westward. The hotel is about 300 yards west-southwest of Old Harbor. Although we have telephones, thanks to a telephonic cable that was laid in November of 1886, the Island does not have electricity.

Our two-story house has gabled windows that face east and overlook the Old Harbor and the Atlantic Ocean. Our second-floor bedroom has a view of the other side of the island, where the Narragansett Hotel, the U.S. Weather Bureau, and the New Harbor dock and Hog Penn[i] are located.

Annie is tall and thin, like our father, and I'm short and thin like my mother and brother. All of us have brown hair that lightens considerably

i Pre-WW1 submarines were small and were required to surface frequently. Sailors on the decks of destroyers or battleships looked down at these subs surfacing and then submerging, over and over. They reminded the sailors of porpoises. Porpoises were also called Sea-Pigs. Hence, the subs were in turn called Pig Boats. When the Navy's subs sailed to Block Island, they always docked in the inner basin of the Great Salt Pond. The inner basin became known as the Hog Penn. The term predates WW1.

during the summer months. Whenever Annie and I walk in the front door, we are reminded of my father and brother. To lessen the winter chill of an island in the Atlantic, they built a fireplace, a smaller replica of the one in the hotel lobby and installed iron stoves. They also installed wall mounted kerosene lanterns. They completed these tasks a few months before they drowned. But that wasn't the only tragedy my mother has faced. Her brother Erwin fell from the roof of the Union House, suffered significant brain damage, and is now living in an institution in Connecticut.

Our uncle, Geo Eddey, is the head weather observer at the Block Island Weather Bureau. He is also our stepfather. Last fall, at his request, the Office of Naval Intelligence (ONI) sent John—we never knew his last name—to Block Island to determine the motives of three mysterious men who suddenly appeared on the Island's isolated west side. The ONI referred to the episode as the Weather House Mission because all action centered around the Weather Bureau.

After the mission ended, John asked Annie if she would consider a civilian position with the ONI. I was surprised when the official offer came through, but not surprised that she readily agreed. The ONI had recognized her talent for solving problems, in this case the identification of German spies on our island.

Last fall I asked John for an explanation why officers become interested in espionage.

"What motivates someone to sign up with the Office of Naval Intelligence?"

"It's a combination of things, Emma. Some officers have a desire for adventure that espionage can offer, especially if you're an agent on the ground."

"What's an agent on the ground?"

"They're agents in the field. They recruit foreign spies for us and provide needed information from abroad. Many officers find going behind enemy lines and infiltrating foreign governments exciting."

"Annie has courage to go behind enemy lines, but I don't. Are there other reasons?"

"In addition to adventure and a sense of patriotism, some are bored and want a more impactful career. And a few may wish to leave mundane relationships behind. And there are those who sign up because of financial issues, but officers with large debt often pose a real risk."

Lillie and her sister operated a private school in the Union House. This continued after she leased the Union House to the Manisees Hotel. The Manisees operated it as an annex, but when the number of summer visitors dropped, they used it for staff housing. Well before it was run into the ground and she closed her school, Lillie became the Postmistress of Block Island's Post Office in Old Harbor Village.

My sister and I had long worried that the prosperity of our island might wane. Fishermen could not fetch fair prices for their catches. Storekeepers had little merchandise on their shelves. And the Great European War showed no sign of ending. Geo's eldest son, our cousin, moved to a town near New York City to become a printer. His youngest son moved to South Carolina to work at a Marconi wireless station. His middle son, Wallace, age 27, remained on the island to work the night shift at Bell Telephone. The switchboard is located on Dodge Street above Darius Drugstore. Wallace is fully aware that he will have to leave his island home for better pay. The owner of Darius Drugs recently calculated that Block Island has lost 27% of its population since 1910.

What would Annie and I do? For greater opportunity we'd leave the Island together, but with Annie's disability was that possible. Everything changed the day the Office of Naval Intelligence telegraphed the Weather House with a coded message for Annie.

High Street; The Union House is the second building on the right

2

December 27, 1916

ANNIE

I was staring at the fire when my mother, Lillie, hung up the phone. When she first answered I pushed several logs into the fireplace with my right foot and became mesmerized by the fire's reflection on the beads Emma had strung on the Christmas tree. Lillie had been on the phone for so long, saying so little, I had forgotten she was in the room.

"Annie!"

I raised my eyes as Lillie walked over. She sat on the couch next to me, her expression one of worry.

I communicate three ways, with gestures, Morse code, and eye movement. For simple yes or no questions, I raise my eyes to say "yes" and move them sideways to say "no." For more complex conversations, I tap out Morse code on a telegraph key or any hard surface. For complicated discussions I use a telegraph machine so that my comments can be recorded.

"Geo received a call from the ONI. John asked Geo to set up a time to talk with you," Lillie said.

I raised my eyes.

"It must be important because he asked when Wallace was working the switchboard."

If John wanted Wallace at the Telephone Exchange, I knew to expect a confidential conversation. Three months ago, when John was on the

Island, he experienced firsthand the lack of privacy when using the Block Island party line phone system. I was eager to talk to him. We saw each other last at the launching of the *USS Arizona* in the Brooklyn Navy Yard.

I tapped, *What night will he call?*

"Tonight at 11:30. Geo's calling Wallace now to warn him. Wallace will clear the switchboard before connecting John to the Weather House."

Where is John now? He travels so much.

"Geo didn't ask. After dinner, we'll drive over to the Weather House so you can set up in the telegraph room."

In October, Geo's assistant, Milton, observed three men on the most secluded part of Block Island. Geo reported it, and John was assigned to investigate whether the men were German spies. But after being on the island for a few days, John admitted the reason he volunteered was because I reminded him of his sister, who had died from a physical disability. Within two weeks, he wrapped up the mission, but it was enough time for us to get to know him, and for him to get to know our family and Block Island.

Geo has been Head Weather Observer on Block Island for years. In 1888, he transferred to Block Island to become the assistant weather observer after training with the Army Signal Service in Oswego, New York. He was fond of saying that Oswego, on Lake Ontario, was the perfect place to understand moving-weather-systems because it was "the land of blizzards and whiteouts." One year after arriving on Block Island he married my mother's younger sister, Nellie.

A few years later Geo began a series of transfers as the Head Weather Observer including at Jupiter, Florida, Green Bay, Wisconsin, and eventually Abeline, Texas. It was during the assignment in Texas that Nellie died of cancer. After a few years, he transferred back east, to the Brooklyn Navy Yard, and eventually returned to Block Island as the Head Observer. After several years he married our mother, Lillie, and she became known as Mrs. Eddey.

"Mom, when are we going over?" Emma asked.

"When the fire goes out."

It is almost out.

"We're going for a phone call?"

"Your sister has a late-night call."

"Who's calling you, Annie?"

John.

"Can I talk to him?" Emma raised her eyes.

"I don't think so, Emma. John asked for Wallace to control the board."

"Oh, Wallace is at the board? Secret ONI stuff. Say hi to John, please."

Though the December temperatures were frigid, the winter evening was calm. There was no rush to arrive at the Weather House, so Lillie pulled off the road along Crescent Beach. She parked between dunes to watch the Atlantic's surf roll in from the east. The three of us were nervous, but for different reasons. I was anxious to hear what John had to say or announce. Lillie, for a mother's obvious reasons, was worried and could not imagine me living alone off-island. Emma said nothing but was aware of her feelings: she would do whatever was necessary to leave the Island to be with me.

Emma felt the tension in the car and rolled down the window. The rhythm of the pounding surf had its impact, as it always does. Gradually I enjoyed the moment, looking out to sea, saying nothing, focused on my future knowing it would separate me from my sister. The three of us were uncharacteristically quiet, and after we entered the front door of the Weather House Geo remarked on it as well.

What's John going to ask?

"I wonder, too," Geo said.

"Will he ask her to work out of the Weather House?" Lillie asked, ever hopeful.

"Eventually, perhaps, but not now, Lillie."

I'll go anywhere.

"You're not leaving the Island, Annie," Lillie said abruptly, as if it was her last stand.

I shook my head but otherwise did not respond. Nor did Emma.

At 10:30 PM Emma went upstairs to bed, Lillie drove home, and I readied myself in the Telegraph Room.

The Telephone and Telegraph Room is in the back left portion of the Weather House, near the kitchen. I positioned my wheelchair in the middle of the table, with my right hand, my good hand, directly in front of the telegraph key. Geo secured the telephone earpiece on my left shoulder, near my ear, to hear John's voice. The telephone's mouthpiece was placed near the telegraph key to allow John to hear my tapping. I would listen, then respond by clicking the telegraph key.

Last fall, when John and two other officers suggested the possibility of working with the ONI as a civilian, I was thrilled. Although no position was offered to me, a young woman with numerous neurological problems felt welcomed! I can't walk, or talk, and need a wheelchair to get around. It would also be a great comfort to be those who understood Morse Code — members of the ONI, the Army's Signal Service, and, of course, Weather Observers. Morsing was necessary to share my thoughts, however, I was prepared for other's *not* proficient in Morse Code to *not* be as accommodating. For them I use hand gestures.

At 11:45 PM the call came from the switchboard.

"John is on," Wallace said. "All party lines are disconnected, and after I put him through, I'll block calls from the mainland. You'll have no more than ten minutes before the main switchboard must be turned back on. Good luck, Annie."

Thanks, and copy.

Two clicks, static, then silence, and John's voice appeared.

"Annie, are you on?"

I tapped hard, *Yes.*

"I heard your tapping. Please say hi to everyone."

Everyone sends love.

"We only have a few minutes. I received verbal confirmation from Commander McCauley that he's approved a civilian position for you. An official telegram will be sent next month, until then say nothing."

A broad smile appeared on my face, and I tapped, *Thank you, John!*

"Commander McCauley approved you for the first training group," John said. "You'll start by attending organizational meetings and training in Washington at the Army War College. Establishing an intelligence organization is complex, and you'll also witness how Major Van Deman structures his MIS. You'll meet a variety of important people, including Brigadier-General Kuhn, the new head of the AWC."

Why will I train with the Army, and not the ONI?

"The ONI is involved with surveillance and espionage, but its operations are limited. Congressional funds are earmarked for the Major's new unit, the Military Intelligence Service out of the Army War College. Eventually, Van Deman's organization will assume some of ONI's responsibilities."

Where does the Major recruit from?

"The Army, but also detectives from the NYPD Bomb Squad."

Did the Bomb Squad find out who blew up Black Tom?

"They know it's the Germans but haven't identified anyone yet. They also have not determined who blew up the plant in New Jersey in January.

"Now, as far as you're concerned, Annie, McCauley will send a coded telegram to you and Van Deman that you'll be one of two ONI representatives at the training meetings."

Okay. I couldn't contain my excitement. *Are other women invited?*

"The ONI has hired women for the fingerprinting section, and I understand two women are being recruited to the first meetings. The reason for this call is to tell you about your first assignment."

I tapped with lightning speed, *I am listening.*

"Here's the background. One year ago, Secretary of State Lansing and his highly regarded diplomat, Leland Harrison, initiated an intel service within the State Department. With limited funding, Leland has to "borrow" agents. One of his borrowed agents believes Germany is placing a spy in Van Deman's ranks."

Where was the "borrowed agent" assigned?

"To the German Embassy in DC."

I raised my eyes.

"Annie, did you hear me?"

Sorry. John. I raised my eyes to say Yes but forgot to Morse my answer.

John laughed, and continued, "The Embassy keeps a large staff, but Bernstorff, the German Ambassador, may be on his way home. If so, the staff will remain.

"Mr. Harrison's agent has good reason to believe they will try to insert someone into the first training group. His intel could represent negative intelligence, nevertheless we want you to be our eyes and ears."

What is negative intelligence?

"We're using the newer term counterintelligence. It includes the planting of false information by an enemy. Or an ally as you surmised at the end of October's mission."

Who is the special agent?

"Mr. Harrison recruited a guy who goes by Bill, from Wilson's Secret Service. He's an expert investigator and has been detailed to clandestine surveillance of the German Embassy."

Does the German Embassy know he's spying?

"He's working in the open as the escort for Bernstorff."

Are all of Mr. Harrison's agents from the Secret Service?

"Most are from the Postal Service Inspector's division."

Does our Postal Service do clandestine work?

"You're not supposed to know, but yes, our Postal Inspectors are modeled on the Brits intel services. With respect to your assignment, what better person to be our eyes and ears than you. The trainees will learn how smart you are, but it's doubtful any will think you'll be observing them."

They'll certainly look at me.

"We'll teach you how to observe individuals before you arrive."

Besides you, Mr. Harrison, and Commander McCauley, who else knows about my assignment?

"We'll notify FDR, the Assistant Secretary of the Navy, and head of the ONI, before you report for training."

Why not tell Major Van Deman?

"He understands the intel but we didn't share with him your assignment, but will as needed."

I raised my eyes.

After a short silence John asked, "Did you raise your eyes?"

I tapped, *Yes. Sorry.*

John laughed again. "If the spy realizes you're on to him, it could be dangerous."

I tried not to show a sudden jolt of fear. *I understand.*

"He may try to kill you. If you identify him, he cannot know you know."

I took a deep breath to muffle a gasp, but John heard what I could not hide.

"I mentioned last October that working in espionage means imminent danger is to be expected."

I regained my composure, *Who do I stay in contact with?*

"Commander McCauley or Mr. Harrison. You'll also have a supervisor that you can trust. But say nothing unless you feel you're in danger, or you've identified the spy. The spy must not see you engaging anyone, except during the meetings. As I mentioned, Van Deman will be told when necessary."

Understood.

"The last item is your cover. It will be the U.S. Weather Bureau. Everyone will recognize you as an employee of the Weather Bureau."

A series of clicks appeared, and the call was disconnected. Geo walked into the Telegraph Room when he heard the static.

"How did it go?"

John offered the position but in a strange way.

"How so?" Geo sat in the wooden armchair in the corner of the room.

I will get a telegram with the offer. But he focused on my first assignment, that will not be mentioned in the telegram.

"Well, that's better than expected. Best not to share that with Lillie!"

I looked at Geo, and tapped, *I cannot share with anyone.*

"Keeping secrets is part of training."

We retired to the parlor and spoke for a short time.

I think keeping secrets is difficult. Last fall John shared an opinion.

"And ...?" Geo asked.

That the requirement to keep secrets, and lying to do so, weighs heavily.

"He would know, that's for sure," Geo said.

He mentioned something else.

"What was it?"

If a spy gets things wrong, you could be blindsided. But if you are correct and no one sees it, you risk losing credibility.

"I wonder if he was preparing you then for working in espionage."

We sat for a while before Geo went upstairs. I slept on the couch in the parlor, knowing I'd have difficulty falling asleep and did not want to wake my sister.

John's warning to be discreet resonated. I had nearly died once, but the experience wasn't as devastating as when I struggled to save Emma. It was small comfort, but I understood that survivors bore the heaviest burden.

3

Block Island, an island of rolling hills, stone walls, ponds, and unmatched beauty, lies in the Atlantic Ocean off the coast of Rhode Island. No one denies its allure. Standing on the top of the Mohegan Bluffs looking west one sees Montauk Point. Looking east, if the weather is clear, one might see Portugal. But not everything is as perfect as the Island itself. Its beauty masks the burdens of those who call it home.

Block Island has seen a slow decline in prosperity. The precariousness is felt by all, except owners of large hotels and other thriving businesses. Those who don't own such enterprises must raise, plant, or fish for every meal. They dig peat to heat their homes and scour the shoreline for coal washed ashore from passing barges. My cousin has a block of coal as large as a chair that he found on the beach at the end of Cooneymus Road.

Block Island, twelve miles south of the Rhode Island coast and twenty-two miles west of Long Island's Montauk Point, is a place where drowning, fishing accidents, and deaths from alcohol are not easily shaken. Add the winter's isolation, and the Island can foster a level of comfort with uncertainty and hardship or do the opposite and drive people back to the mainland.

During wartime islands anywhere in the Atlantic Ocean are vulnerable. For example, my grandfather's grandfather, Isaiah Ball, and his own father lived through the American Revolution *and* the War of 1812. During the Revolution, the government abandoned Block Island. During the war of 1812, the British overran it. Recently, German U-boats (Unterseeboote) sailed the waters near Block Island.

In May 1912 Emma turned fifteen. I crafted a memorable birthday for her by offering three gifts: one I made, one I chose carefully in Providence, and one was meticulously arranged.

*

May 1912

"Annie, where did you and Mom go last week?"

"Point Judith. Mrs. Conway drove us to Providence."

"Why?"

"You'll find out."

"Oh, come on, Annie!" Annoyed, Emma stood up and looked out the window.

Emma was upset the moment she realized Lillie and I were taking the ferry to the mainland. She said nothing then, but never liked being left behind. The two of us were inseparable and had been from as far back as I could remember.

"We bought a birthday present for you," I said, with a sparkle in my eye.

"Really? Thank you. I can't wait!"

In Providence, at the Westminster Arcade, I begged Lillie to buy Emma a certain gift. "No," she said. "But Mom, it's her fourteenth birthday!" She refused, repeatedly. But I was determined, and, after a child-like tantrum in front of Mrs. Conway, the saleswoman relented, and I carried home a 12-inch square box. I held it on my lap the entire two-and-a-half-hour journey back to the Island. I could not wait to see Emma's reaction when she opened it!

"You can carry it home," Lillie said, "but it's staying in my closet until her birthday."

A day before her birthday Lillie gave permission.

"Emma!" I called out as I walked in the front door. "Where are you?"

"Up here."

I bounded up the stairs, skipping every other step. Emma was sitting on her bed, looking out the window that separated our beds. Our room was wide enough for two beds, set against opposite walls. The window, and its view of the New Harbor area, served as a focal point for our conversations.

"I made something for you. Geo helped me."

"What is it?"

"You'll have to wait till tomorrow evening," I said coyly.

"Annie, what is it?"

"Geo will bring it tomorrow. But I have something for you, now."

Emma sat back down.

"Two presents, for me? Really!"

"Mom said I could show you. I'll be right back."

I retrieved the one-foot square beige box from Lillie's closet.

"Here it is. Happy fourteenth birthday!"

I placed the box on her lap, and she read aloud my cursive italic script written under the store's logo, "'Emma, I love you, Annie.' It's from Westminster Arcade!"

Emma struggled to untie the meticulously tied knots holding the top securely fastened to the box.

"Thank you! Someone in that shop sure knows their knots," Emma said.

Eventually she pulled out a black hat with a wide brim. A smile quickly replaced her whatever-that-face-was.

"It's got a strong tie, like a cowboy hat. It wouldn't blow off your head."

Emma put the hat on, tied it under her chin, and looked in the mirror. My tantrum was worth it!

"You can wear it anywhere. Even sailing."

"We're going sailing, too?"

"Yup."

"That's three presents!" Emma was ecstatic. "When?"

"I'll check with Geo. I don't want to get stuck in a calm."

The day after we celebrated Emma's birthday, I jumped on the horse drawn trolly and took it to the New Harbor where the Weather Bureau is located. The Weather House has always been the home of the Head Weather Observer. It houses a telegraph, numerous weather instruments, and on its grounds stands one of the Island's storm warning towers. Flags flying from the Weather House tower can be seen from the east, west, and north. Ships approaching the Island out of the Atlantic from the south will first see the storm warning tower at the Southeast Light. There are towers at the lifesaving stations as well.

When I arrived, Geo was in the telegraph room Morsing weather information, in code, to the Weather Bureau's headquarters in Washington, DC. He waved me in, and I watched with awe at the speed he Morsed message after message.

"Good morning, Annie!" He didn't skip a beat while we talked.

"Hi, sorry to interrupt."

"It's okay," Geo said, pausing long enough to show he welcomed my presence. Geo is a serious man, some call him Major, his rank in the Army Signal Corp, others call him Mr. Eddey, and some call him George. We call him "Gee-oh," preferring the casual form.

"I'm borrowing a boat to take Emma sailing. When will the wind be favorable?"

"That depends what boat you're taking."

"I have permission to use the small double-ender in the Inner Basin."

"The one in the Old Harbor?" Geo asked to confirm.

"Yes. It's rarely used, but the sails are still good. I've sailed it before, alone."

"That's a safe boat in any weather. It's heavy, so you'll need a good breeze. Tomorrow the winds will blow from the north."

"Tomorrow looks good?"

"Yes, but if a low-pressure system moves up the coast, I'll raise storm warning flags right away. But you'll be safe if you sail the Island. A good wind will help teach your sister to sail."

"I hope she listens this time out."

"While you're here, let's practice Morsing to increase your speed."

"Can I finish telegraphing your messages to Washington, DC?"

"I finished those. You can send these to friends in the Brooklyn Navy Yard."

For the next half hour, I sent a series of Morsed messages to his former colleagues, and then a few to Mrs. Conway, the only woman serving as a Head Weather Observer in the United States. I thanked her for driving us to Providence and shared that Emma loved her new hat. When I sent a second message ... Geo tried a new technique to increase my speed.

"This time I'll distract you but keep up your speed."

"Do trainees go through this type of exercise?"

He answered, "It's helpful to increase speed and accuracy. Now, while sending the message, tell me how it gets to her office in Narragansett."

I continued to Morse, and answered, "The dots and dashes travel in the submarine cable that connects our Island to Narragansett Pier."

"Your speed is dropping a bit."

I concentrated on Morsing and asked, "Geo, do all islands in the Atlantic have submarine cables that run to the mainland?"

"All large islands in the Atlantic have underwater cables, but Great Britain and Ireland have hundreds of submarine cables."

"Who owns submarine cables?"

"The companies that fund them," Geo said.

"Geo, where did you learn the importance of understanding context that's embedded in Morsed messages?"

"It's there for the taking. Where did I learn how? At Oswego, with the Army Signal Service."

After my "lesson" I thanked Geo and walked back home. I bounded up the stairs to find Emma sitting on her bed doing homework.

"We're on for tomorrow, Emma. Winds should be favorable, and Geo thinks the seas will calm by morning."

"Are we sailing around the Island?"

"That's the plan, sail the Island." I raised my hand and drew an outline of Block Island.

Emma looked up with some hesitation. "Mom will pack food and water in the basket that you made for me. But should I bring my hat?"

"Gusts might blow it off. I'd leave it here. We'll use my satchel to pack extra clothes." We picked a top and shorts and stuffed them inside.

"Annie, have you noticed Mom's worried about us sailing? She's never worried before."

"Maybe because the *Titanic* sunk last month?"

"Possible. I understand one child died, a little boy from Finland," Emma said.

"Where did you learn that?"

"In the *Providence Journal*. Was Geo worried?"

"Not if we sail the Island. He gave me another lesson at the telegraph. I telegraphed Mrs. Conway and sent a few messages to his old workmates in Brooklyn."

"About what?"

"A 33-year politician in England, a guy named Churchill, became the First Lord of the Admiralty. They were impressed."

"What did Geo say?"

"Geo responded that if Wilson is elected president, he might appoint a young politician from New York to a similar position in our Navy. Someone Geo's brother-in-law knows."

Emma found sleep right after we turned out the light. It was before 10 PM. The next morning, I woke first and hurried downstairs to wash up. When I returned, Emma was sitting up rubbing her eyes, looking out the window.

"Sun's up, sky's clear, it should be a good day on the water," Emma concluded.

"Yes, it will." I then yelled across the hall, "Mom, we're up. We're heading to the Inner Basin, soon."

"I'll help with unfurling the sails," Lillie said, as she walked in our bedroom. "Geo said he'd arrange the ballast." Double-enders used boulders from beaches for ballast.

We were at the Old Harbor's Inner Basin in no time and were surprised that the sails on the main and mizzen masts were unfurled, and ballast added midship.

"Geo must have been here, or maybe Wallace," Lillie said.

A few moments later we looked up and Wallace called out from the entrance of Barber's restaurant. He gave a quick wave, walked onto the dock, and handed me a basket of food.

"Here's Barber's Old-Harbor-Lunch for you," Wallace said, using the phrase Islander's called the restaurant. For years it was one of only four restaurants on the Island.

Emma and I stowed the baskets of food and my satchel under the rear seat. Double-enders are open to the sea and "stowing" meant placing objects under seats, away from the ballast.

"Happy fourteenth, Emma," Wallace said.

"Thank you," Emma said with a huge smile.

"Thank you for readying the boat, Wallace," Lillie said.

"You're welcome. Girls, the wind's out of the north, gusting a bit. The seas are a few feet, rolling in from the east. Should be a great day on the water but stick to your course around the Island. The west side has no seas to speak of."

I looked over the East breakwater to the Atlantic. "The wind is brisk, but the surf's not breaking over the east wall. It'll take me more than a few tacks to clear the breakwater."

"I think so, too," Wallace said.

Within minutes we raised the sails, gave Lillie goodbye hugs, and thanked Wallace for lunch and pushing us off.

My third present to Emma was underway.

I took the rudder and handled the mizzenmast, and Emma controlled the mainsail. It took two tacks to exit the Inner Basin and five more to exit the harbor and round the East Wall. Using dead reckoning I set a course for southeast and let out both sails. Within twenty minutes we'd reached Old Harbor Point and I let Emma take the helm, to build confidence in her sailing skills. When we were a half mile south of Old Harbor Point, Emma changed direction to due south and let out both sails on opposite sides of the boat. A long day of running with the wind had begun.

Conversation dwindles at sea. There's the effort required to keep the boat on course, the tendency to be captivated by the beauty of the ocean, and the necessity to look for floating hazards. And of course, passing ships or whales. Conversation that does occur that's not sailing related usually involves one's inner dialogue, like growing up and going to school on Block Island. The number of children in a class is rarely more than one or two and most classes are combined. That's Island schooling. Sisters become a greater part of one's life on an island, but not always, as hardships can drive siblings apart. No one can figure out why. For Emma and me, we've always been close, and hope we'll always be inseparable.

"Emma, the Storm Warning Tower at the lighthouse is coming into view."

We'd been sailing for almost thirty minutes, and I was bow sitting on the gunwale, keeping my eyes trained on the Southeast Lighthouse grounds.

"Tell me when you see it," Emma said, as she adjusted her sail.

"I see the top of the tower. But I can't make out any flags."

"If there are no flags flying ... can we continue to run with the wind?"

Emma looked comfortable at the helm, handling the rudder and mizzen sail effortlessly. It was her birthday, and I agreed. It was a beautiful day for sailing, but in retrospect it was the biggest mistake of our lives.

We ran with the wind and changed course once when the following seas increased to five feet. Emma change direction to southeast, bringing both sails to starboard, to increase speed and to better handle the following seas with more precision. The new course would bring us to North Africa if we were at sea for a month. But I was happy to relinquish the helm to Emma.

Several hours out, the Island no longer visible, we kept what I thought was a southerly course.

"Annie, look!"

"What?"

"Off port, a whale and her calf."

"Oh, and they are close. Coming toward us."

Emma kept a steady course, hoping the whales would come closer, and they did. They accompanied us for a short time, long enough and close enough for us to have a conversation. A few fishing smacks were in the far distance, and although we were now far from land, we did not feel alone.

Emma stayed at the helm for hours. She was in total control of the boat, becoming ever more comfortable with sailing. I couldn't wait to tell Geo of her progress.

Suddenly, long after the whale, her calf, and the fishing smacks disappeared, I felt something change. A look back to Emma saw confusion on her face, too. She said nothing, but I turned in the direction where she was focused. Over the starboard bow, a fine white mist was appearing in the distance. Clouds grew before our eyes where none had been before. An uncanny quiet was followed by the crescendo of a roar.

Emma looked more confused. The northern sky was clear, with a few scattered clouds. I looked, again, over the starboard bow, and within thirty seconds I realized what had arrived. I ran back to the stern.

"Annie, the winds have picked up but they're from the south! What's happening?"

I took the rudder from my sister.

"What's going on?"

"Tie both of us up to the mast. As quickly as you can."

"Is that a White Squall?"

"Yes," I said, "and they get violent, fast."

Freed from the helm, Emma grabbed two ropes packed under the aft seat.

"What'll happen?" Emma asked, her hands shaking as she tied us to the mizzenmast. Approaching was the swirling mist, and high winds.

"Look up. See the darkening sky? Hear the noise?"

"It was quiet a moment ago. And why is it so loud?"

Not waiting for an answer, she tied the lines to the mizzen using bowline knots, the short line to her waist, and the longer line to me.

"It's the first White Squall I've been in, Emma. Can you handle the main mast? We need to come about."

"I can do it."

We could barely hear each other. I turned the boat to starboard, into the squall's mist and violent winds. Could these southerly winds turn this double ender around, and quickly? Yes, it could.

"Emma, look, I can't believe it." The noise of the squall became deafening, and suddenly, almost violently, the boat turned into the wind. We didn't have time to adjust the sails. But it didn't matter.

"Annie, I'll flip the main sail around, but I wouldn't need to bring it in."

"I never thought a boat could come about without bringing in the sails." We were both yelling over the roar of near hurricane strength winds.

"Annie, have you seen the wind change direction like that within seconds?"

I yelled, "Never" but she couldn't hear me. The boat healed to starboard, but the boat's weight kept us from capsizing.

"If this was a catboat," I called out, "we'd have capsized by now."

"Thanks for the reminder," Emma yelled. Within seconds the sails were full, and we were heading north-northeast and back to the Island.

"That was fast," Emma said. "No wonder ships at sea are lost in White Squalls."

Before it hit, I couldn't wait to tell Geo about Emma's progress, but now I wondered if we'd make it back to the Island. The strain on the rigging frightened Emma, and she walked back to the stern and wrapped her arms around me.

"One moment the skies were clear, then the haze, then the winds from the opposite direction. How did you know, Annie?"

"It couldn't be anything else. The good thing is if these southerly winds increase, we should reach the Island sooner. But I doubt we'll make Old Harbor."

"Let's get there first," Emma said.

"It's two systems. No wonder the flags weren't flying. The northerly weather system disappeared in front of our eyes. The southern front ate it right up."

"Did someone forget to raise the weather flags at the Southeast Light?" Emma asked.

"Maybe," I said, not wanting to know the answer. "Make sure our lines are tied fast to the mizzenmast."

There was good reason to be frightened. But experiencing a White Squall was only the beginning of our problems. We later learned that this hurricane strength southern weather system was first identified by a Naval vessel 150 miles off the coast of the Carolinas, escaping detection by our National Weather Service.

"Stay with me, Emma. We must stay close." It was all I could say. The roar of the wind came with the darkest daylight sky I had ever seen.

"The water's lost its blue color, its black now. Total darkness down there." Emma's voice trembled. "I feel isolated ... I didn't ten minutes ago. I wish the whales were with us."

"Keep your eye out for anything unusual," I said without thinking. "We're not alone."

"What are you talking about? Are we going to see a man walking on water? Some birthday present that would be."

The rain came and went and came again, but it didn't matter because the wind blew it sideways, and little entered the boat. For an hour and a half, the seas behaved strangely, like a rip current. But the deep and wind-driven-surface waves from the south took over and we were, once again, in a following sea.

"Keep an eye out for a wave that might crest on the stern. It would fill the boat, and we'd have another problem."

Emma rolled her eyes. "Don't remind me."

Emma's resilience returned and I asked her to take the rudder. I kept my eyes directed south, to watch for following waves that might wash over the stern. The double-ender's two "bows", a design made for following seas, divided the waves with the stern's high gunwale.

The seas reached eight feet, and I took the helm back. Emma sat at my side, holding my left leg. With these seas, if there was a dying wind for a few cycles, one wave could fill the boat.

And then it happened.

"Annie, look," Emma screamed, "it's breaking over the boat."

A 15-foot following wave. The wind kept up and I reached back and touched it.

"That was nothing, but a wall of water," I said, as if it didn't matter. I knew we were saved by the wind.

"Annie," Emma looked up. "Are we going to make it?"

"Yes, we will." I crouched down and gave her a hug. "Look for waves coming in from the northeast. Waves from the south are surface waves, but waves from the east should be deep waves from Georgia's Bank."

"Why are you telling me that?"

"Making conversation."

"Annie, is our luck is gonna run out?" Emma asked in all seriousness.

"I'll get us back to the Island, I promise."

We were sailing at an incredible clip, and soon we made out the outline of Mohegan Bluffs. We were a few miles away and coming into a reasonably shallow area of the Atlantic Ocean. Due to the erosion of the Island moving north over the past ten thousand years, it was much shallower than expected and an area of shipwrecks.

"Emma, watch for waves breaking."

Emma spotted another rogue wave but there was nothing we could do. It washed over the boat, knocking us both forward. The ropes held and we quickly regained our positions. I held the rudder and Emma worked feverously to bail.

Ten minutes later she yelled out, "Another one, but it's at a different angle. Look how big it is!"

The fear in my sister's voice was palpable.

"I see it, hold tight."

We crouched low and held the seats. But the wave was too strong for Emma, and I heard her scream my name. "I can't hold on, Annie!" Then silence, except for the roar of the wind. I called her name, but I knew she was under water, and hopefully not under the boat.

I grabbed her line and followed it into the water. She was still attached to her line but when I dove overboard, I couldn't find her. I needed to reach her before she panicked and started "breathing" water. Were we celebrating her last birthday?

I took a deep breath, followed Emma's line, and grabbed her tight around her chest. But I still could not move her, and I started to panic.

She pointed to her line, that it wouldn't move. It was stuck in a splintered board on the bottom of the boat. She was gulping water and started to go limp as I finally unwrapped the line from the board and brought her up. When we surfaced, I pushed her to the gunwale and let her breathe. We were in a trough and the boat was stationary. Emma held me tight. She took breath after breath and coughed up water, and then vomited.

The boat was turning sideways, and I had to get her onboard before the next wave. I pulled myself over the gunwale with my left hand, the other holding my sister tight. At this point she let go of my chest and was able to grab the gunwale. Simultaneously, I reached under her arms, turned her around and somersaulted her into the boat. My left hand smacked the gunwale, and I was sure it was broken.

A calm came over me as Emma held me and wouldn't let go. She was crying between coughs. I dragged her to the stern and took control of the rudder.

We were alive. Yet, if we were to go under again, I wasn't sure we'd make it. But at least we'd perish together. I remembered a story about a fisherman who got knocked overboard, lost his bearing underwater and calmly asked himself, should I surface, or just die. At that point it didn't matter to him. He surfaced to tell his story. As long as we died together, in each other's arms, I understood why it could go either way.

Emma sat on the bottom of the boat, near my feet, and looked up, still coughing, "I'm okay. How can I help?"

"Just rest. We will be okay." I looked at my sister, she was staring up at me, and I wanted to cry.

A few minutes later, I heard her say, "Annie, thank you for saving me."

Tears poured from my eyes and mixed with the rain. But I had to concentrate on sailing. For a good fifteen minutes I could not look down.

Until the winds picked up.

"Emma, it's getting worse. The gusts have got to be hurricane strength."

"And it's spring," Emma said, trembling.

"I see the lighthouse. The waves are breaking from the bottom of the bluffs out to here. We must be two miles away."

I let the wind and seas push us home while I focused on avoiding submerged boulders. A beam from the Southeast Lighthouse pierced the mist and rain. We were getting closer.

I'd lost track of time but guessed it was at least 8 PM. We were beyond exhausted. Emma became quiet, occasionally coughing, from the impact of water in her lungs.

"I'm going to beach the boat below the lighthouse," I said, my weariness now evident even to me.

"Can't we make it to the harbor?" Emma asked.

"I'm too tired, Emma. These boats beach easily if I stay clear of the boulders."

"But you can't see underwater boulders," Emma argued, raising her voice. "Can't we try?"

But I didn't listen or change course. Dozens of ships, from fishing smacks to oil tankers, coal barges, large sailing vessels, have all run aground off the rocky shores of Mohegan Bluffs.

It was a small favor that we had not come out of the sea halfway between the Island and Montauk Point, the mouth of Block Island Sound. Sailing into the Southwest shoals, equidistant between Block Island to Montauk Point, in a storm like this, would be certain death. I was grateful we were not near the most treacherous shoals on America's East Coast and said a prayer of thanks.

Less than a mile from the bluffs waves routinely broke over the stern. But the boat remained stable even with three feet of water sloshing around. Emma bailed as much as she could. She stood up and held the rudder, to give me a rest.

The winds pushed us closer to the Island, but I knew it was giving a false sense of security. The shallower the water, the greater the hazardous due to submerged glacial erratics.

We'd been knocked about quite a bit. Gashes on our faces, arms, and legs, but it was the cuts in our scalps that would not stop bleeding. Periodically, Emma would wipe the blood from my eyes. And then there was my hand. When she was falling over and grabbed my arm I screamed in pain.

"I'm sorry, what did I do?"

"It's my left hand and arm."

"It's swollen."

"I broke it ... against the gunwale."

The sharp pain gave a jolt, but I quickly regained my composure and avoided several massive boulders. But, suddenly, about twenty yards from the beach, I hit a submerged boulder. The unrelenting surf pushed the boat sideways against the boulder, but it did not overturn.

I have no memory of what happened.

*

EMMA

Annie and I both fell forward when the mizzen mast snapped at the base. The mast hit Annie on the head, bounced off her and landed on the gunwale. Blood flew from her scalp.

The mast was still attached to the boat by its lines, but the broken mast freed the lines that were holding us to the boat. With the next wave, before I could reach her, Annie washed overboard. We were close to shore, and I wasn't worried about staying on the boat. Nor was I worried about the large boulder that the double-ender had struck – I'd use it to brace myself against the surf and the undertow.

I knew my sister was knocked unconscious before she went overboard, and I had to keep her head above water. I jumped in and was able to grab her right away. I held her tight and called her name, but she did not respond. The blood from her head wound mixed with the ocean and got in my eyes. I couldn't see until the next wave washed over us.

The double-ender was thrown back against another large boulder, missing us by inches. It was then I saw the mast and its sail float away.

"Annie!" I yelled again and again, but she didn't answer.

The surf continued to break over our heads, and I rode each wave closer to the beach. I braced us against every boulder I could when the powerful undertow dragged us back to sea. But with each wave we got closer to the beach at the base of the bluffs, and all the while I kept Annie's head above water.

When I lost ground to the undertow I screamed, "I'm not giving up!" And did it repeatedly. Annie remained limp and did not respond to my cries of anguish. I couldn't help but think she'd died. The love one feels is never greater than when the end is near for those you love.

I looked up and saw that the beach was but a stone's throw away, but the undertow made it feel like an endless journey. I fought the fatigue and braced myself on the next submerged boulder. I waited for the next wave to carry us to the shore, and that last breaker brought us up the boulder-strewn beach. I dug my feet into the sand and struggled to pull my sister up to a safe spot, as close to the base of the bluffs as possible, where the surf could not reach us. I lay down and held her head in my arms, exhausted.

"Annie, Annie," I cried into her ear. But she wouldn't answer. She was breathing, but why didn't she hear me? I remember little else, except that we lay next to one another. Annie never woke up, and at one point I lost consciousness, too.

After midnight two members of the West Side Lifesaving Station spotted debris near Black Rock Point, almost two miles to the west of where we landed. Their search eventually shifted to the rocky area below the Southeast Lighthouse. During the wee hours of the early morning, well before dawn, I awoke to the sound of the men calling our names. I remember someone saying: "The younger one's alive, not sure about the older sister." I've never forgotten those words, and when alone, openly cry, when that sentence plays in my head.

4

EMMA

The West Side lifesaving crew came upon us at the base of the bluffs, and I was never so relieved. I saw and heard four of them, but there were probably more. Two interviewed me and asked question after question: Are you alive? Can you wake up? Emma, you're awake, good. Your sister, is she breathing? Where's the blood coming from? What happened?

"Yes, she's been breathing all night," I said softly, not fully awake.

"What happened?"

"Annie saved me from drowning and then I saved her," I said, holding back tears.

The lifesaving crew saw I was okay and attended to Annie right away. When I was more awake, I tried to explain the circumstances of Annie's head injury, but I wasn't sure anyone was listening. They were preoccupied with securing my sister to a board. Then several of the crew carried her up the steep 150-foot incline to the top of the bluffs.

I yelled out, "She broke her left arm. Be careful." But I don't think anyone listened to that either.

I did not see the men carry her to the top but heard their boots crunching into the clay cliffs as they ascended. Soon they were out of sight and earshot. I couldn't help but worry. She was breathing but pale and not awake. I said a dozen David Copperfield prayers that she would be okay, then I cried. She saved me, and I did the best I could to save her. I gained my strength and climbed to the top of the bluffs with the help of the wife of a member of the lifesaving station.

The lifesaving crew had alerted the Newport Naval Station and the Coast Guard about us being lost at sea. When they called to report we were found, a nearby patrol boat responded. By the time Annie had been brought to the Old Harbor, the 40-foot Naval patrol boat was a mile away. Within two hours Annie was in Newport. Geo and Wallace accompanied her to the hospital.

Lillie, who couldn't stop crying, brought me home. I knew what her thoughts were, mine were the same. She had lost her husband and only son to the sea, her brother incapacitated from a fall, and now her oldest daughter might have a similar fate.

Island living could be cruel, and had taken yet another toll on our family.

Lillie bandaged my cuts and bruises as I sat on the sofa, staring out the window at the harbor. The reflection of the setting sun in the clouds. I couldn't enjoy the scene. All I could think about was Annie. We sat together for a long time.

"She'll get better, and we'll be together again." Lillie didn't sound convinced, then added, "We have each other, Emma, and hope."

She brought me upstairs and lay me on my bed, and continued to bandage my wounds, while wiping her tears. I told her the story of our day at sea. I took full blame for convincing Annie that we should sail south instead of sailing the Island. But I don't think mom was listening. I had to avert my eyes from her face, the anguish too much for me bear.

That night Gladys from the switchboard called, said she was sorry, and put Geo through from Southwest Newport Hospital. My mother and I crowded around the phone.

"Is she okay, Geo?" Lillie asked, her voice trembling.

"Yes, Lillie, she's moving her right leg."

"Is she awake yet, Geo?"

"Not fully. But she opened her eyes, and a nurse heard her groan."

I could tell Lillie was skeptical, believing Annie would die.

"Geo, how's her head?" I asked.

"Her skull is fractured, on the right side."

"Where the mast hit her?" Lillie asked.

"What about her broken arm?" I asked.

"I didn't know it was broken," Lillie said.

"It is broken," Geo confirmed. "When did that happen, Emma?"

"When I was washed overboard, about an hour out from the Island."

"She handled the boat with a broken arm?" Lillie asked.

"Yes, Annie did everything," I avowed.

"On the ferry I moved her swollen arm, and she showed no pain," Geo added. "But now she's more alert and winces when it's touched."

"Maybe she'll awaken, Geo," Lillie said, holding back tears.

"Annie will wake up! I know she will," Geo said with conviction. "I Morsed on her arm that I loved her, but she hasn't responded, yet."

I took the phone from Lillie. "Geo, I must see my sister! Can I take the next ferry and see her? Please!"

"I'll ask the doctor, Emma. But it might be too soon."

"Please," I pleaded.

"It's too soon, Emma," Lillie said, and then sobbed uncontrollably.

I said goodbye to Geo and hung up the phone. Before Lillie stopped crying, I made up my mind to see my sister, with or without permission.

"Mom, we're going to visit Annie."

*

The next day a nurse observed that her right side moved, but not the left. Alarmed, Geo rang up an old friend stationed at the Newport Naval Base, who immediately came over to visit. He explained that the Newport Naval Corps had increased staff training to prepare for the United States entering the European War. In that regard they had sent two enlisted men to Reed College to complete a new four-month program in Physiotherapy. The Newport Hospital physician invited the Naval physiotherapists to evaluate Annie.

A few days later, when we arrived from Block Island, the physiotherapists were in the process of their evaluation. I wanted to run to Annie's bedside but of course I couldn't. So, we entered the room quietly. Three other young patients were in the large room. Annie saw Lillie, but not me. I took a seat near the bed of a young boy, diagonally across the room.

Lillie was introduced to the physiotherapists who called themselves Reconstruction Aids. They mentioned their recent training. Along with the Newport Hospital physician and nurses they discussed Annie's physical condition. Speaking in hushed voices I could tell they focused on her left arm and leg. I overheard that her alertness was improving but they did not discuss her ability to talk. But none of that mattered — I wanted my sister back home.

Geo walked with the staff into the hall leaving Lillie and me in the room. I immediately jumped on the hospital bed and hugged my sister. In an instant I knew Annie would be okay.

"Emma, get off the bed!" Lillie yelled.

"Annie, I love you!"

Annie's eyes opened, and a partial smile returned. She tried to speak but could not. Lillie reached over and placed a book under her right hand, and Annie started to Morse a message. She tapped softly. I moved closer.

I am okay, Annie Morsed with her good hand on my arm.

"Mom, she's going to be okay," I looked at my sister and I could sense that she'd make it back home. I fought back tears, and I was partially successful.

Two days later, Geo and I took the ferry home while Lillie remained at the hospital until Annie's discharge. Lillie's overwhelming anguish troubled me, but I was comforted by Geo's understanding of the situation. He had started to communicate with Annie using Morse Code and believed she would make it back to Block Island. I stayed at the Weather House, along with Wallace, until Annie was discharged.

Lillie called every few days at 11:30 PM when Wallace was on the board. We don't know who first suggested to Annie to communicate using her eyes. It could have been the Reconstruction Aids from the Naval base, or it could have been Lillie, or Mrs. Conway who visited for a full day. But soon Annie was communicating using simple "yes" and "no" responses by using her eyes.

"She understood right away," Lillie said. "To say yes, she will raise her eyes."

"How will she say 'no', Mom?" I asked.

"She looks to the side readily, Emma, so that will be her 'no'."

"Any improvement in her arms and legs?"

"She can move her right arm and leg. Her movements are not smooth, but she's getting there. But not much on the left side."

"How will she get around the Island, Mom?"

"The physiotherapists from the Naval Hospital will make a wooden wheelchair."

"Will she talk again?"

"She makes squawking sounds, but that's it."

One month later, even I could see that Annie would be paralyzed on the left, and she'd never walk again. It was doubtful she'd talk. The Reconstruction Aids from the Naval Hospital brought the wheelchair the week she was discharged; the nurses glued soft cushions on the seat, back, and sides. Soon, she was sitting up and used her right hand to move a few feet in the wheelchair.

One doctor was hopeful that she could recover more function, but I knew that was not true. She would never be the same. I wished I could be the one paralyzed, but I knew that was not possible.

Seven weeks after admission she was ready to be sent home. The physician gave Lillie a handwritten letter upon discharge that explained the extent of the damage from the falling mast:

"The mast that fell on Annie Rose's head caused a cranial fracture and hemorrhage on the right side leading to brain damage and subsequent paralysis on her left side. It appears a small portion of the left frontal area was impacted, too. This will affect her ability to speak. Due to the heroics of her younger sister, we do not think she suffered hypoxia from being underwater. She will require a wheelchair for mobility. It is doubtful she will talk, but we can hope. To communicate we recommend the use of hand signals. Her mother, Lillie Ball, explained that she is expert at Morse Code. Hopefully her right hand will improve, and she can tap on a telegraph key. The extent of her inability to swallow food and drinks without causing aspiration, termed dysphagia, is not yet clear, and this is concerning. Unfortunately, we do not know how diffuse her brain damage is and cannot make a prognosis about her reasoning or thinking ability. Please continue to utilize the practices of the Naval Physiotherapists to prevent contractures in her extremities, from disuse."

"Mom, of course Annie can use Morse to communicate," I said, after Lillie read the report over the phone. "And tell that doctor that I know Annie will regain her adventuresome spirit and will want to go on long outings with me in a wheelchair."

"I hope you're right, Emma. Two weeks ago, when she started Morsing at a fast pace on the side of the bed I started crying and the nurse had no idea why."

"You explained to the nurse, I hope."

"Yes, after I stopped crying."

"When will you be home?"

"Friday, early afternoon. Meet us at the ferry."

Before the accident Annie and I slept in separate beds. Before she returned from the hospital I pushed our beds together, and from then on, we shared the same bed. I'm not sure about much, but if it's possible, we became closer than we were before the accident. Yet, as time wore on, and perhaps this is a paradox, at the same time our sibling rivalry, our competition, took on a different dimension.

No damage to the cognitive regions of her brain might be considered a miracle. But it was just as reasonable to think it was pure luck. Within a few months it crossed my mind that perhaps the damaged portion allowed her more concentrated effort to the undamaged portion of the brain. Could this be possible?

Her recuperation took about a year and a half, and, unfortunately, as the physiotherapist at the Naval Hospital had thought, her ability to speak did not return. Physicians call this dysarthria. But, her swallowing function did. Over the years she focused on keeping her muscles active, a term they called physical habilitation.

The easiest part of her recovery involved using the Telegraph Machine. Her right hand functioned perfectly and her speed and understanding of Morsing to communicate was relearned quickly. Mrs. Conway would Morse almost daily with her, to improve her skills, and soon, Annie could communicate complex ideas and thoughts faster than if she could talk. Two years out from the accident even Geo was surprised that she could now routinely "read between the lines" of copy, to discern those subtle, hidden meanings in telegraph transmissions. The ONI would eventually appreciate that skill and it would become quite useful during her training at the Army War College in Washington, DC.

If you saw her sitting in a wheelchair, let's say in Old Harbor looking at fishing smacks unload their catch, you'd be forgiven for not thinking she could communicate well, or was intelligent. But if you understood Morse Code and engaged her in a conversation, you'd quickly find she had a mind like few others. The part of her brain that controlled movement by and large did not return, especially on the left side. But the part that controlled reasoning was unaltered. By the end of October 1916 officers in the Office of Naval Intelligence realized she was brilliant and began discussing her future.

5

January 1917

ANNIE

In October, at the conclusion of the Weather House mission, John returned to his ONI office in the Brooklyn Navy Yard, I volunteered to help Lillie at the Post Office, and Emma signed on as a deck hand on a fishing smack out of the Hog Penn in New Harbor. I hoped a position with the ONI would materialize, as John had stated. I was aware that the Secretary of the Navy agreed to approve the hiring of women for many noncombat roles, and I remained hopeful. For now, sorting mail would keep me busy, but Geo mentioned that there was an opening for a telegrapher at the Ocean View Hotel.

The Bell Telephone Company on Dodge Street is on the second floor and its inside space limited, making it impossible for a wheelchair user to be employed there. But the Ocean View Hotel's public Telegraph Service is on the first floor, and yesterday Emma pushed me up the long walkway leading to the hotel. I met with the manager, but the interview didn't go well because he did not know Morse Code. I was expecting his sole telegraph operator to be present for the interview. In the end, I was rejected at the end of the interview.

"The Ocean View didn't take you on?" Geo, asked at dinner that night. He looked up, surprised, and then at Lillie, who looked away.

I tapped, *He said maybe, then said no.*

"I think he was afraid of Annie," Emma interjected.

After a few moments Geo said, "It's too bad we don't live in England."

Geo was referring to England's vast telegraphic and telephonic network that was the responsibility of the Royal Post Office. I would certainly have a position there.

The manager should have interviewed me with his telegrapher.

Geo paused, not sure what to say. "Finding a Morsing position will be difficult on the Island. Why don't you help me until something comes along?"

I had helped Geo before.

On the evening of August 28th of last year, the Hygeia Hotel, located diagonally across from the Weather House, caught fire. By morning it had burned to the ground. The flames and smoke frightened more than the guests and Islanders. The inferno could be seen for fifty miles in every direction. That night I telegraphed dozens of messages for Hygeia's guests, to their families and friends on the mainland. In the early hours of the morning, I began Morsing updates on the progress of the fire to editors at newspapers throughout the Eastern Seaboard, including the *Providence Journal* and *The New York Times.* It was a long and difficult night, but I helped everyone. This freed up Geo and Mitchel to remove weather equipment from the roof, to avoid damage from flying embers. Emma was stationed on the porch with pails of water, to extinguish embers that landed at the front of the Weather House. Every ten minutes she'd run back to the telegraph room, give me a report, and fill the pails from the kitchen sink.

Fires were not the only non-weather-related telegrams that were transmitted from the Weather Station. As the Head Observer, Geo routinely kept newsrooms informed of Island events, including shipwrecks and storm damage assessments. A week after the loss of the grand Hygeia Hotel, another historical and near-tragic event occurred. This, too, was a late-night event and caught the attention of newsman throughout the United States.

The well-known Lawrence Sperry "crashed" his Curtiss Model F aeroplane at the base of the bluffs. More accurately, he guided his plane to a soft landing at the water's edge below the Southeast Lighthouse. He was flying a clandestine military flight, but Geo could not report that or that Sperry had a bomb onboard. Geo telegraphed editors that Sperry was safe and that a tug out of New London was on its way. The tug towed the Curtiss aeroplane to the New Harbor for repairs, which Geo did report, as well as when Sperry successfully flew his plane off the Island days later to complete his mission. We never did find out where he dropped the bomb.

This week Geo had me telegraph newsy information about the Navy leasing the Narragansett Hotel to house Naval officers. The arriving enlisted sailors were setting up a tent city in the back of the hotel. I followed that by Morsing to editors that Naval patrol boats were docking in the inner part of the Great Salt Pond, called the Hog Penn. Most importantly, as soon as any Islander spotted a U-Boat, I telegraphed that as well. This kept me busy, but I wondered if the officers in the ONI had changed their minds? I don't mind volunteering, but is that all that I will be asked to do?

6

February 1917

"They haven't contacted you, but if they do, Annie, you're not reporting to DC," Lillie insisted.

I tapped, *Mom, I can do it!*

"For God's sake, Annie, how would you manage? You're in a wheelchair, and who'll take care of you?"

I turned and stared out the window. I expected my mother to continue to resist my leaving the Island. She's aware that war's coming, we all are, and she knows I cannot enlist. But here's an opportunity to train as a civilian with the ONI.

I tapped hard on the windowsill, *How can I turn down an offer to join the ONI?*

Emma spoke up, "Mom, Annie's eager to contribute."

I tapped harder, *I can take care of myself!*

"No." Lillie was emphatic. "You are not signing up for a dangerous task."

It is not dangerous, and I can contribute as a coder and maybe more.

"I know war's coming. The evidence is everywhere. But be reasonable, you're NOT going to DC alone." Lillie did not waver.

"I can go with her," Emma interjected.

"Emma, they're not going to allow you to go to DC with her. And I can't go to DC because I need my job at the Post Office. If the ONI wants you, they'll let you work from the Weather House."

Signs of war were mostly seen in the New Harbor Area where Naval construction projects abounded, including a building rising adjacent to the Hog Penn. We often stayed with Geo, and our bedroom on the second floor of the Weather House looked out on all of this – Trim's Pond, the Naval patrol boats at the Hog Penn, the Narragansett Inn now converted to Naval Officer housing, and the Great Salt Pond with the various larger naval vessels, docked or anchored. Every week more Naval Officers in full dress uniform reported for duty. Two submarines tied up at Payne's Dock, although they quickly sailed away. Without submerging, in no time they were through the Cut and into Block Island Sound.

Another sign war was inevitable was the event in Newport Harbor last October. A German U-boat, courtesy of President Wilson's neutrality policy, sailed up to the big wharf in Newport. A German sailor jumped to the dock, went for a stroll, and grabbed a few newspapers. Back on board the captain of the submarine determined from the newspapers what ships were scheduled to sail from New York Harbor to Europe. And when. Why? The very next day that U-boat torpedoed ships sailing near the Nantucket Light. Did this U-boat deposit the three mystery men on Block Island? Or did they arrive on a ferry? We'll never know. But one thing was certain. Geo learned that the captain of one of the ships was a distant relative from England. Fortunately, Captain Lyle was saved, along with all his crew.

On the east side of the Island, on a routine basis, Islanders see destroyers sailing to and from the Naval War College. This past summer destroyers brought dozens of sailors in full dress uniform to participate in Block Island's Independence Day Parade. The ships dropped anchor a nautical mile offshore. Although President Wilson believes the US can remain neutral, no one in the ONI or on Block Island think so.

Our mother, Lillie Ball Rose, wears her grey hair long, is slender, and is Emma's height. When standing together side by side, their anguish is palpable when I insist that I will leave the Island. Lillie's because she refuses to believe I can fare well off Island, and because of our family history of heartbreak. And Emma's because she wants to be with me, and because it is our plan.

After a month of this back-and-forth, I devised a hand signal that meant, *Mom, I can do it!* I'd raise my left hand, to just below the level of the armrest and turn it up and down twice. Hand signals repeated twice meant I was emphatic.

Lillie wouldn't let up. "I don't want you to go! They'll have to let you work from here, on the Island."

"Mom, even I know that that isn't a compromise," Emma said. "The ONI could use her skills but not before she's trained."

"She'll be there for more than the training, that I can sense," Lillie said with sadness.

My ultimate assignment will depend on my performance in the meetings and training.

"Annie," Emma said, "I wonder how you'll fare, alone, without me."

I'll be okay, but I'll be better if you join me.

Lillie put her head in her hands. I turned and stared back out the window and remembered how helpful I was when I assisted the ONI to locate the spies. And how appreciative the senior officers were of my concern that "false flags" could be used by anybody. I felt honored to contribute, and now they wanted me to join their mission. But when would they call?

I tapped angrily, *Mom, I proved myself and I can be independent. The ONI will provide for me.*

Lillie glanced at both of us, her head still in her hands, "After training, you'll have to report somewhere. And you know that work the ONI is assigned is dangerous. You know what John has been through!"

"I don't want Annie to leave either," Emma said.

"Aren't you worried about your sister?"

"I think she'll be okay," Emma said.

"Aren't you worried about anything, Emma?"

Emma thought for a moment and confided, "Yes. I'm worried the ONI will assign another caregiver."

"They will not let you accompany her," Lillie said with finality.

*

In January 1917 my major concern was how to convince Lillie that

I should report to the ONI. I would love to have Emma with me. She's more than the engine behind my wheelchair, and although she's become expert at pushing, Emma is the best confidant a person could want. Surely, she could board a ferry, after I settled, but it broke my heart to think we'd be separated. In addition, Emma helps me develop hand signals to communicate with those who do not understand Morse Code. And she has been helpful learning different forms of communication, and I suspect I'll need her help learning the language of spies.

Island living is not for the faint of heart. Islanders are forced to deal with what living in the Atlantic hands out. The seasons are harsh, the weather systems are unpredictable and stay around longer than expected. After summer, gray skies are always above and green vegetation long gone. When snow falls, what doesn't melt, the wind blows back to sea. Pushing me in the wheelchair in the winter was not Emma's favorite activity. But she rarely complained.

*

It was late evening when the phone rang. Emma was upstairs in bed, and I was with Lillie downstairs when she picked up. I heard my sister get out of bed and figured she was listening to Lillie's portion of the conversation. But Lillie didn't say much, and Emma must have crawled back into bed and fallen asleep.

"That was Geo. The ONI telegraphed the Weather House. You're to meet a boat at the Hog Penn early tomorrow morning."

I'll think of this as my first orders — to attend an early morning meeting.

"You'll have to get up early to get there on time."

What time? And what boat?

"Sorry to say, 4 AM."

I rolled my eyes, then raised them to say, *Yes*. Then I tapped, *What boat?*

"A small tug with two stacks will tie up at the Hog Penn, adjacent to a Naval Patrol boat. I'll get your wheelchair ready with warm blankets in case the winds don't die down by morning."

Emma will hope the winds are non-existent. Pushing my wooden wheelchair up even the smallest of hills and into the wind isn't easy.

Emma was fast asleep when Lillie helped me to bed.

"I'll wake you at four, and you can wake your sister," Lillie said.

I rolled my eyes and gave a hand signal for a sarcastic, *Thanks.*

"Annie, this is a meeting with John, but you're not going off Island."

I rolled my eyes, again.

At four o'clock Lillie called my name. I shook my sister with my good hand, and when I had her attention, tapped on the headboard, *Wake up! We must get to the New Harbor.*

"This early?"

Hurry! And no, mom cannot drive us.

"I know. She's gotta sort mail. Is this what the phone call last night was about?"

I raised my eyes, *Yes*.

When the possibility of working with the ONI surfaced in December, Emma and I agreed that it would be a good organization for me. Because most ONI employees were proficient in Morse Code, I could communicate with everyone using a portable key, by telegraph, or by tapping on hard surfaces. I still feel that way. Communicating through Morsing allows me to demonstrate my skills. Officers in the ONI learned that I felt comfortable with uncertainty and thrive on it. I also want an adventure off-island, and very much need a job.

I was sure the ONI understood that I have adjusted to my disability, and that I wouldn't stop trying to accomplish anything. With my sister at my side, I forged ahead and soon, nothing, nothing at all, seemed to bother me. But having my sister at my side was not going to happen.

"If you knew we had to get up this early, why didn't we spend the night at the Weather House?" Emma asked. She mumbled her complaint, "And what direction is the wind blowing? Will I have to push into it?"

I did not respond to either question and went about getting dressed. I had partial use of my right leg and full use of my right arm and hand, and rarely, except for buttons, needed help getting dressed. But when I did need help, I asked for it in a "matter-of-fact" manner.

Emma returned from the bathroom and watched me struggle to put on a dark blue flannel shirt and dark blue pants, both official men's

Naval issue that John gifted us last October. My matter-of-fact approach appeared shortly after our accident, when I learned to acknowledge help with a slight nod of my head, sometimes with a smile, but just as often without.

"Annie, what's so urgent?"

Will explain on the way.

"When there's a task at hand there's no way to change your mind. You're driven, Annie," Emma said, with a touch of sarcasm.

But I get things done quickly, and efficiently.

"Yes, yes, yes, like before the accident."

Emma made sure that I would never change because she encouraged me all along. She continued to give a running dialogue, mostly to herself.

"You always put things in motion, and only share the *why* at some point down the road."

And that's bad?

"Well, that way it's too late to try and talk you out of it. You are my sister, but most times you're the 'person in charge'."

And what's wrong with that?

In October, John mentioned that ONI officers must not disclose information learned from working on missions. And that I'd have to learn to ignore some of Emma's questions. My sister and I shared much about the Weather House Mission but when I didn't, Emma knew it was my signal that I held confidential information. A consequence of not answering her questions was that I'd have to listen to her yarning, like this morning.

"What's it going to be this time? And why is it so darn important it can't wait 'til later? It's freezing outside."

7

ANNIE

"I'll help Annie down the stairs," Lillie said, as she walked into our bedroom. "When you get to the Hog Penn, it's important that no one sees you board the tug."

Lillie had placed my wheelchair at the base of the stairs and was fully "dressed". A gray winter coat, without markings, provided by the ONI last October was draped on the seat. On top was another navy-blue cape. The overcoats fended off the winter wind when it blew under the seat. John had given Emma and me official overcoats without insignias and Emma flung hers over her shoulders.

"Muffins are in each of your pockets, but Geo will provide breakfast, too."

"Thank you, Mom," Emma said.

The sun was three hours from rising and there was plenty of time to board under the cover of darkness. As Emma guided me down High Street, we noted that there was very little wind. She started pushing as we approached the statue of Rebecca at the bottom of the hill and turned left onto Water Street and through the heart of Old Harbor Village. In the center of Water Street, we passed the U.S. Post Office.

"No one's in town. Only one fisherman in the inner basin. He's struggling with his sails," Emma said as she looked out to the Atlantic.

I tapped, *He wouldn't get far in that boat if the wind doesn't pick up.*

We turned left on Dodge Street and when Old Harbor Village ended, we continued straight on Ocean Avenue toward the New Harbor. It was a half mile before it intersects Beach Street. But, as Emma always reminds me, not before the rutted dirt of Ocean Avenue begins its steep uphill climb.

"Why are you so quiet Annie?"

I was going to tap my thoughts, but it was too long to Morse. And, I had other things to worry about. Instead, I tapped the obvious, *I wonder who is on the boat, and why we are not to be seen?*

"What's going on?"

I didn't reply, and Emma let it go for a third time.

We were halfway to the top of the hill and Emma stopped pushing to catch her breath. It wasn't just the hill that wore her out, it was the ruts in the clay and sandy road that made pushing even more difficult.

"These ruts, this road needs smoothing."

Before Ocean Avenue was made, we would have had to go the long way ...

"I know the path here was turned into a road twenty years ago, but it's still a lot of pushing."

We continued past the foundation ruins of the massive Hygeia Hotel that burned five months previously.

The boat we're meeting is a tugboat.

"That's a rarity on Block Island."

Lillie says it has two stacks.

We reached the top of the hill and descended on the other side. Right away the Hog Penn came into view. But it was dark and all I saw were patrol boats. I did not see stacks on a tug. The Hog Penn was a few hundred yards on the right, on the other side of the stone bridge over the tidal Trim's Pond.

Straight ahead, a half mile away, was the end of Ocean Avenue and the main wharf, where large ferries docked. To the left of the Ferry Dock was the Narragansett Inn, but we couldn't see the tents in the back.

Without sunlight it was impossible to make out vessels anywhere in the New Harbor. I strained my eyes but could not see a tugboat in the Hog Penn.

We continued down the hill, crossing over the rails for the horse cars.

About fifty yards from the Hog Penn the fishing smacks came into view, along with that two Naval patrol boats at the far end of the Hog Penn near the new building. Then I saw a vague shadow. I was dumbfounded. Without light from a moon above I wasn't sure what I was seeing.

"I see it! Is that the tug?" Emma asked.

Yes! At the end of the Hog Penn.

"On the other side of the patrol boat but set back. Is that it?"

I raised my eyes, *Yes*.

"That's not a tug, Annie. If it's a boat, it's the most grotesque thing I've ever seen in the water."

I shook my head and brought my right hand toward my belly and turned it up and down. It was my sign for, *What the heck is that?* Emma and I often used that hand sign, especially in class where nobody knew what it meant. We stared for another minute. The boat was painted black or dark gray, and we could see that it was powered by steam engines, because of its two short stacks.

"It has a hull, with a high bow and a stern with a low gunwale, so I guess it's a boat. What's that structure on the deck? It's square, as tall as it is long, and it's two large square 'portholes' make it look like a floating office. But it isn't a tug."

I tapped, *Looks like a cabin was dropped on the deck of a patrol boat, and now it's disguised as a tug.*

Emma guided the wheelchair toward the Hog Penn. The uneven ground at the edge of the water was treacherous in a wheelchair. The few uneven wooden planks were in a constant state of disrepair. I wasn't sure what was worse, the ruts on Ocean Avenue, the rails of the horse trolley, or at the water's edge of the Hog Penn. Last summer Emma accidentally pushed me into a rut near the edge, and the wheelchair tipped over, and I tumbled into the water. I surfaced quickly and we laughed. It is difficult for many to understand that I do not feel as disabled when I swim underwater, so it didn't matter that Emma inadvertently dumped me in the drink.

"Why didn't the tug tie up at the main dock?"

Better hidden here, behind the Naval Patrol boats.

"Closer to the Weather House, too."

Suddenly a figure emerged near the shadow of the boat and walked into the street. There was no doubt he was heading in our direction.

Who is this?

Emma saw him first, her eyesight better than mine. My fear turned to elation when I realized it was John. Emma called his name and ran to him.

"I've missed you," Emma said softly, hugging him, forgetting that he had frightened us. "Did you come off that ugly boat?"

"Great to see you two! Let's get your sister out of the street and on deck."

Great to see you, too, I said using the sign I created in October for John. It's a good thing it was dark because tears clouded my vision.

"Where did the boat come from?" Emma asked. "Is it modified to look like a tug?"

John nodded and pushed me onto the dock, and then hoisted me out of the wheelchair. "Let's get on board. Bring the wheelchair, Emma, please."

"Did you sail out of the Brooklyn Navy Yard or Newport?" Emma asked.

John didn't answer.

"And how fast does it go?" No answer to that question either. We both figured he'd tell us what was going on when he was good and ready.

The cabin door opened inward. I was startled to see another man from the Navy sitting below deck, in plain clothes. At six feet tall, it's a good thing this guy didn't approach us in the street.

John carried me to a plush chair near a wood burning stove and introduced us. Lieutenant Fabbri of the Naval Reserve held the same rank as John. But did not appear to be John's supervisor. We later found that Fabbri was on board for a secret mission. John would leave Fabbri in Maine, and would then return to Washington, DC before setting sail to the Caribbean Sea for another assignment.

"This is Annie Rose, and her sister Emma Rose," John said to his shipmate.

"Hi," Lt. Fabbri said. "Good to meet you. I understand that you two know Lawrence Sperry."

"Oh, yes, we do!" Emma said without hesitation. Her palpable enthusiasm brought a chuckle from Lt. Fabbri, and a broad smile to everyone's faces.

John turned to Emma. "Geo has a packet of information for me. Could you run up to the Weather House and bring it back?"

"He might not be awake," Emma said hesitantly, not wanting to take leave of the Ugly Tug.

"He's awake. He wired that he has breakfast for us. Would you please bring that back, too?"

"Of course." Emma complied and hurried out the cabin.

We heard her jump off the gunwale and land on the dock, then she retraced her steps up Ocean Avenue toward the Weather House. I'm sure Emma was thinking the same thing I was: Why did John and Lt. Fabbri arrive in the cover of night? But with John sending Emma to the Weather House, it was clear that they had something more to share with me, most likely information about my secret mission.

With Emma off the boat, Lt. Fabbri eventually excused himself and went for a walk in the direction of the Narragansett Hotel. John explained what I knew, that my conclusions about the Brits attempting counterintelligence against us were not happily received by Admiral Benson, the Chief Naval Officer, or by the Army's Chief of Staff, General Scott. Yet, others in the ONI were impressed with my hypotheses, even if I was wrong. And how I asked questions no one else bothered to entertain.

"It's not a longshot, Annie, that you can make an impact if you join the ONI. I know you can't walk or talk, but you've got remarkable reasoning ability. And despite having no formal training in my field, you can figure anything out."

I gave my hand signal for *Thank you.*

"Major Van Deman at the Army War College was impressed when you identified an operation that had as its intent to *disguise* the actual source of the responsibility of the operation, and then pin the blame on another party. Do you know what that's called?"

Is this what's called a false flag?

"Yes! It's a very old term that's used when there's an attempt to disguise the source of responsibility of an enemy action. And always includes blaming another party. It was first used in the late 1500s and continues to be used today in military operations. You're figuring this out on your own is one reason we believe you'll become an impactful member of the ONI."

I listened intently and tapped, *Thank you.*

John added, "And your intuitive understanding of what Major Van Deman calls negative intelligence and its impact on policy made him realize you understand a lot more than most."

Thank you.

"Have you heard of Winston Churchill, Annie?"

Of course. Geo spoke of him, and he is in the newspapers.

"Years ago, Churchill and a mystery professor, Alfred Ewing, modernized a section of their Secret Intelligence Service, a far more robust version of our ONI. In part, they established listening posts worldwide. The ONI needs to expand our wireless system in America, and, to that end, Lt. Fabbri and I are sailing to northern Maine. He's showing me an ideal, secluded spot to establish a wireless listening station."

Only a receiving station?

"The Navy will eventually add transmission capability."

Did the British Secret Intelligence Service do that, too?

"Yes. As far back as 1901 they placed wireless telegraphy equipment on Royal Navy ships. After that they set up listening centers throughout their country, and then the world. This is top secret. But you will learn this in your training sessions. Room 40, as early as 1908, was able to intercept wireless transmissions anywhere in the world. We've gotta catch up," John said emphatically.

Can Germany do that?

"Yes. Their wireless transmission system extends to the Ottoman Empire."

Can the SIS eavesdrop on cable transmissions, too? And decipher coded messages?

John wasn't totally surprised by my question. "I wish we knew."

But then he put his head down. "This is a good time a time as any to share top secret information. We suspect that Churchill and Ewing, long ago, set up a system to intercept cable transmissions throughout Great Britain. But we can't figure out how they do it."

Room 40 is part of the Royal Navy?

"Room 40 is part of the SIS, and is based in the Admiralty."

How did they figure that out?

"Good question. That's where Professor Ewing comes in. He understands the science of wireless and cable transmissions, how to intercept them, and how to decipher them. It took an engineer to figure that out and that's his calling."

Do we have an engineer like that?

"Yes, and those folks are creating the Radio Corporation of America. Some are working for the ONI and some with the Army Signal Service. I believe RCA is trying to buy the Marconi Corporation. But Ewing was also an early cryptologist, too."

John went quiet for a few moments, then looked up.

"Annie, the other information I need to share impacts you directly."

I read his face and John's demeanor had changed.

"This is top secret at the highest level. First, the good news. Commander McCauley approved your recruitment and participation in the organizational meetings and training program that Major Van Deman is organizing. The Commander also approved your assignment that we talked about on the phone. This can never be shared with anyone, including Geo or Emma, or anyone else in the ONI."

John took a deep breath. "I'll explain as much as possible before Emma returns to the boat. You must attend the several weeks of sessions at the Army War College in DC. It's a combined ONI and MIS training that will introduce you to cryptology, the nature of classified information, and espionage techniques."

I raised my eyes and tapped, *Must I attend the first training?*

"Yes. You will be one of only two from the ONI assigned to the first training. You must attend because of the possible spy.

"Agents have different motives when joining an intelligence service. You'll read about that in the packet of information I have for you. I also want you to be aware of a recent form of a spy, a double agent, and that there are now spies who are journalists."

Do double agents want to betray their country?

"Depends on their motives. They often do, but not always. We'll share what we've learned about each of the trainees. It's important that if you identify new or different aspects of their lives and motivations that we did not know prior to training ... that could be a clue that that man is a spy."

I raised my eyes, and after a pause, John continued.

"You'll be introduced as a civilian member of the ONI, to train as a coder. Being that you're a young woman in a wheelchair with a disability who cannot talk, it's unlikely that anyone will suspect that you've been given an assigned mission. Most likely you'll be ignored by most, although some trainees will be friendly. Don't worry if you're not taken seriously. That could be helpful."

I will have three covers. My disability, being a young woman, and working for the Weather Bureau.

"Well said, Annie. Your training group will consist of many individuals, but not everyone will be present for the first week. As far as I know, two members are transferring from the Army's Signal Service. Sergeant Yardley has been with the Signal Service and State for ten years. His assistant has worked with him, but we know very little about him.

"One well researched trainee comes from industry, and we only know that he's interested in industrial espionage. There are several detectives from the NYPD Bomb Squad who have been invited. One will work with the ONI. We have a soldier transferring from an assignment at the Army War College. There's also a well-regarded lawyer from the Army, and another from the Army originally from West Virginia. But there are others. Except for you and Barnitz, all have been chosen by Major Van Deman."

Who is Barnitz?

"He's a detective and the Deputy Director of the Bomb Squad, under Tunney."

He's experienced and I'm not! What resources will I have?

"In this folder are details of each trainee. Please memorize the information, then destroy it. As far as resources, you'll have the same access to those the trainee group has. For example, an old model Telegraph Machine will be installed in the conference room."

I know old Telegraph Machines.

"I remember that you and your sister clean the salt from the cabinet!"

We got distracted by voices on Ocean Avenue. When they got louder and approached the Hog Penn, John left the cabin to identify the source. Soon the commotion stopped but John didn't return right away. When he reappeared, he explained that he'd walked four very drunk sailors away from the Ugly Tug and back to their tents behind the Narragansett Hotel.

"Annie, how do you think Emma will fare when you leave?"

I was glad John asked the question because it needed to be addressed.

I Morsed slowly, *Neither Lillie nor my sister want me to leave, but for different reasons. Lillie feels I will not be taken care of in DC. Emma and I want to leave the Island, for a better future, but we want to leave together.*

"I think your mother will eventually agree that it's best for you. It's a remarkable opportunity for you. One reason I'm here is to convince her of that. And about Emma, that situation will work itself out in a few months. She'll understand."

Emma is worried she'll be replaced by another caregiver.

"She's realistic," John said. "Your new caregiver will be Mrs. Lynch, from the Army War College."

8

ANNIE

More voices walking toward the docked patrol boats irritated John.

"I must talk to the captain of the patrol boats. We're carrying a crate of depth charges, and we don't want anyone near them."

Last October, John came as close to being family as anyone we'd ever met. I felt comfortable sharing with John a conversation my sister and I had last weekend.

I explained that we had stopped to look at the tide rushing in under the old stone bridge on Ocean Avenue. The channel under the bridge connects the two parts of Trim's Pond. When a mid-ebb tide comes in, we often peer over the edge, mesmerized by the current and get lost in memory. For those who know small channels, at mid-ebb tide, the current speeds up, a function of the bridge's narrow opening rather than the tide itself.

I tapped, *Emma was holding me as I looked over the bridge to the current below. Emma was resigned to my leaving.*

"She may be resigned, but she's not prepared for it," John said.

I raised my eyes. *She spoke of David Copperfield's life – the loneliness of his life.*

"It's been a long time since I've read Copperfield."

Our teacher said it is an autobiographical novel. Emma sees us in the book. Copperfield lost his mother and a younger brother, and my sister and I lost our father and a brother. But his life was lonelier than ours.

Dickens writes a lot about being "houseless" in this and other writings. We have never been houseless.

"Do you ever feel, 'David Copperfield Lonely'?"

Sometimes. That day on the bridge she dwelled on me leaving. We are inseparable. We go to school together, we are very good friends, and after the accident we have shared the same bed.

"And you almost died together."

I looked down and tapped, *It is hard to believe we are still alive.*

"You're both here and we're the better for it."

She is my heart outside my body. She said what we both know ... that I will die young, before her, and she will never be able to see my sweet face again.

"Copperfield walked for days to reach his aunt's house, only to find out she didn't know what to do with him. She allowed him to stay in the top floor with a view of the ocean, and he thinks, finally, he's no longer houseless. And will never be alone again."

Yes, and he thinks about his mother and his sister, looking down from heaven watching over him. Before I fall asleep, I often gaze out to sea and imagine my dad and brother looking down from Heaven, keeping a watchful eye on us.

"If I ever see your sister leaning over the bridge, I'll know she's worried about something. Or she's saying prayers, one blessing the dead, and one asking God to bless you."

John put his head down and I knew he was saying a prayer for his late sister.

*

EMMA

I walked in the front door of the Weather House to the noise of the Telegraph Machine receiving and printing messages, a small reminder that the Weather House is an active Weather Bureau of the United States Government, and not primarily a home.

Geo was waiting to serve breakfast.

"Geo, that's not a tugboat," I proclaimed before I took a seat at the kitchen table. "But it's got a wood burning stove and a comfortable chair. But it's still an Ugly Tug."

"Looks like a floating black box, doesn't it?" Geo observed. "But under that cabin is a mighty fine boat."

"Why do you say it's a fine boat?"

"Those twin stacks represent two powerful engines. Remember, what appears is not always what is. Those engines are there for a reason – underneath is a fast Navy patrol boat."

How many times has Geo given Annie and me mini lectures, all with the same theme, to challenge us to learn *how* to think, rather than learning *what* to think? He also had the great skill of turning anything into a moral dilemma. Annie would soon meet someone very much like him.

"Below deck is a desk, a stove that looks like a fireplace, a small head, three bunks and a hatchway to the engine room."

"They're bringing me a new wireless transmitter. A replacement for the one we have."

After a few moments I asked the question I most feared, "I know Annie will eventually be called to Washington, DC, but are they taking her today?"

"I don't think so, but it will be soon. Are you going to help at the high school today?"

"They don't need me, and I'd rather spend the day with Annie."

"That's fine. I support Annie working with the ONI, and one reason they're on Island is to explain why it's a good decision for your sister. Hopefully your mother will agree."

Geo's comment sent me reeling but I sat quietly and said nothing.

"We all know that Annie needs to be challenged, and never coddled because of her disability. I am certain that working for the ONI will make her happy, because she needs to make a difference."

I looked down.

"Emma, I know you understand she needs to leave the Island."

"I understand, but I need to leave, also," I insisted.

Geo said he understood. "One day you will leave the Island, too, for more opportunities."

"We can live together, and I can find a job in the same area."

Suddenly, I hesitated and thought of an incident that came to mind from several years ago.

"What is it, Emma?" Geo prompted.

"You know that Gloucester fisherman occasionally tie up in the Old Harbor. When they arrive, they're a tad arrogant and always point out that their small city is named after Gloucester, England, near the Cotswolds. There was a fisherman from one of those boats who treated Annie like she was retarded. He sat on the stern asking stupid questions. Annie played along with facial and hand gestures."

Geo raised his eyes. "What did you do?"

"I didn't do anything. I was standing near the fish houses, and she signaled me to come over. When I got close, she blinked me Morsed instructions. I wasn't sure what she was up to, but the closer I got I saw how rude and condescending that guy was."

"Uh-oh, then what?" Geo rolled his eyes.

"I casually pushed her along the dock as if we were going home. Annie helped me steer across one of the ruts in the dock. Of course, the front wheel jammed, and Annie ejected herself out of the wheelchair and in one motion rolled off the dock into the water."

"Oh, no. That poor fisherman."

"I thought he was going to have a heart attack."

"Then what?"

"I started yelling and he jumped into the water. But he couldn't find her because she was holding her breath, hiding behind the pilings. He surfaced then dove back down but came up again for air. Finally, he dove in a third time, and she came out from behind the piling, and he brought her up. She pretended to gag, but I knew she was okay."

"Did the fisherman apologize?"

"I'm sorry, I'm sorry. You alright? Lesson learned.'" I imitated him.

"I never heard that story."

"There's more. Remember when Lillie had a lot of tuna and swordfish?"

"Was it from that fisherman?"

"Yup."

Geo shook his head.

We finished our oatmeal, with milk from the Mitchel Farm that was left by Wallace at the back door. Wallace, the most difficult of Geo's three boys, had caused much grief to Lillie for various reasons, and tried her patience over and over. Yet at the same time he was responsible and lovable. He was a quiet person, rarely interacted with but a few Islanders, and loved being at sea. He had difficulty socializing in large groups and found a perfect home and made good friends working the night shift at the Bell Telephone switchboard. He also kept secrets, an important attribute for someone working a party line switchboard. Recently he built a bungalow on Mohegan Bluffs, near the expansive land of the Vaill Hotel and the judge's house, and within walking distance to the Mitchel Farm. He displayed the name of his home, *Eddey's Shanty*, in a porthole bolted to the front of his home and surrounded it with blue hydrangeas.

"Emma, you should get back to the boat. Take this folder, along with the basket of food."

I thanked Geo for breakfast and left out the back door. The sky was beginning to lighten, earlier than the scheduled sunrise; its light reflected off the top of the masts of the fishing smacks.

Geo walked into the telegraph room while I stood on the top wooden step and gazed beyond the Hog Penn to the Great Salt Pond beyond. I heard Geo tapping a Morsed message. It was too faint for me to make out entirely, but the only words I could hear were my sister's name and the word "deception".

What was that about? Who was going to be deceived?

9

ANNIE

While Emma was having breakfast with Geo, and Lt. Fabbri was still visiting an officer at the Narragansett Hotel, John elaborated on my question of why the Major wasn't told about my mission. His answer served as an introduction to "human sources" that ONI agents try to recruit.

"Commander McCauley and Mr. Harrison will be the only two at the meetings who know of your assignment. In general, espionage services rely on human sources, if we can, otherwise we plant human sources to observe. Of course, if we can intercept crypted messages that's great."

I tapped for clarification, *Human sources provide information about spies, and some are spies?*

"Yes. And remember that if there is a spy in the training room, he may try to recruit you to be a human source for Germany."

I raised my eyes, twice.

"Annie, everyone you meet will know that you, and Barnitz, are on assignment from the ONI, but none will be privy to your mission. Do not confuse the three groups of people, your supervisors, your colleagues in the training sessions, and the very few senior intelligence officers that know about your assignment."

I understand.

"Remember, never expose sources. As times goes on, you'll figure out that it's better not to know too much."

How do we recruit human sources?

"The ONI has been doing it for years. You'll learn in the training how it's done. Van Deman's MIS will struggle doing that. But our ONI has been in existence since the early 1880s and we've developed human sources that are embedded in many country's embassies, and especially their ports of call, and their ships. We recruit readily from the docks, where allegiances, as they say, change with the wind."

Will I meet a human source?

"You'll meet one agent outside your training and, if you stay at the Hamilton Hotel, you'll meet a few sources. They must never be exposed."

Who is the agent that I might meet?

"U-1 embedded an agent in the German Embassy to monitor the German Ambassador's activities. Remember, no one knows about your mission or U-1! You're being alerted because you may meet a senior agent who goes by 'Bill'. That's not his real name. He dines at the Hamilton and is a member of the Cosmos Club. That club and the German Embassy are within walking distance of the Hamilton."

How many in the training room know of the existence of U-1?

"The trainee from the Army War College assignment knows, Yardley, and his assistant."

Emma entered the cabin and John shifted to generic non-espionage information that Emma could overhear. Soon Lt. Fabbri returned.

"Here's the food and the packet from Geo," Emma said. "The stove sure does heat up the cabin. It's warmer in here than in any house on the Island."

"Yes, it does, and thank you, Emma." John handed the basket of food to the Lieutenant and placed the documents in a secure drawer.

Emma sensed that she had returned too early, and said, "I want to walk up to the Narragansett Hotel for a few minutes. I'll be right back."

"I'll join you, Emma," Lt. Fabbri said. "But would you take me up to the Weather House? I'd like to meet your uncle."

"Of course!"

"My hobby is wireless telegraphy. I've built a wireless receiver and transmitter. Can you Morse as well as your sister, Emma?"

"I'm not as fast as her but I can Morse well. Everyone in my family can."

After they were off the boat, John talked about the importance of using the metal file folder. He explained how to use the lock and handed me a

12-inch by 14-inch thin metal file to attach the lock. He handed me a slip of paper with the combination 2 – 9 – 5, and after I memorized it, he threw the paper into the fire. Using my right hand, I moved the dial with relative ease.

"You'll store documents in this file. It's heavy but it will stop a bullet if need be. We've been using the locks for five years, and the long bar can be used to attach the file to your wheelchair.

"Here's general information about the ONI. You'll have three other supervisors besides me. I'm the lead, but when I'm on assignment other individuals will fill my role. You know Mrs. Conway and she agreed to help but I don't think she'll be able to. Harriet Lynch works for the Army War Department. She's been a trusted confidant with clearance in the Army for several years and has volunteered to supervise and oversee your well-being while in DC. Major Van Deman will also supervise."

I tapped, *You said there was a fourth supervisor?*

"Both the ONI and Van Deman are trying to recruit Elizebeth Smith from Riverbank Labs. Along with Parker Hitt and his wife, Genevieve, and Elizebeth's fiancé, Bill Friedman, Elizebeth is the only other trained cryptologist in the United States. She can code and decrypt. Unfortunately, the officer we sent to Riverbank to recruit her doesn't think she'll join the military."

Sorry to hear that. Mrs. Conway told me about her.

"There would be no better mentor."

What about Mrs. Hitt?

"I believe she'll be stationed in Texas if we enter the war. You'll meet her husband. He's scheduled to give a lecture at the meetings. Last year the Army published his manual for solving military ciphers. Van Deman wants him, also, but McCauley told me that he'll be assigned to the intelligence group of the American Expeditionary Forces.

Next to your name are three words, "The Offshore Division." What is that?

"The ONI has an Onshore and an Offshore division. After the MIS becomes operational the ONI will hand over most responsibilities of the Onshore Division to the MIS. I've always been assigned to the Offshore Division."

Why is the Weather Bureau getting a new wireless transmitter?

"It's possible Germany, either its U-boats patrolling Block Island Sound or land-based agents, have spliced cables that Block Island's submarine cables connect on the mainland. It's easy to do that with a relay switch. A new wireless receiver and transmitter will circumvent any problems.

"Germany started using wireless after the Royal Admiralty cut Germany's cables in the English Channel the very night Britain declared war on Germany."

Geo told me that the U.S. Signal Service tapped underwater cables in 1890.

"Intercepting cable transmissions probably began soon after they were laid."

It says on my sheet that I must learn Swedish. Why? I thought Sweden was neutral.

"Nobody is truly neutral. Germany uses Sweden's cables for international transmissions. It's obvious that Sweden favors Germany. Like we favor Great Britain. Neutrality is as pragmatic as it is honest. You'll also have to learn Spanish codes, as messages can be routed through South America and back north to North America."

Will I learn the extent of that cable system?

"Yes, there's a sophisticated submarine cable system that crisscrosses the Atlantic Ocean. I'll make sure Leland Harrison gives you a reference manual."

Our meeting ended when Emma and Lt. Fabbri returned to the tug. We said goodbye and Emma pushed me to Payne's Dock. It was light now and sailors from the tent city behind the hotel were up and about. A Naval patrol boat started its engine and headed through the cut into Block Island Sound.

Emma asked an odd question, but then I realized it was about a word, "deception", that Geo had tapped out. "Annie, are you being deceived?"

I don't know what to what Geo was referring, but deception is a part of negative intelligence.

"Is this negative intelligence an area you're interested in?"

I raised my eyes *Yes, very much.*

"But what if he was Morsing a real concern that someone was deceiving you?"

10

ANNIE

Emma and I stayed on Payne's Dock to give time for John and Lt. Fabbri to plan their trip north. Early the next morning they'd set a course for the Cape Cod Canal, on their way to Maine, to the site of Lt. Fabbri's family land near Bar Harbor. They had to pick up a passenger in Boston Harbor, one of John's fellow naval officers, Ray Cole. It turns out that Alessandro Fabbri was a friend of FDR, who arranged to have him become an ensign in the U.S. Naval Reserve Force. The extent of Lt. Fabbri's substantial contributions to the United States, in war and in peace, would become clear during training, I learned that he was donating his land on Otter Point to the Navy to build the finest receiving tower for wireless in the world. It was safe and used for allies to communicate directly with President Wilson.

As small as Block Island is, without a compass, understanding the geography of the Island is difficult to comprehend. Yet, for European navigators sailing to our continent, the Island itself has been a well-known geographic marker for centuries. A popular navigation book used in the 1600s includes a chapter titled, "When Coming Out of the Sea at Block Island." I think the best way to approach me is head on, too. And I've come to think the phrase "coming out of the sea at Block Island" as a metaphor to understand me and my disability.

The sun was up, the absence of a red sky suggested it would be a pleasant winter day. The wind was barely perceptible. Would this be a mild winter? It had been years since both harbors froze over.

Emma held me on the bench as we watched Naval officers walk in and out of the Narragansett Hotel, while enlisted men walked about their tents behind it. The smell of campfires permeated the entire area, competing successfully with the smell of dead fish.

A Naval patrol boat entered the cut with such speed that its wake was more prominent than the boat itself. As it approached Payne's dock every boat at anchor or docked rocked back and forth. The Naval presence on Block Island was the best sign that war was near. Yet, President Wilson continued to say that the United States would remain neutral. In my mind we were already at war. And I learned from John that almost every intelligence officer knew with certainty that we would eventually enter the Great European War.

"When I first saw John walking into the street to greet us this morning, it made me think of October. Remember that night when Lillie made him an honorary member of our family," Emma said.

I tapped, *I remember. It was a Saturday evening, at dinner.*

"And after that, Lillie gave us an order to attend church. Do you think she was aware someone was going to get killed that next day?"

I will never forget when Lillie looked at John and said, "And that includes you, John." I think she could see the future.

Lillie had a premonition one or more people would soon die and was worried it might be one of us. It was important for us to all attend a Sunday morning together at her Methodist Church. She was correct of course; three men were shot. The ONI agent brought in by John from the Mainland lived, but the two others died. One was a German spy, but the other may have been an itinerant fisherman working at a North End fishing camp. His allegiance was still unclear.

*

We returned to the Weather House and Emma helped carry and assemble the new wireless transmitter. Lt. Fabbri and Geo continued their talk of all things wireless. Emma helped string new transmission wire to the top of the signal tower, where weather flags are designed to fly.

By late afternoon Lillie informed us that she'd had a busy day entertaining a special visitor. We'd been up since 4 AM, saw the sun rise over the Old Harbor and were now seeing the sun set. We were pleased she would drive over and pick us up. Emma pushed me back to Payne's Dock and we sat on the same bench to wait for Lillie.

Mr. Mott, the owner of the Narragansett Hotel, was walking about with a naval officer in full dress uniform, including his white cap. They walked over to say hello.

"This is Commander Lieutenant Vanderbilt," Mr. Mott said. "This is Annie and her sister, Emma."

The Commander nodded and reached to shake my outstretched right hand. Emma stood up and shook his hand as well.

"I'm Emma Rose."

"Nice to meet you both."

I was worried that the Commander would see my new metal file under my cape. I deftly changed the subject by Morsing a question. I didn't know if Mr. Mott understood Morse Code but surely Lt. Vanderbilt did.

I tapped at my usual speed, *That patrol boat entering the harbor earlier came in very fast. Why?*

"I saw that too," Commander Vanderbilt acknowledged.

That wake could have capsized a small fishing smack.

"True. Those patrol boats have powerful engines. May I ask, Annie, where you learned to Morse so well?"

I tapped quickly, *Commander, that's top secret, sir.*

He laughed. At this point Mr. Mott interjected, "Annie Rose's uncle is the Head Weather Observer at the Weather Bureau and a Major in the Signal Service."

Is that your yacht, SP 56, docked on the end of the wharf?

"Yes, I gave it to the Navy. You're welcome to come aboard. It was great meeting you two," the Commander said, and he and Mr. Mott continued their walk around the hotel's grounds.

I often took time to *express* my thoughts but *formulating* them was a different story. My answers to questions came lightning fast, and I was as quick and witty as anyone. I strived to be strategic in all my responses and learned early on to take into consideration the setting, and to alter my response time as needed. All this varied given the situation, of course. With the Commander I wanted to ask a question to distract him, if by chance, he saw the metal case. So, I communicated a simple thought about the Naval patrol boat. My speed at Morsing changed the Commander's expression. Diverting conversations was a skill I possess, one that, perhaps, the ONI could develop.

Lillie arrived shortly thereafter, and Emma helped me to the back seat. She placed my wheelchair in the boot. I clutched my metal file close to me.

"I had a visitor today," Lille said. "She asked if I've ever wondered if one's life is nothing more than working hard toward a goal, and then, waiting for those special moments when dreams come true?"

I tapped, *What was that about*?

"She was talking about you."

Who was it?

"I'll tell you in a moment. But first, when is John leaving the Island?"

Later tonight, at high tide.

"They're leaving tonight?" Emma gasped. "I didn't say goodbye."

"You'll see him again. He's coming to dinner, and there will be another guest, too."

"And who's that?"

Suddenly Lillie became distracted and yelled out loud.

"What is that?" Lillie asked in disbelief. "It can't be seaworthy. Those stacks make it top heavy. Who would build such a thing?"

Emma and I couldn't stop laughing at Lillie's decidedly uncharacteristic reaction to seeing the Ugly Tug. I laughed so hard that I rolled off the back seat. Emma reached back to pull me back up. When laughter took hold, it wasn't unusual for me to partially collapse, due to lack of muscle coordination. With my sister and I, bursts of laughter, when we were alone, took on a life of its own, despite, or just because of, me literally losing it. But we let loose only with each other, or in the company of Lillie.

When we'd calmed down Lillie asked, "Aren't you interested who's on Island?"

11

ANNIE

"The visitor has to be a fisherman, because there's no ferry running today," Emma reminded us.

"You both know who she is," Lillie hinted.

I tapped, *Mrs. Conway?*

Lillie nodded to confirm.

"What boat brought her here?" Emma asked.

"A fishing trawler dropped her off in Old Harbor. The trawler put its engines in reverse and backed in where the ferry docks, and Mrs. Conway jumped right off. The captain left with its engines roaring, smoke billowing from its stacks, and within minutes they were on their way to George's Bank."

Margaret E. Conway is the Weather Observer in Charge of the US Weather Bureau in Narragansett Pier. First appointed in 1891, she's one of the most senior and well-respected observers in the United States. She's the only woman observer in the Weather Bureau with forecasting privileges, a rare privilege accorded to very few local Head Observers.

After my recovery and the magnitude and permanence of my disability became apparent, Mrs. Conway "spoke" to me regularly via telegraph. Geo helped increase my speed, but Mrs. Conway encouraged me to use Morsing as a "conversational language". She understood it would be essential to express complex thoughts – if the other person knew Morse Code of course.

Lillie glanced over her shoulder. "She brought documents for you to sign."

"Will we get to see her?" Emma asked.

"Yes, she'll be at dinner. She wants to explain how to work with Naval personnel, and she'll tell you what she knows about one of your supervisors. She'll take the ferry back to Newport in the morning."

"Is she one of Annie's supervisors?" Emma asked.

"I'm not sure."

"Mom, Annie is gladder if that's a word, than she's been in a while. But I'm sadder, and I know that's a word. If she leaves the Island, I'm going to go with her!" Emma was defiant.

I tapped, *If you were present at my meeting, you would understand. I will be very busy.*

My responsibilities were more than I anticipated, and although honored to be assigned my secret mission, I worried about being alone in the Washington, DC, too. How would I fare without Emma? My self-confidence will have to hold up, but perhaps I'm NOT as independent as I think. But whenever I think that, Geo's voice pops up in my head: "It doesn't matter if you're worried ... don't let it interfere with your work."

Lillie turned right at High Street and my mind returned to Mrs. Conway. When she turned into the narrow lane that led to our home in the back of the Union House Hotel, I looked for Mrs. Conway. As soon as we approached the front entrance, she walked right out the front door. She was short yet gave the appearance of being taller in her long green dress. Her dark gray hair suited her age of 68, but the bounce in her step made her look much younger. She walked toward the car, and it hit me. Tears flowed from my eyes. Because, except for Emma, *everything* was falling into place, and Mrs. Conway was the great reminder of how far I have come.

Lillie had not turned off the ignition when Mrs. Conway opened the back right car door and enveloped me in a big hug. I didn't want to let her go, and tapped on her arm, *I have much to share!*

Emma removed the wheelchair from the boot and placed it a few feet behind Mrs. Conway. Our prolonged embrace prompted thoughts of what we'd been through, individually, as friends, as family. Episodes such as this gave pause to reflect on how different we were now. Different as a family, and as individuals.

Mrs. Conway helped transfer me to the wheelchair, while I clutched my metal file.

"I brought papers to review," Mrs. Conway said.

I looked at Emma and gave her one of my little-used hand signals, *Is this happening?*

Emma smiled and closed the back door of the car. I know what she was thinking, that it was happening for me, but not for her. It was our dream that we'd both leave the Island, to explore the world, together. Leaving without her was not part of our dreams. But I wasn't worried, we'd figure out a way to be together again. I'd make sure of that. But I couldn't risk sharing my thoughts of how my sister could follow me to Washington, DC. But if she came at the beginning, she'd be left alone most of the time.

Mrs. Conway and I gravitated to the far corner of the living room near the fire, which she had thoughtfully stoked prior to our arrival. Speaking softly under the cover of the crackling fire she handed me the package and we discussed the contents.

"The first sheet of instructions lists your four supervisors. I'm one of them, mostly because I know Mrs. Smith of Riverbank Studios."

What's Riverbank Studios?

"It's a private research compound near Chicago. She's a cryptologist and the ONI is trying to recruit her."

John mentioned that her friend discouraged her from working for the Navy.

"If true, that's too bad, because she's brilliant."

We were interrupted by a knock on the door, but before anyone could stand up, it swung open and in walked Geo, John, and Wallace. Lt. Fabbri stayed back on the Ugly Tug.

We promptly sat for dinner, but soon Lillie's dinner turned into a "recruiting" session – for me. I tried to keep track of everything, but it was difficult. At first, Geo, Lillie, and Mrs. Conway retreated to the kitchen to review my hiring letter. The letterhead made clear that my cover and paycheck would come from the U.S. Weather Bureau. This explained why Mrs. Conway was assigned the task of bringing Weather Bureau documents to the Island.

Lillie then joined John in the living room. They moved to the far side of the fireplace, in a corner of the living room. I remained at the table, but Emma deftly positioned herself near the indoor pile of firewood. She was far enough to not attract attention and kept busy stoking the fire. She picked up a copy of the John Rathom's newspaper and wondered what the *Providence Journal* would say tomorrow.

John got right to it. "Lillie, I know you're not going to like this, but Annie needs to start in a few weeks."

"How is Annie going to function, alone, at the Army War College?" Lillie said, shaking her head.

"I understand your concern, but Mrs. Rose, you are aware of your daughter's skills and her desire to work with the ONI."

"I'm aware. And I agree that this intelligence business comes naturally to her. And she gets the big picture, but she has much to learn."

"She 'doesn't get lost in the trees', as my professor at Yale was fond of saying. And it's amazing that her speed and accuracy of transmitting Morse Code is better than ninety percent of telegraphers."

Lillie gave a curt smile. "Have you thought about how she'll be taken care of? I do not want Annie to leave until someone here can accompany her."

"We will provide individuals to help."

"We love her, and I don't know how the sisters will deal with being separated." Lillie's voice cracked, holding back tears.

"Annie understands negative intelligence. Last October it didn't matter that she was wrong, she correctly understands possibility must be raised."

"What is this about?"

"Your daughter was one of few who thought a close ally would use intelligence against us."

"Does it have anything to do with President Wilson's steadfast desire to remain neutral?"

"It might. Let me explain. Recently, Wilson upset Churchill when he ordered our Navy to monitor wireless receiving stations – powerful enough to receive messages from European nations – to prevent an adversary from using them, and that included the British.

"But that's not important for us. Let me discuss the team we put together to help Annie."

Lillie sat back in her chair. "Where will she live? Who'll take care of her?"

"Annie will live at the Hamilton Hotel, not too far from the White

House. As you know, the Hamilton is owned by someone from Block Island."

"Yes, Irving." Lillie nodded. "He left the Island twenty years ago. He's a nephew of Block Island's famous Nicholas Ball."

"Irving will be there, of course, and he'll be told that Annie is attending a training at the Weather Bureau headquarters in DC. He will not be privy to anything, and it's essential that no one from the Island learn about Annie's assignment."

"Who will look after my daughter?"

"We'll assign someone experienced with her condition to her on an everyday basis. Someone who works for the Army War College and has clearance."

"I'm glad you thought about that."

"Lieutenant Fabbri and I will take the boat to Maine for two weeks. After we pick up one of my colleagues in Boston Harbor, we'll head to Maine to complete a mission.

"When we return, we'd like for you to agree to let us take Annie to DC. She's 22 years old and we don't need written permission, but we want you to feel comfortable with her becoming a civilian in the ONI. After that, I must travel to begin an international mission. We'd like her to be settled in before we leave the States."

Lillie surveyed the room. Geo and Mrs. Conway were still in the kitchen. I was at the table talking with Wallace. Emma was "reading" the newspaper.

"Annie was a motivated, fearless child and her disability doesn't faze her," Lillie said. "I don't know what will become of her." Tears appeared in her eyes.

John fully understood Lillie's apprehension, but he recognized that her watery eyes suggested Annie Rose would soon leave the Island ... and with her mother's blessing. Fortunately, Lillie was not privy to my secret mission. If that was shared, there's no chance in hell that she or any mother would let a daughter be recruited. And for very good reason.

12

ANNIE

Throughout the evening, Emma overheard bits and pieces of conversations that she knew not to ask about. But before we fell asleep, she wanted me to explain the difference between codes and ciphers.

I tapped, *A code is a made-up language, that uses letters and numbers from any alphabet. Sometimes codes will include symbols that have nothing to do with the alphabet. Symbols are difficult to break.*

"That's all a code is?"

It's more complicated. Groups of letters and numbers are given certain meanings, like words in English have meanings. In a sense, a code becomes a new language, but uses an existing alphabet.

"Letters have different meanings than in the original alphabet. But what's a cipher?"

Ciphers hide an existing language. English, German, French, or any language can be hidden in a system. And cipher machines scramble words.

"Who makes sense of it all?"

The analyst or cryptologist. Ciphers use existing alphabets but mixes up letters to create words that have different meanings. Cipher machines do this instantaneously all the time. These are almost impossible to break.

"Understanding ciphers and codes is a lot of work," Emma said. "I hope you can learn this stuff."

I raised my eyes, and knew that if I could not learn it, I would not last long at the ONI.

*

The next two weeks were a blur. Emma finished reading the last few chapters of *David Copperfield,* and I studied the packet of information that Mrs. Conway brought. It was practically thick as a bible. Frankly, what I could not understand I memorized. I learned to memorize whatever I do not understand, because the day I have a better grasp of the information, it comes together quickly.

After John and Lt. Fabbri sailed to Maine, Emma saw worry on my face. She was right, I did not smile that first week, but by the second week my normal facial expressions returned. I even put lipstick on.

Emma always marveled that I rarely complain. "You just work, Annie. You don't stop."

I'd respond, *"Emma, learning is hard but fun. And I don't do easy.* It has become my favorite phrase.

When Emma finished reading Dicken's novel, I noticed she discretely put aside her clothing in a corner of the closet. Two days later I saw the clothing had been wrapped in a tight bundle. I wasn't sure how she'd get to Washington, DC, but she'd find a way.

But what if she never made it to DC?

13

ANNIE

At 7:30 PM on Sunday, March 7, John sent an urgent wireless message to the Weather House: "German U-boats off New England coast. Will dock at Hog Penn early Monday morning. Have Annie packed and ready to depart at 02:00. Need cover of night to avoid U-boats."

Geo immediately called Lillie. "I received the 'go' message from John. The Ugly Tug will arrive after midnight."

"Oh, no. It's happening, Geo," she said, gasping.

I was ready for bed when Lillie came upstairs to deliver the news.

"Annie, tonight's the night."

"What?" Emma practically shouted, "Annie has to go now? NO!"

It shook Emma in a way I should have anticipated. I wish she could accompany me, but John was adamant she could not. It was out of the question due to legal issues.

"Yes, Emma," Lillie said, also visibly shaken.

I decided to Morse at my fastest pace, so that Lillie could not understand. It's how we communicated privately with each other. I felt for Emma, she was so sad, and we'd been through so much together.

I tapped with lightning speed: *Emma, I'm sorry, but I must go. You will not be far behind. I promise. Do not worry. Pay attention to me.*

Emma raised her eyes then buried her face in her pillow and shook her head. Lillie put a few last items in my duffle bag. I was certain that I was the only happy person in the room.

I fell asleep but Emma had difficulty. At 1:15 Lillie woke me, helped me dress and carried me downstairs. Geo was waiting outside, having already stowed my wheelchair in the boot. Geo appeared calm, but not Lillie. Emma was in a daze.

The roads were deserted as we made our way to the Hog Penn, the only sound the crunch of the tires on the gravel. We were early. Geo decided to take the long route, entering the New Harbor from West Side Road, and parked across from the Hog Penn. There we waited for the Ugly Tug to enter the cut.

The silhouette of the Naval patrol boat disguised as a tug was unmistakable, with its two stacks and box-like cabin. But so too was its massive wake. A few minutes later, the tug docked in the Hog Penn, bow first, and in the shadow of the new Navy pavilion. John had with him another Naval officer. He filled the boat with a thousand gallons of fuel from tanks installed by the Navy while John secured the boat.

Geo carried the baggage to the dock and Lillie pushed me. Emma refused to carry anything or help in any way. When the front wheels of the wheelchair got stuck in the rails of the horse trolly, she made no effort to lift the wheels over the rails.

I tapped at my fastest speed, *Emma, listen to me carefully.*

She looked surprised but nodded.

After the tug was secure, Geo passed the luggage to John. Emma was upset to the point that she couldn't muster a hello to John, but did say hello to the new officer. She stayed by my side.

"After the accident, I vowed that I would never leave you, and now I failed you," Emma whispered.

I blinked Morse Code so that no one else could see: *You didn't fail me. Going to need you.*

"What?" Emma tilted her head to the side.

"Lillie," John emphatically said, "I give you my word that the men in the first meeting sessions and during training will look after Annie. They are a good sort, and one of them has been ordered to do so from Lawrence Sperry! Mrs. Lynch will also be with her."

Lillie smiled at the mention of Sperry's name. Everyone does.

When the new Naval officer had finished refueling, John formally introduced him.

"Geo, this is Lieutenant Cole. He's been with the Navy as a radio operator for several years."

After a few minutes of exchanging pleasantries, John announced it was time.

"Okay, let's move. I'll carry Annie on board. Geo, can you lift the wheelchair on board?"

John went to pick me up and, using my eyes, I gave Emma my "get ready" hand signal. Then, I went into action. I locked my right hand around the armrest and my right leg around the bottom of the wheelchair frame. This prevented John from lifting me. Trying to carry both was obviously too dangerous.

"What's going on, Annie?" John asked.

I tapped, *Not going without Emma*. I tapped it twice, for everyone to hear. After all, this was an audience where everyone understood Morse Code.

John stepped back. "Annie, be reasonable, please, and let me carry you onto the boat."

Reasonable? Watch this.

With my good hand, I yanked backward on the right wheel, simultaneously propelling the chair past the edge of the boat and spinning it clockwise. The moment it was clear, I twisted, pitching myself out of the chair, but unfortunately, I fell off the dock, and into the water. I didn't care that I twisted too hard. I went with this unexpected "difficulty" and pretended to sink like a rock. The water was ice cold.

Everyone froze in disbelief. Except Emma. She also wasn't expecting me to go into the water, but without thinking she followed me.

Underwater I could hear Lillie reacting. "My daughters!" It took a moment before she realized what Emma had done and I would be okay. Emma dove under the water to me, grabbed my shoulders, looked closely into my eyes and saw my smile. She shook her head and returned my smile and then we surfaced. They reached down to pull us to safety. Geo wrapped a blanket around us while Emma and I sat there, catching our breaths. Out of the corner of my eye I saw Lt. Cole break into a smile of his own.

I tapped, *I trust my sister with my life.*

Geo shook his head from side to side. He looked at John and then they too started smiling.

"She drives a hard bargain," Lt. Cole said. "It's what we need in our ranks."

"She is determined, isn't she," John responded. "Lillie, Harriet will watch over them. And Geo, perhaps you can find job for Emma at the Weather Bureau in DC?"

Geo said he'd try. Lillie looked at us, wrapped in blankets and grinned. We must have been a pitiful sight, huddled together on the dock, wet hair, under the blanket.

Lillie turned to Geo, raised her for yes, and said, "Okay, let them both go."

Within minutes we were at the Weather House, getting dry clothes. Downstairs, John was explaining to Lillie that he'd mail her an official document to sign giving them permission to bring me along, but for now, verbal consent was all that was necessary. Lt. Cole was getting a tour of the Weather House's telegraph room, suggesting a more powerful transmitter was warranted.

Emma leaned over and whispered in my ear. "Annie, I had it all planned. I saved money to pay for a train to New York. Tomorrow I'd jump on the ferry to Providence and take the train to NYC and stay with Geo's sister in Upper Manhattan. I hoped that she would give me the rest of the money to take the train from Penn Station to Union Station in DC."

Clever, but you wouldn't have had to do all that. I realized convincing John to take you on board was the safest way to get you to DC. All other options were risky because you would be alone.

"What do you mean?"

Not for one second did I intend to go without you.

"But John said I couldn't be with you. Why didn't you tell me?"

I gave my good shoulder a shrug and tapped, *I like surprises – but you had to look surprised, too.*

On our way to the Ugly Tug for a second time we laughed uncontrollably when Lt. Cole summed it up, "This is a morning I'll never forget."

Washington, DC

Winter 1917

14

The second round of goodbyes went a lot smoother, and tears were barely perceptible. Geo assured Lillie and John that the weather and seas would be clement, and a routine trip to NYC could be expected. At 02:30 the Ugly Tug set sail. John explained that if plans did not work out as expected he would put Emma and me on a train to Washington, DC. Harriet Lynch would pick us up at Union Station and drive us several miles to the Washington Navy Yard. He didn't explain what would happen if his plan DID work out.

"Sail the open ocean or Long Island Sound, either way you'll have a good trip," Geo said.

John took the helm and Lt. Cole supported me in the comfortable chair, using a wide strap around my waist. Emma tied my wheelchair to the deck, securing it safely for me to use, if I wanted to sit in the stern.

"This converted patrol boat is powerful," Lt. Cole explained. "If it's rough in spots, I don't want you falling from the chair. Emma, feel free to use the bed in the forward cabin, but you must find a safe spot to sit, too."

"Okay, thank you. How fast can this go?" Emma asked.

"After the conversion, upwards to 40 mph. A little faster in a following sea and wind. I understand you and your sister understand following seas and high winds very well."

"Oh, yes, we do, Lieutenant Cole," Emma said with a smile, fully aware of the reference to our near tragic sailing trip years ago. She sat on two Navy blankets, on the floor close to the stove. We both needed sleep, Emma more than me, but in the aftermath of my planned and rather unique method of securing Emma's passage, we were, unexpectedly, unable to fall asleep right away.

Emma looked up from her cozy position on the floor, "So far so good, Annie."

I nodded and smiled, then tapped on Emma's sleeve, *Working with John and his colleague is a breeze. I hope it is the same at the meetings.*

"You'll figure them out," Emma said.

Will I get along with my new supervisors? I tapped for everyone to hear.

"That will go fine, I'm sure," Lt. Cole said.

And what about my fellow trainees?

"As long as they can keep up with your Morsing, everything will be fine," John interjected.

My status will be lower than everyone in the training. Plus my disability.

"Your disability might be an issue, but I think that being a highly intelligent young woman will be a greater problem for some of them," John said.

Effortlessly, but not quietly, John backed the boat out of the Hog Penn and turned it up, not at all concerned about the large wake the Ugly Tug would leave in its path. After clearing the Cut into Block Island Sound, he cranked it up to full throttle. With the engines roaring, and the Block Island Sound tide in the direction of the Atlantic Ocean, they decided on a course to New York Harbor two miles out into the Atlantic Ocean. Sandy shoals are often found two miles off the coast of Fire Island, and sometimes as far as three miles offshore from Long Island's barrier island. But with calm seas John expected an uneventful trip.

A course was set to the Montauk Lighthouse, with its beam flashing every five seconds. John swore he could see the beam for miles farther than its reported 22-mile reach. With it being high tide and less than one-foot seas, there was no danger of running into the Southwest Ledge. After passing Montauk Lighthouse, the next tall light we'd see would be the Fire Island Lighthouse. Its beam flashed every eight seconds, but that was two hours away.

Emma had fallen asleep in the berth, but I was awake. John asked if I'd like to sit outside and helped me to the stern.

"We can reach NYC faster with this converted patrol boat than taking the train from Providence," John said, then asked, "How are you feeling about leaving home?"

I tapped, *I hope I can learn a lot and find the spy, if there is one.*

"You're not nervous?"

I raised my eyes, *I am, worried about being accepted by the trainees.*

"You can do it, Annie. Nothing's easy. Pay attention and you'll learn a lot."

What do I look for when observing someone?

"Pay heed to the soft-spoken word. If you see a change in facial expression, it might be an important clue to what they have on their mind. Watch faces to learn to read faces, especially when everyone's attention is focused away."

I smiled, gave my hand signal for, *Thank you,* and tapped, *I feel comfortable Emma is here. She understands how others interact with me.*

"She's a good observer, isn't she," John pointed out. "I should have suggested to the ONI that she accompany us. Do you have questions about your assignment?"

At dinner you mentioned that the head of U-1 was going to assign someone to watch over me.

"Harriet Lynch will introduce you to Lieutenant Edwards. He's quiet but very helpful. Look over there." John pointed along the barrier island. "Look at the silhouette of Fire Island. No more than four or five feet above sea level, it has a few lifesaving stations, three lighthouses in different styles, but only two tall ones, the Montauk Lighthouse, and the Fire Island Light."

I see a lot of one-story bungalows.

"There are a hundred of those scattered about. It's a lawless stretch of the coast."

Are there spies on Fire Island?

"Yes. It's easy to come ashore from a U-boat, or any boat, like Block Island."

John offered, "When I met you last October, you were reading *Moby Dick*. Melville spent the last summers of his life on Fire Island? And did you know that he wrote poetry, too?"

Poetry? Now I know why his novels are difficult read.

We both laughed out loud. "I brought him up because he'd be a great spy."

How do you know?

"He's a great observer of behavior and can write about it."

Emma was asleep and I dozed. At 4:55 we came abreast of the Fire Island Light. An hour later we entered the New York Bight and found the Ambrose Channel into New York Harbor.

John nudged Emma and me and said, "Staten Island is to port. Brooklyn will be off starboard. When we sail through the New York Bight we'll have entered New York Harbor, and straight ahead will be Governors Island."

Governors Island is a sliver of a low-lying island, five nautical miles from where Staten Island reaches out and tries to touch Queens. The island is a kilometer from the southern tip of Manhattan and separated from Brooklyn by the quarter mile wide Buttermilk Channel. Before it was dredged, at low tide, you could walk across it to Brooklyn.

"The Brooklyn Navy Yard is a mile farther north up the East River, beyond the Brooklyn Bridge," John explained.

I tapped, *What's on Governors Island?*

"It's an Army base, with a landing strip for aero planes."

After a few minutes, I asked Emma to help me to the head, to change into my new red dress. I braced myself against the wall and used my right hand to wash up, then slipped the dress on me. I loved the dress, especially the way the material puffed out around the shoulders and upper arms. It was the style now, in Europe and the United States, and it covered my legs when seated. Emma came and brought me back outside.

The harbor was calm, but the gentle lapping of the waves against the boat was mostly drowned out by the twin engines. I could see the Statue of Liberty off to the left of Governors Island, and the Manhattan side of the Brooklyn Bridge over the East River.

While we were in the cabin, we heard Lt. Cole tapping out a message on the wireless transmitter. John said he was Morsing with Lawrence Sperry. Both Emma and I smiled. Known to everyone, from Hollywood to the White House, one of the most famous persons alive today, Lt. Cole was Morsing him about mutual friends on Mount Desert Island.

"Sperry? Where is he?" Emma asked, looking at John.

"He's on Governors Island, with three Army pilots, waiting for us."

"He knows we're on board?"

John winked.

Emma sat on the gunwale, and I in my wheelchair, watching the fort at water's edge on Staten Island as we sailed by. Fort Wadsworth, a relic of the Civil War, stood as a silent witness to the passage of time. Manhattan Island lay to the north, the bright rising sun reflecting off the buildings of Wall Street. Governors Island was low to the waterline and at this distance barely distinguishable.

"The Statue of Liberty looks like it's in New Jersey," Emma said.

"Before last summer," John explained, "there were three islands close together. The two larger ones are Ellis Island and Liberty Island. Black Tom Island extended into New York Harbor behind the Statue of Liberty."

"Where is it? I don't see it," Emma said, standing on tiptoes.

"That's where the massive explosion in New York Harbor was. The man-made Black Tom doesn't exist anymore."

"I remember, John," Emma said. "That was a huge explosion. What happened?"

"We're not sure yet but the NYPD Bomb Squad is looking into it. There have been other explosions including the major explosion in January, at the Kingsland Factory. I understand that the Bomb Squad thinks they are the result of German saboteurs.

"Now, look ahead. We're about five miles from Governors Island. Most of that island is flat. It was enlarged using the sand, soil, and rock from excavating Buttermilk Channel, as well as the Lexington Avenue subway. We're heading to the runway, on this side of the island, and that's where Sperry is waiting for us. He's flying another Curtiss prototype, a much larger plane than the one you were in last fall."

I cannot believe we are going to see Sperry, again!

"He always asks about you two. I mentioned to Lillie that I had spoken with Sperry by phone when I was in Maine. He said he'd fly us to Washington, DC, if we could get to Governors Island. Much faster than taking the train. Sperry and I scheduled meetings at the Washington Naval Yard later today, one with the assistant to the Army Chief of Staff. After our meetings, we'll fly back to NYC.

"When we land, I'll introduce you to Harriet Lynch, one of your supervisors. Lt. Cole has already sent a wireless to the Army War College letting her know that she should meet us at the Anacostia Air Field. Harriet will show you the Naval Yard while we have our meetings, and then after we say goodbye, she'll drive you to the Hamilton Hotel."

I raised my eyes in agreement.

Before I could ask why four aeroplanes waited for our arrival, John offered up the explanation: "There's a ton of military mail sent between New York and DC. Recently, the Army instituted this *aero mail* trial. At times one plane will make a stopover in Philadelphia but the other three fly directly to DC. They used to fly out of an airfield near Belmont Park, but for some reason the Army assigned the mail aeroplanes to the Governors Island Air Field."

I tapped, *A new aero passage to Washington.*

John took out his binoculars and tried to locate the dock on the southeastern portion of the island, near the runway. After a minute he identified a few pilots in military dress standing near the water's edge, but still no dock in sight.

A few minutes later he announced, "There it is. We should be able to navigate close enough to avoid having to sail around to the main dock. Looks like the dock is small. We'll have to back in."

The dock consisted of four pilings, two on each side, extending about fifteen feet from land, with a very narrow gangplank connected to trees on shore. I recognized immediately that it was going to be a challenge to carry me off the boat, across that narrow plank, and up the six-foot embankment. The docking came up fast. Lt. Cole stayed at the helm, and John unloaded the bags first, then lifted the wheelchair to a second man standing on the plank. The plank sagged but did not appear in jeopardy of breaking.

I was meeting men I'd never seen before, except for Sperry of course. I felt uncomfortable and was grateful my sister was with me. It wasn't fear, perhaps I was embarrassed about my condition and the help that I needed. But I forged ahead and accepted everyone's help in my usual matter-of-fact attitude.

John lifted me to a third man on the plank. Then Emma, then John jumped off the boat. John stayed on the plank to pushed off the tug. Emma waved goodbye as Lt. Cole backed away from the small dock and motored into Buttermilk Channel. He was heading up the East River to the Brooklyn Navy Yard where he would complete his report on the highly-secretive site for the ONI's newest international radio receiver, one that would rival Germany's Nauen Transmitter.

We moved briskly along the grass runway toward the planes. I was carried by one of the pilots, who, after he said hello, said something funny that got me laughing all the way to the plane. Another pilot carried the wheelchair. John, the third pilot, and Emma handled the luggage.

Sperry hopped out of a plane to greet us, and quickly made a round of introductions, although in all the excitement, I forgot everyone's names. John wasted no time discussing the flight plan with Sperry. They wanted to reach Washington, DC before noon and return tonight, if possible.

"The wind's favorable." And just like that, Mr. Sperry beckoned Emma. "Emma let's get going. Great to see you two again. I knew we were waiting for your sister, but what a surprise to see you, too!"

"Long story, Mr. Sperry," Emma said with a mischievous smile.

"Knowing you two ... I'll bet it's a long story." Everyone laughed before climbing in the cockpit.

John and I were assigned to the largest plane, and the pilot and John lifted me into the rear cockpit. The luggage and the wheelchair were placed in the third plane. The fourth plane was scheduled to stop in Philadelphia and was loaded with parcels.

I was amazed at how efficiently things went. Getting us and the baggage off the tug, loading everything, including ourselves, into the one of the mail aeroplanes took little time. It was as if everything was preplanned. *Is this the way the Army always works?* I wondered. It wasn't like this on Block Island, except at the Weather House. Now I understood why Geo worked fast and accomplished tasks promptly.

When John reviewed the flight plan with Sperry and the other pilots, I heard mention of a "General Scott" and a minute later I heard the word "Maine". I assumed they were talking about the new wireless listening station in Maine. But who was General Scott? He was not a Navy person.

Once in the aeroplane John used cushions to support and protect me in the rear seats of the cockpit. The mail was placed neatly in each of the four planes. We sat side by side. Sperry's plane had a smaller cockpit and Emma sat directly behind him. She could lean forward to have a conversation. The fourth plane was unique in that the mail packages were placed in the first cockpit and the pilot sat in the rear cockpit. Better to balance the load I supposed.

I tapped, *John, who is General Scott?*

"He is an old fashion general and is now the Army's Chief of Staff. He moved up the ranks quickly, first in the Calvary where he gained a reputation for settling difficulties with diplomacy. He's known for solving issues with the pen. There are many examples, here and abroad."

I tapped, *Is he a supporter of the Office of Naval Intelligence?*

"Frankly, Annie, General Scott's opinion on intelligence gathering is backward. That's all I'll say. But Major Van Deman's MIS is in the Army War College, and Brigadier General Kuhn, who runs the War College, understands the necessity of intelligence, and more importantly, developing our own intelligence services. If the MIS remains under General Kuhn, Van Deman has nothing to worry about."

Be thankful for small things.

"But, if we enter the war, and I truly believe it is inevitable, the Army will undergo a reorganization. And if that occurs, Van Deman will be moved under a division in the General Army, and Scott will become his ultimate boss."

Oh.

"Scott ran the Military Academy at West Point and during that time he developed a close working relationship with the leadership in the Royal Armed Forces, including the Admiralty and Room 40. He's continued those relationships and believes the Brits should take the lead for us in the intelligence arena. But let's change the subject."

Good idea. I have been reading about officer's motives who want to be spies.

"Any questions?"

How can I determine if someone is or isn't patriotic?

"We need them to be patriotic to our country. It's an individual with a sense of attachment to one's country, and someone with unquestionable integrity."

Integrity is an absolute requirement.

"I believe so, Annie."

Accurate background information can be used as a measure of integrity, right?

"Yes. What's difficult is identifying those who shift allegiances easily, because they have debt, or other reasons."

Our conversation ended when Sperry gave the signal for the other three pilots to get ready to take off. Soon, one after the other the planes followed Sperry and taxied into the wind. Within minutes all four were airborne, and the sights of New York Harbor drifted below.

The planes were noisy, but John and I were able to Morse throughout the flight.

I tapped on John's arm, *This is breathtaking, my mother's favorite word.*

Sperry banked a wide left turn just below the tip of Manhattan. I saw Emma in her seat behind Sperry, and only then did it occur to me that I'd not said goodbye to her – it had all happened so fast.

The Statue of Liberty appeared to be raising its arm to say hi, so I turned and waved a goodbye. The four planes fell into final formation over Staten Island, and we were on our way.

Emma told me later that she and Sperry didn't talk much, due to the noise of the plane's engine. But when she had a question, he idled the plane and explained things in detail. With forward momentum and a tailwind, the plane glides easily. Enough time to tell a couple funny jokes and point out geographic features. It was clear Sperry loved to fly – with or without the engine. Breaking formation over Asbury Park, New Jersey, he turned off the engine and the two of them had their first conversation. Emma asked about something that puzzled me since last fall.

"Mr. Sperry, what's an Air Scout?"

"It's a new term that we're using to describe the process of spying from the aeroplanes. If there's a battle going on it is easier to scout out the battlefield from the sky. That's why we call it an Air Scout."

"I have another question. Annie wonders about that German cargo submarine that docked in New London, Connecticut last fall. So many people showed up to welcome it to the Town Pier. I had no idea cargo submarines existed."

"Ah, yes," said Mr. Sperry with a knowing nod. "That was the Deutschland. She was on a spy voyage."

"Geo said that it landed a few months ago in Baltimore."

"That's correct. The German government offloaded secret documents, possible new code books, a large amount of money, and medicine. John may have more details."

Sperry restarted the engine when the fourth plane left the formation for Philadelphia. Today, the tailwind was our friend and he thought it ensured an earlier than expected arrival. We approached Washington, DC from the south, and flew up the Potomac River. This time our pilot took the lead and Sperry followed.

From the plane, on the other side of Washington was the White House and the Washington Monument, still under construction. They both seemed like miniature buildings, as if they were made of nothing more than paper and glue. The new Providence Hospital, not too distant from the Anacostia Air Field where we would land, loomed larger, its red brick walls and orderly rows of windows stark against the blue sky. Beyond that was the U.S. Capitol and, behind it, was Union Station. From the sky the cars and trucks looked like toys and the people were no bigger than ants.

John pointed to other landmarks: the Washington Naval Yard across the Anacostia River from the landing strip, and the Army War College, beyond the Naval Yard. "You'll be spending a lot of time there."

The aeroplanes landed one after the other on the newly opened grass runway of the Anacostia Air Field, like a fleet of cormorants settling in the shallows of the Great Salt Pond. The single runway field is at the confluence of the Anacostia River and the Potomac, and managed by the Division of Military Aeronautics, or Air Corp, and used by the Army and Navy.

After the aeroplanes landed, I noticed John and Sperry were anxious, and I assumed because of their scheduled meeting. Emma transferred me into the wheelchair and brought me to Mr. Sperry, and I became nervous as well. The source of Sperry's nervousness turned out to be the ONI, too. A good lesson that everything is intertwined in this business.

15

ANNIE

After collecting the packages from each aeroplane, the military mail truck drove off the grounds of the Anacostia Airfield just as an olive-green car without markings entered.

This new car would take us from the airfield to the Washington Naval Yard, about a mile away. The new bridge over the Anacostia River made the trip less than ten minutes.

"There's our car," Sperry said.

"Is that a Cadillac?" Emma asked.

"Yes. Harriet Lynch often drives the Army Chief of Staff's cars. She serves with the ONI and at the Army War College."

Emma and I were surprised when a Negro woman wearing civilian clothing stepped out. She was a woman of medium height, had a graceful walk, and a warm smile.

I tapped, *Oh, that has gotta be my supervisor.*

She walked over, nodded to Sperry, and reached out to shake our hands. "Welcome to Washington, DC. I'm Harriet Lynch. John told me all about you." She seemed kind and capable. "And you are the younger sister?"

"Yes, I'm Emma."

"John tells me you both grew up on Block Island."

I raised my eyes, and Emma asked, "Have you heard about our Island?"

"I have. There's a small community of people of color on Block Island."

"Yes, it's near our church. I haven't heard that phrase 'people of color'?"

"Thanks for asking, Emma. Frederick Douglas, who lived in my neighborhood, has asked us to describe our people that way. I'll share more later."

John walked over and greeted Mrs. Lynch. "I'm glad you guys have met. I've told Mrs. Lynch a lot about you two."

"She was telling us about Frederick Douglas."

"I'm sure she was. She lives near his old estate," John said.

After a few moments, Sperry reminded everyone we had to go. "Harriet, John and I must get to ONI. Let's load the luggage and the wheelchair in the boot."

Sperry and Emma sat on either side of me, John was in front with Mrs. Lynch. On the way to the Naval Yard, Mrs. Lynch explained its unique nature.

"Annie, you might be overwhelmed when you see the Navy Yard. It's also called the Naval Gun Factory, because the long guns for battleships are made there."

"Mrs. Lynch, were the *Arizona's* long guns also made there?" Emma asked. "Last November we saw the launch of *Arizona* in the Brooklyn Navy Yard."

"Yes, they were. I'll show you the building."

Sperry was nervous. He reminded Mrs. Lynch that he had two meetings. One with General Scott's officers, and the other with his father and an ONI officer.

"Lawrence, I didn't know your meeting was with your father," John said, surprised.

"Yes. FDR has just recruited a former diplomat to open the ONI's NYC office. He'll work with the NYPD Bomb Squad and Van Deman's MIS to protect plants from German sabotage. His first task is to evaluate my father's plant in Brooklyn. It's all related to the Black Tom and the Kingsland explosions."

"Mr. Sperry," Emma said, "we saw your father at the launching of the USS *Arizona*."

Emma was nervous, too. But bringing Sperry's father into her conversation for no apparent reason was in fact quite telling. She needed to anchor our new experiences with experiences from our past, to help adjust to this new world.

"My father was there, Edison, and other industrialists," Sperry said.

"They're an important part of our ability to prepare for war," John added.

"Mr. Sperry, does General Scott have an office in the Yard?" Emma asked, abruptly.

Emma felt she could ask Sperry anything, but I thought she couldn't stop dwelling about General Scott. Did she think he was the one person who could make my life miserable? We all need demons, and, apparently, Emma chooses him.

Mrs. Lynch was surprised by her question. "No, Emma, he's downtown in the War Building."

"Will Annie be meeting with him?" Emma asked.

"Perhaps in the training sessions," Mrs. Lynch responded, again surprised.

John and Sperry couldn't contain a laugh. Mrs. Lynch shook her head. She often gets called to drive the General around DC and has always found him to be gracious.

"Does he have a problem with females?" Emma asked.

John interjected, "Emma, Emma. Let's change the subject, there's no reason to worry about General Scott."

I smiled, but we soon were distracted when Mrs. Lynch slowed the car. We were approaching a highly unusual structure. The nine-foot-high brick wall that enclosed the Naval Yard soon became part of the exterior wall of a long two-story building. In the middle of this long building was a gate.

Before I or Emma could ask, Mrs. Lynch explained, "It's called the Latrobe Gate. It looks like a driveway through a building, which is exactly what it is."

Once through the building, or gate, we saw men and a few scattered women, all dressed in civilian clothes.

I tapped, *Who are the women?*

"We call them the Yeoman (F) women. They were hired right after the

Navy allowed women to work as civilians."

"They're in civilian clothes? Shouldn't they be in uniform?" Emma asked.

"Workers from the local area *are* civilians, but the Yeoman (F) women will be issued uniforms," Mrs. Lynch said.

The air was thick with the smell of smoke and iron. The Navy Yard was noisy, the roar of the machines in a few buildings was deafening, and, occasionally, the ground shook beneath our feet. When we peered into a building, my eyes widened in amazement. It was lined with giant machines, all of them working at a furious pace. From a distant building the sound of metal grinding against metal permeated the Naval Yard. This Yard was different from the Brooklyn Navy Yard.

I tapped, *Where are the ONI offices?*

"Our offices are across the street from the War Department. We just moved from the Mills Building and to a new building two blocks away," John said. "We have a small office in the Latrobe Gate."

Listening to Mrs. Lynch and John made me realize how lucky I am to be in Washington, DC, to be a part of the Navy, and to train with the ONI. My dream was coming true. And my sister was by my side!

Mrs. Lynch parked, and John and Sperry hopped out first. "Would you get your sister's wheelchair from the boot, please," John asked.

Emma removed the wheelchair from the boot and wheeled it forward so Mrs. Lynch could help me transfer. She was as comfortable with me as anyone I've met. After I was seated, she pointed to a section of the Yard.

"See that building over there? That's where ordinance is made. And next to that, torpedoes are assembled. We'll head over to the building across the grounds, so you can use the restrooms."

"We'll see you in an hour," John said. He and Sperry walked quickly away from us to a nearby building.

"Annie, do you need anything, besides the restroom?" Mrs. Lynch asked. "I can find some food in one of the offices."

I smiled and raised my eyes, *Yes.*

"Mrs. Lynch," Emma interjected, "Annie and I developed hand signals that serve as shortcuts. We use them when we're in rush or when Morsing would take too long. I'll interpret them for you if necessary."

"Could you show me an example?"

I brought my right hand, the good hand, toward my belly and turned it upside down. Twice.

"That hand sign means, 'Heck, what's that'?" Emma said.

"I'm sure Annie has other signs that will be just as helpful." Mrs. Lynch started to laugh and shook her head. "Girls, I Morse, but I'm a tad slow."

After a minute, an awkward silence came, as though Emma and me and Mrs. Lynch were suddenly aware of the vast difference between us. Mrs. Lynch must have recognized this, too, and stopped suddenly. Right away she brought in, for a second time, Block Island, to help us feel comfortable.

"Girls," she said, "I still do not believe you met Lawrence Sperry when he crashed on Block Island."

"Oh, yes, we did!" Emma's smile went from ear to ear. "It's true. We met on the wharf in New Harbor the day after his aeroplane was towed from where it crashed."

"Where did he crash land?"

"At the base of the bluffs, near the Southeast Lighthouse," Emma said.

I tapped, *He was on his way to drop experimental bombs, near a German U-boat.*

"I can't believe you know that!" Mrs. Lynch said.

"Block Island is secluded," Emma said, "and we learn a lot."

Mrs. Lynch flicked a wrist. "The crash didn't deter Sperry. He makes headlines all over the world and is currently a favorite in France. A month after that crash Sperry successfully dropped a bomb. Unfortunately, our testing aviator, Clarence Bronson, wasn't so lucky."

Emma flinched. "What happened to him?"

"One day, flying over Indian Head, the bomb he was to drop exploded in the cockpit, killing him and the pilot. We'll remember him for his work, and for changing the meaning of the term, 'bombers'. It used to refer to infantry tossing hand grenades, but now refers to aeroplanes that drop bombs."

The restroom Mrs. Lynch brought us to was huge, ten times larger than the head on the boat. She left us for a few minutes while Emma and I relaxed. We said nothing but needed to say nothing. We were comfortable, but hungry. Mrs. Lynch returned with two sandwiches and iced tea. Soon were on our way to the water's edge.

Just before we reached the bulkhead on the Potomac River, I raised my good hand. It was my signal to my sister to stop pushing my wheelchair. I then twisted my hand, my signal to turn me around.

I had developed a unique skill since the accident. I could visualize the social interactions of those in my immediate area – as if I'm looking down from above. Essentially, I could see, without seeing, and ... that included how individuals reacted to me. I could monitor my surroundings, know things without knowing how or why I know them.

"Annie, what's up," Emma said as she turned me around.

We were startled to see a big, muddy dog, about fifteen yards back, running at full speed toward us.

"Annie, the dog has eyes for you. I hope that's all she has."

"Don't worry, this is Fritz. He's been in the Anacostia River," Mrs. Lynch said, moving in front of the wheelchair.

The dog ran right up and sat before me, then we locked eyes. He wasn't frightening at all, and not once barked. I'd never seen anything like it. He stayed seated in front of me for a few minutes, until a loud whistle came from behind a building near the Latrobe Gate. He turned, took off running, and disappeared.

I tapped, *Whose dog?*

"Nobody's," Mrs. Lynch said. "He showed up here one day. Goes back and forth to the Army War College. Some of the officers think he might've fallen off a boat somewhere in the Potomac River, or at sea. Presumably, no one on board saw this. Maybe it happened at night? He eventually found himself here."

Who takes care of him?

"Anybody and everybody. He's got the run of the yard. Different officers feed him. That's what's happening now. It's time for Fritz to eat."

We continued to the bulkhead to find the SS *Boothbay*, its name printed in large black letters on the bow.

"This steamship looks like a ferry we see on Block Island," Emma said, surprised.

"It was built as a cargo ship and the Navy uses it to transport the long guns and munitions to other Naval shipyards," Mrs. Lynch explained.

I understood why Emma sought reminders of home. It was only the first day of my new journey, and I, too, looked for places and objects to anchor me. The Boothbay's resemblance to a ferry on Block Island provided a source of stability, similar perhaps to a how religion provides a sense of security.

"Mrs. Lynch, can we walk down the bulkhead? I see two small beaches up there," Emma asked.

"Sure. I've never walked that far up."

The bulkhead ended thirty-five yards from where we were standing. There were no other boats docked on the bulkhead. A small sandy beach stretched for twenty feet and then the bulkhead resumed for another ten yards before another sandy beach appeared. We were now behind the long buildings cranking out the long guns.

Emma shook her head. "I can see why you never come back here, Mrs. Lynch."

"It's quieter on the weekends, I'm sure. This sand is beautiful, isn't it. The Navy Yard must have trucked it in because the Potomac doesn't have sand like this."

Emma must have felt Fritz could provide a sense of security because, without telling us, she let loose a shrill whistle that startled Mrs. Lynch. Would he come running back? Sure enough, in less than a minute Fritz appeared, wagging his tail. Emma whistled again, to show Fritz that it was she who had whistled. But he ran right up to me and sat. He inched closer, momentarily stared at my debilitated left hand, and tilted his head to the side.

"Annie, Fritz understands," Emma said, raising her eyes.

"Is that possible?" Mrs. Lynch asked.

"We think so, Mrs. Lynch," Emma said.

John finished his meeting and having heard Emma's whistle, walked down to the bulkhead and saw us at the beaches. Even from that distance, he couldn't miss what the three of us were observing: Fritz's head on my lap as I petted him.

John picked up his pace and joined us. He took it all in. "Emma, we heard your whistle from the other side of the yard. It's gotten louder."

He gave Fritz's head a little jostle. "You've got a new friend. Fritz is a Portuguese Agua, or water dog. You'll appreciate his power when you see him swimming against a current."

"When will we see you again, John?" Emma asked.

We all looked at John. A stillness came over us.

"Within the week I'll be in the Caribbean Sea, near South America" John shrugged. "I'm not sure when I'll be back to the States."

I looked at Fritz to pet him and to shield anyone from seeing my watery eyes. Would this be the last time we saw John? It couldn't be easy for him, his missions are always filled with uncertainty and danger. Even the mission on Block Island last October was dangerous, with three men killed, one being a friend and fellow agent.

Without saying much, we traversed along the bulkhead and to the front gate. Fritz on my right, John walking ahead, side by side with Mrs. Lynch. Perhaps giving her last-minute instructions about me? Before we reached the Latrobe Gate he turned around.

"Don't give Mrs. Lynch a difficult time when I'm away." He smiled. "I'm glad to see you've gotten acquainted."

"Yes, we have," Mrs. Lynch confirmed.

"Sperry no longer enjoys night flights, so we must return. Mrs. Lynch will drive you to the Hamilton Hotel, and introduce you to your long-lost cousin, and your assigned housekeeper."

I raised my eyes.

Mrs. Lynch turned to John and asked about his meeting.

"Could've gone better. Scott still wants us to rely on the SIS – the Brits Secret Intelligence Service for intel, and to a lesser extent the French. He's beguiled Van Deman for years, but the General's willingness to rely on the Brits, unfortunately, is held by others. Fortunately, General Kuhn understands the necessity of having our own intelligence services, and right now he's in charge of Van Deman and the MIS.

I tapped, *John, is the Brit's SIS the formal name for Room 40?*

"Room 40 is a component of the SIS. They are decoders and have the word's best cryptologists. They appear to have significant oversight of all thing's intelligence, but officially Room 40 does not exist."

Why does Scott want them to do our intel? Will he become a problem for me?

"He's a problem for some, but he means well. Sperry's father had an issue with him agreeing to use a French intelligence manual for instructions on how to use wireless 'aeroplane-to-ground' communications. After an argument, Scott agreed that Mr. Sperry could write the manual."

"Best not to talk too loud in the Yard," Mrs. Lynch reminded John. "What's Major Van Deman's thinking about Industrial Security, to prevent sabotage? Last week he mentioned that he'll appoint the head of Industrial Security from this first group of trainees."

"Until he gets funding, the ONI will continue to oversee it, and we'll work with the NYPD Bomb Squad, too. We're making a big effort to protect the GE plant as well as Mr. Sperry's aviation and gyroscope plants in Brooklyn. I do think the Major will use the meetings and the training group to choose members of several sections. But he'll get advice from an advisor, soon."

John's comments were a small window into how complicated this business is, everything is intertwined in many ways, and numerous unnamed individuals often participate in decision making.

John walked by my side until we reached the Latrobe Gate. Sperry was talking to a Naval officer he'd corralled into driving them to the Anacostia Airfield. John and Sperry became uneasy when the goodbyes started. If the military was efficient, it was evident in the goodbyes. A simple nod of the head, a tepid smile, and a handshake. And just like that John and Sperry were on their way to the airfield. Frankly, I was relieved the goodbyes were fast because I did not want to dwell on the possibility that I may never see John again. He was worried because of the obstacles I'd face, but I knew being given the opportunity to explore a new world would carry me through any doubts that surfaced. I tried to ignore the thought that I might not see him again, but it returned again and again. If discouragement came, or if my life was at risk, I'd think of John, to prove him proud.

Although I knew my life might be in danger, what I never expected was that my sister might suffer the same fate.

16

ANNIE

"Emma, hold Annie when we hit bumps," Mrs. Lynch instructed. "A lot of potholes in these Washington, DC roads."

"We call them puddle holes because they're always filled with water," Emma said.

We drove through the Latrobe Gate onto the streets of Washington, DC and the streets were in no better shape than the roads on Block Island. A major difference was that the air was thick with the smell of exhaust fumes. In this part of the city the roads were hard packed dirt, although intersections were made with concrete. The exception were streets with trolley cars; cobblestones lined either side of the rails.

Adjacent to the Naval Yard were two- and three-story wooden houses. Front yards were small, side yards nonexistent. The closer we got to Union Station the wider the roads and most were paved. The smell of fumes even more pronounced.

We passed a few bicycle riders and drove alongside cars and horse drawn carriages. I raised my eyes, as did Emma, when we saw men riding horses in suits and overcoats – to and from work Mrs. Lynch said. We'd never see that on Block Island. Then there was the horse drawn truck that delivered laundry. In bold letters, *West End Laundry* was printed in bright gold on three sides.

Before long Emma started asking questions. I could tell she felt comfortable with Mrs. Lynch.

"You know about Annie's condition. How's that?"

"When I was younger, I worked in a section of Providence Hospital called habilitation. That helped me figure things about patients with disabilities, and I became comfortable with everyone."

"Was it difficult?"

"At times. Some nurses and aids never felt comfortable, and they moved to another section of the hospital."

"How long have you worked at the Naval Yard?"

"About ten years. First as a civilian assigned to the ONI Security Office. Five years ago, I moved to the Army War College."

We passed a new hospital, and I tapped, *Is that where you worked?*

"That's the new Providence Hospital, I worked across town at the old hospital. It's one of the few hospitals with a habilitation unit."

The White House and Hamilton Hotel were on the other side of the city. We turned on New York Avenue which was paved and wide enough for new automobiles to park in the center, with ample room to spare on either side. As we approached the White House, the houses were different. They were brick and many had ornamental marble. Some were five levels high. I did not see but a few wooden homes in this area. Block Island was the same as it had been for a century, except for the wooden hotels that burned to the ground. But Washington, DC was a city during transformation.

"Mrs. Lynch, will Annie have difficulties in the meetings?" Emma asked, continuing her questioning.

"Annie, any thoughts?" She passed the question to me.

I tapped slowly, *I am one of two representatives from the ONI. John smoothed things over with ONI staff who were skeptical of hiring me. But from the Army, we will have to see.*

"Don't expect everyone to be friendly," Mrs. Lynch cautioned. "I'll help you present yourself and point out when you need to stand your ground. Your idea about the British Secret Intelligence Service creating an explosion in the East River had some officers unwilling to accept that."

I gave a hand signal, *I was wrong.*

"But, to your credit, raising the issue impressed Major Van Deman. He was surprised that you understood the concept. He has long been interested in what he calls negative intelligence.

"But, on the other hand, Annie," Mrs. Lynch went on, "Germany has been funding sabotage events in our country for the past few years. You must have heard of the explosion in New York Harbor last summer."

"Yes, Mrs. Lynch," Emma interjected. "Folks from our Island heard it when they were in Manhattan that night. It shattered windows in their hotel."

"Annie, don't be surprised if you're cautioned for thinking that Britain created an explosion in the East River."

I tapped, *I am aware of German sabotage efforts because the editor of the* Providence Journal *reports everything.*

"Ahh, the *Providence Journal.*" Mrs. Lynch smiled. "We always wonder what it will say in the morning."

I wanted so much to learn, to contribute, to make a difference. But I had such worry that I would not impress anyone with my skills or my desire.

"Annie, do you have any questions?"

How much will we see of you?"

"Oh, Annie. I'm your designated supervisor. I'll look after you and Emma. Although I was not expecting you, Emma!"

Emma laughed. "I'll not say a word."

"Every morning I'll pick you up at the Hamilton, bright and early."

I was relieved and let out a sigh of relief. Yet, there was no way to know how impactful Mrs. Lynch would be on my journey to understand and navigate the world of espionage.

"Let me share a story of a woman," Mrs. Lynch opened. "This woman was from outside the government and the military. She argued that General Scott is wrong that the United States need not create a Military Intelligence Service. She didn't have the impact some think she had, but it's a good story. The woman is a famous novelist, and it shows how serendipity may play a role in important decisions."

What did she do?

"The war in Europe distracted her from writing novels, and she wanted to help the war effort. She had known the Secretary of War, Newton Baker, for a while, and he gave her an assignment. Would she write a report about the situation at Army training facilities in the Washington, DC and surrounding area? The story goes that her assessment was to be given to him and not General Scott. Secretary Baker is Scott's boss."

"Then what happened," Emma asked eagerly.

"One day, the Secretary asked her to spend the day with Major Van Deman. They toured local military sites without aids or military police. Except the driver."

Were you the driver?

Mrs. Lynch smiled but said nothing.

What triggered Mr. Baker to give the novelist that assignment? Sounds like the novelist may have been a cover for something else.

"Maybe you're right," Mrs. Lynch replied. "At any rate they had a productive day visiting the training facilities, and along the way the Major explained that he tried for years to establish an intelligence service in the Army. The novelist was aware that the Brits had significant accomplishments using espionage, and the U.S. Army should do the same. She asked what stood in the way of Major Van Deman creating his own independent Security Service."

What happened next?

"The Major explained that General Scott forbade him to *discuss* the need for a Military Intelligence Service with the Secretary of War, Mr. Baker."

Scott forbade Van Deman from discussing this with the Secretary of War?

"The novelist thought it was wrong, too, and met with Baker to discuss Van Deman's ideas and plans. It worked, and soon a funding request was sent to Congress."

"It's a nice story but I doubt funding came after a novelist meets with the Secretary of War," Emma said. "I agree with Annie."

Is the novelist a spy?

"She's well-traveled, but, no, she's not a spy. I cannot share her name, but she is *the* most famous American woman novelist alive today."

After a long silence I tapped, *If the story is true that she had an impact, it has to be Willa Cather. I loved her novel about a girl named Thea.*

Mrs. Lynch smiled. "Annie, after you get to know Major Van Deman, let it slip you know about Cather."

Emma's eyes lit up. "Do you know any spies?"

"There was a woman, a former slave, who spied for the North during the Civil War, but she didn't get newspaper coverage. She spied for the Navy."

What was her name?

"Mary Touvestre from Virginia. Have you heard of her?"

"No," Emma said.

I moved my eyes sideways.

"I thought you might've, because your stepfather's father may have met Mary at the Continental Shipyard in Brooklyn."

Geo's father, Carnes, may have met Mary at that Green Point shipyard? What spy-work did she do?

"This story I know is true. Mary uncovered the Confederacy's intentions to build the first ironclad ship. That information led directly to the Navy funding the building of the USS *Monitor*."

"Geo's father worked with John Ericsson who designed the Monitor. It's possible she met him but Geo never mentioned that," Emma said.

I tapped slowly, *The obituary for Carnes mentioned Ericsson.*

"We have 45 submarines in our Navy, and one of them is a Monitor class submarine from the Civil War," Mrs. Lynch said.

Suddenly Mrs. Lynch become distracted, and her focus went back to driving.

"Too many cars, too much gasoline smell in the air. And too many people walking across the streets. It's always like this around the White House. I was going to drive around to show you the Cosmos Club, but it'll have to wait for another day. It's on that corner over there." She pointed a few blocks away. "Annie, John mentioned that he'd told you about Cosmos."

Yes.

Emma always sensed when she should not ask questions and made no comment on my reference to the Cosmos Club. Later, I explained to her as much as I could of its history and purpose, but withheld that it was a gathering place for our own ONI and MIS staff, as well as enemy spies. Established as a private club, membership was limited to men of distinction in literature, science, exploration, and politics. Wives, or women in general, were allowed to visit, but only through a side entrance. The club had purchased the adjacent Dolley Madison house, a very suitable place to recruit spies due to its small, private rooms. Emma took my explanation in stride, but I could tell she was intrigued.

Within minutes Mrs. Lynch had parked in front of the Hamilton Hotel, and the story of Mary the Spy, and others who frequented the Cosmos Club, would have to wait.

17

The Hamilton is one of Washington's grand hotels. Located at 14th and K Streets it overlooks Franklin Park. Its renovated palatial lobby, beautifully decorated rooms, and large dining room is the "home away from home" for elected Senators and Congressman, businessmen, and dignitaries from around the world. In one direction it is a fifteen-minute walk to the White House and in the opposite direction a ten-minute walk to the German Embassy. Although the Hamilton plays a significant role in the history of our nation, it also has a strong connection to Block Island.

That connection was Nicholas Ball. *The New York Times* referred to him in life, as well as in his obituary, as the *King of Block Island*. Commensurate with that 'title', Ball was no stranger to President Grant's White House. And Grant was no stranger to Block Island. In 1869, President Grant and his family were guests at Ball's Ocean View Hotel, built with Gold Rush money. During that first trip to the Island, Ball convinced Grant of the need for a substantial lighthouse on the Southeast Mohegan Bluffs. Although the Lighthouse Board agreed with the need for a lighthouse at that location, its funding policy for land-based structures fell far short. After Grant's visit, once back in the White House, he signed a bill (that he wrote) appropriating $78,000, a far cry from the $14,000 the Board had allocated. In 1875, Grant visited Ball on Block Island again, this time with Rhode Island officials. The outcome of that visit was the eventual funding of the submarine telegraph cable, a necessity to establish the Weather Station. Ball's contributions to the Island could fill a book, and did. His service to our federal government could fill another book. In due time, Ball recommended his young nephew, Irving O. Ball, for the role of manager of the Hamilton Hotel. It wasn't long before Irving was its sole proprietor.

Mrs. Lynch pulled up to the front of the hotel and Emma jumped out to find Irving. She passed two bellhops fast walking to the car as she opened the heavy doors to the lobby. At the front desk she saw our distant cousin, Irving. We'd never met him, but he sure looked like a Ball.

As *advertised*, he was standing talking to a guest. It wasn't difficult to recognize the characteristic large forehead, a feature Emma and I have been spared. By the time he recognized Emma, and interrupted his conversation to walk over to her, Mrs. Lynch had pushed me through the doors into the lobby.

"You must be Emma, am I correct?" he said, extending his hand, a faint New England accent still apparent.

"Yes, we're here," Emma replied, taking his beefy hand. "Nice to meet you, Mr. Ball."

"Good to meet you, too. No need for formality, Emma. Please call me Irving."

Emma looked left and right. "This is a beautiful lobby. I love the chandeliers with so much crystal hanging between the light bulbs."

"Thank you, Emma," he said, smiling. "I imported the chandeliers from France. I take it your sister has a caregiver?"

"Yes, and a couple bellhops are attending to our baggage."

"How is your sister? I hear from your mother she's doing well."

"Yes, she's doing very well," Emma replied. "She's excited to be in Washington."

"Your mother said Annie is following in Geo's footsteps and starting a career at the Weather Bureau," he added.

"Uh-huh," Emma said, going along with my "cover" story. "And I'm along to help Annie communicate her needs to those who don't Morse."

Irving looked up and immediately saw me and Mrs. Lynch. She had slowed pushing me toward the front desk, to give Emma time to introduce herself. After seeing me, Irving returned his attention to Emma.

"I - I didn't realize your sister was still in a wheelchair," he said, slightly nervous. "I must have missed that. Now ... I understand why Lillie said there'd be a caretaker from the Weather Bureau."

Irving was clearly put off by my disability, a reaction of many people. I'm used to it, but it's another reason I am grateful to travel with my sister. Emma knew how to respond in a matter-of-fact manner.

"Annie's doing fine, Irving. She's ready to get to work. Mrs. Lynch has a boot on the back of her car to stow the wheelchair, and she'll drive us to the Weather Bureau. With a wheelchair it's difficult using taxicabs, especially the horse-drawn carriages."

"How long will you stay?" Irving asked. "Two or three weeks, right?"

"The training is scheduled for three weeks."

I introduced myself to Irving with a quick wave as we approached the desk. Irving did not Morse, so I used hand signals, which Emma translated.

"I'll pick up Annie every morning and take her to her training at the Weather Bureau," Mrs. Lynch explained to Irving. "Is it possible to speak with the maid assigned to their room?"

"I'll check to see who that will be," Irving said, quickly shuffling some papers on the desk. "But I think we'll have to change rooms. Initially I assigned the girls in a well-appointed room with a view of Franklin Park, but I'm afraid it's too small for Annie's wheelchair to maneuver around the furniture. I'll change them to a larger room."

The Weather Bureau is now part of the Department of Agriculture after being transferred from the Army's Signal Corps. It would serve as an ideal cover. I had been instructed to never mention the ONI, the Naval Yard, or the Army War College. Or flights with Sperry, the one last fall, or today's from Governors Island. John even asked Emma to never mention that she's even met Lawrence Sperry. It was a strange world, the world of spies. But it was a world that I had chosen to live in. And I wanted to serve my country.

Emma and I understood the necessity of cover, though she did not like lying. She was upset to not mention Sperry, but I had spoken to her a few times about being secretive, and that lying was not lying in this business. She did not agree, and frankly, I was glad she did not agree. But she would have to accept that part of my new life. Would I get used to this kind of subterfuge? Sure, but my sister? Probably not. But I also knew I would never get used to lying to my sister.

Lillie had called Irving to explain everything before we arrived, but he did not grasp the extent of my disability. He greeted me without making eye contact. It was subtle but Emma picked up on it, too. He raised his voice to say hello, as if I were deaf. I let it go with a smile. When Irving turned his attention away, Emma raised her eyes. "Annie, you're always gracious when people ignore you."

I tapped, *At least he's not staring at me.*

Bellhops brought the suitcases and bags and secured the elevator. I suspected that Irving would continue to feel uncomfortable with me and instead of talking to me would initiate idle conversation. Sure enough when the elevator door closed, Irving told a story about Nicholas Ball. He also referred to his uncle as King.

"The King stayed here all the time and ate with friends and politicians in the dining room. He dined frequently with his friend Crosby Noyes, the publisher, and journalist, of the *Washington Star*. Crosby's paper was known for being a 'purveyor of clean, sound, and active facts'."

"Irving, didn't the *Washington Star* print a story about their trip to China?" Mrs. Lynch asked.

"Yes, it was twenty-five years ago when they travelled to China for the government. They were both New Englanders but met for the first time at the Hamilton, sometime in the 1860s. My hotel was Ball's home away from home."

"And for the foreseeable future," Emma interjected, "it will be ours, too."

The bellhop opened the elevator door, and Irving led the way to our reassigned Room 207. It was spacious with two single beds but devoid of a view. I could see Emma's disappointment when she looked out the window and saw the back of another building. But I liked the room, tucked away at the end of the hall. Even though it was the farthest from the dining room.

Emma flopped on the bed, and I was exhausted, too. But I had the comfort of my wheelchair. It had been a long day, and our fatigue wasn't lost on Mrs. Lynch or Irving. Less than 24 hours ago we boarded the Ugly Tug in the Hog Penn. Minutes after arriving at Governors Island we climbed aboard the aeroplanes that flew us to the combined Army-Navy Anacostia Air Field. On the grounds of the busy Washington Naval Yard, we got to know Mrs. Lynch, and Fritz! Then came short goodbyes, and soon after we were being driven to the hotel.

Irving and the bellhop stepped into the hall while Mrs. Lynch surveyed the room. "This is a good location, near the service elevator. Away from things. I think you're in good hands. I'll be back at 7:30 tomorrow morning," she said with a smile. "I'm going to talk with the housekeeper assigned to your room before I leave."

We said goodbye and Emma thanked Mrs. Lynch with a long hug. A sudden burst of pride for my sister hit me. I was thankful for Emma's presence, because I was nervous about the other trainees, and my secret mission.

Irving came back in the room and offered to send dinner. We couldn't have been more relieved.

"If you need anything, just ring," Irving said to Emma directly. Mrs. Lynch, Irving, and the bellhop departed together, and Emma closed the door.

"I'm determined to teach Irving how to communicate with nonverbal people," Emma said, slightly irritated.

No need, Emma. Gives me cover.

"It doesn't make sense," Emma protested. "You stand out to some, and to others you're invisible. We should address Irving avoiding you."

I understood my sister's concern. She'd covered for one lie tonight and didn't like it. Now I was asking her to ignore Irving's uncomfortableness.

I tapped slowly, *I need your support.*

Emma could not think of a response. She pushed the two beds together and lay down to rest. I crawled in, too. Thirty minutes later, dinner arrived on two trays. Emma sliced my meal into small pieces, and we finished in twenty minutes. Emma put the trays outside the door as Irving had instructed, then helped me wash up.

I opened the duffle bag John had repacked and retrieved our night clothes. Emma secured the two beds together with twine she found in the bag John had rearranged, and we climbed back in bed. It was a chilly room and Emma placed my wool shawl over me.

We were excited and sleep evaded us for an hour or more. Footsteps in the hall and the back stairwell made Emma get up to make sure the door was locked. I tapped a few thoughts on the headboard, which had become our nightly ritual, and eventually we fell asleep.

At 6:45 AM, a firm knock startled us awake. Then a voice announced something that was impossible to understand.

18

ANNIE

Emma rolled out of bed and opened the door. A short, older woman in a maid's uniform greeted us with a grin. She was Emma's height, which is to say that if I could stand erect, I'd look down to meet her eyes.

"Come in, please," Emma said, gesturing.

I waved hello from the bed. Our assigned housekeeper introduced herself as Sarah Powers and asked, "Will eggs, bacon, and toast be okay for breakfast?" She spoke with a Canadian accent and offered up that she was from Nova Scotia, and we could call her Miss Sarah. Some of her sentences ended with a lilting "eh".

"Yes," Emma said, "eggs and bacon are fine, thank you. Eggs must be cooked hard for Annie."

"I'll be right back with breakfast." She held up a finger. "And, oh, don't forget, Mrs. Lynch will be waiting downstairs at 7:30. You two get ready, eh. It's very nice to meet you both."

I tapped, *Thank you.* Emma translated.

We washed up together, more thoroughly than the previous night's bathing. Emma was helping button my dress when we heard Miss Sarah knock and repeat the word we'd hear each morning: "Housekeeping."

She brought two trays and a large wooden stand to set them on. When she spoke, she looked directly into our eyes. Her voice was gentle and kind. She took a few minutes to ask about us, and I was convinced she was genuinely interested in both of us.

"How are you feeling being away from home?" "Let me know if you get homesick, sometimes I get homesick, too." "You can use the office phone to call Block Island."

We were taken by her warm manner, as we were yesterday with Mrs. Lynch, and I wondered if they were friends. She wasn't intimidated by my disability and did not speak loudly or in an uneasy tone. She seemed to understand that I was the same person as I was from before our accident at sea, even though I could no longer walk or talk.

Emma explained how I raise my eyes to say "yes" and look to the side for "no".

"Thank you for showing me. I appreciate and understand," Miss Sarah said. "A family from Chicago visit every year with their son with *parálisis cerebral*. I heard he died recently."

I used a hand signal, *How old was he?* Emma translated.

"I think he was twenty," she said. "I don't understand Morsing, so thank you for using hand signals."

I'm sorry, Miss Sarah.

"Let me help you with breakfast, Annie." And with that Miss Sarah began her day, and ours.

After breakfast Miss Sarah straightened out my dress. She cleaned my face with a soft wet towel, like Lillie used to do. Finally, she meticulously combed my hair.

"I love your dress, Annie," Miss Sarah said.

"Our mom made it, and the one she wore yesterday, too," Emma said.

The day was fair, and I wanted to put on my bright green dress that flowed to a few inches below my knees. It had black shoulder pads, and the sleeves were puffed and balloon-like. I felt comfortable in the dress and hoped it would lesson my nervousness about meeting new colleagues. Miss Sarah eagerly helped me pull it over my head, as if she was aware that it was my great opportunity to start a career open to very few. I worried my hands would shake, especially my left hand and arm, they especially were prone to shaking if anxiety came over me. I wanted to look my best, to prove wrong those who felt I did not belong. Above all I wanted to make John proud.

"Today starts a new adventure," Emma said, as Miss Sarah helped transfer me to the wheelchair. It was nearly 7:30. Emma gathered our coats and we both took a deep breath, looking left and right, worried we might have forgotten something important.

"Let's go girls, we don't want Mrs. Lynch waiting, eh?" Miss Sarah urged. "I'll come back and clean up."

She led us to the service elevator around the corner from our room and we were in the lobby in a minute. Even if Irving thought to put us in Room 207 to keep us out of sight of the other guests, this was a good location.

Mrs. Lynch entered through the front lobby doors and walked up to greet us. She and Miss Sarah exchanged greetings in a way that indicated familiarity with each other.

Irving was at his usual post, the front desk, and when he caught Emma's eye he waved. Miss Sarah walked with us to the car, the same Cadillac Mrs. Lynch drove yesterday. Emma lifted me into the front seat, helped me to the middle and jumped in beside me. Miss Sarah placed the wheelchair in the boot.

"Girls, did you sleep well?" Mrs. Lynch asked.

"Yes, but it took a while to fall asleep," Emma replied. "Mrs. Lynch, do you know Miss Sarah?"

"I know her well," Mrs. Lynch replied. "She helped monitor a German businessman who was staying at the Hamilton. Don't repeat what I say, or she says, to anyone else. If you accidentally repeat something, you must let me know. Things like that do happen. Occasionally, Sarah helps the ONI with guests who need to maintain a low profile, and that's why she's assigned to Annie. You can feel safe talking to her."

I raised my eyes, and Emma added, "We feel safe."

"Thank you for telling Irving that Annie is here for Weather Bureau training," Mrs. Lynch said with visible relief. "No one can know that she attends anything at the Army War College, or even knows about it. We learned a long time ago that Irving cannot keep a secret."

"I understand, and John said it was important," Emma said, then frowned. "But I wish Irving wasn't so uncomfortable with Annie's condition."

I am okay with his attitude. He may or may not come around.

"We'll use Irving's discomfort to our advantage. Moving you to a room at the back of the building near the service elevator was helpful," Mrs. Lynch said, but Emma's face registered a different opinion. "The less the other guests see of you two, in the dining room or the lobby, decreases the chance of someone looking into Annie's cover story of training at the Weather Bureau. The editors of DC's newspapers, and dignitaries, dine at his hotel. Journalists digging for information can be a problem for the ONI. Can you imagine one of them seeing Annie eating, then talking to Irving and finding out she's in training at the Weather Bureau. What a human-interest story that could become.

"That's why it's best to keep a low profile. Emma, you can teach Irving how to treat Annie in a year from now."

"I see your point," Emma said.

"And now, let me continue the story of Mary Touvestre. You may not remember that the Union Army burned USS *Virginia* to the water line, but the newly formed Confederate Navy salvaged the hull. Mary was a seamstress and a housekeeper in Norfolk, Virginia, and the man she kept house for was the Confederate naval engineer who redesigned that ship with iron plates on the hull. It would become USS *Merrimack*.

"One day, Mary saw his plans lying about and in her own hand she copied them. Soon, transportation was arranged, and she brought them to the Capital to give directly to the Secretary of the Navy, Gideon Welles."

"It's amazing that the housekeeper was a spy," Emma gushed.

I can't believe she risked her life.

"She was a brave woman, a patriot," Mrs. Lynch said, "and she made a great contribution to the Union cause."

"What happened next?" Emma asked.

"Those hand-drawn plans led to Congressional funding of Ericsson's new boat design that became USS *Monitor*. Now you know the story Mary Touvestre, the spy," Mrs. Lynch said.

"It led to the building of the *Monitor*. Geo's father helped build that, in Brooklyn," Emma exclaimed.

It was another connection to our family, but I was more interested in knowing that Mary, the housekeeper, was a spy, an agent on the ground.

Mrs. Lynch's story distracted me from my angst, but it returned as we entered the gate of the Army War College. How would my fellow trainees accept me? I knew I was hired as a civilian coder, but I wanted to be a spy. I had my cover, but that wouldn't gain respect from my colleagues.

Mrs. Lynch drove to Roosevelt Hall and parked at the base of the granite steps. It was the newest and largest building on campus. Emma retrieved the wheelchair from the boot and pushed me to the base of the first set of granite steps. The first six steps ran along the entire length of the building. Emma and I had long since determined that with my wheelchair it's best to spin it around and pull me up the stairs backwards. And that is what Emma did. Mrs. Lynch followed, somewhat amazed at how easily we negotiated the steps. At the first landing we paused, turned around and looked up.

"Impressive building isn't it?" Mrs. Lynch pointed out.

"Theodore Roosevelt Hall" was carved in the long granite beam below a giant eagle. Above that, at the top of the building, was carved, "Army War College" and scattered along the roof line were a few ornate sculptures.

"It's beautiful. Who designed the building?" Emma asked.

"McKim, Mead, and White, in the Beaux Arts style. The bald eagle is fifteen feet high."

Twenty steps up to the next landing took some concentration and muscle. Soon we stood between two massive three-story granite columns. We gazed out onto the open fields of the campus, and the Potomac River.

A guard, who was a friend from Mrs. Lynch's church, walked over from his desk and opened the lobby doors.

"Annie and Emma, this is Sergeant Lightfoot. Annie, every day he'll check you in. Sergeant Lightfoot Morses, too."

"Welcome to the Army War College," he said with a generous smile. "Mrs. Lynch mentioned you'd be here today."

I tapped quickly, *Nice to meet you, sir.*

He brought us to a manned elevator and gave the okay for us to be taken to the fifth floor. His full name was Sergeant Frederick Lightfoot. He was a quiet, tall Native American man with short gray hair, who wore his Army uniform with pride. He supervised the guard desk located at the front of the rotunda where it merged with the lobby. He checked all who entered, and had a memory for faces, and knew everyone. The nonverbal communication between Mrs. Lynch and Sgt. Lightfoot suggested they had known each other for a long time. Picking up on nonverbal communication was second nature for me, for obvious reasons.

The entire west wing of the massive building was an open space, five-story library. Mrs. Lynch asked the operator to stop on the third level so we could look inside the beautifully designed vaulted room. We saw five balconies, connected at the top by bridges, and a long central corridor below. The remarkable design was perfect for a cavernous library.

I looked down to the first two levels and the central corridor that went from one end to the other. On the first level numerous officers in uniform were standing or seated at tables. The officers at a large table appeared to be in a meeting; their voices did not travel to the third level. A few officers studied at desks on the second level. Everywhere were metal shelves, some empty but most filled with books.

"On this level, in the back of the stacks, there's a balcony where Leland Harrison has an office. Tom Yardley has a desk there as well. You'll them at the meetings. Major Van Deman's office is on the first floor.

I tapped to softly to confirm, *Mr. Harrison runs the State Department intelligence service.*

Mrs. Lynch nodded, surprised. "Some call it U-1."

We walked through the third level. Emma and I were in awe because this was the most beautiful building we had ever seen.

"We're a long way from Block Island," Emma said.

"Emma, there's a comfortable reading area on the third level, below the balcony," Mrs. Lynch instructed. "You'll have to check in with Sergeant Lightfoot, but he'll be happy to grant access."

"Are those Army officers here to study at the AWC?" Emma asked, peering down to the first level. "They look older than most students."

"They're senior officers," Mrs. Lynch explained. "The Army War College is different than West Point, where students study the history of war and war theory. Officers attending the AWC learn practical skills, such as how to issue complex verbal orders and tactical instructions in the field, and how to design war campaigns. A lot of emphasis is placed on studying and creating maps. Major Van Deman lectures at the War

College, and this year General Kuhn is charged with recruiting the Army War College's first permanent faculty."

She went on, "Annie, if war funding comes through, in a few months, Major Van Deman and his MIS will move to new office space in an apartment building in downtown DC. It'll be near the Secretary of War's offices, closer to the White House. The ONI office is on New York Avenue, but will move to the new Navy Building after it's built on Constitution Avenue."

We took the East Wing's elevator to the fifth floor and walked to the end of a long hallway. Along the way, Mrs. Lynch pointed to a door leading to the roof. "There's a great view of Washington, DC, up there. You can see Union Station, the Capitol, the White House, the Washington Monument, and across the Potomac to Arlington. You can also see the Lincoln Memorial, which is still under construction. The city is beautiful in the early evening when the streetlights turn on."

Can we see your house from the roof?

"Yes, and I can point out Cedar Hill, Frederick Douglas's mansion."

At the end of the hall two doors led to a secluded conference room. This would serve as our meeting room. Lectures for officers were always given on the first floor in the West Wing's large auditorium. But this conference room was for classified discussions, and few knew of its existence. In a few days, everyone would be astounded when a guest speaker requested armed guards at the doors. At first, we thought it was because General Kuhn was in the room, but when the speaker was revealed, the seriousness of the meetings and it's demand for secrecy became obvious.

Before we walked in, Mrs. Lynch paused. "Annie, the Major explained to the officers that you're with ONI and are highly intelligent. He explained that you have a paralysis and use a wheelchair. They understand you'll communicate using Morse Code and are to be treated no differently than any other member of the group."

I hoped she was correct.

"Are you ready?" Mrs. Lynch asked. "Emma, I'll introduce you, too, but you won't be able to stay long."

My sister and I took a deep breath. Mrs. Lynch went first, then Emma pushed me through the door, whispering, "You'll be fine. I'm not worried half as much as the night the double-ender capsized at the base of the Bluffs."

I gave my hand signal for, *It will be okay*.

I looked around the room and how it was set up. The long table, a podium at one end, in front of the largest blackboard I'd ever seen. It struck me, again, that the danger of my first secret mission *also* placed my sister in danger. No wonder John and the ONI did not want Emma to accompany me, but there was no turning back.

Emma could never be privy to my mission and would never realize that her life was in danger, too. Did I make a mistake to encourage her to accompany me to Washington, DC?

19

The only other person in the room was seated near the head of the conference table, an officer in full dress uniform. Mrs. Lynch recognized him from the Army War College but did not remember his name. She'd heard he was from West Virginia. His rank of Second Lieutenant was emblazoned on his uniform.

He stood right up. "Hello, I'm Lieutenant Peter Gordon."

Mrs. Lynch shook his hand. "I'm Harriet Lynch. This is Annie Rose, and her sister Emma. Annie will be attending the training sessions."

"Hi Mrs. Lynch. Hi Annie, I've heard about you." He looked directly at me, bent down and Morsed on my wheelchair arm, *Nice to meet you*. I could tell right away he wasn't put off by my condition or that I was in a wheelchair.

I smiled and tapped, *Thanks, and you as well.*

"I transferred from the quartermaster at the War College to join Major Van Deman's MIS," he said.

I tapped quickly, *I'm a recruit to the ONI.*

He shook Emma's hand, and offered, "If need be, I'll help your sister if you're not around." Then he turned to me and asked, "How long have you been in the wheelchair?"

About seven years.

"Lieutenant Gordon, what does a quartermaster do?" Emma asked.

"We store and provide, when necessary, equipment, supplies, and provisions for the entire U.S. Army. There's a lot to keep track of, including where our troops are stationed everywhere in the world. My major responsibility is, or was, the security of highly-secret geographic and military maps stored at the Army War College. And, please, call me Peter."

"Were you assigned to the Map Security Section under Major Van Deman?" Mrs. Lynch asked.

"Yes, for several years, Mrs. Lynch," Lt. Gordon answered.

I could tell from the look on Emma's face that she, too, was comforted by Peter's matter-of-fact approach. I didn't mind that she kept asking questions to continue the conversation, because it gave me time to relax a bit.

"Peter, have there been famous quartermasters?" Emma asked.

"Oh, yes. President Grant started his career as a quartermaster."

Peter was a warm individual and I liked him immediately. Emma felt the same and pushed me next to his seat.

After several more questions from Emma, Lt. Gordon excused himself as two other men entered the room.

Mrs. Lynch whispered, "The older man in formal Naval dress is Commander Ed McCauley, the head of the ONI. The other is Major Ralph Van Deman."

A third officer followed, Sgt. First Class Tom Yardley, from the Army Signal Service. All were well known to Mrs. Lynch.

I noted that Sgt. Yardley gave a wary, almost askance look, when he first laid eyes on me. But after Commander McCauley and Major Van Deman acknowledged my presence, each with a quick wave, he walked over.

Mrs. Lynch introduced us, "This is Miss Annie Rose and her sister, Miss Emma Rose."

"Hello," Sergeant Yardley said in a low measured tone, while looking over my wheelchair. I raised my right hand to acknowledge him, but his body language suggested he wasn't interested. Later, Emma would agree.

He stepped away to greet another officer in a more friendly manner. Mrs. Lynch explained Yardley's rank is the highest a specialist can attain in the Army's Signal Service and that he advanced the field of Signal Intelligence, which was originally pioneered by the Brits. If he were in the infantry, he'd be a First or Second Lieutenant.

Yardley looked handsome in his military uniform, almost appealing, his polished brass buttons closing his uniform right up to his neck, but Mrs. Lynch knew full well who he was. She later explained that he was a poker player, a risk taker, often garrulous, and, some thought, a louche. But he was very accomplished. An early U. S. Army Signal Service decoder, he was secretly assigned to the State Department. His permanent desk was on the third-floor balcony, near Leland Harrison.

I tapped, *Mrs. Lynch, is Sergeant Yardley a cryptologist?*

"Although he deciphers messages, technically he is not a cryptologist. I think Parker Hitt is the closest our Army has to being a true cryptologist."

Do the Brits have cryptologists?

"Yes, they do, and their SIS have been working at it for years."

I liked Second Lieutenant Peter Gordon much better than Yardley. He was younger, respectful, kind, and down to earth. He also had proven his abilities with his work at the AWC. His full head of hair, something Sergeant Yardley was rapidly losing, was a bonus.

The room filled with a few more men, all but two in uniform. Mrs. Lynch pointed out the man in a dark suit was Mr. Harrison, the director of U-1. He readily acknowledged Mrs. Lynch with a short nod and a slight wave of his hand. The other suit, Lt. Edwards, was much younger and took his seat to my right. He was, Mrs. Lynch explained, commissioned as a Second Lieutenant in the Army but wore plain clothes due to his assignment with Mr. Harrison at State. Neither were overly friendly, but they were respectful.

Commander McCauley stepped away from Van Deman and came over to say hello. He was a most distinguished man, with a slightly round face who wore his Naval hat high on his head, showcasing small ears. Mrs. Lynch mentioned little about his background, except that he wore "many hats" and was deeply involved with almost everything at the ONI. His rank was Rear Admiral. He coordinated information concerning enemy communications, and, on the ground, he oversaw agents in the Investigative Section, who increasingly had been working alongside the NYPD Bomb Squad.

"Hi, you must be Annie Rose. I'm Commander Ed McCauley." He reached down and shook my hand. "It's a pleasure to meet you and have you on our team. A few months ago, John and Mr. Sperry told me all about you, and your sister." He looked at Emma and nodded. "In fact, I believe we crossed paths in the Brooklyn Navy Yard last fall."

"We were there," Emma said, and I nervously tapped, *Hi, sir.*

Commander McCauley was the oldest in the room but looked fit enough to run up five flights of stairs without breaking a sweat. Despite also being the highest-ranking officer in the room, he emanated a warmth that made everyone feel at home. He turned to Mrs. Lynch.

"Hi, Harriet. Good to see you." He reached out and shook her hand.

"Hi, Commander," Mrs. Lynch responded.

He turned to Emma. "Thank you for helping your sister, Emma. I'm here for opening remarks, but I'll be back to discuss progress ONI is making to identify U-boat activity. I'll also be back later in the week to listen to a guest speaker."

He made no reference to my secret mission. It was a great lesson: Be careful what you say. Speak only when necessary, and even then, think twice.

I glanced up to notice Major Van Deman talking to another man who'd walked in. He, too, was in civilian clothes. The Commander gave him a wave. Mrs. Lynch leaned over and said that she thought this was the special guest. She had never seen him before, but from his accent knew he was British. He had a receding hairline that made him look about 45 years old. From what I could see he was accompanied by an armed guard who remained in the hall. Much later I'd learn who he was, and that he was well known to many industrialists.

Commander McCauley wished Annie good luck and turned his attention to Major Van Deman and the gentleman with the British accent, who were standing at the front of the room. Mr. Harrison soon joined them in conversation. The Commander's quick handshake to each of the men in suits were different, one brief and one warm. I registered those interactions.

Lt. Edwards was introducing himself the armed guard in the hall and Mrs. Lynch to the opportunity to say quietly that Mr. Harrison was a graduate of Harvard Law School, and before establishing U-1 was a very well-respected member of our Foreign Service. "I've gotten to know Mr. Harrison, and admire him, greatly," Mrs. Lynch said. "He and Major Van

Deman think that Lieutenant Edwards is destined to be an exceptional practitioner of the craft of espionage and will most likely be assigned to the State Department."

It was obvious Lt. Edwards was a quiet man. He interacted, when necessary, was thoughtful, kind, and kept his head down to read a packet of information he brought to the meeting. He smiled when he nodded hello. I waved back and immediately took a liking to him, as did Emma. Even without knowing his background, I hoped he'd become a strong ally.

To my left was Lt. Gordon and to my right was Lt. Edwards, Mr. Harrison's protégé. Across the table the chairs were being filled by my fellow trainees. All of them went right up to Major Van Deman after choosing their seats. Major Van Deman was not what I expected a major to look like. He was tall and thin, wiry almost.

A few minutes later he walked over to welcome us.

"Annie Rose, pleasure to meet you. I'm Major Van Deman," he said with enthusiasm. He leaned over and shook my good hand, and then Mrs. Lynch's hand. "John told me so much about you." He took a step toward Emma, shook her hand, and smiled. "Emma, welcome. I wasn't expecting to see you!"

We all laughed, even Mrs. Lynch, who added, "Neither did I!"

"But you should know," the Major continued, "that Lawrence Sperry took great joy telling me how you guys met on Block Island."

"Oh, I'll never forget his crash, and that thankfully he was okay," Emma said. She was wide-eyed, clearly in awe of Commander McCauley and Major Van Deman. And so was I. Both welcomed me and seemed pleased to have me on the team.

"Annie, in addition to being on the staff of the War College, I'm also a physician," the Major continued, "and I will help if the need arises."

I tapped at my fastest rate, *Thank you, sir, very much!*

"I look forward to working with you," he said genuinely. "It's too early to say, but after Congress approves funding for my division, I may need someone with your interest in negative intelligence."

My broad smile appeared, and I tapped, *I would like that*.

The Major excused himself and walked over to say hello to the other participants who had taken their seats on the other side of the conference table.

"After Major Van Deman became a lawyer," Mrs. Lynch added, "he attended medical school"

Annie tapped, *Do you know him?*

"We've known each other for a few years. He's a very well-studied man and loves the adventures the Army has afforded him." Mrs. Lynch paused, surveyed the room, then said, "Emma and I are going to step back and sit against the wall, next to the Telegraph Machine. We'll stay for a short time, and then leave."

I raised my eyes in acknowledgement.

They took their seats and Emma immediately explained about that model of a telegraph machine.

"This is an old ciphering telegraph, identical to the model installed at Block Island's Weather House. Geo is getting a newer model with a wireless transmitter, but Annie and I learned to Morse on the old machine."

"John mentioned you know a lot about telegraphy."

"Everyone in our family are telegraphers. We know how telegraphs work and can repair them, too," Emma said proudly.

I turned my attention to Lt. Gordon and Lt. Edwards who both seated. They each moved closer to me, and I began my first fast-paced Morsing conversation at the Army War College with the two Lieutenants. I tapped on my right armrest, and they did, too! We tapped softly to avoid being overheard by the rest of the group. Lt. Edwards worked with Mr. Harrison, and he mentioned to Lt. Gordon that fact. I was surprised he acknowledged that fact, but then realized that they both worked in Roosevelt Hall.

Lt. Gordon tapped, *Lieutenant Edwards, who trains your agents at U-1?*

Lt. Edwards tapped, *We borrow senior special agents, mostly from the Postal Inspectors, but occasionally from the Secret Service. Of course, we also have Naval Attachés assigned to certain State Departments throughout the world. We will expand that service working with the ONI soon.*

I tapped, *Does ONI perform domestic surveillance?*

Lt. Edwards tapped, *The ONI is trying to prevent German spies from infiltrating war-related manufacturing plants. I heard that one of our former State Department diplomats has been assigned to the ONI's New York City office."*

I tapped, *Do we work with the British?*

Lt. Edwards tapped, *The Brits helped uncover a plan to blow up a bridge connecting Maine to Canada, but I don't know how they are helping us.*

I was being introduced to sensitive, top-secret information, and it was the reason Emma was not invited to Washington, DC.

Although John mentioned the enemy spy in our training group would probably be the least obvious man, I thought it unlikely that Lt. Gordon or Lt. Edwards were spies. Both Lieutenants worked on small, top-secret projects while assigned to offices in the Army War College. And Lt. Edwards did not divulge information about U-1. I did not get a chance to explore their personal lives, but at this point I wasn't worried.

I glanced back. Emma was at the Telegraph Machine. She was showing Mrs. Lynch the back of the machine and presumably, how to take it apart. Lt. Edwards looked up, surprised to see someone he knew walk in the door.

He tapped on my arm rest, *Lt. Gordon, do you recognize that man?*

"I don't," he said softly.

Lt. Edwards tapped, *I believe that is Mr. Whytock. The Major is considering him for a position dealing with the Port of New York.*

He walked to our side of the table and took a seat next to Lt. Edwards. He introduced himself in an outgoing and confident manner. I was reminded of John's suggestion, that when activity occurred, it was a good time to look around the room to read the faces of those observing the commotion. It was good advice.

But it wasn't the looks of the trainees that I noted. It was the expressions of Van Deman and his British guest that I won't forget. Whoever Major Van Deman's guest is, he must be someone important. His measured stare changed to a wide-eyed man who was unable to return to his usual blank stare when he laid eyes on Mr. Whytock. Major Van Deman was similarly affected. They were pleased with his arrival, perhaps they expected him to be a late arrival. But here he was.

20

EMMA

"I can take this machine apart and reassemble it in no time," I said, pointing to the telegraph Mrs. Lynch and I were seated next to against the wall.

"How did you and Annie learn this?" Mrs. Lynch asked. "You know more about these machines than most in the room!" She was astonished.

"Geo taught us. Salt air permeates the Weather House, and Annie and I have to clean it every few months."

"Do you know how it works?" Mrs. Lynch asked.

"Yes, of course. Geo's telegraph had a recording device added to it a few years ago. It records messages, whether it's manned or not."

"Does this telegraph record all transmissions?"

"Yes, it was added on, probably last year. You can see it through the gap in the cabinet."

After my explanation I think Mrs. Lynch looked on me as more than simply Annie's younger sister. I was hoping I could stay in the room, but when I asked, Mrs. Lynch reminded me that I did not have clearance. I am determined, for the time I'm allowed in the training session, to observe how the men interact with my sister. It is my self-assigned responsibility. After all, I've had years of experience pushing Annie around and observing folks interact with her. I can pick out those who will treat her poorly, but also, my seat against the wall near the telegraph machine was as good a spot as any to watch the men the Major hoped to groom for the Army's new Military Intelligence Service.

Mrs. Lynch leaned over and directed my attention to the front of the room. "We have the three directors of our government's intelligence services: McCauley, Van Deman, and Leland Harrison. And of course, the British guest must be from the British Secret Intelligence Service. The Service that doesn't exist!" She winked.

My mouth flew open. "It doesn't exist. What does that mean?"

"What it means is that no one acknowledges its existence."

"Oh, but the blackboard behind the podium exists," I said, to make my point and change the topic. "It's massive. Why is 1801 carved in it?"

Mrs. Lynch couldn't contain her laugh. "That was the year West Point installed blackboards. They were the first to do so, and now classrooms all over have them. Do the classrooms in your school on Block Island have them?"

"Yes, but they are very small."

I continued to observe everyone in the room. Subtle facial expressions, eye movements, grimaces, body movements, that confirmed or belied feelings. It helped that Mrs. Lynch explained where the men were from and why they were recruited.

Except for the man from the SIS and Mr. Whytock, she knew everyone, including the two former members of the NYPD Bomb Squad. I observed a subtle nod between Mr. Whytock and the two former members of the Bomb Squad. Did Annie observe this?

Capt. Johnston sat to the right of Whytock, and across from Detective Barnitz. Barnitz, Mrs Lynch explained, was recruited to the Office of Naval Intelligence, not Van Deman's MIS. He was the second in command of the Bomb Squad, under Tunney, and highly regarded. Capt. Johnston is a blond, blue-eyed man who left the NYPD to join the Navy, but soon returned to the Bomb Squad. He was muscular, tall — six feet four — a fit man who was surely the only recruit who could outrun Commander McCauley in a race. Van Deman recruited him because of his military service, and his service on the Bomb Squad.

Mrs. Lynch leaned over and explained that intelligence operations often utilize former detectives for on-the-ground work. Johnston's title, "Captain", was a holdover from his early NYPD days where he was the youngest captain in his precinct, before joining the Bomb Squad. I lost focus looking at his largeness. I did not realize until later that he never made eye contact with my sister. But I did notice that he never introduced himself.

Detective George Barnitz of the Bomb Squad looked much older than his 42 years. It was common knowledge that he always had a cigar – in his mouth or in his hand. Although not while on the grounds of the Army War College. Slightly overweight, his coarse appearance went along well with his permanent frown. Although clean shaven today, he was not shy about a handlebar mustache that he could grow in no time at all.

Directly across from my sister, and in my direct line of sight, sat Clark Holder. He was recruited, according to Mrs. Lynch, from industry. She was not sure if he was in the Navy but was recruited soon after January's massive explosion at the Kingsland Munitions plant in Lyndhurst, New Jersey. Six months before, the Black Tom Munitions depot in New York Harbor was blown up, all but obliterating the man-made island. Black Tom was located a few hundred yards behind the Statue of Liberty before it sank into the Harbor. It is expected that Holder will become part of the Major's Industrial Security section of his MIS. Barnitz will assume a similar role in the Office of Naval Intelligence.

"There was an article in the *Washington Star* last week that gave accounts of sabotage carried out by German spies in several industrial plants," Mrs. Lynch said. "I'm sure the *Evening World* reported on it as well, but I didn't see that paper."

"Mrs. Lynch, who's in charge of the German spies?"

"We are now certain that it is run out of the German Embassy, right up the street from the Hamilton Hotel. You can walk there in ten minutes."

"The Embassy has spies?"

"Yes, although some are referred to as attachés."

"Mrs. Lynch, what's Holder's rank?"

"I think he's an Ensign."

"He's handsome, don't you think? As good-looking as John Barrymore!"

While Mrs. Lynch smiled, I kept staring at the guy. It appeared from my observations that he's modest in conversation but not withdrawn or quiet. When Annie looked at him, did I see an interest that only a sister can identify? Mrs. Lynch explained that he worked with his father, an associate in William Rockefeller's oil business. Was it at the Sleepy Hollow Club in

Scarborough, New York where Holder became interested in Industrial Security? I appreciated Holder's matter-of-fact manner when he interacted with my sister. But his calm exterior and Hollywood handsomeness got me hooked.

Across from Lt. Peter Gordon was another Second Lieutenant, Royal Weller, a portly fellow with dark brown, closely cropped hair. On the Ugly Tug, John mentioned Royal was a classmate in college, although they were not friends. Lt. Weller grew up on the Upper West Side of Manhattan, and because he spoke five languages, he was recruited to develop translation services for the MIS. He joined the Army after Yale Law School. I wondered if he played things too close to his chest. He asked Annie to call him Roy when he introduced himself, but I couldn't get a feel for him. Perhaps I was observing his lawyer-like attitude.

Sitting next to Holder was Sgt. Bill Byer. And sitting next to Bill Byer was Yardley.

From the outset it was my opinion, regardless of how highly Mrs. Lynch thought of Byer, that he was a sidekick of Sgt. First Class Tom Yardley. He was Yardley's subordinate in the Signal Service and would always be subordinate to him. Byer followed Capt. Johnston's lead and never introduced himself to Annie. A clear sign of disregard. He was introduced by the Major as someone who was recruited to help establish coastal "listening centers" for the Army, like the site John was directed by the ONI to evaluate on Mount Desert Island in Maine.

I observed the men's nonverbal reactions to Annie while she Morse coded a conversation or answered a question. A few whispered things along the lines of, "Why is this pretty young woman here?" Over the years, by focusing on everyone in the room, I've gained insight into what Annie's nonverbal communication reveals in others' nonverbal gestures.

Sgt. Yardley had commandeered his seat near the end of the table the moment he walked in the room. When Byer eventually took his seat, Yardley patted him on the back and nodded to Capt. Johnston. The subtle reactions of Sgt. Yardley and Sgt. Byer caught my attention. I witnessed the lack of interaction when Clark Holder asked a question. I was surely the only person observing Yardley and Byer while my sister tapped out her answer.

Holder, from across the table: "Annie, what's it like living on an island in the Atlantic Ocean?"

Annie tapped on the table: Most Islanders are farmers or fisherman. Some lucky ones are pilots, who bring the large steamships in from the Atlantic to port. *The weather is a great part of everyday life. Unless your family owns a hotel, life can be a struggle to make a living. But until now I know no other life.*

A reasonable answer, I thought, but Yardley and Byer looked away from Annie, after previously staring at her. They whispered to themselves before chuckling. After that whenever Annie Morsed they'd talk to each other. At one point, when they disagreed with her, they simply started voicing their opinion before she'd finished tapping out her sentence. This was disturbing, but even I could observe that Sgt. Yardley knew his Morse Code and understood nuances in my sister's messages.

I had seen hundreds of people look at my sister as I pushed her wheelchair and got good at figuring out reasons why they looked uncomfortable. When I saw the face of "uncomfortableness" it generally meant two different things. It could reflect an uncaring or unkind person, who looked down upon her with pity. But in some it reflected a simple fear of the unknown, and these individuals would eventually show their kindness, after Annie had spent time with them.

And then there are some who look at her with a mixture of annoyance, as if she were an inconvenience. If given the chance I'd tell them how wonderful she is; but I'm rarely given that opportunity. Annie is not fragile, and she certainly is not an inconvenience. She loves swimming under water, and she's smart and independent. But I know there are many people who do not see her that way. I marvel at how she always deals with her disability with grace and dignity, especially when she is not treated with grace or dignity.

The stares of Yardley, Johnston, and Byer seemed to be filled with contempt — but I did not see that in others. Is this behavior the product of callous men. If so, for what reason? I did not see it with Barnitz, Edwards, Gordon, or the heads of the intelligence services. My initial gut feeling was that they could not handle seeing a young woman, and one with a disability sitting in a wheelchair, in the training group. But there was the possibility that it could have nothing to with her disability – and everything to do with her being a young woman.

Conference room with names of participants

Standing against the far wall: L. Harrison | British Guest

2LT Royal Weller | ENS Clark Holder | SGT Bill Byer | SFC Yardley | Det. Barnitz, NYPD

R. Van Deman --

Podium **Conference Table**

E. McCauley

Chair

2LT Peter Gordon | Annie Rose | Lt Edwards | Ross Whytock | Capt. Johnston, NYPD

Telegraph Machine against the near wall **Doors**

Major Van Deman, Commander McCauley, and Mr. Harrison had wrapped up their conversations and took their positions. The Major at the podium, McCauley in the comfortable chair, and Harrison standing alongside the Brit against the far wall. I did see Leland Harrison make eye contact with Lt. Edwards, but other than that I observed little else.

Major Van Deman peered at his pocket watch after adding another sentence to his welcoming message on the blackboard. *Welcome to the Army War College and the Military Intelligence Service's first training.* The Major glanced at his watch as it approached the turn of the hour. He was a stickler for starting promptly — must be the lawyer in him, physicians are rarely on time. A subtle clearing of the throat brought the attention of the training class, and the session began.

"As most of you know, Commander McCauley is Chief of the ONI and the senior most intelligence officer in the United States. He has a few opening words for us." Major Van Deman nodded to McCauley and said, "Commander."

Commander McCauley stepped to the podium. "Good morning and welcome to one of several Military Intelligence Service organizational meetings. This will serve as the first training session, and we welcome those who are new to Roosevelt Hall and the Army War College. We do expect more invitees to travel to Washington at the end of the week.

"The United States is fortunate that the new MIS will be under the direction of a very capable Major Ralph Van Deman. Few are aware that the ONI was established in 1882 and has been the only permanent intelligence division our country has ever had. This despite the Major's efforts to create a similar intelligence service in the Army. We need a strong Army-based espionage division to complement what we do, and the Major knows that we will assist the MIS to coordinate surveillance activities at home, at sea, in Europe, or anywhere the American Expeditionary Forces require espionage services. If we enter the European War, General Pershing will establish an intelligence group with French and British allies.

"As an introduction to the breadth of the ONI's surveillance efforts, including how we approach adversaries overseas, I'll share a report we recently completed. We are experts in liaison with other entities worldwide because intelligence efforts, at sea especially, require coordination with parties throughout the globe. We submitted to the White House an extensive report on Germany's U-boat capacity. These findings required the input of observers on ships, merchant and Naval vessels, military staff, information from the Royal Navy and the French Navy. The data is sobering."

Commander McCauley paused to observe the reactions of everyone in the room.

"How many U-boats do you think Germany operates under waterways and oceans around the world?"

No one ventured a guess.

"Take a guess?" McCauley prompted.

"Thirty-five," Byer hazarded a guess.

"More than that," Yardley blurted out.

McCauley nodded, "That's right, many more. Along the coasts of

Europe, in the Caribbean, in North America ... we estimate the total number of ocean-going U-boats at 101. And in addition to those vessels, there are fifty coastal U-boats in action in Europe, North America, and the Mediterranean. In addition, we've discovered another eighty-six U-boats that are laying mines.

"Germany launches three submarines every week. And, for the most sobering information: Not one of our merchant ships has been spared the wrath of German submarines. Since February, when Germany initiated unrestricted U-boat warfare, *every cargo ship in the United States' Merchant Marine has gone down to the sea.* As of today, nineteen U.S. Merchant ships have been sunk. Nineteen!"

Yardley raised his hand. "Commander, have vessels under sail been impacted?"

"Yes. As you might expect, square rigged ships are easy prey for U-boats," Commander McCauley said. "This war might put an end to using large sailing vessels to ship cargo."

Annie raised her right hand and tapped at lightning speed, *Numerous smaller fishing smacks have been torpedoed and sunk, too. Our Island's Captain Sanchez was sailing his fishing schooner on Georgia's Bank, and it was bombed by a U-boat.*

McCauley looked impressed. "I'm aware of those sinkings, Annie. Germany does control the North Atlantic, as well as the North Sea."

Yardley asked one of the more astute, and classified questions: "Are we making progress on anti-submarine measures?"

"Yes, but slowly. The ONI works closely with scientists and our industrialists, especially Edison. Edison is helping us develop underwater sensors to detect submarine movements. The Royal Navy's devices, unfortunately, have not been successful. I think our new 'listening' devices will have the capability to pinpoint the location of any underwater vessel. This is top secret, but it will take a while to manufacture and deploy this type of undersea equipment. Mr. Edison, we all thank you.

"Any questions?" Again, the Commander surveyed the room before continuing his lecture.

"Unfortunately, at this point, the United States is in dire straits. If there was a battle of the Atlantic this month, we would lose."

The commander's comment shook the room. Except perhaps for Yardley. No one said anything until Annie started Morsing a question.

Annie tapped with lightning speed, *How can that be? All I saw on Block Island was one warship after another, sailing to and from the Naval base in Newport. And the USS* Arizona *was launched in February.*

"I have spoken the sad truth. We are playing catchup to the Germans, because their industrial strength is unmatched anywhere in the world. And the Royal Navy has suffered defeats like they have never known. Shortly the ONI will send Admiral Sims to England to survey the situation."

A quick glance at Annie confirmed that everyone but Yardley was surprised to hear that as well. The room remained silent. It was as if everyone froze. They waited for the Commander's next comment. It was a revelation that taught so much about intelligence and policy makers and politicians. Although Annie and I could not appreciate this lesson until months had passed.

"We are already at war, aren't we? All the intelligence officials know." The Commander continued in a methodical manner, "You must understand our current situation ... because your responsibilities and actions ... in the MIS and ONI ... will help determine the outcome of the war."

The Commander paused long enough for the information to sink in. There were no questions. Ed McCauley, the highest-ranking intelligence officer in our country, looked over at Mrs. Lynch and me.

"Have I discussed classified information? Yes, so you must refrain from repeating anything ... and that includes anything that you will soon read in the *Washington Evening Star* or the *Evening World*."

Mrs. Lynch turned to me. "Emma, time for us to go." I smiled at the Commander and gave him a quick bow, to thank him for allowing me to stay this long. He acknowledged me with a nod of his head. I thought the morning was a good beginning for my sister, but I was concerned more than ever about how the undercurrents of the group would play out. There were a few who would be supportive, a few who would not be, and the rest somewhere in between.

21

ANNIE

I noticed the Commander's gaze in my sister's direction. I thought it generous that the Commander and the Major allowed Emma to remain in the room for as long as they did. This raised the issue of Emma being privy to secret information and suggested they trusted us to be careful not to divulge anything heard, here or elsewhere, going forward. I raised my eyes twice and Emma responded accordingly.

After Mrs. Lynch and Emma walked out and closed the door, the Commander asked if anyone had questions about the U-boats, or the industrial capabilities of Germany.

I raised my right hand.

"Annie Rose, your thoughts?" the Commander asked.

I started tapping at an extremely fast rate, but realized I was 'telegraphing' my nervousness and I slowed down. *About our development of undersea listening devices, how soon can they be operational?*

"Not soon enough, Annie. A comprehensive naval strategy includes listening devices, and our goal is to plant them off the coasts and in shipping lanes. Eventually, in all areas of the oceans. It will take years to do this but eventually we'll cover much of the Atlantic. This will be done in complete secrecy. Just like so much of the ONI's responsibilities. Most do not know that we have been operational for decades. I hope that this war will be a reminder to Congress, future presidents and our own military of the importance of espionage for our country."

The Commander finished up with an encouraging comment.

"We are counting on everyone in this room to learn as much as you can, to support the intelligence initiatives to save our country. This training group is, in part, where this effort will originate. It's vital to national security. Do not underestimate how important you all are."

He walked from the podium and did not entertain questions.

I was motivated beyond what I thought possible and vowed to excel in the training. But suddenly it struck me that not only had I completely ignored the rude behavior of Yardley and Byer, I also took my mind off observing the other men in the room. If I had observed the *responses* to the Commander's comments, it could have been extremely helpful to figure out who the enemy spy was. I missed that opportunity and I vowed to not let that happen again.

Major Van Deman retook the podium.

"I hope everyone appreciates the Commander's insight that intelligence is not only essential to military strategy, but that it is vital to diplomacy and developing policy in our government. I sincerely hope that after the war in Europe ends our country continues to support a permanent intelligence community.

"Mr. Harrison is a senior diplomat in our State Department and has been assigned to Embassies in adversarial countries. In the past year, he was called back to the Army War College to develop liaison protocols. He knows better than anyone that the politics of self-interest can and will start wars. He also directs the State Department's new intelligence agency. Mr. Harrison."

Leland Harrison took a few steps forward and addressed the group with brief comments from the side of the room. "Your training is more than understanding codes and ciphers. We are all here to protect the security of our country. And, while each of you will develop your own specialty, you must learn to work closely with your teammates. When you help each other, you will learn at the same time. In diplomacy we work with individuals everywhere in the world.

"What is the role of intelligence in diplomacy? Mostly to understand geographic intelligence and near-real-time intelligence with respect to motives of leaders of other countries. We must understand cultural issues, including the desires of its citizens, especially when they are not congruent with their country's leadership. We are also responsible for the safety of the military attachés assigned to our Embassies. I cannot imagine developing effective State Department policy without the benefit of intelligence gathering.

"As everyone knows, the dual monarchy of Austria-Hungary had annexed Serbia, and then a Serbian assassinated Archduke Franz Ferdinand and his wife. That set off a complicated series of events that included Germany supporting the dual monarchy of Austria-Hungary. But then Germany quickly declared war on Russia, because Russia backed Serbia. At the end of that summer Germany had invaded France and that led to Great Britain declaring war on Germany.

"The war started after the assassination, but the underlying cause was widespread nationalism, hastened by poor economic conditions. Having a strong Foreign Service is essential and, unfortunately, war can be the consequence of failed diplomacy. Germany and Austria versus Russia. Although a Consulate cannot stop a war, if another nation-state is uncompromising. But understanding hidden motives helps to prepare for consequences.

"The State Department's Foreign Service has a long history of working closely with the Office of Naval Intelligence. In the 1880s the ONI started placing trained Naval Attachés to our Consulates around the world. It's no secret they've been a great source of intelligence.

"Concerning negative intelligence, Major Van Deman has struggled to convince his fellow officers in the Army to understand its importance. Frankly, our Foreign Service offices have been overwhelmed by such efforts of the Germans. To some it's propaganda, but it goes further than that. At this point we are no match for them. Tunney's Bomb Squad, and our own Secret Service, are aware of this situation. We welcome the Commander setting sail to Europe next month to address this issue. He wlll personally meet with our Naval Attachés.

"But no one is in a better position to understand negative intelligence than the gentleman standing to my right. Major Dansey. He is a Naval attaché at the British Embassy."

And just like that, the man with the British accent had a name, and a title.

I looked around the room. Everyone looked surprised, except Yardley and Whytock. No one else had a clue that Dansey represented the British Secret Intelligence Service. Perhaps we should have, given the armed guard that followed him about the War College campus. Perhaps Lt. Edwards was also aware, but his head was buried in his papers.

Major Van Deman continued the conversation. "Major Dansey and I will distribute old transmitted, encrypted messages to help you learn to decipher messages. I'll distribute messages sent by our Foreign Service Attachés to the State Department. A few were sent by Edward Bell, a career diplomat at our London Embassy; he previously worked in Cairo, Teheran, and Cuba before being reassigned to London four years ago.

"And of course we do not need to remind anyone that this information is top secret.

Van Deman nodded to Mr. Harrison. "Sir, do you have anything to add?

Mr. Harrison stepped forward. "The German encrypted messages provided by Major Dansey were obtained from the home office of the Admiralty. These are especially helpful to learn how to decipher German messages. Some will contain intel from human sources. Thank you, Claude, for sharing these encrypted messages.

"Finally, everyone must understand Major Van Deman's responsibility is to develop a comprehensive and integrated intelligence agency within in the Army ... but our nation's security here in the United States is equally important. We must ensure that the new MIS, the ONI, and my service, U-1, work together to lead our national intelligence efforts. We are fortunate that we have members of the NYPD Bomb Squad in attendance, representing the ONI and the Army. But we are most appreciative of Major Dansey's involvement, and it is wonderful that we have the support of the Director of the Army War College, Brigadier General Kuhn."

Mr. Harrison's sobering words were more instructive than I could have imagined. His message added to the seriousness of the atmosphere in the training group. After talking confidentially with the Major, he left the room with Commander McCauley.

22

ANNIE

An armed guard appeared at the doorway and signaled to Van Deman, who nodded back. "Decipher those telegraphed messages. I'll be back shortly," he said to the room as he and Dansey departed.

We first tackled the encrypted messages sent from our London Embassy to our State Department. Yardley took the lead, being the most proficient at decoding our own messages, but also because, as he admitted, he had already seen this message. It was sent by Eddie Bell. Two other messages sent by Ambassador Page were also easily dispatched with. While reading these messages we learned that Bell kept in touch with colleagues at his old posts, in Teheran and Cairo. I learned, although everyone else in the room already knew, that Colonel House was a close friend of President Wilson and his unofficial foreign policy advisor. House was a Texan who supported Wilson early in his campaign, but his "wealth" was more than money. He had a broad perspective on national and global affairs.

The most distressing message we deciphered was sent by Ambassador Page on January 19, 1915, to President Wilson. It was an eyewitness account of when German Zeppelins dropped bombs on the city of Great Yarmouth, killing 20. Five days later, Yardley explained, Page sent an extensive message that detailed the Brits sinking of the SMS *Blücher*.

We learned a lot about Edward Bell from Yardley. Bell was a friend of FDR and loved being a diplomat. Yardley said that he was down to earth, a masterful negotiator, and by all accounts a student of diplomacy. His only weakness: he loved whisky.

While this was going on, and with the Major still out of the room, I figured it was an ideal time to observe for a potential enemy spy in the group. It also struck me that with only attendees in the room, I, a civilian woman, was the only one aware that sitting at the table was perhaps a German spy. But my observations of the men gave me no clue. John's admonition that I treat *everyone* as a potential spy reflected good judgement. Still, I had a sense from the morning that Lt. Gordon would become an ally, as would almost certainly Lt. Edwards.

A few of my concerns date back to when I was offered the position. Will some men become detractors, regardless of reasons? Women have been allowed in the Navy, as civilians, for only a few months. But it's doubtful that the men will believe I belong here. There's my wheelchair and having to rely on Morsing to communicate. My grasp of negative intelligence probably didn't matter to any of them.

Major Van Deman and Dansey walked back in the room. He returned to the podium and Dansey took his position against the wall.

"Annie, do you have any questions?"

I tapped, *Not yet, except I have a lot to learn.*

"We're glad you're here, Annie. You'll learn that gathering and analyzing intelligence is complicated, that it's as much an art as it is a science. Placing interpretation of data into context is difficult, especially when it is presented to politicians and policy makers."

The Major turned to Dansey. "Now that you've finished decrypting messages from our London Embassy, Claude will help decrypt the German messages he brought from Whitehall. Room 40, a section of the SIS, decrypts messages from around the world. Claude can easily discern meaning from decrypted messages.

"Annie, one other thing, please remind your sister that secrecy is imperative when overhearing intelligence data. You can tell her that even George Washington stressed secrecy, and that he, too, established spy rings. He also established the first secret fund called the Contingency Fund."

I tapped, *That she will be interested in. What was it for*?

"It was for negative intelligence purposes."

Can I ask a question? If Washington understood the value of negative intelligence, why can't General Scott understand the need for it?

Most everyone in the room chuckled or laughed, but only Whytock couldn't contain himself. He laughed out loud.

Ross Whytock spoke up, "May I add that President Lincoln understood the value, too, and he also established a similar fund."

"Well said, Ross, and welcome to DC," the Major said.

I raised my hand, and after being acknowledged by Van Deman, I tapped, *Why did we not maintain intelligence agencies between wars?*

"The Brits, the French, and the Germans maintained their spy networks. Unfortunately, only the ONI maintained their division, but not the Army. Ten years ago, I directed a reconnaissance mission in China, to learn about logistics capabilities, but that was as part of a military program. I'll talk about that mission in my lecture."

With that he walked to the podium and began his introduction. It was clear from the beginning that he enjoyed lecturing and was good at it.

Five minutes into his lecture he introduced me.

"As you may know, the ONI has two parts, the Offshore and Domestic divisions. We have one participant from the ONI, Annie Rose, who most of you met when you came in. She represents the Domestic Division. The ONI officer who recruited Annie is currently at sea, and he represents the Offshore Division.

"Welcome, Annie," he said, then directed his attention to the others. "For those who didn't introduce yourself to her, please do so during our lunch break. She's a courageous young woman who communicates using Morse Code, which you are all proficient in, too, or you wouldn't be here."

Ten minutes into his lecture he returned to the story of his mission to Eastern China to discover logistical information, which I found interesting. But that wasn't the reason he brought it up. It was the lesson learned he wanted us to remember.

"During the mission I knew we were being followed by Japanese spies, but I had no idea that there was a spy from China, too. Where was he, I wondered, when I was asked to leave the country?"

Lt. Weller raised his hand. "Did a Japanese spy turn you in?"

"It wasn't a Japanese spy, it was my damn housekeeper! I should have known, because housekeepers have a long history of spying. The ONI has used them and are an example of 'espionage on the ground'."

After a brief discussion of China and Teddy Roosevelt's desire to prevent China from being split up by the major powers, Van Deman focused on signal intelligence. That included knowing the location of underwater cables. I looked around the room and found puzzled faces, except for Yardley, Byer, and Whytock.

"What's the term for underwater cables?" Major Van Deman asked, returning to his serious side. "And what year was the first one laid, and where?"

Bill Byer and Capt. Johnston hung their heads as if embarrassed they didn't know the answer. On the other hand, Weller, Holder, and Edwards eagerly awaited the correct response. The Major was ready to offer an explanation, but I raised my right hand.

"Annie, your thoughts? If anyone in the room can't keep up with Annie's Morsing let me know." He chuckled, but there was no laughter from the men.

I tapped on the table at my usual rate of speed, which was twice as fast as anyone in the room. The men on either side listened attentively or appeared to understand. Before I finished my answer, a few men started complaining, that they could not hear my tapping, or were pretending they couldn't hear. I took note of who they were.

But the mumbling got worse. I stopped tapping when Yardley called out, "This was a bad idea, Major! What's she trying to say?"

I knew Yardley could understand everything. I saw Lt. Weller and Sgt. Byer shake their heads. Then Johnston, to my far right, uttered words under his breath that everyone heard: "Why is she here?"

Their dissent was about me, a young woman, who was trying to give the answer that they themselves did not know. I was afraid this would happen, but the test would be, how long it would continue, and who would be the major offenders. On Block Island, Emma was my eyes and ears, but here, I'm on my own. I became intimidated and insulted. But it got worse.

The grumbling intensified, and then I got angry, and responded by tapping faster and louder. As loud as I could manage without decreasing my speed. The sour mood got worse, especially on the other side of the table. A quick glance to my right and I saw an expression of disbelief from Whytock. I later found out that his father was a physician and cared for children who had similar conditions.

How I wished Emma was in the room. At times like this I'd move my good hand, turn it back and forth – my signal to Emma that I needed help. It was no fault of my own, and I was as surprised as much as I was hurt, that most didn't attempt to understand my Morsing, or care.

I started my answer over, tapping loud on the table and Morsing with lightning speed. *In 1845 Ezra Cornell placed the first underwater cable in the Hudson River, from Washington Heights in Manhattan to New Jersey. The laying of underwater cables is called submarine telegraphy. Once they are laid on the ocean or river floor, they are called submarine cables.*

The Major had sat in the large chair as I Morsed my answer. After I finished, he remained seated for a few moments. He gazed at each trainee. During that moment of silence, we all waited for his response. I'm sure the men, or some of them, were hoping I got it wrong. I thought my answer was correct but did not want to be wrong and become further embarrassed. Nor did I want to appear smarter than my new colleagues in the room.

"That is correct, Annie," Major Van Deman said, returning to the podium. "I'm impressed."

I smiled, sat up as much as my body would allow, and scanned the room. Except for the men on either side of me, none were happy, and the grumbling continued. Now that I knew my answer was not only correct, but that I impressed the Major, the negative responses did not bother me. A lesson learned. I was happy but the Major was annoyed with what he observed.

"Does anyone want a further explanation?" he said, raising his voice slightly. No one said anything. "Annie, when did the Brits lay their first submarine cable?"

The room became silent once again, and I gathered my thoughts. Before I started Morsing the answer, the Major demanded everyone's undivided attention.

"Listen up!" Major Van Deman said, "Annie has as much right to be here as any of you. She's earned her seat at the table. You men will accord Annie with the same respect that you do to each other. Are we clear on that?

"Annie, continue with your answer, please."

I formulated a lengthy answer in my head and tapped rapidly, *The British laid their first submarine cable across the English Channel in 1851. The following year they laid a cable in Canada, between Prince Edward Island and New Brunswick.*

The first cable laid across the Atlantic Ocean was in 1858. It's a complicated story with a lot of problems but that year Ezra Cornell taught Peter Cooper the intricacies of laying submarine cables. Peter Cooper went on to fund a Transatlantic Cable between Newfoundland and Cape Clear in Ireland. Cooper also funded the American Telegraph Company.

"I wasn't expecting you to know all that," the Major said. "Unfortunately, that first Transatlantic cable broke, and they had to lay down a second one using a different route. But it was operational by late August of that year. An important point of this discussion is that, in the past sixty years, cables have been laid the world over, on land and under water. Now there are thousands of underwater cables in the world."

I could not have been more appreciative of the Major's admonition to the men, but I didn't expect him to continue his tirade.

"Are we CLEAR on what I said before?" he demanded.

"Yes, sir," various men responded in hushed tones.

"You're all in this training upon my invitation. I reviewed hundreds of men who were interested and selected you guys. I can easily un-invite you. Keep that in mind."

This was a side I wouldn't have expected, given how warm he was when he introduced himself. Major Van Deman waited for a few moments before continuing in his normal voice as if his outburst had never happened.

23

EMMA

I didn't like having to leave the room with Mrs. Lynch. I was appreciative that I was allowed to stay in the conference room for as long as I did. But I was worried about my sister. Always will be and if I get faulted for that I do not care.

The elevator took a few minutes to arrive to the lobby and I took the opportunity to ask questions that I wasn't sure I should ask.

"Mrs. Lynch, how do I get clearance, so I can stay with Annie?"

Mrs. Lynched smiled. "I know you two are inseparable, but Annie has to do this on her own."

"I know but is there a way for me to get clearance?" I pleaded.

"To be in that room would require top level clearance."

"But Annie doesn't have clearance, and I'm guessing that except for Yardley, and Gordon and Edwards who've been at the Army War College, I doubt the others have clearance. Am I right?"

"Emma, you are correct. But after they complete training, they'll be eligible."

I wasn't getting anywhere and changed the subject. "Have you heard the Major lecture before?"

"He teaches at the War College. I've attended his lectures on strategies for surveillance based on his expeditions to China."

I looked up to Mrs. Lynch, and even though we'd only met, I enjoyed her company. I hoped she wasn't disappointed to have been assigned to my sister. I looked down at the gray marble on the elevator floor, and before the doors opened, I said a prayer for Mrs. Lynch. And then another one, that she would always be our friend.

Praying helps me. I learned this when my brother and father drowned. And I learned how good it made me feel when I thought Annie would die. But I didn't pray when I almost drowned, instead, all I thought of was how would my sister be, without me? When I pray, I usually kneel, usually at bedtime, with or without my sister present. Annie doesn't pray much but sometimes she asks me to say a prayer for her. Which I do of course. I once said, "Annie if you died, I don't think I could handle it. Because how do you pray and cry at the same time?"

As the door to the elevator opened, seeing nobody in the hall, I asked another question, "I overheard Lieutenant Edwards mention a man by the name of Spencer Eddy. Who's that?"

She raised her eyes. "I do know that there was a Spencer Eddy who was a colleague of Mr. Harrison, but I'm not sure where he is right now. If I remember correctly, he left the State Department for personal reasons."

We walked to the lobby and waved goodbye to Sgt. Lightfoot, who stood on the far side. Once outside Mrs. Lynch grabbed my arm in hers. I took her arm and we walked slowly down the granite steps of Roosevelt Hall.

"Finding facts about events is tough, isn't it Mrs. Lynch? Like trying to determine the story of Mary Touvestre. With much of her life is unknown."

"It's difficult to piece together her life. Lives of slaves, even freed slaves are invisible. Their families, their homes are invisible, to white folk for sure. Being invisible may be good for a spy but not for the rest of us."

We got in the car and in no time were in front of the Hamilton Hotel.

Before I stepped out, I asked a final question, "Do you think there's a job for me at the Army War College?"

Mrs. Lynch smiled and shook her head. "You don't give up, do you, Emma. I'll return between 3:00 and 3:30 and we'll pick up Annie together."

*

At 3:15 Mrs. Lynch arrived back. I had been waiting outside for ten minutes and wanted to find out about Annie. I missed her terribly but at least I wasn't stuck on Block Island. How I wished Mrs. Lynch could find a job for me.

I opened the car door and was surprised that she looked sad. Or tired. I couldn't tell so I asked about her day.

"I drove officers back and forth from the War College to the War Department, across from the White House. Some of the officers aren't very nice."

"I should be with you in the car, as a chaperone. I'd give them a hard time."

Mrs. Lynch burst out laughing and responded to me in the most wonderful way, "You would need clearance. I'll ask around, there must be something on campus you can do. It would be good to be around to help your sister during mealtime."

I opened my eyes wide and raised them, twice. "Really?"

We drove the rest of the way to Roosevelt Hall in silence. When I opened the car door at the base of the steps of the Hall, I startled. Fritz was waiting. I jostled with him as he followed us up the steps and into the lobby.

"We're back, Sergeant Lightfoot," I said, showing off Fritz at my side.

He waved with a flick of his wrist.

Mrs. Lynch gestured to Fritz. "Tell him to 'stay' and he'll wait for us. He'll listen to you now."

I looked directly at Fritz and said, "Stay." He obediently backed into the corner of the lobby and sat.

The fifth-floor training room doors were closed. No sound issued from the other side. Mrs. Lynch knocked lightly, then opened the door. Several of the men, including Major Van Deman, were standing around Annie. We could barely see her but heard a distinct rapid clicking. I recognized the sound; the Major had brought Annie a telegraph key. Now everyone in the room would hear her Morsing, loud and clear.

Yardley and Byer were in their seats, arms crossed, on the other side of the table. Johnston was with them. The three were talking quietly amongst themselves. I noticed Whytock was not in the room.

Five groups of a series of letters were written on the chalk board, arranged in what appeared to be a completely unintelligible sequence. Below that was a question. Annie was answering that question. The officers watched in amazement as Annie tapped out the correct answer. Mrs. Lynch and I took seats by the door, and she whispered, "The letters on the board are part of a training cryptogram. It's a great way to start learning cryptography. But I don't understand the question below it."

"It sounds like my sister has stumbled onto something new." I leaned over to Mrs. Lynch. "Annie read the packets of information John sent to the Island, and it's always amazed me how fast she absorbs information."

"Your sister is something else, I'd say." Mrs. Lynch shook her head in wonderment.

Major Van Deman acknowledged our presence with a wave and came over.

"How did my sister do at lunch?" I said nervously. "I worry when I'm not with her."

"I'd ordered food suitable for her," he replied. "John had mentioned she had dysphagia, and I instructed the staff to prep the food for her."

"Thank you, Major."

"Clark Holder pitched in to help as well," Major Van Deman let loose with a brief smile. "Your sister is taken by his good looks."

"I noticed him this morning. He's handsome enough to be in the movies."

"Speaking of movies, I was surprised you know Sperry. His fiancée is an up-and-coming Hollywood movie star."

"Really? Who?"

"Winifred Allen. But he dates a lot. Before her, Sperry was involved with Dorothy Sims, a wild and wealthy woman. Her father builds our submarines."

At that point Major Dansey walked over to say he was leaving. I took the opportunity to introduce myself, while the Major and Mrs. Lynch stepped aside to continue their conversation.

Dansey was a short man, a few inches taller than me.

"Nice to meet you, too, Emma," he said cheerfully in his English accent. "I appreciate that you're a great help to your sister."

I smiled but being nervous I responded only with a simple thank you.

"When I get the chance, I'll tell you and your sister about a remarkable disabled women in London. But I've got to get to the British Embassy."

"Thank you, Major," I said.

"Emma, you can call me Mr. Dansey. Do you know the gentleman waiting for me at the door? He's a diplomat, a friend of Mr. Harrison."

I glanced at the door and in the hall was a tall man, dressed in a suit. I shook my head.

"He's an Eddy, too. Is he part of your uncle's family?"

"I don't recognize him."

"He's been with the ONI. Annie will meet him, soon. He'll be at a few of the meetings."

Just then I saw a booklet drop from Annie's wheelchair. Lt. Gordon reached down and got it first. I walked over and said hello.

"Annie's doing a great job." From his tone of voice, I could tell he liked her, which made me like him even more.

I returned to Mrs. Lynch and the Major and caught the tail end of a muffled conversation.

"... I can't believe the two of them did *that* in an aeroplane," Mrs. Lynch said. She seemed to be blushing.

"It was three years ago, today. Surprising, I know. But over Long Island Sound Sperry started the Mile High Club."

I had no idea what they were talking about. The Major's interest in movie stars seemed odd, but Mrs. Lynch informed me he enjoyed Hollywood gossip.

"I'm surprised at how Annie Rose is so quick to learn," he said, returning to his professional demeanor. "After an hour of small group assignments using our training cryptograms, Annie solved the first part of a new one that's up on the board and helped the others with it. Now she's the only one answering the question on the board."

"She works well with others," Mrs. Lynch said, putting on her supervisor hat. "I suspect that by having to adjust to her condition, she can recognize right away when she needs help. And, just as quickly, she can offer help if possible. She's got a valuable skill."

The Major recognized this, too, but no one else in the room did. Nor would they. Annie and I struggled to adjust after the accident. She was always the first to do something, never afraid, very independent. Learning how to sail solo at a young age is an example. But after our accident Annie had to let go of her need to accomplish everything on her own. It was no longer possible and gradually she embraced being reliant on me at times – and that set the pattern for how to interact with everyone. It became her manner. I've never seen anyone besides Major Van Deman comprehend that within such a short period. Last October John recognized it and explained there's word for that: "Annie's interdependent."

"And Morse Code is definitely her ally," Van Deman continued. "She's lightning fast, accurate to almost forty words a minute, few ever attain that speed. And Harriet, for your evaluations of her, after the group deciphered that message, Annie went on to explain how to garner information by reading between the lines of code. Including how she discerns feelings and perspectives of the person telegraphing it."

"John mentioned she could do that," Mrs. Lynch said.

"Geo taught her that," I added.

"It's a rare skill and she has it already," Van Deman said. "Although my objectives for the class remained, she altered the way the session unfolded."

"Emma, how does she absorb and apply information so quickly?" Mrs. Lynch asked.

"She's always been that way. She's got a great memory, and the accident seems to have made it even better, if that's possible. She methodically thinks through problems and believes her most important skill is the ability to discern what's right and what's not right. She likes to use that word, discern, a lot. What fits and what doesn't fit. I think it's part intuition, part reasoning. Somehow, she just keeps on figuring things out."

"She *is* a quick study," Major Van Deman reiterated.

"I'm sorry, Major, we've got to get to the Weather Bureau," Mrs. Lynch interjected. "We're creating Annie's cover identification, so folks on Block Island, who know everything, won't know this time."

"I know that Island," he affirmed. "Everyone finds out about everything because of that party line phone exchange."

"How did you know that?" I asked. "Have you been to the Island?"

"I have not, but I know the exchange is located above the drug store. Your Island has a problem. It's not only the phone calls, but telegrams are wired from hotels. Everyone knows everything, you can't conceal anything." Major Van Deman shook his head. "I fail to understand why the Island's Weather Bureau calls are routed through the public switchboard. I hope things change when the Navy takes over the Narragansett Hotel."

"It's an isolated Island community, we had a hard time finding which family harbored German spies." I did not mention that there are Islanders who have never been to the southwest part of the Island.

"And that's why cover for Annie is essential," the Major said.

Major Van Deman excused himself, announced to the group that he had a meeting to attend. After packing up his lecture notes, he took a quick leave. "See you tomorrow at 8 AM sharp."

Ensign Clark Holder was standing near Annie. He leaned down, put a hand on Annie's shoulder and said something in her ear. She raised her eyes, *Yes.*

He took hold of the handles on Annie's wheelchair and pushed her over to us.

"Here she is," he said, beaming. "She taught us something today."

"What was that?" I asked.

"Nobody can talk behind *her* back – or push her around – without permission."

We all laughed, attracting the attention of everyone.

"See you tomorrow," Clark said and headed for the door.

The men filed out of the room. Royal Weller disappeared on the heels of Major Van Deman. Lt. Gordon and Lt. Edwards came up to say goodbye, then left together. Sgt. Yardley, Sgt. Byer, and Capt. Johnston exited quietly along with a supervisor from the Bomb Squad, Detective Barnitz.

"Annie, where did the journalist go?"

Annie tapped, *He knows how to Morse! Before he left, I had a short conversation with him about London. A very smart man, one of the smartest I've met.*

Soon the three of us were on the elevator.

Annie radiated contentment. She Morsed and used hand signals, *We reviewed training cryptograms, and after that, I was the third person to decipher a new cryptogram. Yardley and Byer deciphered it first.*

"After we left this morning did the men continue to be rude?" I asked.

Annie tapped, *Even after Van Deman's comments, some continued to shoot cloaked daggers. I realize that to some men I will be a threat. Remember Geo's favorite phrase, Emma? 'What Peter says about Paul says more about Peter than it does about Paul.' I understand what that means, that some men will never be on my side.*

Annie changed the subject, *Dansey carries himself in a manner that makes it impossible to know what he's thinking. I didn't think he could smile, grin maybe, but not smile. He has a poker face.*

Mrs. Lynch gave an all-knowing smile.

"He was very cordial to me and asked if we knew the man in the suit named Eddy."

Annie tapped, *That's a senior recruit to the ONI, a friend of FDR and Mr. Harrison.*

"There are a lot of people involved!"

"That's an understatement, Emma. It's a huge endeavor to build the Army's intelligence service. You'll see a lot of different faces in addition to those you saw in this room," she assured me.

We entered the lobby to find Fritz still sitting in the corner. As soon as he saw Annie, he ran up, tail wagging furiously. He placed his paw on her lap, and then his head, looking into her eyes. We continued outside, and I worked the wheelchair down the granite steps. Fritz stood guard and walked alongside us.

On the way to the Weather Bureau, Mrs. Lynch shared a most bizarre story.

24

ANNIE

Thirty minutes later we pulled up to the Weather Bureau headquarters at 2416 M Street, NW. Emma stayed in the car, and we went in through a side door. Immediately we were greeted by an administrator. Few words were spoken throughout the entire time we were in the building, but at no point was an explanation needed.

The assigned photographer asked me to transfer to a wide bench, then he took my photo. Twenty minutes had passed when the administrator produced several signed documents and placed them in my lap. All he said was, "The photo will be ready in one week. Good luck, Annie, I hope things go well for you."

Back in the car I asked if we could drive around the Hamilton Hotel neighborhood before dropping us off. Mrs. Lynch readily agreed. I hoped we'd see the German Embassy that was not too far from the hotel. If the Germans recruited a spy, visualizing the Embassy might be helpful. Because I could not share anything about my secret mission, I was relieved Mrs. Lynch did not ask for an explanation.

But I needed not worry because Mrs. Lynch had something on her mind. She spoke to us about a phone call she'd received earlier in the day from Miss Sarah.

"Miss Sarah asked if I'd give permission for you two to be introduced to a guest at the hotel. The guest had asked Irving a question about Block Island, but he didn't know the answer. When she found out you were from Block Island, she asked Miss Sarah."

I tapped, *Did Irving suggest she talk with us?*

"I think so," Mrs. Lynch replied. "Her name is Miss Muriel. She's a retired journalist from Canada."

"Why is she in DC?" Emma asked.

"She mentioned that she's on business and visiting friends. Apparently, she's well-traveled, has studied in France and Italy, and published a novel."

What's her question?

"Apparently, her good friend died on Block Island at the Ocean View Hotel, where she was working as a maid. She was close to the owner of that hotel. Miss Muriel wants to know if you two know anything about their deaths."

That was twenty years ago! I remember the stories about Nicholas Ball dying from apoplexy at his hotel.

Emma exclaimed, "Twenty years ago! I wasn't born yet. Why is she asking us?"

"Miss Muriel explained to Miss Sarah that her friend died a day or two before Ball."

"That's not a Block Island connection I want to hear about," Emma said.

I was glad Emma asked her questions. But I tapped, *Emma, I have other things on my mind. Can you deal with this?*

"That's a good idea, Annie," Mrs. Lynch chimed in, "Emma, are you okay with that?"

Emma let out a sigh. "Will do."

After Mrs. Lynch pointed out the Dolley Madison House, she drove up 14th Street, past the Hamilton Hotel, and continued for a few blocks, drove around Thomas Circle onto Massachusetts Avenue, I saw this huge brick mansion.

Without me having to ask, Mrs. Lynch pointed to it. "That's the German Embassy." Mrs. Lynch then turned left on 15th Street and circled back to the Hamilton.

She dropped us off and reminded us once again that if anyone asked, to say I was attending a Weather Bureau training. We nodded agreement, and as Emma helped me into the wheelchair, I gave Mrs. Lynch a quick wave goodbye with my right hand.

We saw Irving at the registration desk talking with guests before Emma pushed me through the lobby doors. He smiled when he saw us, but gave the appearance of being too busy to walk over and say hello. But he did take a few steps toward us and said in a low voice that a guest wanted to ask us a few questions.

"About?" Emma asked.

"A question about Crescent Beach and the Ocean View," Irving said, then quickly got back to his guests.

We avoided the backup of guests waiting at the main elevator and took the service lift at the end of the hall. We were looking forward to resting before dinner. But we weren't alone for long.

The knock on our door brought Miss Sarah, and our dinner. "Welcome back," she said enthusiastically, as if she'd been waiting all day. She let us know what we'd already suspected, that Irving requested we eat in our room.

Emma turned to me. "Annie, I know you don't care, and Mrs. Lynch thinks it's for the best, but he's keeping us out of the dining room because he doesn't want the other guests to see you. He thinks *everyone* feels awkward around people in wheelchairs."

I let my eyes drift down to my lap, rolled them, and tapped, *It's best for our security, Emma.*

"I'm not done," she protested. "The only way to get Irving and everyone comfortable with someone in a wheelchair is for them to see you and interact with you."

"Emma," Miss Sarah said, "remember what Mrs. Lynch said?"

I could see Emma was frustrated with the situation. She shrugged her shoulders and said, "Yes, I know, she wants dinner brought here, too."

I tapped, *If that is the way it has to be, then so be it. I'm tired but also excited about my first day of training.*

Miss Sarah seemed amused by my sister's short tirade. "There's one very important thing I must mention to you. Ross Whytock, from New York, is staying at the Hamilton. You must not say hello or acknowledge him in any way. I think you know not to ask questions. Am I right?"

"Yes, Miss Sarah," Emma replied. "He was at the meeting this morning.

Annie spoke to him. Do you know him?"

"He doesn't know who I am, but I've seen him here, and we have spoken a few times."

I raised my eyes, twice, to acknowledge Miss Sarah's instructions.

"And when I come back to pick up the trays, if it's okay," Miss Sarah said tentatively, "I'd like to introduce you to Miss Muriel. She has a few questions for you."

"Mrs. Lynch mentioned that you had called her."

"She's from Halifax, and a former journalist. Before she retired, her assignments brought her to the States. Whenever she's in DC she stays here."

What newspaper did she work for?

"The *Halifax Herald* I believe," Miss Sarah said, opening the door, "I'll be back in about an hour."

Emma waved goodbye, and after we finished dinner, we climbed into bed for a rest. Emma started with the questions: "What happened after I left? I still worry when I leave you among strangers."

In that room there are those who feel I belong, and those who don't. It's not fun to be ignored by some of the men, but I'll get used to it.

"When we picked you up, there you were the center of attention! How'd that happen?"

I gave my right shoulder a shrug. *I don't know what you're talking about.*

"Very funny," Emma sneered. "Don't be coy."

If we weren't both tired, Emma would've pushed me off the bed. And then thrown pillows on top of me, until I answered her question. But she knew I'd tell her at another time.

Sometime later, three soft knocks on the door woke me up first. I poked Emma, but she didn't want to move. I poked her again.

"Okay, okay." Emma got up and opened the door. Next to Miss Sarah was a very thin older woman, a few inches taller than me. Emma welcomed them into our room with a hand gesture.

"This is Miss Muriel," Miss Sarah said.

"Hi, Miss Muriel. I'm Emma Rose, and this is my sister, Annie. Come in please."

"Nice to meet both of you," Miss Muriel said. She took a seat on the wooden chair.

Emma was intrigued and puzzled at the same time by Miss Muriel's story, but I had questions. Why would she ask us about the death of her friend from years ago? How did she know we were here? And why did Irving say she wanted to know about the beach on Block Island?

Miss Sarah began, "Years ago, Miss Muriel's close friend, Dalia McGrenn, died suddenly on Block Island. She wants to know if you know anything about her death."

As we had agreed, Emma handled the questions, some of which I hand signaled for her to ask. All the while I observed Miss Muriel as she told her story.

"Was Dalia from Block Island?" Emma asked.

Miss Muriel replied, "She and I were born and raised in Halifax, Nova Scotia. In her early twenties she travelled to the States and found work at the Hamilton. She started as a housekeeper and stayed her entire life. During the summers, and only during the summers, she worked at Nicholas Ball's hotel on Block Island."

Miss Muriel's Canadian accent was less pronounced than Miss Sarah's – and she didn't end her sentences with the rolling "eh". I thought she was a bit stiff, not warm like Mrs. Lynch or Miss Sarah. But other than that, I would withhold judgement.

"When did you meet Dalia?" Emma asked.

"I was assigned to write a story in Washington for the *Toronto Week*. I stayed at the Hamilton for almost a month, and it was then that I met Dalia. She was a supervisor at the time. I should add that she was the daughter of a friend of my mother's, back in Halifax. The two of us had much in common, being from the same place, and in no time we became great friends."

"Tell me and my sister what happened on Block Island?"

"It was June of 1896," Miss Muriel recounted, "and Dalia invited me to stay with her in her room at the Ocean View Hotel."

"To clarify," Emma asked, "Dalia only worked at the Ocean View during the summers. Do I have that right?"

"Yes," she answered.

"What happened?"

I noticed a reticence from Miss Muriel. What was the real reason she wished to meet us? So far there was no mention of Crescent Beach.

She offered a little smile and said, "When I found out that one of your distant relatives was Nicholas Ball, I thought I'd ask you a few questions."

"Irving, the owner of this hotel, knows more about Nicholas than we do," Emma responded.

Miss Muriel shrugged. "I asked him, but he didn't know anything about Dalia."

"How did you get to Block Island?" Emma asked, hoping for an explanation of why she wanted to talk to us.

"It was difficult. I boarded a fishing smack out of New London and sailed into the New Harbor. I remember a bell buoy being set near the entrance to the Great Salt Pond. I must admit that when I got on the Island, I was surprised at how poor it was."

"Why do you say that?" Miss Sarah asked.

"The Island is beautiful, but it's no Nantucket. I wrote an article on Nantucket. It became famous for its wealth from whaling, and the women walked about in long fine silk dresses. And Nantucket had heroes, in novels and real life. As far as I can tell the only famous person on Block Island was Nicholas Ball, although the Dodge family of ocean-going pilots are a close second."

Miss Muriel was highly intelligent and was right about our Island taking a very long time to develop. But why was she telling us this history?

I tapped, and Emma translated, *It's better now, Miss Muriel. We have numerous hotels, fishing camps, fishing and lobster smacks that supply Islanders and the mainland. We also have a horse-drawn trolley. But there's still much catching up to do.*

"What happened?" Emma asked, again.

"I was writing a story explaining why there was a migration of Halifax youth to Rhode Island and decided to visit Dalia. The Ocean View Hotel had 200 guest rooms. The largest and most famous hotel in New England. I stayed with her, and we had a great time."

And our Supreme Court of the United States held summer sessions at the Ocean View.

Miss Muriel's eyes lit up. "One day, I saw P.T. Barnum and Phillip Armour and John Jacob Astor in the dining room. The next day I saw General Adolph Greely, too."

"Famous guests have always vacationed there," Emma pointed out.

"Dalia introduced me to Mr. Ball. I'd met him at the Hamilton, but he didn't remember me. He was a big man, big. I always had the impression that the two of them were ... well, more than just friends."

I thought, okay, here's a reason for her reticence, they were more than friends.

Emma pressed, "Miss Muriel, what happened to your dear friend?"

"We had a great visit. She was in good health, and we walked all over the Island. Then I returned to Canada. But a few weeks later, in early August, I read a wire service report that Nicholas Ball died."

"Nicholas Ball has a massive gravestone in the Island Cemetery, a few feet from our grandfather's stone," Emma added. "But what's that have to do with Dalia?"

"The last paragraph in his *New York Times* obituary explains why I'm here. It said that they both died within a day or two of each other." Miss Muriel looked down at her lap and there her eyes rested for the greater part of a minute.

When is she going to look up, and I don't remember the obituary, maybe Lillie remembers it, I thought to myself.

"Can you tell us more?" Emma asked.

Miss Muriel raised her head. "Ball's obituary stated that Dalia died in her own room at the Ocean View, one day before Nicholas Ball died."

"Really?" Emma exclaimed.

"And there's more. He paid her a visit the day before she was found dead."

A housekeeper's death noted in his obit. Another reason for her reticence to get to the point. This could be interesting, but why wait until now to ask questions of us? And how did she know we were here the day after we arrived?

"It's highly peculiar that Dalia's death would be noted in the last paragraph of a famous person's obituary," she pointed out.

"It does seem odd," Emma said, after a short silence.

Miss Muriel looked perplexed. "Why did she suddenly die? I need to know."

Emma turned to me. "Do you know anything about that, Annie?"

I looked sideways, twice.

Miss Muriel continued, "The *New York Times* obituary said he died of a stroke, or apoplexy. No cause of death was listed for Dalia, but I suspect that's not unusual since it wasn't her obit."

I broke my silence and tapped, *What else can you tell us?* Emma translated.

"She was in good health ... and then she was dead. Just like that." Miss Muriel looked down, again, and said, "I'm certain something happened to her in her hotel room. At the time, my editor at the newspaper discussed the case with the detectives of the Royal Canadian Police. They called the Block Island and Providence Police Departments but found no family members to talk with. They could not uncover information other than what was in the *New York Times* obit."

"She was in good health and then she died ... the day before Ball died? Were they close?" Emma asked to clarify.

"She wasn't ill when I saw her, and the detectives said it didn't fit the pattern of a lovers' quarrel. Even though they knew each other for a long time. The only thing that confused them was ..." her voice trailed off.

"What confused them?" Emma prompted.

"... the large amount of money in her possession."

"What?" Emma gasped. "A housekeeper with a large amount of money?"

I ignored the money issue and tapped; Emma translated, *We'll ask our mom the next time we call her. She might know about this.*

"Thank you," Miss Muriel said.

Emma started to ask further questions, but a knock on the door startled us. Someone called out, "Miss Sarah, are you in there?"

Emma opened the door to reveal a young housekeeper, who blurted out, "I'm sorry to bother you, but we need help upstairs."

"What's the matter?" Miss Sarah asked.

"A guest is drunk, passed out in his room, left the bath water running. Now it's overflowing. We need help with him and help mopping up the water before it leaks to the room below." The housekeeper explained, anxiously.

"I'll bet I know who it is," Miss Sarah said. "Muriel, we should go and let the girls rest."

"If we learn anything we'll let Miss Sarah know right away," Emma offered.

Miss Muriel put her hands together. "Thank you."

Emma bade Miss Muriel good night and closed the door.

I tapped at a rapid pace, *It's an interesting story, and after all these years she still misses her. They must have been close. Or she's lying.*

Emma gave me a mischievous wink. "I'll snoop around and see what I can find or hear about Miss Muriel at the hotel. It will give me something to do while you're at the training."

I raised my eyes, then tapped, *What are you going to do first?*

"I'll look for Ball's obituary in old newspapers at the AWC's library. They should have old copies of *The Providence Journal*, the *New York Times*, the Newport paper, and the *Washington Evening Star*. Maybe you can ask Whytock to check out his *Evening World*."

Nicholas Ball was a good friend of the Washington Evening Star's editor and publisher.

"How do you know that?" Emma asked.

Geo has a copy of his memoirs. I have read it a few times. It mentions they travelled to China together.

I reclined on the bed and looked at the ceiling. Miss Muriel was strange. All these years later she seeks us out and asks questions.

I tapped on the headboard, *Emma, ask Irving what he said to her, and what were her questions to him.*

25

ANNIE

I put aside Miss Muriel's anguish and turned our attention to my first day of meetings. I made a few friends, but it was clear certain men would never be won over. Although I expected some hostility, not so much of it on the first day. I wanted to keep my uneasiness to myself, but it bothered me enough to tell Emma. We washed up and climbed into bed.

I tapped, *I never thought I'd work with men so mean.*

Emma sat up straight. "I know. Mrs. Lynch took note of that," she offered.

The Major sensed it, too. It was only a few, but it hit me on the way back to the hotel.

"Maybe military men are like that," she offered.

Emma, last fall, did we ever meet a mean ONI officer?

"No. Is that why you were so quiet in the car?"

I raised my eyes, *Yes.*

"Why did we drive around the neighborhood?"

I wanted to see this part of DC.

Years ago, after discharge from the hospital, Emma and I started a tradition. Before falling asleep she would ask a question, and I'd respond with simple hand signals or Morse detailed answers on the headboard. We almost never missed a night. Through this nightly ritual I opened the doors of the training session to Emma, if it wasn't classified. Tonight, she wanted to compare notes about our observations of the men in the room.

"Who was most unfriendly?" Emma said excitedly. "I have my list."

Yardley, cold and unkind.

"Did it get worse after I left?"

Yes.

"I'm not surprised. How about the others?"

It's only been a day, but I'm comfortable with Lt. Gordon, Lt. Edwards, and Clark Holder. And Mr. Whytock is very interesting, I'm sure he has stories to tell.

I showed Emma my new hand signals for Lieutenant, Ensign, and Sergeant. I explained how Lt. Gordon taught me the differences in rank and we figured out the hand signals together.

Lt. Gordon looked me in the eyes when he explained the difference between First and Second Lieutenant. He was proud to be in the Army and determined to succeed. He leaned on the arm of my wheelchair, and I sensed he wanted to look after me.

"I could see right away that he was at ease Morsing with you. He was natural and matter-of-fact when he interacted with you. I could see it in his facial expressions, the same kind I see when you're talking to a friend."

And he was willing to teach.

"If he listens when you teach him ... then that's all we need to know. That's key. I liked him a lot, too."

Lt. Edwards communicated with me nonverbally as readily as he did by Morsing. He used subtle facial expressions, was good at it, and I wondered if he had experience with someone like me. Gordon and Edwards got along well.

"I didn't notice how Lieutenant Edwards greeted you. But I liked that he pretty much steered clear of Yardley."

I couldn't share anything about my secret mission with Emma, or anyone else. But I wish I could share it with Lt. Edwards. As a trusted member of Mr. Harrison's State Department secretive intelligence service, I wonder if he was assigned to look after me, if need be.

I expect he'll be supportive and perhaps a friend.

I moved on to Johnston, *I learned Capt. Johnston comes with quite a reputation. Detective like. Not friendly, and certainly not modest. He ignored me.*

"I noticed, Annie. But he never interacted the whole day?"

I looked to the side, *No.*

"No sense of warmth or kindness from him? I'm sure he's no fan of women – and vice versa. He's not a happy guy and maybe he's someone who could never be happy. A smart man with angry skills."

He's like a fisherman who goes to sea alone, because he cannot get along with anyone.

"He's probably a 'disciple' of Yardley."

They don't know each other. Time will tell.

"Can you avoid Yardley?"

I don't want to. He has great technical skills. Has worked with State and the Signal Service for years. And he's the best cryptographer. I can learn a lot from him.

Yardley could not be the enemy spy. But a spy could readily latch on to him. He was indispensable for more reasons than his skills in cryptology, which are renowned. Of course, I could not share any of these thoughts with my sister. All I said was, *He has strong prejudices and may not want me in this training.*

Emma responded, "You weren't invisible to him, that's for sure. But he didn't interact with you in a respectful manner, and that hurt MY feelings."

My sister and I marvel at the many different reactions of people toward me. Most are variations on a few themes. Facial expressions of *pity* differ from faces filled with *sadness*. Sometimes its *curiosity*. Others show *fear*. Almost everyone shows signs of *avoidance*. But frequently we see *sympathetic* faces with *avoidance*. We realized early on that the most comforting satisfying interaction, one that we like best, is a matter-of-fact acknowledgement of my condition, without sadness, pity, or sympathy.

A smooth talker perhaps, and one who likes women but not in the Army.

"Lillie says about men like him that, 'They like women in the old-fashioned sense'. What about Royal Weller?"

Weller asked detailed questions about Morsing and codes. He speaks with a melodic voice. During a break I asked if he was interested in politics.

"What did he say?"

He smiled and said his father was a friend of Congressman LaGuardia. He wasn't conversational with anyone, but he did not ignore me.

"From where I was sitting, I looked directly into Weller's eyes. He looked at you frequently and his facial expressions were more curious than sympathetic. He didn't disregard you, but maybe he's good at disguising his emotions. He might become your friend, Annie."

I thought about her comment then tapped, *Weller and Edwards are the quiet ones in the group, but in different ways.*

"Good point. If Weller is indifferent, he's indifferent to everyone. What about the handsome one?"

I tapped out questions and comments to Clark throughout the day. After a while he couldn't keep his eyes off me. I was flattered. I hope he's not a smooth talker, too.

"Did he get along with the Lieutenants?"

Yes, very much.

"Can you work with Clark? He has the look of someone who is curious."

I think so.

"Byer?"

I tapped, *Byer?* Then looked askance.

"No, huh?"

He didn't ignore me, but I wish he had. He's rude. He whispered to Yardley that I was a show-off. He's a follower, and prone to ridiculing. I bet he has mastered that art! Obsequious.

"When I was in the room, Byer would scowl at you, but only when you weren't looking. I think you're right, his way of expressing distain is ridicule."

I agree. His skill is talking under his breath.

Emma said with conviction, "Byer should not be trusted."

I don't think Lt. Edwards likes him, although he would never say anything.

"Byer's someone to watch, that's for sure," Emma said. "You haven't mentioned Dansey."

He's very important, and I am determined to figure out why. He's been a British spy for a while. He reviewed the history of British Intelligence but never gave details because no one is supposed to know that the SIS exists. My assessment: Trying to figure him out will lead nowhere, but observing him will be invaluable.

"Did he mention negative intelligence?"

Oh, yes. I think that's where the Major got the phrase from. Dansey discussed Churchill's early interest in espionage. I gather he was involved early on with British intelligence. With respect to negative intelligence, he mentioned Abraham Lincoln's use of it in Europe during our Civil War.

"What was that about?"

Lincoln funded both negative intelligence, and sabotage, both on British soil. Even Major Van Deman did not know that Lincoln paid saboteurs to blow up a ship built in a British shipyard that was ordered by the Confederacy.

"Really!" Emma sat up when she heard that.

Yes, and it was blown up on the very day it launched. Lincoln also established a worldwide public relations campaign against the Confederacy.

"Why did he discuss that?" Emma looked confused.

He was referencing the German Embassy's campaign of disinformation against our country. I learned today that this kind of influence occurs all the time. And has for centuries.

"We never learned that in history classes, and Geo never mentioned it was part of war," Emma observed.

Over the years, Geo shared a lot of Army history with us, and it helped to talk about that information with my sister. To talk it out helped both of us see things better. There have been surprises, of course. But without Emma having clearance I could no longer have these conversations. That pained me. I could no longer share everything but would continue a long-standing tradition of talking before we fell asleep – if it wasn't classified information.

Tonight, we tried to figure out members of the group, who to trust, who could be won over, and who was a lost cause. I was hoping for more friends than foes, but now I was not sure.

"Annie," Emma offered, "I think your worst treatment came from Johnston."

I agree. The expressions of Yardley were obvious from the moment he introduced himself. Johnston's scorn slowly emerged. Yardley's reaction we've seen before, a lot. But Johnston's was different. He looked right through me, as if I didn't exist.

"I doubt it has anything to do with your disability. I think it's because you're smart and a young woman, and a pretty woman at that. You're in the same meetings as him. He has been through a lot, in the Bomb Squad, and in the military. Geo says those guys can become unemotional."

I wonder if he is beyond that.

What I couldn't say to my sister was that Johnston belonged on my list of potential enemy spies, despite being a detective on the Bomb Squad, due to his personality. Was I right or wrong?

26

ANNIE

Tuesday, my second day of training, began with an unexpected snow shower. If you are not used to snow it can delay everything, and not surprisingly breakfast did not arrive.

To enquire, Emma took the back stairwell, near the service elevator, and entered the kitchen through a rear door. She was back within minutes.

"No one uses those back stairs, and it's a great way to enter the kitchen. The woman said there's a staff shortage. That's the problem, but she'll put together take-out packages for us and have them ready before heading off."

I tapped, *Who did you talk to?*

"A friendly, older woman. She knew who we were, even our names."

I gave my hand signal for, *Interesting.*

"She asked if we'd seen Miss Sarah."

I repeated my hand signal, *Interesting.*

"Let's get to the lobby, and I'll run to the kitchen."

I dwelled on what transpired since leaving Block Island, but I couldn't let anything deter progress on my secret mission. Nor could I allow the training to consume my attention. I was determined to do everything expected of me, and more.

I waited in the lobby while Emma walked through the dining room to the kitchen. I saw Irving behind his desk talking to a bellhop. Shortly, the bellhop asked if I wanted to be pushed outside to wait for my ride. I moved my eyes to the side, but before I knew it, I was on my way through the doors of the hotel. I waited at the curb, as Mrs. Lynch had not yet arrived. The snow had stopped but the wind was brisk.

When Emma returned to the lobby she looked around, confused. She caught the eye of another bellhop who gestured to the street, and quickly joined me at curbside.

"Why'd you come outside, Annie? I have breakfast and milk." Emma helped me take a few sips from the mug. "We have four hard-boiled eggs, two biscuits with a scoop of spread and two mugs of milk. The lady said to me, 'You need this nutrition, Emma, and so does your sister. Oh, and please return the mugs."

The same lady as before.

"Yes. Why are you outside?" Emma reiterated, louder this time.

Irving had a bellhop push me here.

"What?" Emma said defiantly, and I couldn't help but laugh.

Mrs. Lynch arrived, and we were on our way.

"Thank you for waiting outside," she said.

"It wasn't our doing." Emma tossed her hands. "While I was in the kitchen, Annie was waiting in the lobby and a bellhop brought her out."

"Oh, I see," Mrs. Lynch said.

Emma did not explain it was Irving's doing.

After a few moments Mrs. Lynch asked, "How did you like Miss Muriel? Miss Sarah called last night and explained that Miss Muriel's friend died on Block Island. A long time ago. If we'd known that, we wouldn't have given permission."

Emma replied, "She said Irving suggested she talk to us, thinking we'd know something. But her friend died twenty years ago."

"Annie, you're too busy to deal with her request," Mrs. Lynch insisted.

I agree. I told Emma it was hers if she wanted it.

"I'll figure it out," Emma said with confidence. "I know my first steps."

"And what will those steps be?" Mrs. Lynch asked, eyes wide open.

"I want to know if her story is accurate. I'll start in the library and read a few obituaries. Does the library have copies of old national newspapers?"

"Old newspapers are on the third floor, near the balcony. Why do you want to read obits, and which ones are you interested in?"

"Miss Muriel mentioned that the *New York Times* had a long obit, so I'll start with that. The *New York Times* has written about Nicholas Ball several times. They refer to him as, 'The King of Block Island'. I'll also look at the Providence, Rhode Island papers, including the *Providence Journal.* Then I'll read the *Washington Evening Star.*"

Mrs. Lynch's brow furrowed. "Why those?"

"The *Evening Star* because he was friends with the editor. And editors may edit things out of their friend's stuff. In the case of the Providence papers, it's likely the family submitted information that they wanted printed."

"It's good to start looking for differences in the obituaries," Mrs. Lynch said approvingly.

"Rhode Island papers will probably publish information provided by family or friends."

"My first thought was to ignore this woman's request, but it may be interesting," Mrs. Lynch said.

"It's a Block Island story that we didn't know. But if she's not forthright we need to know that, too."

Emma has a good point, and it will keep her occupied while I'm at the meetings.

"It's important to figure out if Miss Muriel has a motive," Mrs. Lynch said. "It does sound a bit suspicious to me."

"We'll figure her out," Emma said.

"Oh, Emma, this morning I spoke with the Major," Mrs. Lynch said. "You cannot get clearance, but he'll allow you to help Annie at lunch in the conference room. Help her eat, take her to the restroom."

Emma was elated and I was relieved. At least she'd be on campus a portion of the day.

"Thank you," Emma gushed. "Did you ask about a job on campus?"

Mrs. Lynch gave a wry smile. "One thing at a time, my dear Emma!"

We entered the grounds of the AWC, and Mrs. Lynch announced she would return in early afternoon for Emma. She parked at the base of Roosevelt Hall. We looked up to find Lt. Peter Gordon and Ensign Clark Holder ready to walk into the lobby. I thought they'd come down and take me up to the conference room, but they disappeared into the building. I know better than to be disappointed, especially with my secret mission – because keeping my distance is a good thing. But the feeling of rejection returned, as it often does in new situations.

Emma jumped out, left the door open, and retrieved the wheelchair from the boot. I slid onto the wheelchair, and Emma pulled me up the granite stairs, backwards.

But then out of nowhere Lt. Edwards appeared and offered to help pull me the rest of the to the lobby. Once inside, Sgt. Lightfoot walked over and reiterated what Mrs. Lynch had told Emma that the Major had given her permission to help me with lunch.

"Sgt. Lightfoot, may I sit and read the old newspapers on the third floor of the library?"

Sgt. Lightfoot raised an eyebrow. "What are looking for?"

"Old newspapers from August of 1896."

"They're filed in boxes on the shelves to the left of the couches. You may use the library whenever you want."

Emma broke out in a wide smile.

We said goodbye to Sgt. Lightfoot, and Lt. Edwards and Emma brought me into the elevator. Before Emma got off on the third floor, I tapped, *Lieutenant Edwards, Sergeant Lightfoot always makes eye contact with me.*

"When I was first assigned to the War College, he taught me how to visualize every person, at any given time, anywhere within the walls of this building. There's a name for that but I forgot what it is."

After my accident, I look around, constantly, visualizing where everyone is, where they might be heading, and note buildings or cars where someone might be behind. It's second nature now.

Emma exited on the third floor. While Lt. Edwards offered, "Good luck with the old newspapers, Emma." I thought about John, what he taught me about intuition. That it can fool you and I should not rely on it, but I do not think Lt. Edwards could be an enemy spy.

27

EMMA

I exited the elevator on the third floor. The librarian showed me to the leather couches near a long table where current newspapers were strewn about. A sign indicated the location of old newspapers from the United States and Canada. They were in tall, narrow gray boxes, and labeled with the city and dates of publication.

I reached for the most recent *Washington Evening Star* lying on the table. It was one of two newspapers that covered the District of Columbia. I sank into the plush leather couch and opened it randomly to an illustrated, full-page advertisement.

"Easter Hats. Tailored. $10 to $12."

But the short articles about the war on the opposite page drew my attention. Officials in Connecticut discovered the German government trying to influence American opinion among German-speaking citizens. The second article reported that a local Washington, DC high school teacher, of German descent, hung a picture of Kaiser Wilhelm in her classroom. The next day a student ripped it off the wall! Disciplinary action was taken against the teacher, and two days later a photo of President Wilson hung in its place. I wondered if the teacher had been manipulated by articles planted by the German Embassy. I was beginning to understand more than I had anticipated.

On the next page an original German article transmitted from the Berlin wireless tower was reprinted, word for word. It was far more ominous: "German Naval Cruiser Captures 22 Merchant Steamships, including 5 ships powered by sail." Germany confiscated them all, including the oceanic sailing ships. Under that was a half-page article titled: "$24,000,000 Raised by the Efforts of a Canadian Citizen." The article referred to monies for Canadian families whose sons volunteered to fight with Britain. When I read the mention of explosives in the middle of the article, I thought the money was related to the war effort.

The article about China sending men to help the British and French saddened me greatly. The title: "The future of China and the United States will always be linked." When I finished reading it, tears were in my eyes. It was about men taking risks, to fight in a war on the other side of the world. Men who would never see their families again. I relived my own near death, and it took a lot to hold back tears. The Province of Shandong was under German rule for years, but when Japan became an ally of Germany, the Chinese ousted all German diplomats from Beijing. Geo had always mentioned that Teddy Roosevelt was an ardent supporter of China. And so, too, was the King of Block Island. In graphic language the article reported that the French ship *Athos* was sunk by a U-boat, and over 500 men from China drowned. These were only a few of the 37,000 Chinese "workers" who sailed to Europe to fight alongside the French Army. I learned that over 100,000 men from China fought with the Brits. For the rest of my life, I'd wonder how many never saw their families again and vowed to include the men in my prayers.

The newspaper's editorial criticized Wilson's neutrality position. "The war is decimating the British. It's about balance of power, it always is." I felt frustration with the President's position.

On the front page there were two headlines that confirmed the precarious state of the world. "Sinking of the *Healdton*, a U.S. Merchant Marine Ship by U-boats." Was this ship included in the data the Commander presented at his lecture?

The second headline was about our Navy: "DC National Guard Readied for Deployment to Naval Warships Within 45 Days."

I leaned forward on the couch. "The war is here already. Wilson must have changed his mind," I said out loud.

Someone tapped me on the shoulder, and I startled. It was Sgt. Lightfoot.

Realizing he overheard me, I asked, "Isn't it pretty much a given we're entering the war?"

"German aggression leaves us no choice," Lightfoot said gravely. "Have you looked for the old newspapers, Emma?"

"I've been reading this from a few days ago. I haven't pulled the old ones, yet."

"Let me help you."

"I'm looking for Nicholas Ball's obituaries in several papers. He died August 8, 1896, on Block Island, Rhode Island. I need to start with the *New York Times*, then the *Providence Journal,* and finally the *Washington Evening Star*."

"We have a few copies of the *Providence Journal* on the table. Are you familiar with that paper, Emma?"

"Oh, yes," I said in an animated manner, "On Block Island we're always quoting their byline, 'The *Providence Journal* will say tomorrow.' Or variations, 'What will the *Providence Journal* say today?'"

Lightfoot chuckled. "You must know of the editor?"

"Everyone in Rhode Island knows of him. My uncle, Geo, knows him. Whenever there's a serious weather event on Block Island, they talk to each other. Geo always says, 'John Rathom. It's hard to fathom John Rathom'."

The sergeant could not contain a hearty laugh. "He's been quite helpful over the past few years. Your sister will learn about him."

As he pulled boxes that contained the August 1896 newspapers, he remembered a call from Mrs. Lynch. "She won't be back on campus until 5:00. That will give you ample time to be with your sister for lunch and come back here to finish reading. But you may also want to walk outside. The snow's gone and it's beautiful."

"I will," I enthused.

He handed me a pencil and a piece of paper from a nearby desk, and said, "When you're finished, place the papers in the boxes, but leave the boxes on the table. The librarian will reshelve."

I thanked Sgt. Lightfoot, and for the next hour I reviewed the obituaries. As expected, the *Washington Evening Star* made no mention of Dalia or the money. The *Providence Journal* was alarming. It stated Dalia was from Providence! And, in another article, it stated that Dalia died after seeing Ball so very ill in his room at the Ocean View. The editor of the New Zealand paper focused exclusively on Dalia's money. I jotted the details of the newspapers and highlighted the differences. I need to find his obits in other Providence papers or the Newport paper, before coming to a conclusion.

I tried to understand Miss Muriel's story, her situation, her fears, her lost friend. I was convinced Miss Muriel had her facts correct. But did she live those experiences, or simply read about them? Mrs. Lynch is correct, we must determine her motive.

I took the elevator to the lobby.

"Thank you, Sergeant Lightfoot," I called out.

Lightfoot waved back. "You're welcome. On my rounds I saw Mr. Harrison."

"I saw him yesterday on the fifth-floor conference room."

"I mentioned you were in the library reading. He was quick to say that Major Van Deman was impressed with how your sister handled herself yesterday. She has a friend in Mr. Harrison."

"I'll tell her tonight," I promised.

"Emma, after helping Annie with lunch, take a walk along the Potomac River side of the Army War College campus. Start where the Anacostia River flows into the Potomac. You wouldn't see ships like the Naval Yard."

I reached up and gave him a hug.

Halfway down the granite steps Fritz came running. "Fritz!" He bounded up the steps, water dripping from his thick, dark coat but he wasn't bothered by the cold nor was he tired.

I surveyed the campus. In the center of the parade grounds was the original building of the Army War College. It had a curious sign: "Drafting".

"Fritz, let's go for a walk." Fritz led me to the river's edge, which was bulkheaded but not to the extent as the Navy Yard. The riverbed was filled with Fritz's footprints going in and out of the river. This area was smaller than the sandy beaches behind the buildings at the Navy Yard. Then I walked to the building in the Parade Grounds, but Fritz followed slowly behind. "Fritz, come on, let's see what's at the drafting studio."

I read the plaque on the outside of the building, then went inside. Curiously, Fritz did not follow and stayed outside.

28

ANNIE

At 11:30 AM the group left for lunch, and I waited for Emma. Major Van Deman and I were the only ones in the room. He struggled to change the paper in the Telegraph, and I assured him that Emma would help. And when Emma walked in, as if on cue, she walked right past me and up to the Major standing at the Telegraph.

"Hi, Major," Emma said cheerfully. "Can I help?"

"Hello, Emma. The key doesn't open this machine," he said with a note of frustration.

Emma waved a hand. "You don't need a key. I'll show you."

The Major was dumbfounded and stepped aside.

Within minutes Emma had opened the cabinet door, closed it again, and showed the Major how to open it without a key. She pushed on the door from the bottom, then on the frame of the cabinet laterally.

"My sister and I have taken this model apart many times," she explained. "The frames of these cabinets bend when you push here. See where my hand is? Then you reach in and unlock the door. See in there? It's the roller."

The Major stared at the machine but said nothing. In one smooth motion, Emma stored the used roll of paper on a small shelf inside the cabinet and took the roll of paper from the Major's hand and slipped it on the roller. She then closed the cabinet door.

"You know this old machine, don't you," the Major said, still surprised at what just happened. "Thank you."

"You're welcome. I can be useful for more than helping my sister. If there's a job I can do at the War College, please let me know."

"You two are something," he said, shaking his head.

Before leaving for lunch, he sat with Emma and me for a few minutes.

"Annie, Dansey disagreed with you, but the evidence suggests that you're right about two German codes." He turned to Emma, "I gave the group the first of many complicated wireless assignments, and your sister did well."

I tapped, *Why didn't Mr. Dansey agree with me?*

"Annie, Major Dansey has his reasons." Van Deman replied cryptically.

"How did Annie reach her conclusion?" Emma asked. "Or is it classified information?"

"It's not classified, but it's a good time to mention, Emma, that you must not repeat *anything* you hear. Or, more importantly, especially with you two, you must never repeat things you figure out on your own."

"I wouldn't," Emma promised.

"I handed out encrypted German messages that Dansey brought from Room 40 in London. He says that the messages were intercepted by the Royal Navy in the Mediterranean Sea."

The messages Room 40 sent along with Dansey are very helpful to learn decoding.

Van Deman nodded, "Yes, they are. We're lucky he's here."

Major Van Deman, I did not know the Royal Navy patrolled the Mediterranean Sea.

"Only the Western part," Major Van Deman clarified.

If the group finds decrypting messages from the Western Mediterranean is easier than the ones from Cyprus, that suggests further that there must be two codes.

"Germany has close ties with Ottoman Empire countries and have been sending messages, mostly wireless, to them for years. And that includes Turkey," Van Deman said.

"Where does Germany transmit the messages from?" Emma asked.

"Germany's powerful Nauen transmitter is located near Berlin. We don't have one that powerful."

We will soon, Major. It will be in Maine.

"I heard that from the Commander. About this afternoon's session. We'll focus on intercepted transmissions picked up from the towers on Long Island and the across the Potomac at Fort Myer. These messages were received in the middle of January and will give everyone more experience decoding German messages."

Major, earlier, Yardley agreed with me that there might be two codes. But why did Holder nod in agreement with Dansey?

"You're observant," Van Deman acknowledged. "Clark has no idea about codes. He met Dansey a few years ago and was simply agreeing with him."

The Major thanked Emma, again, and asked, "Emma, where were you this morning?"

"In the library, looking at old newspapers. Last evening Annie and I were introduced to a Miss Muriel, from Nova Scotia. She had questions about a friend who died on Block Island in 1896. She wanted to know if we knew anything."

"That was a long time ago," Van Deman pointed out. "What was she doing asking you two?"

"She'd asked the owner of the Hamilton Hotel if he knew, but he referred her to us. I went to the library to read a few obituaries and found that her facts are correct, about everything. I compared different newspaper obits for Nicholas Ball, and sure enough her friend was mentioned in those obits."

"I still don't know why she asked you," the Major said. "By the way, Whytock, who sat near you today, is staying at the Hamilton. Don't talk to him if you see him at your hotel. I'll mention what you said about Miss Muriel and let's see what he can uncover."

"Tell Mr. Whytock that Miss Muriel says she's a journalist from Canada," Emma said. "And she's written novels."

She knows who we are, but we don't know who she is.

"Maybe she researched Dalia's death, like I did," Emma suggested.

"You could be right, Emma," the Major said.

I raised my eyes, twice.

"Major, in the library I read an article by Mr. Whytock."

"Was it in the *Evening World*?" The Major asked.

"Yes, in mid-March. He wrote about the famine confronting Germany. And then he wrote about being embedded with our Ambassador to Germany, James Watson Gerard. Was Mr. Whytock always a foreign correspondent?"

"He has had many roles as a newspaperman, with the *New York World* and before that in St. Louis. He was in the Missouri National Guard for many years. Whytock met General Kuhn in our Embassy in Berlin."

I tapped, *Did General Kuhn recruit Ross?*

"Ross has been involved with a few intelligence missions for well over a year. Best not to ask any questions," the Major said.

We both acknowledged his command and he returned to the podium, and we settled in for our lunch.

While Emma and I ate lunch I thought about my secret mission. A thought from last night stayed with me. If there is an enemy spy in the group and Miss Muriel is connected to the German Embassy, is it possible that someone inside the training group tipped her off about us at the Hamilton? And did a connection exist between Miss Muriel and the German spy killed on Block Island last October? Or were we wrong, and Miss Muriel was only a love-lost older woman whose behavior was a bit crazy?

On the other hand, she did know about the navigational buoy placed at the entrance to the cut into the Great Salt Pond. I know what buoy she speaks of; I see it whenever we fish for flounder at the Cut. Also, in her favor, only a few would know that sailing to the New Harbor from Connecticut in the 1890s was commonplace. Add to that her knowledge of Nantucket and an ability to compare it to Block Island.

Emma chopped my lunch, thickened the milk with mashed potatoes, to minimize the risk of choking, while I answered her questions.

"What else did you learn this morning about the men in the room?"

I tapped a summary of a conversation between the Major, Yardley, and me: *This morning, Yardley agreed there might be two German codes while Dansey knew of only one German code.*

"Could you read facial expressions?"

I smiled, and raised my eyes, *I could read everyone's except Dansey. The topic jumped to negative intelligence, and it got heated. After Dansey left, Yardley said, "How effective can our negative intelligence be if Room 40 is embedded with us?" Is that a paradox? Dansey is helping Van Deman, yet Yardley's point is well taken.*

"You like paradoxes. Yardley supports your ideas, and hasn't ignored you, after all," Emma offered.

I recognize paradoxes, but I could do without them. I thought initially Van Deman was keeping Dansey at arm's length, but the reality is the opposite. They've forged a close relationship.

Emma cautioned, "Don't get on the bad side of Dansey."

I raised my eyes. *General Kuhn will be in the room tomorrow when Dansey lectures. Armed guards will be posted at the door whenever he lectures.*

"You're opening more than the closed doors of the training."

I raised my eyes. As far as Dansey, I reasoned, he cannot be the enemy spy because he is the ultimate spy. So far, I've ruled out Dansey, Gordon, and Edwards. I'm sure I'll add Yardley and Whytock to the good list, too.

"Annie, what about Royal Weller?"

He's not rude, but I cannot figure him out. He's a sphinx.

"He's a lawyer, right? Not surprising. What will you do?"

Bide my time, until he plays his hand. I overheard he loves racehorses.

"He goes to the races?"

Yes, at the Freehold, New Jersey track. He'll show his cards, either on purpose or accidentally.

"How about Clark?" Emma flashed a sly grin.

I wondered when Emma was going to ask me about Clark. *After two days of sitting across from Clark, I wonder if he is smitten.*

"Here we go. Be careful. Thinks can happen fast." Emma sat up and listened.

At break, Peter Gordon left to do an errand, and right away Clark came over.

"Well, well, well." Emma raised her eyes and kept them raised. "Be careful, or did I say that already?"

I smiled.

"He's got a British accent."

His parents live in London.

"What's he like in class?"

He's a listener, not a talker, and smarter than he looks. But he tries too hard.

"Do you like his attention?"

It's better than the negative attention of the others; they who hide their disdain for me when the Major is in the room. But when he's not here or if he's looking away, they don't hold back.

"I'm not sure what that means." Emma frowned. "You're sitting at a table across from two men. One's glaring and the other's staring, one's welcomed, and the other isn't. Don't forget what Mrs. Conway taught us about 'encroachment' and other unwelcomed behavior from men."

It means that Yardley is indispensable. He's the best cryptologist. He advanced the field of Signal Intelligence. If he knocked over my wheelchair there's no way he'd get kicked out.

"Annie, the Major can change his attitude," Emma insisted.

If Yardley wants me out of the training program, then it will be me who must convince him that I belong, not the Major.

"How?"

I don't know, with Byer and maybe Johnston, it'll be tough, but I'll figure it out.

"When does the afternoon session begin?"

They'll be here soon. One more thing. I found a connection between Dansey and Clark.

"What?"

I tapped rapidly, *Clark's stepfather owns plants in Great Britain and Long Island, and they live in Manhattan and London. Clark met Dansey at the Sleepy Hollow Club, a private club for industrialists, on the Hudson River.*

"How did that come up?"

Clark spoke about his interest in industrial security. At that club, Clark learned that Dansey developed security protocols for Rockefeller plants, and his father's plant. Yardley was in that conversation, too.

"So, that explains his interest in industrial security. You didn't finish your conversation with Yardley."

At the end of the conversation, Yardley, for no apparent reason, pointed out that there was a long list of Brits who thought Room 40 had the exclusive right to develop negative intelligence.

"Why say that?"

Only to suggest Dansey is on that list.

Emma nodded. "Got it. The Brits have the best spies in the business, don't they?"

I raised my eyes. *There's a lot to figure out.*

Emma and I finished lunch and waited. Byer and Johnston walked in first, and, surprisingly, both nodded in my direction. I raised my eyes and gave a quick wave of my right hand. I wasn't ignored but quickly found out the reason: Moments later the Major and Dansey entered the room and with them was a uniformed armed guard.

Dansey came over to Emma and me, while Major Van Deman and the guard spoke for a few minutes.

"Hi there." He extended his hand to Emma, and then me.

"Hi," Emma said softly.

I tapped rapidly, *Hello Major Dansey.*

"Not so fast, Annie. I'm a slow Morser."

We laughed for a moment, and he turned to my sister.

"Ralph tells me you know these old Telegraph Machines!"

My sister could not contain a smile. "Annie and I have a lot of experience taking them apart."

"Can you Morse as fast as your sister?"

"Not as fast, but I'm good. It's a family tradition," Emma said with pride.

"Ah, very well then. My family has a few, too," Dansey said, then turned to me. "In London there's a disabled British suffragette named May Billinghurst. I know her because Scotland Yard has arrested her, and that's where I met her. She uses a modified tricycle as a wheelchair."

I raised my eyes, *How did she modify it?*

"I'm not sure, but I'll bring you a photo."

I gave my hand signal for, *Thank you. Why was she arrested?*

"When demonstrating for the right to vote she used what Scotland

Yard calls, 'illegal tactics'. She's done a lot to fight for a women's right to vote, and she does it from that modified wheelchair."

Emma interjected, "The women on Block Island have been fighting for the right to vote, too, and erected a statue in the center of Old Harbor Village for that."

I tapped, *Emma, the purpose of the statue was to get the men on the Island to stop drinking.*

"That's not a bad idea, either!" Dansey chuckled. "Smart women you have on that Island."

"Well, Annie, I like to think the statue has to do with voting," Emma said with indignation.

"Your small Island is *not* a quaint place, is it? More like an island community for hardy souls, who work hard to survive."

New Englanders are hardy folk, but we Islanders experience true hardship.

Dansey put a hand on my shoulder. "Do you have any questions for me, Annie?"

Mr. Dansey, can I ask a question about negative intelligence? What advice do you have?

Dancey smiled. "I know you have a talent for it. Negative intelligence has many purposes, and it always involves confusion, so that the process appears unclear. Ralph will cover that during the meetings. Tomorrow, I talk about another highly sensitive topic, so Emma, you wouldn't be able to be in the room. And Annie, you must not say anything about what you learn, except to supervisors."

I raised both eyes as he turned to rejoin the Major at the podium.

"Annie," Emma said as he walked away, "he shared Billinghurst's use of a tricycle. He respects her, and you."

I tapped on Emma's arm, *I hope he likes me, too, but there is a distance to him, something I cannot put in words.*

"I think the word you're looking for is …" she whispered, "*he's a spy*."

Emma cleaned up, and she was about to leave when Major Van Deman came over.

"Emma, Sergeant Lightfoot mentioned that Mrs. Lynch wouldn't be back until 17:00. We're not discussing confidential information this afternoon, but tomorrow you may not be in the room."

"Mr. Dansey explained about tomorrow."

The Major walked to the podium, and after a few minutes announced the afternoon's objectives.

"We have another cipher assignment courtesy of Room 40. It's repetitious but will increase your skills deciphering German codes. I suspect it will take all afternoon.

"The group on Lieutenant Gordon's side of the table will decrypt intercepted transmissions sent to German ships in the Atlantic, and Yardley's side of the table will have the opportunity to decrypt messages sent to Turkey or somewhere in the Eastern Mediterranean near Cyprus.

"First, determine if the messages start with Preludes. As you learned yesterday, all top-secret messages sent by Germany include them, whereas low-level secret messages do not. After identifying messages with Preludes, the tasks for each group differ dramatically.

"Now Annie," Van Deman said without explanation, "I want you to help your sister clean the Telegraph Machine, but you'll observe how each group handles their tasks."

I was not sure what the Major's intentions were by assigning me to an observational role. But I suppose I'd find out as the day wore on.

Major Van Deman handed out Room 40's intercepted messages.

"Now, remember," the Major continued, "don't get distracted by nonsense messages."

Lt. Gordon, Edwards, Johnston, and Whytock were able to identify a Prelude right away, but after that their progress was slow. I did not see an early success from Yardley's side of the table. I went back to the Telegraph Machine to help, or watch Emma open the cabinet, but instead of cleaning inside, she handed me a paper roll of sent messages.

After two hours of trying, my side of the table announced that they had deciphered one message. It was in the old German code. But Yardley's group struggled to decode any messages.

"Yardley, how far have you gotten," the Major asked.

"We've identified Preludes, and we're working on one small message, but haven't accomplished much so far."

From my vantage point I observed the continued frustration of

Yardley. The others in his group had largely given up. If Yardley was having a difficult time, I knew he was dealing with a new code. I tapped loudly on the metal cabinet, *Your difficulty is not your fault. It's logical to conclude that Germany is sending messages toward countries of the Ottoman Empire in a second code*. Yardley nodded agreement.

"I agree with Annie. It's not surprising you haven't deciphered one message," the Major said. "Lieutenant Gordon, what did you guys pick up?"

"Our messages are in the German code that we've always seen. Two messages appear to be nonsense. Tom, would you look to see if they're in the second code?" He pushed the messages across the table to Yardley.

"Now," the Major said, "for the remainder of the afternoon, here are a series of messages received on January 16 or 17 at our towers. These wireless messages were supplied by the telegraphers across the Potomac. It'll probably take the rest of the afternoon. Tomorrow morning, we'll discuss your findings in detail."

Lt. Edwards raised his hand. "Major, are we sure there are two codes?"

"If our best cryptologist cannot decipher messages received in the Eastern Mediterranean, it suggests two German codes."

I looked at Dansey and waited for the argument to begin.

"Those messages are probably nonsense messages. We can't learn anything from this exercise," Dansey argued. "It's preposterous that a second German military code exists. I stand by my comments."

I was fascinated by Dansey. I couldn't tell what he was thinking even when he was speaking. John taught me spies deny and evade, regularly. But why is he doing that? It had nothing to do with Machiavelli's phrase, 'Keep your friends close and your enemies closer'. That did not apply because everyone's on the same side, the same values, the same wishes. And it did not apply to the two Majors in the room. They were getting along famously, as if they had a previously close relationship.

Emma and I were still at the Telegraph Machine. Major Van Deman remained at the podium shuffling papers. At this point Emma caught my attention.

"Annie, look at this message. It was sent to the NYPD Bomb Squad. You'll never believe who sent it." She spoke in a barely audible voice as she pulled out the roll that she had previously stored in the cabinet.

It took seconds to "read" the message. Johnston sent it, apparently to a colleague in NYC. It read as follows: *The ONI has sent two attendees to these meetings. Good old George Barnitz, and a young mentally-retarded twenty-two-year-old girl. She sits in her wheelchair. She's pretty, but can't talk. What's going on? Also, do you know who this guy Dansey is? He must know Gaunt.*

Emma cringed. "What do you think, Annie?"

I gave her my hand signal for, *Idiot.*

"Do you think the Major saw the message and wanted you, and I, to see it, also?" Emma whispered.

I tapped, *Perhaps, as a test of my will, but also Johnston should not be talking about Dansey.*

"Perhaps both messages are for you, and me," she theorized. "First, to learn what Johnston said about you, and second so we'd realize that keeping secrets in this room is essential."

I raised both eyes. *Possible*.

"What are they talking about now?"

Emma and I had become distracted by the Johnston message, but I understood what was transpiring at the podium. Dansey was discussing the coded messages that Room 40 had generously shared with our training group, and that Van Deman had, moments before, distributed to the class. Dansey was emphatic that the messages were picked up wirelessly, rather than through intercepted submarine cables. There was an undercurrent of disagreement

I tapped on Emma's arm. *Dansey is saying that we are deciphering intercepted wireless messages. Not messages intercepted from cables.*

"A reminder that right after we cut Germany's cables in the English Channel, in 1914, the German's resorted to their tower." Dansey was firm about his answer.

Van Deman responded carefully. "True, but Claude, the Germans *do use* the Swedish cable for non-military purposes." He looked around the room. "Anyone have questions? Get as much done this afternoon as you can."

Royal Weller raised his hand. "Wireless messages received from

Europe should be the same on the Sayville, Long Island, and towers in Alexandria, Virginia. Even with different technicians taking the messages off the towers, the odds are good that they'll be the same."

"That is correct," Major Van Deman said.

The use of the phrase 'the odds are good' by Weller made me think of his enjoyment at the racetrack. It was the first question he had asked, but I wasn't sure what purpose it served.

The Major continued to let the groups finish their tasks. Putting aside I wasn't assigned to either group, the exercise was straight forward in that Major Van Deman appeared to be setting up the two groups to make a point, and it occurred to me that he was using this exercise as another way of disagreeing with Dansey. They had become good friends and I thought that this was one way for them to disagree.

When my name wasn't called, I took it as a learning experience. But when Van Deman and Dansey stepped out of the room for a short break, Johnston ridiculed me, and my emotions surfaced. Even Yardley said, under his breath, 'Finally, the Major has come to his senses'. Things had not changed.

The Major was correct that it took until 4:30 to decipher the messages. He collected our work and dismissed us, saying the discussion would take place tomorrow morning prior to Dansey's lecture.

Emma took me to the lobby and down the granite steps where we waited for Mrs. Lynch. Except for Emma's statement that there might be armed guards at the doors tomorrow, there was not much conversation in the car. Emma retrieved the wheelchair from the boot and pushed me through the lobby doors. We were surprised to see Mrs. Lynch had already entered the lobby and was at the front desk. I heard her ask a bellhop about the whereabouts of Miss Sarah, and Irving.

"She left early today, and Irving is at a meeting across town," Mrs. Lynch informed us.

Their absence changed Mrs. Lynch's facial expression. A crinkled forehead replaced her usual calm demeanor and foretold frustration. I waved goodbye with my good hand and realized I should have asked how her day went.

Emma pushed me to the service elevator, and we were in Room

207 within minutes. We sat and talked about Emma's assessment of the obituaries. After washing up, a new housekeeper we'd not previously met, or seen, brought us dinner.

"Hi, Miss Sarah is not here. I'm Jamie. Miss Sarah asked me to bring dinner."

"Thank you, Jamie," Emma said. "That's very nice of you."

"Can I do anything else?"

I was sitting on the bed leaning against the headboard and did not make eye contact.

"Thank you, but we're okay."

"Okay, fine," she said, and turned to leave. As Emma was closing the door Jamie popped back in and said, "Oh, there was an older woman asking for you. Should I say you two are in?"

I flashed hand signals to Emma, *No, we're busy*.

"We're tired from a long day," Emma said, picking up on my concern, "Please let Miss Sarah know about her request in the morning."

Emma closed the door and said, "Didn't want to talk to Miss Muriel, eh?"

I smiled and let it go. Emma prepared my plate. Surprisingly, we spoke very little while we ate. Instead, I pondered my mission. I had ruled out Yardley as the enemy spy, and doubted Edwards or Gordon were spies. Whytock was beyond reproach. Dansey was certainly a spy, but the kind we all want to be.

"Annie, I enjoyed talking with Sergeant Lightfoot at the library."

I raised my eyes but kept eating.

"And I liked my short conversations with the Major and Mr. Dansey, too."

I raised my eyes, again.

We were more tired than expected. Emma left the trays in the hall, locked the door, and put the wooden chair against the doorknob. We washed up and got ready for bed. For some reason I avoided our nightly ritual of "talking" before finding sleep.

Emma drifted off to sleep quickly before I warned her about Miss Muriel. I let it go until the morning, but couldn't get out of my mind that she was either a love-lost crazy elderly woman, or a dangerous spy.

29

ANNIE

"I locked the door last night, right?" Emma asked, as she stepped into the hall.

I raised my eyes, *Yes, and you put the chair against the door.*

"It's not locked, and last night's trays are still here."

I tapped, *Hopefully, you unlocked it without realizing it.*

No one was in the hall. Emma shrugged her shoulders and came back in.

It was now apparent that I put my sister in danger by having her accompany me to DC. It was the first week and I wanted her on campus with me, to help, sure, but to protect her from harm's way. There wasn't any safer place than the War College campus. I did not want to be distracted by an unlocked door and the worry that it brought. It was Wednesday and for the moment I had to concentrate on my secret mission, not my sister's safety.

Miss Sarah's recognizable knock on the door had Emma greeting her with open arms.

"Good morning, Miss Sarah."

"Hi, girls. How was last night?"

I tapped, *A young housekeeper brought our dinner.*

Emma blurted out, "Ah, yes, and the trays are still in the hall. And our door was unlocked when we woke up! The housekeeper mentioned Miss Muriel wanted to talk to us. But we said no."

"I'll make sure she doesn't contact you," Miss Sarah said firmly. "Now, are you both set for the day?"

"We're still waking up," Emma replied, "but yeah, we're ready."

Miss Sarah smiled and tidied our room, but she wasn't in a talkative mood. It was most unusual for her, but maybe she was up late, too.

"Is everything okay with you two?" she asked with concern.

"Yes, we're fine," Emma said.

When someone asked if we were okay, it could be a genuine sentiment, but it also could mean Miss Sarah was worried about something. Had she spoken with Mrs. Lynch? She wished us a good day using the word 'eh', and left the room.

"Annie, I'm not staying at the hotel."

Okay. Read at the Library.

Mrs. Lynch pulled up at 7:30 and before Emma helped me into the passenger seat, she asked, "Can I stay at the Army War College when I'm not allowed to be in the meeting room?"

"Yes, and you can still help Annie at lunch. In the morning I must observe your sister, to report to John when he calls this afternoon. In the afternoon you'll have to leave the fifth floor. I'll be downtown at the War Department building."

Along the way Emma asked the question that I wanted to ask. I was worried that I'd said or done something wrong.

"Isn't it too early to evaluate Annie?"

"We've learned that Annie participates regularly, learns quickly and independently when necessary. John wants me to assess two other important abilities. Does she demonstrate leadership qualities? And how well does she routinely interact with colleagues?"

Emma was agitated. "But why so soon?"

"Your sister's progress will determine where she gets placed."

I tapped, *How do you evaluate for leadership?*

"Does a person inspire and motivate others? Or does the individual simply follow direction to get things done."

Emma, what will you do before and after lunch today?

"I'll research more obits. Maybe walk the grounds with Fritz."

Mrs. Lynch, our door was unlocked this morning.

"What!"

"Yes, it was," Emma said.

Mrs. Lynch clearly wasn't pleased. "I'll call Miss Sarah, again."

We drove the rest of the way in silence until we entered the grounds of the War College. Immediately we saw a greeting party at the bottom of the granite steps.

Emma pointed out the window. "Annie, look, Clark and Peter."

A welcome distraction, but why this morning, I wondered.

"Good morning, good to see you," Clark Holder called out as Emma opened the car door.

Lt. Gordon chimed in, "Good morning, Annie, we're your assigned welcoming party."

Emma brought the wheelchair from the boot while the boys argued who'd help me into it.

"Would you like the honors, or me?" Clark asked.

I raised my right hand and brought it to my chest.

"That's her sign for she can do it herself," Emma said.

Clark chuckled. "I'm sure she uses that sign a lot."

I turned sideways, slid to the edge of the seat, and used my right hand to hold onto the wheelchair. I was about to slide out of the car when Clark reached in and grabbed me. He pulled me forward and guided me to the wheelchair in one quick motion. Peter was surprised, withdrew a bit, but then steadied the wheelchair. I marveled at the ingenuity of Clark, edging out Peter, but it was all in good fun.

Emma leaned over and whispered in my ear, "Your smile confirms your pleasure of two handsome men fighting over you."

It was then that I remembered John's warning on the Ugly Tug when we were sitting in the stern, with Fire Island to starboard. He'd said, "It's an art to never let your guard down. Yet, at the same time, you must appear relaxed and remain engaged, including with adversaries."

Clark Holder and Peter Gordon weren't adversaries, but for some reason John's comment had come to mind. They brought me to the training room, while Mrs. Lynch and Emma trailed behind.

"Are the guards going to be there?" Emma asked.

"Only in the afternoon," Mrs. Lynch said. She suggested to Emma that she accompany Sgt. Lightfoot on rounds and see the view of Washington, DC from the roof. And that is what she did.

The morning session was awkward. Mrs. Lynch sitting against the wall observing my performance. Clark's antics. Dansey leaning against the far wall, alternating between staring at his feet and observing the trainees.

I stopped dwelling on the distractions when the Major stood at the podium and began summarizing yesterday's session.

"From yesterday's assignment we've learned of the distinct possibility of two codes being used by German Military and their government. One directed to the East of the Berlin tower and the other to the West, in our direction. This despite Mr. Dansey's persuasive argument that only one exists.

"We also demonstrated the use of Preludes in all top-secret German transmissions. This has long been known, due to the diligence of Room 40. We also know that Germany sends secret, but not Top Secret, transmissions without Preludes.

"Finally, we learned that Germany uses wireless, mostly."

Mr. Dansey interjected his thoughts, "As I mentioned yesterday, as of 1914, Germany stopped using cables to transmit confidential information. The night Great Britain declared war on Germany, our Royal Post Office cut all of Germany's English Channel cables. Second, while I applaud your class assignment, as I said yesterday, I believe the second code is purely a nonsense code, used to confuse."

Was Mr. Dansey's comment regarding the lack of evidence for a second code more of his distraction? Whether it was or not, it served as a great teaching point.

"Claude, another reminder that Germany uses those Swedish cables, and you know that they remain untouched throughout the world."

From this short exchange, I noted two things. Only Van Deman called Dansey by his first name. And all seemed straight forward, but at the same time, it was a great way for one Major to disagree with the other Major.

"Also, a reminder that our Room 40 guest, Major Dansey, will lecture this afternoon starting at 14:00. Only a few will be invited to his lecture because of the top-secret nature of the information that he'll present. General Kuhn will be in attendance, as will armed guards. General Kuhn and I have agreed that this presentation is important to help us organize the MIS.

"Guards will be stationed at the elevators, as well as this room, and no one will be allowed on this floor except us. The following members of the training group should show up at 13:00: Yardley, Gordon, Rose, Barnitz, Weller, and Edwards. Mr. Harrison will also be in attendance. Any questions?"

There were no questions, but those that were not invited appeared miffed, except for Whytock, who was quite happy to have the afternoon off. Everyone called me Annie and most, if not all, did not remember my last name.

"I'm handing out portions of Cypher Telegrams provided by Major Dansey. I'm not sure where he obtained them, but let's decipher them. Everyone is encouraged to work together, but we'll keep the same groups."

I raised my hand, and the Major nodded in my direction.

I tapped, *What days in January are these transmissions from?*

"January 16 or 17."

At this point everyone in the room realized that I wasn't assigned to either group. My concern of being left out was overshadowed by my secret mission and the need to observe everyone's behavior. I read Yardley's lips when he said, "The Major has come to his senses – now the *men* can get the work done, and get it done properly." Byer nodded agreement.

Suddenly, Ensign Holder spoke up, "Sir, what about Annie?"

Out of the corner of my eye I saw Captain Johnston gloating. He must have been upset about being excluded from Dansey's lecture.

"I was getting to that," the Major said. "After Annie finishes her meeting, she'll be available to help either group. Or you can feel free to direct questions to her."

"Direct them to *her*?" Yardley wondered out loud.

His comment caused quite a stir with Yardley's sidekicks, Byer, Weller, and Johnston. Even Clark raised his eyes, but I saw no such reaction from Gordon or Edwards. Whytock seemed frankly amused. I became convinced that from that side of the table only Bernitz, from the NYPD, was acting mature. I wanted to get to know him.

I tapped rapidly on the telegraph key, *I think I understand the reason behind this class assignment. I'm looking forward to seeing if I'm correct.*

"Annie, is there anything else you want to say to the group?" The Major looked annoyed.

Yes, I have something to say. I would like to tell the person who wrote an unencrypted telegraph message to the office of the NYPD Bomb Squad that ... I am not mentally retarded.

"Well, I wonder who wrote that, Annie?" the Major said. "Tom, the reason that Annie will oversee this assignment is three-fold. Like you, she has a remarkable feel for obtaining meaning embedded in Telegraph messages. She has an interest in negative intelligence. And, thirdly, I want to give her the opportunity to supervise, even if only twenty-two years old."

It may have been my comment or the Major's comments, but either way the class let it go, and I heard nothing further.

I came to realize it was Major Van Deman's method of testing me, and testing Yardley to see if he could work with me, a young disabled woman. In other words, an exercise in dealing with uncertainty and adversaries. Observing everyone would also help me ascertain who might be the enemy spy in the room. Johnston's immaturity suggested he was a possibility. But so too were the others seated on the other side of the table. I've added Barnitz, along with a fellow New Yorker, Whytock, who probably were not spies.

My review aside, the episode left me troubled. Not because I took things personally, but because it caused me to doubt myself.

The session went smoothly and was dominated by Yardley, because he recognized the telegrams as short segments of one of the Zimmermann Telegrams. I had little to add. He had been privy to seeing bits and pieces of it in February at State. They were in fact encrypted in the old German code. Yardley also taught the groups as much as he knew about the old code and tricks to doing so. The Major was pleased.

Our discussion ended at 12:30 PM and Mrs. Lynch was pleased with my interactions in the room. She took her leave. Emma stayed with me to help with lunch. Whytock was the only person who stayed with us.

Whytock approached me and said, "Hi, Emma. I'm Ross. Nice to have a chance to say hello."

"Hi, Mr. Whytock. We understand that you're staying at the Hamilton, but we're not supposed to say hello. But I haven't seen you there."

"I'm there. My room is on the fourth floor. I saw you guys from my window getting into the car driven by Mrs. Lynch. But you're right, we cannot interact there, only here, at the War College."

"Could I ask you a favor?"

"Sure."

"There's this journalist from Canada who came to our room last evening, asking about her friend, Dalia, who died on Block Island ..."

Whytock cut her off abruptly. "Emma, I know. Mr. Harrison mentioned it this morning. He asked me to investigate her life story. I'll call my editor at the *Evening World* to find out if she's active as a journalist or playing the role of a journalist from Canada."

"This morning our door was unlocked, and I know I locked it last night," Emma insisted.

"I will keep an eye out for her. Where are you staying?" Whytock asked.

"We were assigned to a room on the second floor, near the back stairwell. I think Miss Muriel is on the fourth floor."

"I'll look into it," he assured us. "But remember we can only be seen together at Roosevelt Hall and not at the Hamilton or anywhere in DC."

Emma and I nodded, and I gave my hand signal for, *Thank you, sir.* Then I tapped, *You are not attending the afternoon session?*

"I've worked with three other members of the SIS, although it wasn't until yesterday that I met Major Dansey. I've also worked with Detective Barnitz from the Bomb Squad, and it's great to see he's involved with the ONI."

You've worked with British spies in NYC?

"Yes, and I've travelled to London, but I cannot tell you about any of that," Whytock said. "And if you haven't figured it out, Dansey is extremely secretive and very important to British intelligence. Few know who he is. I'd suggest that you follow his lead and keep a low profile, too."

Does he have skills that others don't have?

"He's well-read, well-rounded, and has a tremendous intellect. He has this capacity to know where everyone on the planet is located, at any given time."

"Now that's got to be an exaggeration, Mr. Whytock," Emma said.

Whytock smiled. "Only a little, Emma. Dansey is as committed to Great Britain as much as Winston Churchill. In fact, I'm told that they're friends. Apparently, Dansey got his fearlessness from his father."

With that, the man whose full name was Mr. Roslyn Whytock took his leave, quite content to be excused from Dansey's lecture.

I turned to Emma and tapped, *When you took a quick break and left the room, where did you go?*

"I went to the restroom but ran into Sergeant Lightfoot on rounds. He was on his way to the roof, and I joined him. It was windy up there, and the view was like being in a low flying aeroplane. I saw the Capitol and Union Station, on this side of the city and the White House to the Northwest. The Lincoln Memorial is still under construction. And on the other side of the Potomac I saw the towers at Fort Myer. In the other direction, Sergeant Lightfoot pointed out Cedar Hill which was Frederick Douglas's mansion."

Did you go to the library? You were gone for a while.

"I saw Mr. Harrison and showed him my notes on five obituaries."

Was he interested?

"Yes. Mr. Harrison had read the obituaries. Turns out Mrs. Lynch gave him a heads-up yesterday. He was able to determine that Miss Muriel was a journalist, and grew up in Nova Scotia, on the outskirts of Halifax. Her two novels were based in Canada. Remarkably, he found out that when she visited Dalia on Block Island, she was working on an article about Canadian youth leaving Canada to work in Rhode Island. He also mentioned he touched base with Ross Whytock about Miss Muriel, to see if he could find information about her from his colleagues."

He found all that out.

"Yup. He couldn't get over the title of Ball's *New York Times* obituary: 'King of Block Island, Dead.' He didn't think it was funny, however, to learn about the details of the housekeeper's death. In addition, Mr. Harrison was able to confirm that for Dalia worked at the Ocean View Hotel in the summer for years and was at the Hamilton the rest of the year.

"He thought it was important that Dalia's death occurred *after* Ball had his first stroke, and the day after he visited her in her room. And of course, there was the money. Perhaps $25,000 in securities, but he could not confirm the exact amount."

That could buy two hotels on Block Island.

"The money was found by another housekeeper ... the day after her body was brought to a vault in the Island Cemetery."

Does he think Dalia was romantically involved?

"He didn't say, but when he realized Ball's friend, the publisher and editor of the *Washington Star*, left out all mention of Dalia in his obituary, Mr. Harrison thought something was up."

Did other papers leave out mention of Dalia?

"The Newport, Rhode Island paper did not mention her. While he thought this was interesting, he wanted to determine if Miss Muriel is really Miss Muriel. He said that anyone in Canada could assume her life story because so much information about her life is readily available."

He's worried I suppose.

"Yes. He said one clue she may not turn out to be Miss Muriel has to do with a buoy that that she says was being anchored the day she sailed into New Harbor. She could have read about that buoy in a newspaper clipping and added it to her story for authenticity."

And who would schedule a trip to the Island the first day the new channel opened?

"Mr. Harrison has seen a lot."

This is getting very interesting. I wonder if Ross will add anything to solve the two mysteries, what happened to Dalia, and is Miss Muriel really Miss Muriel?

I couldn't share my next thoughts with Emma, but what if Miss Muriel is not her real name. Could she have a role in my secret mission? Or will it turn out that Miss Muriel is who she says she is: a lonely, retired journalist who was at one time in love with her friend who died unexpectedly on Block Island in the summer of 1896?

30

ANNIE

The Major was back from break, leaving Dansey with General Kuhn. The three spoke about the content of Dansey's lecture – one of several secret lectures he would give at the Army War College – and, most importantly, cleared the attendees who would be allowed in the room later this afternoon. After arranging notes at the podium, he came over and sat with us.

"Emma," Major Dansey said, "I ran into Mrs. Lynch in the lobby. She suggested we find you a job with our Sketching Division, with Mr. Lyle."

Emma perked up. "What do they do?"

"They teach soldiers how to sketch a battlefield."

"Will they hire me?" Emma's eyes brightened in anticipation.

"It's possible," the Major said. "Mr. Lyle is in the brick building in the center of the parade grounds."

"I read the huge brass plaque at the front entrance on one of my walks with Fritz," Emma frowned. "Fritz doesn't like that building for some reason."

"Do you know who is commemorated on that plaque?"

"Elihu Root. Geo has mentioned him and has been to his home on Irving Place in New York City."

"Secretary Root established the Army War College," the Major said. "He's now a diplomat to Russia but was a New York Senator. In 1912, he won the Nobel Peace Prize."

Emma raised her eyes. "Very impressive. He's done everything."

"Mr. Lyle knows him, too. Ask him about Mr. Root. Also ask him to explain the importance of Landscape Etching to military maneuvers in a battlefield."

"How does drawing help?"

"Military sketching teaches a soldier to estimate distances, which is crucial on a battlefield. Sketching both terrain and perspective educates the 'eye' to estimate distances."

"Do they use special paper?"

"Good question, Emma," the Major acknowledged. "Yes, sketchers use pads developed at the School of Musketry. These sketching papers are lined vertically to enable the use of codes."

"Does everyone on this campus use codes?" Emma asked, surprised.

"Yes. Let me know tomorrow how it went with Mr. Lyle," the Major said, then returned to the podium.

Mrs. Lynch arrived, and after a short conversation with Major Van Deman, she brought me down the hall to a smaller room to discuss my review. We spoke for fifteen minutes, finishing up in time for the last part of the morning's exercise.

My performance was satisfactory, but it was too early to decide on a placement within the ONI. She mentioned the difficulties some men were creating for me, and thought that the Major was allowing some disrespect to see how I handled adversity.

"John called Monday afternoon, and again this morning, to see how you were doing. I will tell him on our next call that you are always attentive, ask smart questions, and are slowly developing good working relationships with men in the room."

I tapped, *What did he say to that?*

"He wished Miss Smith had agreed to participate."

She was supposed to be one of my supervisors.

"I'm certain that if she were present, no one would treat you with disrespect."

Why isn't she here?

"I explained to John that Miss Smith is no longer Miss Smith. She's now *Mrs.* Friedman."

Oh, that's why.

"There's more to the story," Mrs. Lynch added, "but let's leave it at that."

Relieved my performance was satisfactory, I returned to the conference room and Mrs. Lynch took the elevator to the lobby.

Although it was easier when someone pushed my wheelchair, I was able to move forward in a straight line using my right hand, while changing my weight to one side or another, to steer the wheelchair. Slowly I'd get to where I needed to go. Oddly enough, I'd learned to use the 'difficulty' of the ruts in the dirt roads on Block Island to help me steer, but the smooth floors throughout the Army War College required less effort.

At the conference room door, I found two armed guards standing erect. Another was farther down the hall standing at the stairwell. I turned around and noticed another was positioned in the opposite direction near the elevator.

Ten minutes into being ignored by every man in the room, I looked up to the ceiling and wished Mrs. Friedman had remained Miss Smith. I envisioned her sitting between Byer and Yardley and looking directly into the eyes of Johnston. I would later find out that Mrs. Smith also enjoyed a low profile, much more so than Ross Whytock.

Each group returned and promptly finished up the morning's exercise.

Yardley took the lead. He said he had already seen parts of the message assigned to his group several few weeks ago. I knew he was assigned to the State Department and was often called to decipher messages for the Secretary of State.

I tapped hard on the telegraph key, *Did that message come off the towers?*

Major Van Deman interjected, "The message Yardley has in his hand was given to us by Major Dansey. The SIS's cryptologists in Room 40 gave permission to bring it on the boat that brought Balfour's contingent to meet with President Wilson. Tom, can you find Zimmermann's name in that message?"

"Yes, I saw his name right away. And it begins with a Prelude," Yardley replied.

"What code is used in the message?"

"The usual German code," Yardley affirmed.

"Let me know when you've deciphered the entire message," the Major instructed. "The other messages were picked up on the towers at Fort Myer, the Belmar, NJ tower, or the Long Island tower. The ONI's tower in Maine is not yet operable."

The Major walked to our side of the table. "And let me know if your messages have a Prelude and the name of the German Foreign Minister."

Thirty minutes later Johnston called out, "What's the purpose of this exercise, Major?"

"Can anyone answer that question?" The Major surveyed the room.

I raised my right hand.

"Go ahead."

I tapped on the telegraph key, *Zimmermann's name is in every newspaper. This exercise has two purposes: To give experience deciphering German messages, and to determine if Zimmermann sent messages that were received wirelessly at U.S. towers on those two days in January. Our group has not been able to identify any of his messages received at any of the three towers in the United States.*

"Annie, could you explain that again, please?" the Major asked.

If we do not see Preludes that suggest Top Secret messages, or his name on those two days ... then the Zimmermann Telegram could not have been sent wirelessly from the Berlin Tower.

I paused and looked around the room. No one had questions and they all appeared to be listening to me. I continued, *If this is true, then it follows that these Top Secret messages of Zimmermann's were sent via undersea cable, and not wireless.*

Lt. Gordon spoke up. "That would suggest that we need to identify what submarine cable the German's used to transmit those messages."

And, more importantly, how they were intercepted, I added.

I thought this was an instructive exercise, but wondered if Commander McCauley and Major Van Deman would use real data to prove something to the Brits. I found it quite interesting and wondered if this was related in any way to my secret mission?

"Let's wrap up. It's time for Dansey's lecture," the Major announced. "You've had ample time to find a Prelude, and the word 'Zimmermann'."

Lt. Gordon answered for our group, "Annie's correct, we haven't found any such messages." He had nothing further to say and sat down.

The Major looked at Yardley.

"Major, only that first one had both," Yardley insisted.

"Did you decipher it?"

"It dealt with disabling all German ships in our ports or in foreign ports, if Germany goes to war with the rest of the world."

"Germany must keep their ships out of the hands of its enemies," the Major explained. "This is a clear indication, something those of us in the intelligence community have long known, that war is here."

"Yardley, any additional thoughts?"

"The message is the first part of longer message sent on January 16 and 17 and I'm wondering why the last part is missing."

No one ventured an answer, and the Major let us take a break while we waited for the arrival of General Kuhn and Major Claude Dansey.

This gave me an opportunity to telegraph Lillie, which I did. Afterwards, I opened the cabinet door and read the paper tapes, my right index finger sliding over the paper, and then returned them to the cabinet within minutes. Word had spread that Emma and I had previously developed proficiency in using this older machine.

Clark came over and said he didn't understand the relevancy of the exercise that we'd completed.

I tapped slowly, *The release of the deciphered Zimmermann Telegrams may have been one of the reasons why Wilson abandoned his neutrality position. He stopped being the "Appeaser in Chief" as some say. Great Britain needs our help. But we can learn something else from the exercise: It sends a message to Room 40 that we don't agree with their explanation of the how's and where's of the interception of the Telegrams.*

Clark looked confused. "I don't understand."

The head of Room 40 told Walter Page, our Ambassador to Britain, that Room 40 intercepted the Zimmermann Telegram wirelessly. And we proved today that it was not sent from the Berlin Tower.

I don't think Clark understood, or he was acting stupid. Or had he not yet learned the difference between lying and the necessity of deception in espionage? Did his background in industrial security make him sound naïve? Or was he just toying with me for fun?

The armed guards walked into the room. They appeared anxious waiting for the General to appear, and wondered if Kuhn would sit in the comfortable chair. I felt a sense of pride when those not invited to stay for Dansey's lecture left the room, and I, the sole woman, stayed.

And then General Kuhn and Major Dansey arrived with another armed guard, who sat in the back of the room. The others remained in their assigned positions in the hall.

The contents of the lecture cannot be discussed. I can report that Dansey, in his attempt to help Van Deman create a comprehensive intelligence agency, gave an overview of the SIS's organizational chart that would suffice for decades to come. It was quite a gift to both Van Deman and members of the Army War College. Much later, Dansey would contribute to the reorganization of the SIS, and become the director of two divisions, one military and one domestic.

*

Emma was not allowed on the fifth floor, and I asked a guard to bring me to the lobby. I was surprised to see Clark waiting for me.

Clark took me to the bottom of the granite steps of Roosevelt Hall. After a few moments, without further coaxing, I transferred myself onto the second step. I started leaning to the left, my weak side, and he braced me with his arm. Without realizing, it dawned on me I was returning Clark's affection. We sat and talked for ten minutes and then he pointed straight ahead.

"Annie, there's your sister!"

Fortunately, and to the surprise of the physicians at the hospital in Newport, the accident at sea had no impact on my vision. I recognized my sister's smiling face from a hundred yards away. But when she saw my empty wheelchair, and realized it was me sitting on the granite steps, a scowl appeared.

I used hand signals, *Clark, would you help me into my chair, please?*

"Of course." Clark helped me up so I could bear weight on my good leg, and I transferred into the wheelchair.

I tapped on Clark's arm, *Thank you.*

"See you tomorrow, Annie."

On the ride home, Emma made no mention of what she'd witnessed, but asked, "Where's Second Lieutenant Peter Gordon?"

I did not answer, nor did I respond when she said, "Clark has the looks of a movie star."

Sensing discord between us sisters, Mrs. Lynch asked, "Emma, did Mr. Lyle introduce you to his instructors?"

It worked. Emma's good cheer returned immediately.

"Yes, the guys were helpful and fun to be with. Many more times than the men in Annie's training."

Mrs. Lynch could not contain a laugh. "How was Mr. Lyle?"

"After he gave me a quick lecture on never repeating anything that I learn or surmise at the Army War College, he explained the reasons for Landscape Sketching. That the Army trains soldiers to be artists for one major purpose: So, they can estimate distances on the battlefield."

Mrs. Lynch dropped us off at the Hamilton and we went to our room straightaway. We were exhausted, but for different reasons, and after dinner we retired early. We needed to find sleep and after washing up we both dozed off.

But Emma started tapping and woke me. She would tap on the headboard when she wanted to say something but did not want me to respond. In other words, she was angry.

Emma tapped, *Annie, are you ever going to tell me about Clark and Peter?*

I gave a hand signal for, *I'm tired.*

Emma tapped, *I do not want to know if you would let Clark kiss you. Do not answer that question.*

I was taken aback.

She tapped again, hard on the headboard. *Do not answer this question either: Was Milton the last guy you kissed?*

I raised my eyes but did not dare tap an answer.

This time she she pounded, *Do not let Clark kiss you!*

31

EMMA

I was mad at Annie, and it took a while for us to fall asleep. I could not remember the last time I was this upset with my sister. Why was she leaning against Clark on the steps of Roosevelt Hall? Where everyone could see her. Last year she was friends with Milton, Geo's assistant at the Weather House, and I had no concerns when she kissed him. This was different.

I walked down the back staircase to the lobby for a glass of warm milk. The lobby was empty except for a bellhop behind the registration desk, and Irving sitting on the large sofa. He was filling out paperwork. We saw each other at the same time.

"What's up Emma?" he asked, raising his eyes in surprise. "Having trouble falling asleep?"

"Yes. Could I get a glass of warm milk from the kitchen?"

The bellhop overheard my question and made eye contact with Irving, who nodded, and the bellhop took off in the direction of the kitchen.

"Are you always up this late, Irving?"

"Not usually. I'm scheduling shifts and ordering for the kitchen before I travel to Providence, for a business trip." He cleared his throat, then asked, "How's it going for your sister at the Weather Bureau?"

"Very well," I said.

"What's she learning?" Irving pressed.

The last thing I wanted was to engage in a lengthy conversation about my sister's cover, so I changed the subject. "A lot of what they're teaching is stuff she already knows. Irving, we really enjoy staying at the Hamilton. Thank you for everything."

Irving may not have been pleased by my answer; he looked at me strangely and said, "Emma, why does Mrs. Lynch pick you up in an Army vehicle?"

I flinched, then said, "It looks Army, but it's a Weather Bureau car."

The bellhop returned with the glass of milk, and I thanked them both.

"So, I should get back. If Annie wakes up and I'm not there, she'll be worried. Good night, Irving."

"Good night, Emma," Irving said, looking a bit perplexed.

Back in bed I wasn't sure the milk would counteract my anger at my sister, or my new worry that I had blown Annie's cover.

32

ANNIE

I awoke to find Emma sound asleep and breathing heavily. Despite poking her, she would not wake up. Ten minutes later I tried again and this time she startled.

"Why are you poking me?" Emma grumbled. "What time is it, Annie. What's wrong?"

I tapped hard on the headboard, *Wake up. Still angry at me?*

"Probably."

I have something to tell you.

"I'm tired. I went downstairs last night to get a glass of milk, but I still couldn't fall asleep. Because of you!" After a moment she settled down and added, "What's so important?"

There's an enemy spy in the room.

Emma sprang right up. "Where? In our bedroom?"

I used my hand signal for, *No, silly,* and tapped emphatically, *in the training group.*

"A real spy?" Emma reacted as if struck by lightning.

I raised my eyes, *Yes. I spent last evening silently debating whether to tell you. It's possible I'm wrong and I didn't want to worry you, but I must put it out there.*

"How do you know?"

On the Ugly Tug, *John mentioned that all spies wonder if an enemy spy is in their midst. It's part of the job. So, it made me think there might be a spy in the training group.*

Emma looked amazed. "If the Major inadvertently recruited a spy, how would you know?"

I can't go into details, but I'll use the Telegraph in the training room.

"Yes, just like the way we found Johnston's nasty message about you!"

The newer Telegraph Machines are complicated. The dots and dashes that a telegrapher keys in are recorded by a Morse Code Perforator machine. The Perforator is inside a locked cabinet and out of sight. When a message is tapped, the Perforator punches dots and dashes that represent the letters in Morse Code onto a roll of paper tape. The message can only be sent when the paper tape passes through the transmitter portion of the Telegraph. The paper tape containing the messages is automatically stored in the locked cabinet.

Reading retrieved, stored messages on paper tape – without access to a manual transmitter – is very difficult. Reading tapes visually requires a unique skill, one that Geo made us learn years ago. Yardley certainly has that skill, but I doubt the Major has it. I suspect only Yardley and I – and Emma – can read them without running them through a manual transmitter.

On the first day of training the Ciphering Telegraph was used to evaluate the attendees' telegraphy skills. The Major observed that some men keyed their messages with complete confidence. Others, like Clark, had trouble, and stumbled along. With the Major over my shoulder, I telegraphed a personal message to Geo and one to Mrs. Conway. On Tuesday, during lunch, I transmitted a message to our cousin Wallace at the switchboard saying all was well at the Weather Bureau training.

"The locked door is easy to open," Emma reminded me. "Just push your wheelchair against the middle of the side panel and the door will pop open."

I tapped, *I opened it twice.*

"Did you read their destinations?"

Most were to colleagues at government stations. But two were sent to Western Union.

"Why would a message that is transmitted to or from a Western Union office cause concern?" Emma looked puzzled.

It would only be concerning if a telegram was transmitted to a Western Union office in Mexico City.

"Did you locate the routing code?"

I raised my eyes and tapped, *On Tuesday, before you came to help me for lunch, the training group went to the library to consult French spy manuals. I stayed back and opened the cabinet, and the message was staring me in the face. The routing was to Mexico City.*

"Why does that cause you such concern?"

That's the same Western Union Office the Zimmermann Telegram passed through.

"Ah, the Zimmermann Telegram again," Emma sighed. "I remember. It was on the first day of March when newspapers reported that the Western Union Office in Mexico City was involved. I can't believe the Foreign Minister of Germany used Western Union to send a top-secret message to the President of Mexico."

It's true, because there are no direct cables from Germany to Mexico City. Our State Department received a copy of that message from that same Western Union office.

Emma gasped. "Are you joking?"

I'm not. My hunch is that it's part of a negative intelligence operation.

She shook her head. "This is confusing."

Sounds crazy, and you are right, they are ALWAYS confusing.

"Does this have anything to do with the enemy spy in the group?"

I think the spy in the group and the Zimmermann Telegram are two different things. If the spy is sending messages to that office, it's his way of contacting other German spies. The German office is in the same building as the Western Union office.

"How do you know that?"

I overheard Yardley.

"Do you think Yardley is the enemy spy?"

I am sure he is not.

Emma eyed me warily. "How can you be so certain?"

Yardley established a new form of espionage. He has worked at the State Department in sensitive areas for years, and he is a confidant of the Major. He is the last person in the room who would be an enemy spy.

"Annie, if Yardley thinks there's a spy, too, then that might break the ice between you two."

I made the hand signal for, *Maybe.*

Suddenly Emma stood up. "Oh, Annie. I forgot to tell you."

I raised my eyes three times. It's not often I see my sister blush, but she did.

"I have to confess, late last night I may have blown your cover."

My eyes opened wide. *What?*

"I couldn't sleep, so I went downstairs for a glass of milk. Irving was sitting on the couch doing paperwork before leaving for Providence."

I gave a hand signal, *What happened?*

"Irving asked about you and the Weather Bureau. When I changed the subject abruptly, he looked at me funny. Then he asked why Mrs. Lynch's car was a military vehicle.

Okay. Not to worry. Let's see how Irving regards me when he returns from Rhode Island.

Emma blinked. "You're not worried?

Not yet. Before Mrs. Lynch arrives, I have two things to share. The Major and Mr. Harrison asked me to meet with them after today's training is over.

"Are they upset with you?"

I'll find out. The other news is that I have a date with Clark.

"What? No, you're not going on a date with him!" She exclaimed, then said with resignation, "When?"

Saturday night, for dinner.

"No!" Emma stomped her foot down. "With all the uncertainty in the training sessions ... you're going on a date?"

He is nice to me. I want to get to know him outside of the training.

Emma shook her head. And when I tapped, *We better get dressed and downstairs, or we'll be late ...* she threw her hands in the air.

By the time we got to the lobby Mrs. Lynch was finishing a conversation with Irving. He didn't appear to have noticed us and walked out of the lobby with two bellhops carrying suitcases to a waiting carriage.

Out of the corner of my eye I could see Emma looked nervous, but it didn't appear that he'd said anything to Mrs. Lynch. Or perhaps she was nervous because she was still angry at me for going on a date with Clark Holder. When Mrs. Lynch turned to us, she gave no indication of concern.

I tapped, *After the session ends this afternoon, I have a meeting with the Major and Mr. Harrison.*

Mrs. Lynch nodded. "I'm aware of that meeting, Annie."

I hope I did not do anything wrong.

"You didn't do anything wrong, but I heard Johnston was reprimanded for telegraphing his buddy at the Bomb Squad asking about Dansey."

"Good. I read that telegram. He should be reprimanded," Emma said with indignation.

"Annie, I'll meet you on the third floor of the library, around 5:30. Then I'll drop you and your sister off here. Emma, will you spend the day with the sketchers?"

"Mr. Lyle won't be there. He's at the War Department, with his supervisor, and he said he'd ask about a job for me!"

"Very good. What are your plans?"

"I'll stay here."

"Are you sure?"

Emma nodded.

She gave no indication that she wanted to stay at the Hamilton. I tapped, *What do you have to do?*

"I'll keep busy." With that she walked to the rear staircase.

On the drive across the city Mrs. Lynch mentioned there was a chance Mr. Lyle would be able to hire Emma a few days a week. But she was concerned that Emma wanted to stay back at the Hamilton this morning.

Thursday, the fourth day of meetings. I anticipated a busy day, with more deciphering of German messages, but I wondered if there was something additional on the agenda. And then there was the meeting at 5:00 PM in the library. What was that about?

33

ANNIE

The Major was waiting patiently at the podium when Mrs. Lynch brought me to the conference room. I was the second to last to arrive for some reason. Without introductory comments he began as soon as the last man, Weller, took his seat at the table.

"For those who were invited to sit in on Major Dansey's lecture yesterday afternoon please remember that not one word can be repeated, now or ever. There was a reason note taking was not allowed.

"Except for Sergeant Yardley, it's clear you need practice deciphering German messages. Yesterday, I asked each group to look for one word, 'Zimmermann' and for the presence of Preludes. And it took too long. Today, you'll work as one group to decipher a message that Room 40 handed to Commander McCauley. The only hint I'll give is that it's a partial message." He proceeded to pass around two telegrams.

The entire group worked diligently, but my suggestions were not received with interest. So I didn't assert myself and took advantage of being ignored to observe everyone in the room. Wheeling back to the Telegraph Machine was effortless and went unnoticed by the everyone. Pulling the right wheel back with my right hand, I turned around without difficulty. Then I used my weight and occasionally my right hand on the left wheel and was back at the Telegraph Machine in no time. I wanted to determine if any messages had been transmitted last evening.

I noticed right away the Telegraph had been unplugged, and the time stamp on messages, sent or received, would not be accurate. If pulled intentionally, someone used it for underhanded reasons. I left it unplugged.

I glanced at the men periodically, but no one appeared interested in me. The technique Emma mentioned to open the locked door worked like a charm. I pretended to adjust the paper roll and reached with my right hand for new messages. I began "reading" the paper tape with my fingers and my eyes.

As expected, another had the code for the Western Union office in Mexico City. I kept "looking" with my fingers but, thankfully, no more messages were sent to the NYPD Bomb Squad.

I pulled the message to Mexico City. I recognized a few words, in English, but there were a series of what looked like symbols, not words. I could not decipher them. My assumption was that anyone using complicated symbols was well-trained, or simply used them as nonsense words, to confuse. Geo, a descendant of the Turtle Clan of the Mohawks, had mentioned that Code Talkers from Native American Indian tribes introduced their symbols to our Army years ago, but I had no idea what they were.

Suddenly, I heard Johnston say, "Look, she's over there." Byer followed up with, "She's no help anyway." I figured the Major had left the room and stared back at the men. I smiled at Johnston before returning to the message. I understood only two things: The word "U-boote" and the phrase, "pick up". Groups of numbers to form a false code finished the message.

With my right hand I replaced the paper tape in the cabinet and locked the door. Johnston's eyes were on me.

I thought to myself that these questions needed answers: How did the German Foreign Minister receive the telegrams? I wondered whatever the case was, these messages had to have been hand-delivered to the President of Mexico. But by whom?

Whatever the case, those messages had to be hand-delivered to them.

When I looked up the Major had returned and Byer asked right away, "Major, the March 1 newspapers reported our State Department's copy of the Zimmermann Telegram came from the Mexico City Western Union. Is that true?"

Major Ralph Van Deman looked at Byer and gave a one-word answer: "Yes."

Whytock raised his hand. "The *Evening World*'s headline that night said simply, 'PLOT STORY TRUE, SAYS WILSON'. We got that line directly from him."

"Why do you think it originated in Mexico?" Weller asked.

The Major looked at Mr. Dansey, but he declined comment. "Anyone have an explanation for Weller? Yardley."

"Mexico doesn't have secure cables running into the country," Yardley said. "Germany sends all messages for North America to the German Ambassador to the United States. Then, the German Ambassador, Bernstorff, forwards them to whomever they are addressed. With respect to the Zimmermann Telegrams, Bernstorff read them and forwarded them to his Minister in Mexico City using the Western Union Office. No one can send a message directly to the President of Mexico."

"According to the SIS someone sent a copy of the original message in German code, along with a deciphered English translation, from that Western Union Office to our State Department. I suspect that Frank Polk and Secretary Lansing hand-delivered it to President Wilson," Van Deman said. "Claude, any comments?"

Major Dansey shook his head. I noted how silent Dansey became when issues of the Zimmermann Telegram were discussed.

"Now, back to today's assignment." The Major addressed the room, "How far have you gotten on deciphering the message?"

Byer took the lead. "We've made progress. We are decrypting the Zimmermann Telegram that is sent using the usual German code. Or a portion of it."

"How can you tell?"

"Sir, the message ends with the code 97556, which is Zimmermann's name," Byer replied. "It is directed to von Bernstorff in Washington, DC, before he forwards it to the German Minister in Mexico, von Eckardt."

"What else have you deciphered?"

"The code, 115, means it was probably transmitted on the 15th but received on the 16th of January. We've just deciphered the word, *schlagen*, which we interpret in this context to mean 'to strike'."

Lt. Edwards continued, "The telegram mentions four countries, Mexico, Japan, England, and America. Their codes are 67893, 52262, 76036, and 39695."

"And the states mentioned are Texas, with 36477, and Arizona, spelled out using four short-numbered codes. So far that's what we've been able to decipher," Lt. Gordon concluded.

"Well, this is a much better start than late morning yesterday. Carry on," the Major said.

"If we break up into groups of three, we can each decipher a sentence," Lt. Edwards proposed. Yardley agreed and the groups formed.

Lt. Edwards, Lt. Gordon, and I worked together. I suggested a specific sentence that included the words *President of Mexico.* We moved back to the wall to keep from being distracted.

Twenty minutes later Major Van Deman asked to see our progress.

He nodded his approval, and added, "When that telegram was sent to President Carranza, he was only the Provisional President of Mexico. Why is that important?"

I tapped, *He receives it without authority to act?*

"Possibly, Annie. Although I believe he is favored to win his election," he said.

A few minutes later we were stuck on one code and decided to ask the training group for help. Lt. Gordon stood up and yelled across the room, "What does the code 5870 mean? Anyone figure that out yet?"

"It's not a word," Yardley answered right away, "it means to insert a comma."

Everyone chuckled. This was the first time the group laughed out loud together.

"Ah, we have two commas in our sentence," Lt. Gordon said.

Within an hour we had constructed the sentence, took five minutes to marvel at our accomplishment, and pondered its significance. We then tackled another sentence, which was easier to decrypt.

With two sentences completed, we called over Major Van Deman. Major Dansey came over from his side of the conference room to listen in.

"We picked two good sentences to decipher," Lt. Edwards said.

"What's the first thing you learned?" Major Van Deman asked.

"That Zimmermann is an arrogant man," Lt. Gordon said.

"How so?" Major Dansey spoke up.

"The way he requests an alliance with Carranza. Who would accept that?"

"We also learned," Lt. Edwards interjected, "that this message isn't meant to be delivered to Carranza."

"What do you mean?" both Majors asked at the same time.

We explained our deciphered sentence as follows: "You (von Eckardt) will inform the President of Mexico – most secretly *and* when the outbreak of war is certain – and tell him that he must add the suggestion that he (Carranza) must – on his own initiative – invite Japan to *immediate* adherence. And, at the same time, mediate between Japan and Germany."

"You're interpreting that sentence to mean that von Eckardt is only to share with Carranza after – and only after – the outbreak of war with the United States?" Major Van Deman looked impressed. But I noted Dansey looked puzzled, as if he wondered why Room 40 gave him that part of the message to bring to the training.

"Major Van Deman, the stipulation regarding Japan seems unattainable," Lt. Gordon mentioned.

Out of the corner of my eye I saw three men walk to the Telegraph, one after the other. The first was Weller, but he walked back to his group right away. Then Clark followed. He plugged in the Telegraph, then sent a quick message and returned to his group. The last person was Johnston, who transmitted a keyed message, but was so slow that Lt. Gordon walked over and asked if he needed help. Johnston did not laugh.

Each of three men had ties to New York City. Germany had a large consular office and a larger presence. With over eighty German ships forced to stay in the Port of New York City, that meant a lot of German citizens walking around, mostly in the docks on New York and New Jersey. Johnston, of course, was one of two in the room who worked for the Bomb Squad. As of yet, I had not noticed Detective Barnitz converse with Capt. Johnston. Weller grew up in Manhattan on the Upper West Side. And Clark's parents rent an apartment near Grand Central Terminal. I put this in the back of my mind. Nothing yet had made me think that Lts. Gordon or Edwards were enemy spies. And I think Yardley's sidekick, Byer, was also not a spy. But John's comment bounced around in my head like a ball. "Don't jump to conclusions. Anyone can go over to the other side, especially for money, at any time."

Back together at the conference table, everyone agreed that the telegram was received on January 16, and it introduced Germany's intentions regarding becoming an ally with Mexico should war with the United States break out, with certain caveats. I was surprised that no one in the room was interested in our second sentence. When Lt. Gordon raised the issue, still no one appeared interested in pursuing its significance. As usual in these circumstances I surveyed the room to look at faces. Dansey's face was motionless, some were confused, most shrugged their shoulders.

I took it for granted that Dansey would not offer an opinion. His silence made it awkward for the Major to answer questions.

Yardley had explained why Carranza did not have a state-controlled cable for his personal use and must use the Western Union Office. But I thought other questions were not answered satisfactorily. The confusion intrigued me, and I wanted an explanation of why it was confusing. Was this on purpose? Knowing that the question might bring the ire of Dansey; I knew it would not help me identify the enemy spy, I was curious.

I tapped, *Major Van Deman, these Zimmermann Telegrams are confusing. A lot of unanswered or poorly answered issues arise in my mind. Zimmermann acknowledged that he sent the message in the third week of February. This message was sent in January. So maybe the confusion doesn't rest with Germany, but Great Britain?*

The Major hesitated and looked to Dansey.

Isn't it important to sort this out?

Dansey stepped forward. "Annie, the ONI played a role in deciphering the message. Let's ask Commander McCauley when he lectures."

I nodded but realized no one else in the room appeared interested. Perhaps, they were aware of the tension, but they could not imagine that I had understood the tension before I asked the questions. "Confusion", "deception vs lying", and "avoidance" were sealed in my memory. As was each man's facial response to my questions and answers.

Just then I thought about Emma. What was she up to at the Hamilton?

34

EMMA

Before Annie and Mrs. Lynch had left the lobby, out of the corner of my eye, I saw Miss Muriel in the dining room with two women.

I noted that she was seated a few tables back from the lobby, in a seat where she could see, over the heads of other diners, the front doors of the Hamilton Hotel. Knowing that Miss Muriel might see Mrs. Lynch take Annie to the car, I decided then and there to figure out Miss Muriel. I quickly wished my sister a good day using our hand signal, then abruptly walked to the back staircase. By the time I had I reached the end of the hall, knowing Miss Muriel was at breakfast with two women, I had a plan.

I took the staircase to the fourth floor and walked back to the wing that overlooked Franklin Square. I remembered her room location on the fourth floor when we first met. I turned the doorknob slowly and to my surprise, the door opened. I looked both ways in the hall and seeing no one I peered inside. Several copies of the *Halifax Herald* were on a round table confirming this was her room. I walked in and quietly closed the door. Miss Muriel must have forgotten to lock her door, perhaps distracted by her two friends.

It was a spacious room, with a large polished wooden round table. On it were numerous pads of paper, and several editions of her newspaper were strewn about.

I did not allow myself to read anything on the pads. Instead, I walked up to the window. The room had a bird's-eye view of Franklin Park; it was much larger than I imagined from the street. To the right, through the leafless trees, in the far distance, was the roof of the White House. Beyond that the top of the Washington Monument.

Footsteps brought my attention back to my mission. It had been a long time since I was in a place that I wasn't supposed to be, and I froze. If I got caught, I'd be sent back to Block Island, for sure. The footsteps slowed in front of the room, and I looked for a closet to see if I could fit, but soon the steps disappeared down the hall.

I took a deep breath and glanced at the round table hoping to find the reason why, after all these years, Miss Muriel remained distraught over Dalia.

A framed photo stuck out from under a pad. I picked it up. Three women were standing together. Miss Muriel was on the right. In the middle a heavyset woman with closely cropped hair. And on the left, a thin, shorter much older woman. At the top of this black and white, faded photo was the inscription: "To Muriel". At the bottom two signatures were unreadable. There was no way to tell if one of the women was Dalia. I stared at the photo and became sad, because if the older woman was Dalia, then this was all about love. I looked for other photos but found none. I scanned the room but saw nothing else that helped. I decided to walk to our side of the hotel before descending the stairs to the second floor.

Few walked the back stairwell. Between floors I paused to look out the window. It turned out to be a good place to be alone.

If Dalia was in the photo, I felt sorry for her, to have lost a friend years ago and still be so very lonely. I thought of Annie. We both knew she'd die first, and when I reached Miss Muriel's age Annie would be long gone. I too would be lonely and feel the pain Miss Muriel lives with. Tears came to my eyes, not so much for Miss Muriel, but for me, and the loneliness of my distant future. I vowed to include Miss Muriel in my David Copperfield prayers.

I enjoyed the solitude that this back stairwell allowed. But my peaceful sense was interrupted abruptly as I looked out the window of the stairwell and identified a woman walking briskly north on 14th Street. It was Miss Muriel. She was walking alone. Where was she going?

I ran to room 207 for my coat, then took the front stairwell to the lobby and right out the doors. Once outside, Miss Muriel was one long block ahead. I crossed to the other side of 14th Street, dodging horse-drawn carriages and a few noisy cars. By the time I reached the other side safely, I saw her crossing against traffic as well. Was she on her way to the German Embassy? It depended on if she turned left onto Massachusetts Avenue.

I ran at full speed. I needed to reach Massachusetts Avenue if I had any chance of seeing her enter the Embassy. I slowed briefly, to catch my breath, but when she turned left onto Massachusetts, I sped up again. When I reached the avenue, I stopped. Should I cross, as she did, against traffic?

It didn't matter. As clear as day I saw Miss Muriel walk into a side door of the large red brick building, the home of the German Embassy. I continued to walk west, not bothering to cross the street. What if she saw me?

I started shaking. I walked to the next intersection, all the while keeping my eye on that building.

35

ANNIE

Knowing Emma was not at the War College, Mrs. Lynch brought me to my meeting on the third floor of the library. I recognized from Emma's description the couches and the table with current newspapers scattered about. I asked Mrs. Lynch if there was a copy of the *Providence Journal*, which she handed to me. What did John Rathom have to say today?

I tapped, *Is this where Emma sits and reads?*

"Yes, these couches are comfortable," Mrs. Lynch said. "Annie, Mr. Harrison asked me to attend this meeting."

I gave my hand signals for, *Okay* and *Why?*

Mrs. Lynch's expression clouded. "You won't believe this, but your sister was spotted near the German Embassy this morning. He's going to ask why she was there."

I tapped, *So, that is why she stayed back this morning. She never said anything.*

Mr. Harrison came down from his balcony office with a book in hand. He did not mention Emma until the Major arrived.

"Hi, Annie. This reference book may help as you move forward with the ONI." Mr. Harrison placed the manual on the table in front of my wheelchair and took a seat next to Mrs. Lynch.

Is this the book on the submarine cables throughout the world?

"Yes. It's been updated since Maury died and includes the path of every submarine cable, in every large body of water, throughout the world. Including the cables to and from Block Island."

Thank you.

"I found it useful to visualize these maps when I was assigned to diplomatic posts around the world." He turned to Mrs. Lynch. "Harriet, have you heard from John today?"

"Yesterday, not today."

"Ah, there's the Major."

Major Van Deman asked Mrs. Lynch to stay for the discussion involving my sister. I knew only one thing. This was not a social meeting.

"Annie," the Major began, "we're aware most of the men that I invited to the meetings do not want you around. Many men do not like working with women, and are worried it will cloud their focus, and affect their judgement."

I am aware of that and try to assert myself. I am not asking to keep anyone in line, Yardley or Johnston or anyone else. I will prove them wrong.

"Yardley is valuable. He's always worked well with everyone, although he hasn't worked with many women," the Major explained.

I tapped, *He knows a lot, and the Army needs him.*

"We're glad you understand. He's an excellent cryptographer, although not as accomplished as Parker Hitt who'll give a lecture next week. I'll make sure Yardley meets Parker's wife, Genevieve, who is also an accomplished cryptographer. That may surprise him.

"But Yardley and the other men are all motivated. We've tried to persuade everyone in the room to accept you. But you must engage them, and for you to have a career in the ONI you must win them over."

I look forward to meeting Hitt's wife. I will win everyone over, I promise. Please say nothing to anyone, because they would resent me more, knowing that a woman got them reprimanded.

I thought I was doing a good job but apparently not good enough. And then came a most distressing comment.

"Tomorrow's session on firearms is at the Naval Yard. You must learn to use a pistol, and I hope you're able to do it. If not, your future in the ONI will be limited."

I will do that, too. I did not expect that comment, and my heart sank.

Mr. Harrison turned to Mrs. Lynch. "Harriet, would you step outside and return in ten minutes, please?"

After she was out of earshot, he continued, "Mrs. Lynch knows a portion of what we're going to say, but there's that secret mission of yours that no one can know anything about. That's why I asked her to leave.

"I think John mentioned to you about my agent, Joe, who I borrowed from the Secret Service. This morning Joe saw your sister near the German Embassy. He was inside, and out the window saw her walking west on the opposite side of Massachusetts Avenue. Did you know she was going to snoop around?"

I tapped at a high rate of speed, *No, not at all. This morning she abruptly walked away from me in the lobby of the Hamilton.*

Mr. Harrison interjected, "We know that Miss Muriel appeared out of nowhere at the Hamilton to ask about her long-lost friend. And we hope she is who she says she is. But as of now I doubt Emma believes her."

Why do you say that?

"Because moments after Joe saw your sister walking along, he saw a woman up ahead of her who he now knows is Miss Muriel."

Where was she?

"She walked in the back door of the German Embassy. Apparently, your sister had followed her from the Hamilton."

I raised my eyes.

The Major said gravely, "We need you to tell your sister to refrain from trying to be a spy. We do appreciate she made a connection that we'd not known about. You and your sister have such spunk, and that's great, but now we need to keep her out of harm's way."

She must have seen Miss Muriel leave the hotel and wanted to follow her. I will find out tonight. I am thankful she is interested in the Sketchers.

"The Sketchers is a good spot for her," Mr. Harrison said. "For now, we'll keep you two in your room at the Hamilton. If anything distressing comes up, we'll move you elsewhere. We do marvel at how, in just a few days, you've made your mark.

"As far as your secret mission is concerned, what progress have you made identifying the enemy spy?"

With the Major present I wondered if it was Miss Muriel that drew him in, or have they identified a potential spy?

Although Yardley ignores me and treats me with distain, I do not believe he is a spy, nor do I believe his sidekick, Byer, is one. I have also ruled out Lieutenants Edwards and Gordon. Bernitz and Whytock are certainly not enemy spies. I wonder if a few of the men from NYC are to be considered suspect.

"Who are they, and what's your rationale?" the Major asked.

I tapped slowly, *I'm aware that the German Embassy is in close contact with their consulate in NYC.*

"That's a good point, Annie. France and Great Britain have large active consulates in NYC as well. We think we know what's going on in each of them," Mr. Harrison said.

"Who are the three?" Major Van Deman asked, again.

I tapped with blazing speed, *Clark Holder, Capt. Johnston, and Royal Weller live in NYC. Clark has also lived in London. Curiously, he has had prior contact with Dansey. Capt. Johnston appears to be an angry man. He is of course NYPD Bomb Squad yet keeps his distance from Barnitz. And Weller lives on the Upper West Side of Manhattan.*

"That's not enough information to make informed decisions, Annie," Mr. Harrison explained.

I know, but Weller goes to the races. And I think Clark will ask me on a date this Saturday. Should I continue with it? And as I just said, Capt. Johnston is an angry man.

The Major raised his eyes. "I'll watch out for Weller. I didn't know about his love of the horses. As far as your date with Clark, don't fall for anyone. It's okay to socialize, and if he asks you out, I don't think it will be a problem. But to be safe I'll obtain a reservation at the Cosmos Club. I'll have someone mention it to Clark, as my guest."

"Spies do meet at the Cosmos Club, Annie," Mr. Harrison added.

Again, I tapped with lightning speed. *There is one more finding I need to report. As you know, I can read the paper tapes in the Telegraph Machine without using the manual transmitter. Three messages were sent to Mexico City's Western Union office. And yesterday I noticed the plug was pulled.*

"I noticed that, also. No one should touch that plug," the Major said. "I'll have Yardley look at the messages."

Does Yardley suspect there's a spy, too?

"We haven't told him, but he'll figure it out after he reads the messages transmitted to Mexico City. You're a few steps ahead of him," Mr. Harrison asserted. "Ross is also very concerned about a spy in the training, after hearing the story of Miss Muriel asking to talk to you on your second day at the hotel. He immediately became suspicious and contacted us."

"Don't give up, Annie," Major Van Deman added. "Learn to work with belligerent people. Soon everyone will look at you with respect, and you'll have overcome their insolence. But you must learn to use a pistol."

36

ANNIE

It was 7:15 PM. Emma was sitting on the large sofa in the lobby when she spotted the car in front of the Hamilton. The ride back to the Hamilton was quick, and I was still shaken by a few comments at my meeting with Major Van Deman and Mr. Harrison. I was never so glad to see Emma walk out of the lobby. She removed the wheelchair from the boot, said goodbye to Mrs. Lynch, but not before embracing me; we were upstairs in no time.

I tapped, *I have two pieces of news for you.*

"About Mr. Lyle?"

I raised my eyes. *Yes. You start tomorrow.*

"That's great," Emma said happily. "Will I get paid, too?"

Yes. You will not be able to stay back at the Hamilton because you'll work every day.

"What's the other news?"

Well. You were spotted near the German Embassy this morning!

Emma sat on the bed and put her head down. "Who saw me?"

I can't tell you who it was, but I have been told to tell you that you cannot pretend to be an agent and spy. Or they will surely send you back to Block Island.

Emma stood up and crossed her arms. "They can't send me home. I have a job now."

That's not funny, Emma. You must demonstrate a seriousness of purpose. But they did thank you for your observation of Miss Muriel.

Despite Miss Sarah bringing a wonderful dinner from the hotel kitchen, we ate very little. First there was the reprimand of my sister's behavior, and then the reminder that I must learn to handle a pistol. And Emma's safety to worry about, and now Miss Muriel.

Emma was quiet as well. I assumed her eventful day kept her thinking to herself. I waited patiently for her to share her day's activities, as Lillie would say. But when she spoke, she only asked about tomorrow's session at the Naval Yard.

I tapped as if answering a question from Emma, *ONI employees must be capable to use a pistol and understand firearms and other forms of self-defense*.

"You're being issued a handgun, or a rifle?" Emma raised both eyes.

I have to learn to use a pistol, or I will not be allowed to continue.

Emma gasped, but didn't say anything.

The Naval Yard has a small firing range.

We finished dinner, washed up, and climbed into bed.

"I'm tired." Emma buried her head in the pillow.

I had waited long enough, and tapped hard on the headboard, *What did you do today?*

She slowly sat up. "I took a walk."

I hand signaled, *Where?*

"I have to talk to Mr. Harrison."

I hand signaled, *Why?*

"This morning, in the lobby, Miss Muriel was looking at us, and I wanted to find out who she really is."

What did you do?

I listened as she explained her story, and tapped at my highest speed, *Tell Mr. Harrison about the photo on her table. I'm glad at least that you did not walk into the Embassy, Emma.*

Glazed looks came over both of us.

Emma proposed, "There's always the chance that Miss Muriel visited the Embassy to interview staff for a newspaper article."

Not really. One of Mr. Harrison's agents saw the entire episode!

"Oh," Emma blanched. "I guess I'm in trouble, but I would never follow her into the building."

I said nothing, but I'm sure the episode opened up the possibility of danger directed at me and my sister. But what if Miss Muriel is an accomplice to the spy in the training group? That would be a real problem.

Tomorrow, after I'm back from the Naval Yard, let's meet with Mr. Harrison.

Emma agreed. She checked the door twice to make sure it was locked, then returned to bed.

I stared at the ceiling, and tapped, *I am feeling anxious about using a pistol, but I now see it as an absolute necessity.*

"You'll learn to handle it," Emma asserted. "And, honestly, aren't you thankful not to be stuck on Block Island?"

37

ANNIE

For all the worry of last night, the day could have been a lot worse. But it wasn't without its trying moments. The firing range session was a learning experience for more reasons than I thought possible. Testing for proficiency was scheduled for next week, and it was obvious to everyone that I would need extra practice time, primarily to gain arm strength to control my aim. I waited in the car with Mrs. Lynch at the base of the steps to Roosevelt Hall, while Emma ran up the steps for her meeting with Mr. Harrison.

Emma had no trouble finding the partially-hidden third floor balcony offices in the library. Mr. Harrison had not yet arrived, but that gave her the opportunity to talk to his assistant, who turned out to be another lawyer. The meeting went well despite Mr. Harrison reprimanding her – less than forcefully – for walking into Miss Muriel's hotel room. Both men made note of the possible significance of the photograph, but after another round of reprimands, they applauded her courage.

Emma stood up and shook Mr. Harrison's hand. "I hope this won't be the last of our conversations, Mr. Harrison."

"Knowing you and your sister I have the feeling it will not," Mr. Harrison said with a broad smile.

She then reported to the Sketchers building, but not before jostling with Fritz on the parade grounds. As Emma was running down the granite steps on her way to Sketchers, Mrs. Lynch and I were driving out of the

War College gate on our way to the Navy Yard. When we drove through the Latrobe Gate I was immediately greeted by my welcoming party of Clark and Peter. Clark pushed the wheelchair and the three of us went diagonally across the small, tree-lined field toward the Anacostia River. Soon we saw the small arms indoor firing range located fifty feet from bank of the river. It was used only for small arms. Everyone from the training group was present except Barnitz and Whytock.

Lieutenant Donald Leehey was filling in for the Officer in Charge. Originally from Kentucky, Leehey was a member of several sharpshooting squads in the U.S. Army, and the story we heard was that he was on loan to the Navy. After this temporary assignment, we later found out, he would enter the U.S. Military Academy at West Point.

The Lieutenant met us outside the narrow building and did not hide his displeasure when his eyes fell upon my wheelchair. His comments were loud enough to be heard across the river.

"Well, I was warned that there was at least one female in this group, but I didn't know that the Secretary of the Navy now allows wheelchairs, too," he groused.

Referring to me as a "wheelchair" instead of a woman was common. Surprisingly, even people with disabilities who walk about would comment similarly. The men laughed, but I understood the context and did not let it rile me.

Leehey demanded, "She can't handle a heavy Colt pistol. Why is she here?"

"That's what we'd like to know," Johnston offered, in support of the Lieutenant's comments.

"Jesus, why *is* she here?" Leehey repeated, as if I was not present.

"We've brought this up to the Major." I wasn't sure who said that, but it sounded like the muffled voice of Byer.

Then Yardley said clearly, "If she can't use a handgun, she can't continue with the ONI."

I looked at the men's facial expressions and saw nothing except scorn. My calm demeanor disappeared when the instructor ridiculed me further.

"What does she know? She can't even talk," Leehey said, shaking his head.

I looked around to confirm that the Major was not present. With not one man coming to my defense, I decided to use the language common on Block Island's west side, and tapped, *Fuck you.*

That caused a few men to break out laughing. Even Yardley couldn't hold a chuckle.

"Why are you laughing?" Leheey asked, oblivious to my two-word Morse.

Clark spoke up, "Annie communicates rapidly using Morse Code. She just told you to go fuck yourself."

"What?"

"Have you anything else to say to the instructor, Annie?" Lt. Edwards asked dryly.

I tapped with lightning speed, *I'll reserve judgement until after the session*. Edwards translated.

Lieutenant Leheey settled down and invited us into his realm. Once inside the firing range he began a one-hour lecture on firearms, starting with rifles and ending with pistols. I asked several questions and remarkably, much to the consternation of some of the men, he started to come around. The Navy's Colt revolver was heavy. I could hold it but keeping it steady using my right hand was a problem. I was relieved when Royal Weller had difficulty, too. My right hand was not strong enough to hold the pistol outstretched, and building enough strength before next week's proficiency test was a concern.

Throughout the morning, despite my strength not improving, the instructor's attitude did. All signs of his intentional ridicule disappeared the moment he brought out a smaller pistol. The Colt 1908.

"Annie, this is the Colt Pocket Hammerless. Without the magazine it weighs twenty-four ounces and is only seven-inches long. It can easily fit in your pocket. The barrel of the Colt .45 is as long as the 1908."

I raised my eyes twice as Leheey placed the Colt 1908 in my right hand.

"Is that how you say, yes, Annie?" he asked me with a smile.

I raised my eyes, again. Why had his attitude toward me changed? It was the fastest anyone had come to understand me in years.

I raised the gun above my head with little trouble, and, unlike the Colt

.45, the 1908 was automatic.

"Annie, the magazine is essential for anyone with one hand," Leehey explained. "It holds seven rounds."

I braced the pistol against the side of the wheelchair and loaded the magazine. For whatever reason, I had won the respect of the instructor and was determined do so with the men in my group as well. I practiced alongside them as they used the Colt .45. Surprisingly Weller also used the 1908. But he is a lawyer.

At lunch Lieutenant Leheey dismissed those with experience and reminded them the proficiency test was next week. I wasn't surprised to see Yardley, Byer, Johnston, and Gordon leave. But I was surprised when Clark walked out with them. That left me, Edwards, and Weller to practice.

Even with the smaller pistol, my hand tired quickly, but so did Weller's. I took the opportunity to get to know him while we sat and watched Lt. Edwards practice with his Colt .45.

To me, Weller was still a sphinx. A lawyer with a gift for languages, he was quiet and reserved, but in a different way than Lt. Edwards. We started laughing because we both had sore right arms. Eventually he opened up. I learned that his mother died suddenly last year, and that's when his father bought a tiny summer bungalow in New Jersey. He mentioned, almost as an afterthought, that as a young child he had twice vacationed on Block Island. They stayed on High Street. I was surprised he remembered the name of the street. Or did he recently learn that?

I could not imagine Royal Weller being an enemy spy. But was there a concern about his father moving to New Jersey and both frequenting the Freehold racetrack? Geo had long mentioned the widespread illegal gambling in that state. And although I was not surprised his family vacationed on Block Island, why had he not shared that earlier in the week?

An hour and a half later, our arms tired and we had to stop shooting. Leheey then sat with us and reviewed the range of foreign-made small arms that we'd encounter, at sea or on land. After that he focused on my wheelchair, and proceeded to add brakes to each wheel, to prevent movement from the kickback of the Colt 1908. After arm strengthening exercises, which he prescribed as if it were a doctor's prescription, he was sure I would pass the proficiency examination. This Naval officer's transformation from antagonist to friend was remarkably fast, and how I wish it was always so.

*

That night I complained about my shooting arm incessantly, to the point of great annoyance to my sister. After dinner, to quiet me, she stuffed our duffle bag with clothes and directed me to exercise. She then propped herself against the headboard and became immersed in Maury's reference book. She focused on maps showing English Channel submarine cables from various European countries. She then studied the routes of the Atlantic Ocean submarine cables from Ireland and England to the Americas.

Emma asked, "Can I bring this book to the Sketchers lab tomorrow? To learn perspectives, underwater."

I raised my eyes, *Yes. And my arm feels like putty.*

"Forget your arm, Annie," Emma scoffed. "Mr. Harrison's assistant is a friend of Lieutenant Edwards. While we were waiting, he said the Major and Mr. Harrison were impressed that you weren't afraid of the men in the room."

I shrugged my right shoulder.

"Mr. Harrison told him that you can figure anything out, and sometimes faster than he or the Major could."

I tapped, *Like what?*

"He didn't say."

I couldn't be sure but it was possible they knew that the Zimmermann Telegrams were not sent wirelessly. If so, perhaps they also knew what cable Zimmermann used to send his top-secret cypher telegrams. I found the comments of Harrison's assistant instructional for two reasons. First, his comments, albeit wonderful for me, should have never been mentioned to my sister. Second, his offhand compliment suggested my questions were reasonable to ask. And perhaps that I was on the right path and could eventually figure out what cable those messages were intercepted on. Although where Zimmermann's telegrams were intercepted was another story.

I was relieved when Emma changed the subject and asked about Clark.

"Did he really ask you on a date?"

I raised my eyes, *Yes*.

"Are you going?"

At the firing range, Clark whispered that the Major had made reservations for us at the Cosmos Club.

"Oh!" Emma said, somewhat shocked. "It ain't gonna be a Block Island date on the beach."

The Cosmos Club is formal. I can hardly contain myself.

"You've only dated one person, Geo's assistant, right?"

Yes, only Milton.

"I gather Clarkie has had many dates," Emma said. "I still think you should *not* date him."

At my meeting with Mr. Harrison and the Major I asked if I could develop a relationship with Clark.

This surprised Emma. "What did they say?"

I should not develop a relationship ... but could go on a date. If I decided to go with Clark, the Major suggested the Cosmos Club, as a safe place.

Emma raised her eyes in surprise and stared at me.

I gave Emma my hand signal for, *I-want-to-try-on* ... then tapped, *my red puffy dress.*

My sister begrudgingly retrieved my wool dress from the hanging closet. I leaned forward as she slipped it over my head and helped me navigate my arms through the sleeves. She then pulled the dress under me, to below my knees.

Emma couldn't help but smile. "You'll look great, and you might as well use the blush Lillie gave us."

I raised my eyes, then stared at my legs.

Emma was dumbfounded, then asked, "Are you serious?"

Yes, unbutton the side leg, please.

"You want to show some of your leg?"

I raised my eyes, *Yes*.

Emma snorted. "Did you ask your bosses about that, too?"

I ignored her last comment. Emma leaned over and unbuttoned two buttons on the right side.

"When you cross your legs, your good leg will show. Are you planning to show your cleavage, too?" Emma asked, shaking her head.

He's picking me up at 5 PM on Saturday.

"How's he picking you up?"

I gave my hand signal for a horse.

"A horse?" Emma raised her voice. "Who do you think you are, Eleanor of Aquitaine?"

A horse carriage!

"Oh, a horse-drawn carriage." Emma tried but could not contain a laugh.

*

The next morning I discreetly checked the Telegraph Machine for Mexico City bound cypher messages. Finding none, I asked the Major if I could practice shooting at the firing range. To increase my odds of passing the proficiency test I was willing to forgo an opportunity to identify the enemy spy. Royal Weller heard my tapping and asked if he could accompany me. The Major agreed, but only after the morning's intensive deciphering session.

At 11:00, Weller and I left together to secure a ride to the Naval Yard. While waiting at the base of the granite steps, Lt. Edwards called out. He jogged down the steps and joined us.

By the time we located Lieutenant Leheey and set up in the firing range it was noon. Weller and I were issued Colt 1908s and Lt. Edwards a Colt .45. For the next few hours we fired dozens of rounds, until the instructor cut us off for using too much ammunition. My right arm and shoulder thought it was a great idea. Surprisingly, neither Weller or Edwards complained.

*

That night, sleep eluded me because of pain on my right side. Emma rubbed my arm for a while hoping it would help, but she fell asleep before me. We slept late and were woken by Miss Sarah's knocking. She brought breakfast, sat with us, and gave us a housekeeper's perspective on surveillance. Confirming that she'd long been acquainted with Mrs. Lynch.

"Occasionally, I observe guests from other countries," she said. "Usually, it's a businessman from overseas."

I tapped, *Who is your contact?*

"I'm not at liberty to say, but he's Navy."

Sorry, I should know better than to ask.

She put a hand on my knee. "It's okay. Last year I saw photographs of an industrial section of the Philadelphia Naval Yard lying on a pillow. I reported that."

"What happened to the foreigner?" Emma asked.

"I don't know, but if I did know, it would be classified." Miss Sarah said, lifting an eyebrow as if Emma should also have known better to ask.

"My contact gave me the heads-up you were booked here. Seeing you, Emma, was quite a surprise."

"We thought Irving had asked you to care for us," Emma said.

"I self-assigned. Another person in the kitchen does the same. We do informal 'espionage on the ground' and although it's piecemeal, it's important. Annie, if you decide to do this when you're older, you'd be successful. Who'd suspect a disabled woman in a wheelchair is one of our spies on the ground?"

Miss Sarah helped me finish breakfast and I wondered if she had seen the photograph Emma had seen in Miss Muriel's room. I didn't want to ask.

"Annie has a date at the Cosmos Club with one of her colleagues," Emma blurted out.

"When is it, Annie?"

Tonight. I smiled, and turned a shade of red.

Miss Sarah was discreet, smiled back, but did not ask questions. "Well, have a good time, Annie," and shortly thereafter walked out with the trays.

*

Saturday's focus was my date, and we stayed in the room. Except, at noon, Emma went looking for Miss Sarah's "friend" in the kitchen. She took the back stairwell and walked in the back door of the kitchen. Emma had interacted with her before, but wanted to make sure it was who she thought it was. It was a busy kitchen, but sure enough, after spotting Emma, she walked right up to her.

"Do you need anything, Emma?" she asked, right away.

"Do you have lunch I can bring back to the room?"

"I sure do. I'll be right back."

Emma returned with enough food for two days. "Yes, that was the woman I thought it was. She's always working."

She placed the food on the desk and handed me a bowl of mashed potatoes.

"I think you'd be good at 'espionage on the ground'. I couldn't do it, but you could. You're not afraid of anything. I'm so cautious," Emma confessed.

I tapped, *You were not cautious entering Miss Muriel's room!*

"The door popped open as if it was meant to be, Annie!" Emma insisted. "You are naturally observant, it's like you have uncanny observation skills."

You and I share one skill.

"What's that?"

Geo calls it "the skill of working hard". Mom has it, too.

"Mom does have it. Remember when she was running the Union House and the private school at the hotel and was the Post Mistress for Block Island?"

I nodded in agreement.

*

The day flew by and at 4:45 PM we took the back elevator to the lobby. We were surprised to see Miss Sarah sitting on the big couch. Emma sat down beside her, and we waited together.

Clark was punctual. He pulled up sitting in the passenger seat of a large horse-drawn carriage. The three of us watched him hop off and bound inside, as if it was one easy motion.

"Oh, Annie, you are so beautiful in your red dress." Clark gazed at me with a look of awe.

Thank you!

He took an exaggerated bow in front of me, gestured out to 14th Street, and said, "Your carriage awaits, my dear."

I raised both eyes.

He took command of the wheelchair and pushed me outside. Emma and Miss Sarah followed. At the curb Clark lifted me with both arms and transferred me to the forward-facing rear carriage seat, then deftly placed the wheelchair on its side in the front next to the driver. I couldn't help but notice the driver's baffled look.

"I'll bring her back early," Clark said, continuing his exaggerated gentlemanly performance, then took his seat beside me. The carriage did a U-turn as Clark instructed the driver to circle around the White House before dropping us off at the Cosmos Club.

Clark placed his arm around me, for stability, which allowed me to turn and see Miss Sarah and Emma wave goodbye. I was pleased my sister behaved. She later said she pictured me sailing off on a ferry, and was thinking of Block Island, not Clark.

38

ANNIE

It had been an eventful week. Being a young woman at the Army War College and the challenges posed by the training was extremely difficult, but an opportunity I was most grateful for – despite the antagonism of certain men. But making slow progress on my secret mission was weighing on me. Determining Miss Muriel's intentions also remained a mystery, but at least the Major, Mr. Harrison, and Ross Whytock were aware. Did Miss Muriel pose a risk to me or my sister? And the proficiency test that I had yet to pass. Could I safely handle a pistol? And, more importantly, would I be able to fire it quickly if need be? Through it all there was Mrs. Lynch. She was more than a supervisor, guiding and caring for our well-being, and had, of course, arranged Emma's assignment at the Sketcher's lab.

I thought about all of this as the horse drawn carriage carried Clark and me to dinner at the elegant setting of the Cosmos Club.

The Cosmos Club was a private social club on 15th Street across from Lafayette Square. It consists of two buildings, the original Dolley Madison House and a new, attached adjacent five-story building. Located in the "The President's Neighborhood", it was one very long block from the entrance to the White House. It was also three very long blocks to the Hamilton, but in the opposite direction. Modelled on the famous Century Association of New York City, it admitted leaders in the sciences, military explorers, artists, writers, poets, and novelists. Because men devoted to government and officers in the military are eligible for membership, I wondered if I'd see ONI officers at dinner.

As a member, Major Van Deman was able to grant a dinner reservation to a non-member. He informed Clark that guests cannot use the main entrance and must enter through a side door. Even wives of club members were required to use that entrance. There is no doubt in my mind that the women of Block Island would never tolerate such a rule.

The carriage driver drove past the Cosmos Club and around the White House grounds before heading back to the Club. He stopped on H Street across from the Episcopal Church. He lowered the wheelchair to the ground and watched Clark lift me into it, in as graceful a manner as possible. His pride of being comfortable with me, treating me as a gentleman would, was written on Clark's face. I appreciated his kindness and wanted him to be interested in me, rather than the experience of being with someone like me.

A guard stood at the guest entrance checking identification. The Major's guest pass allowed us entry. On the back it read: "Please admit Clark Holder and his guest, Annie Rose, for dinner." It was signed and dated.

The guard looked at me and smiled, but turned serious when he asked, "Do you have more identification, Mr. Holder?"

Clark reached into his pocket, again, and brought out a military ID. The guard checked a list of expected guests, appeared satisfied, and stepped aside to let us in.

Once inside, another guard in plain clothes asked if we wanted a tour. We said, yes, and were guided through different rooms of Dolley Madison's original house. Her portrait hung over a magnificent marble fireplace. We then followed the guard to the new building. The walls of every elaborate wood paneled room were adorned with photos and accomplishments of the club's members. It was a half hour before we were seated at a cozy, candle-lit table in the main dining room. Many were already seated. Conversation was quiet and respectful, not library-like, but close.

Dinner of vegetables, soft sweet potatoes, and fish was served on large Cosmos Club oval plates. The club's blue emblem, a globe with wings in the center, was on top, and the words "Cosmos Club" and "Washington, DC, 1878" were embossed in the circular border surrounding the image.

From time-to-time Clark discreetly leaned over and cut my dinner into manageable pieces. He was vigilant about my needs, and when he assisted me, none of the other diners seemed to pay us any attention. I ate slowly, not wanting the evening to end.

"Annie, what do you find most interesting in the training?"

I looked into his eyes, something I had never done during training, and tapped softly on the linen tablecloth, *To learn as much as I can.*

"You ask questions about Room 40. Are you suspicious of them?" He stopped eating and waited for an answer.

I noticed his eyes were trained on my right hand tapping. I gave long answers to his questions, *I am very interested in negative intelligence and very much enjoy the challenge of figuring things out.*

"How do you do that?"

I try to figure out why things occur, and the context of any event. It's important to understand the context as well as the underlying actions.

"It's definitely a challenge figuring out Room 40." Clark raised his eyes.

Why are you interested in industrial security?

"To prevent sabotage at plants."

I understand next week another ONI officer will join the group. He's been recruited to focus on plant security.

"ONI or MIS?"

ONI.

Clark remained attentive throughout the meal and did not ask about Room 40 again. He looked me in the eyes sparingly. He did not appear uncomfortable.

"After dinner I'll take you to a small sitting room in the new building. There's a tall grandfather clock in it, and we can be alone."

When we left the table I turned around, and before leaving the room, out of the corner of my eye, I thought I noticed Ross Whytock. He was sitting with a friend on the other side of the room. I said nothing to Clark.

How did you find out about this room?

"I can't share secrets."

Did the Major tell you?

Clark smiled.

I sat on the leather sofa and supported myself against the sofa's oversized solid cushioned arm. Clark sat adjacent in a high-backed leather chair. We marveled at the carved cabinet of the grandfather clock, the wall of solid oak paneling, and the members' portraits. But we mostly looked at each other, said little, but didn't have to.

I wanted him to lean over and kiss me, but couldn't get the Major out of my mind. Or Emma's attitude toward this date. Nevertheless, I hoped he would take the initiative.

Finally, he looked in my eyes, leaned over the arm of the sofa and pulled me gently toward him. Then we kissed.

"That was nice," he said.

I smiled. I'd only been kissed a few times before and this, I liked a lot.

"Am I being too forward?"

Try it again and I'll let you know.

He kissed me again, this time, a little longer. I reached up with my right hand and ran my fingers through his hair. And then he pulled me to him.

After gaining my composure, I asked him to compare living in New York City and London, and then sat quietly until the grandfather clock struck nine.

"It is late, and I should get you back." Clark was genuinely concerned.

Thank you for the evening.

As we walked out, the guard who had greeted us earlier, asked Clark to say hello to Major Van Deman.

Once outside we didn't see a carriage or a motor taxi.

"Annie," Clark said, looking left and right, "I'm thinking there may not be carriage service this late. Would it be okay if I pushed you back to the hotel?"

I, too could see there were no carriages. I tapped, *Okay. It should be a lovely stroll.*

"It's mild out, and the Hamilton is only a few blocks."

I raised my right hand and gave the hand signal for okay. Truthfully, I was excited to extend the evening a few more minutes.

To avoid the uneven, gravel walkway, Clark pushed the wheelchair toward the paved street, and began to whistle his favorite tune, "Ode to Joy." To my left, down a ways on 15th Street, I noticed a parked car in the shadows of the streetlights. It appeared to be about thirty yards away, and I don't know if Clark saw it. There was no other traffic as he pushed me forward. When we were ten feet from the curb, I noticed the car had started to move forward, without the headlights on. Then, suddenly, it began to weave erratically.

I Morsed hard on my wheelchair to warn Clark, but he was whistling and didn't hear my tapping. I presumed the driver must be drunk.

When we reached the pavement Clark was still whistling, and the car was about twenty yards away. Just as he eased me into the street, the headlights came on and the car suddenly veered toward us. Clark yelled out as the headlights blinded both of us and I realized the driver was going to hit the wheelchair. I felt Clark lose control of the wheelchair.

As I've done many times, I instinctively threw my body weight to the right, while holding tight to the right wheel as best I could, to spin away. I deliberately tipped the wheelchair over, hit the pavement, and quickly rolled to my right, out of the wheelchair and out of harm's way. The car missed me by inches and kept going, its tires screeching as it rounded the nearby corner onto H Street. The wheelchair was hit and pushed up against me as I lay on the ground.

Clark had tripped and fallen backwards. I noticed immediately that my arm was bruised, and my red puffy dress torn. I had no idea I had bruises all over or that my face was covered in dirt. I did not feel the wound on my head or the bleeding into my hair.

"Are you okay, Annie? Are you okay?" Clark beseeched, quite shaken as he scrambled to his feet.

Annie looked up, twice.

"Oh, my God," Clark exclaimed. "Your dress is torn, the sleeve is ripped. And there's blood in your hair."

I tapped, *My arm doesn't hurt.*

He righted the wheelchair, lifted me, and then held me tight, all the while apologizing as if it was his fault. "I should've pulled you back, but it happened so quickly."

It's okay. But hold me.

Clark held me in his arms for a minute and then placed me into the wheelchair. He started to push, but I held up my hand. I needed a moment to myself, thinking about the training and my mission, I tapped, *Please, Clark, do not tell anyone about this.*

"Why not?" he asked, confusion in his eyes.

If the Major thinks I'm in danger, he'll take me out of the training for my safety.

"Danger? What do you mean?" He stared at me in disbelief.

Maybe it was what it looked like. A drunk driver. Or maybe he was aiming for me.

"Why would someone aim for you?" Clark asked, taken aback.

I hesitated, wondering if I should tell him. If I did, I might learn more about him from his comments. I decided it was the right thing to do and tapped, *I am pretty sure there is an enemy spy in the training group, and I think I know who it is. But I need more time to prove it.*

Clark looked shocked. "Who?"

Cannot say until I have positive proof. But we can rule out the "good guys".

"The men who have befriended you?"

I raised my eyes.

"That leaves Johnston, Whytock, possibly Yardley."

I tapped, *Let's get back to the hotel.*

*

At the Hamilton, a startled bellhop saw the dried blood on my face and in my hair and my torn dress. He ran up as we opened the front doors, then went to call Miss Sarah.

39

EMMA

I waited patiently in our room for Annie to return from the Cosmos Club. To pass the time I wrote a letter to Lillie on official Hamilton Hotel stationary, about working with the Sketchers. I did not mention Annie's date, or my disapproval. I picked up dinner from the kitchen before it could be delivered and ate it with the door locked. I dozed early. At 10 PM came two loud knocks.

I startled, and yelled, "Annie is that you?"

"Emma?" Miss Sarah called out, trying to open the door.

I jumped off the bed and unlocked it. All I could do was gasp. Before I could say a word Annie used a hand signal: *I'm okay.*

"You don't look okay. What happened?" I started shaking.

"She's okay, Emma. Don't worry," Miss Sarah said in a calm voice.

"Don't worry?" I practically shouted. "There's dried blood all over, and on her head!"

Annie repeated her hand signals.

"Annie, why is your arm bruised? And your dress is torn, too," I demanded to know.

"Help me get her washed up, Emma." Miss Sarah strived to remain calm.

Annie finally tapped, *Please calm down. I'll explain.*

I was shaking. "I can't believe my eyes."

Her beautiful dress torn, her hair tangled with dried blood, and I could see a large bruise on the upper arm where the dress had been ripped.

"Did Clark do this?" I was angry. My sister's bright eyes and smile were gone.

Annie tapped slowly, *No, not Clark. I'll tell you later.*

"Let me wipe the dried blood from your head and face," Miss Sarah said.

"Annie, I can't settle down." My hands shook too much to be helpful.

Miss Sarah finished wiping the blood, and ten minutes later Annie's hair was untangled. She pointed and said, "Leave the dress on the chair, and I'll have it cleaned and sewed in the morning."

Annie gave a hand signal, *Thank you.*

Miss Sarah closed the door behind her. She left with a more worried look than when she entered.

"When did you get back to the hotel?" I asked.

Annie tapped, *About 9:30 PM.*

"You were in the lobby for a half hour?!"

Annie explained, *When we entered the lobby, a bellhop saw that I was disheveled. He wanted to call a doctor. Clark said no, so then he called the manager. When the manager didn't respond I asked the bellhop to summon Miss Sarah.*

"Where was Miss Sarah?"

Upstairs. When she came to the lobby Clark explained that I looked worse than I felt.

"Did she come right down?"

Annie raised her eyes, twice. *Clark was beside himself as he explained what happened. He apologized over and over. Miss Sarah listened and then assured Clark it wasn't his fault.*

"It had to be his fault!" I insisted.

Annie tapped, *No, Emma, it wasn't. Miss Sarah calmed Clark, and we said goodnight. Then she brought me to the room.*

"Look at my hands. They're shaking and I can't keep my tears back."

I'm okay Emma.

It took almost an hour to bath her and then I helped her to bed.

"Now, tell me what happened."

My hip hurts. Can't it wait till morning?

"Are you kidding me?"

It took Annie twenty minutes to Morse the evening's events. Everything was fine until the end. I cried.

"Annie, you were almost killed, and I couldn't live without you."

Please don't cry.

"There's no way you can comfort me." Tears streamed down my face.

Emma, you're upsetting me.

"Okay." I stopped sobbing and sat in silence. I was never so happy to be with her. After a few minutes I started with more questions.

"Who else knew about your date?"

Everyone knew. A few days ago, during a break, Clark and the Major were talking about the Cosmos Club.

"A drunk driver, or not, it's still Clark's fault. He should've pulled you back off the street!"

Annie tapped, *It's possible it was a drunk driver, and that was what it looked like.*

40

Sunday, Second Week

ANNIE

At 10:00 AM I woke to the loud rumbling of a truck speeding up 14th Street. Before fully awake, I envisioned the Ugly Tug at full throttle entering Block Island Sound from the Great Salt Pond and was transported back to my Island home. Emma was still sound asleep, curled up around her pillow. I watched her shallow breathing, as I had a million times before, and realized that our accident at sea had been far more terrifying than last night's ordeal. These injuries will heal, and I'll be no worse for the wear.

As we made sense of our accident at sea, I had to do the same for last night, and, at the same time, narrow down who was the enemy spy.

We still hadn't determined the motives and true identity of Miss Muriel. It appears she is associated in some way with the German Embassy, but is she involved with the training group? Perhaps with the Major and Mr. Harrison not interfering with my dinner date it suggests they may have identified the enemy spy. But it has crossed my mind that perhaps there isn't a spy after all.

I transferred from the bed to my wheelchair. I was glad Emma was still asleep so that she would not see me grimace in pain. This morning, a large hematoma had developed on my right hip. It was not swollen last evening. Now it was hard to the touch and painful when I pressed on it with my right hand. I transferred slowly back to the comfort of the hotel bed.

It did not seem likely that Clark was the spy, based on his reaction to my near-miss last night. Perhaps it was Johnston or Weller. Johnston, a brute, appeared to be a loner, without family, who jumped around from job to job, although he was reported to be a successful detective in the Bomb Squad. Weller was a different story. An intellectual, a lawyer, who speaks several languages, including fluent German, had signs of financial difficulties. He would not be a traitor in the "I want to sell out my country" sense, but a man in need of money, and a traitor for that reason.

My mind jumped to the firing range. Why did Lt. Edwards attend the special session with me and Weller? Edwards did not need practice. But, more worrisome, what if Weller didn't need the practice either? But who else should I be considering as the spy?

All I had were questions, and no answers. It was frustrating.

When Emma finally woke, she took one look at me, and tears filled her eyes. When she was alert, I tapped, *My sweet Emma, why are you upset? We've been through so much worse.*

For the remainder of Sunday, we stayed in the hotel room, with my sister leaving only to fetch food from her new "friend" in the kitchen.

Emma's most important concerns remained Miss Muriel's intentions, working with the Sketchers, and me of course.

She commented, "I don't like it that her room is two floors above ours."

If she becomes a problem the Major will find another temporary home for us.

"If we can't stay here, I'll feel houseless."

We're not lonely and we're meeting new people.

"I agree, and I feel at home at the Sketchers."

I'm glad.

"Charles Dickens calls good company, 'Capital Company'."

Was that in David Copperfield*?*

"No. It's from an essay he wrote experiencing houselessness. Before he wrote *Copperfield*."

Capital Company. I like it. We're Capital Sisters!

Sunday night we found sleep faster than I thought possible. When I awoke, my first thought was how proud I was to be starting my second week of training.

I tapped on the headboard, *Emma, wake up.*

Her face crinkled as she smiled in the middle of a yawn. "I'm sure my day at the Sketchers lab will be fun." After a long pause, "Annie, should we have called Lillie about Saturday night?"

No. Did we call home after we almost died at sea?

"No, but there was a good reason – we were almost dead."

Neither of us could contain our uncontrolled laughter. The first we'd had since leaving home. We were convinced we were heard down the hall and into the lobby. I put on a long-sleeved, ankle-length dress to cover my arms and legs. Fully dressed, I doubted anyone could tell I'd had a bad fall, and I didn't think my sore arm would affect my ability to shoot a Colt 1908. I was, however, concerned Mrs. Lynch might observe something was off, and ask what was wrong.

Emma wanted to attend today's morning session, and would report later to the Sketchers lab. She carried Maury's reference book proudly.

When Mrs. Lynch arrived, I wasn't surprised when Emma asked her if she could sit in for a short time.

"Not today, Emma. It's another special session," Mrs. Lynch said, using her formal military voice. "Commander McCauley is presenting, and no guests are allowed."

"Armed guards at the doors?"

"No. Only Dansey requires guards."

In the car, Emma placed her arm around my lower back to minimize motion at the hips, to prevent the slightest grimace. Thankfully, no greeting party waited for us at the steps. Emma transferred me to the wheelchair and pulled me up to the front entrance. In the lobby, Sergeant Lightfoot came right over. He congratulated Emma about her new assignment with the Sketchers but repeated that she would not be allowed upstairs. He offered to take me to the fifth floor. Emma thanked him and headed off to work.

Through the open doors I saw the Major and Commander McCauley standing at the blackboard. It was impossible to miss the Commander, in full-dress uniform, his buttons reflecting overhead lighting. On the board was a chart with various entries in two columns.

A few minutes later, Mr. Harrison entered and stood against the far wall. He gave me a welcoming nod. Lt. Gordon arrived and cheerfully said hello. Then Clark came over. He was chatty in a nervous way. He thought the Commander would discuss Zimmermann's telegrams and the effect they had on President Wilson. He believed Wilson's neutrality platform was the reason he won reelection. When Lt. Gordon walked back to the Telegraph Machine, Clark stopped his commentary and whispered, "I hope you're okay. I'm sorry."

I raised my eyes, *Yes*, and tapped, *I'm okay.*

Clark returned to his seat when Lt. Edwards took his seat.

I tapped, *Good morning.*

Good morning, Annie, Lt. Edwards tapped.

What's the chart for?

Lt. Edwards whispered, "Those are Zimmermann's telegrams, but as far as we know only two were delivered to the President of Mexico. Recently, ONI agents on the ground in Mexico City discovered No. 11 was sent from Berlin on February 5."

The Zimmermann Telegrams

January 16th	*No. 158*
January 17th	*No. 157*
February 5th	*No. 11*

February 22nd	*Hall / Page / Thurstan*

No. 11 is new information. What does it say, and what is below the line?

"I'm not sure. I found out from the Commander on Saturday. The February 22 discussion between Hall and Page, as well as No. 11 are classified. Where's your sister?"

Emma reported directly to the Sketchers. Why is the name "Eddie Bell" written below the chart?

"Eddie's been a diplomat in our London Embassy for several years. Not sure why that asterisk is next to his name. Edward Thurstan is in London and is a diplomat for the Brits; he's attached to the SIS."

I memorized the chart, then surveyed the room. Yardley had not arrived, although his sidekick, Byer, was present and staring at me from across the table. I looked at the Telegraph Machine and wondered if I'd have time to check for messages. At the front of the room Commander McCauley had taken a seat in the oversized chair. The Major was standing with Major Dansey. All three appeared to be in a good mood.

At 8 AM the Major centered himself behind the podium and everyone found their seats. As usual Major Van Deman was punctual, but all eyes were on Commander McCauley.

The Major cleared his throat and began, "Today's exercise will be led by the Commander, our country's highest ranking intelligence officer. Last week we stressed that secret messages sent during war are often meant to confuse, manipulate, or deceive. They can also be nonsense messages. But most often they have a negative intelligence purpose and are directed toward an enemy.

"As you all know, Arthur Zimmermann is the Foreign Minister of Imperial Germany. The chart on the board lists the dates of three telegrams that he transmitted from Berlin to Venustiano Carranza, the President of Mexico. You partially deciphered No. 158 and are aware of No. 157. You're also aware that on March 1 the partial contents of No. 158 were made public. In almost every newspaper in the world the two-word phrase, 'Zimmermann Letter', was printed in bold type.

"There are mysteries about the telegrams. We've touched on a few already. In what code were they transmitted? How were they transmitted? Or what route did they 'travel' to reach the President of Mexico? How were they intercepted? Who intercepted them? Who deciphered them? Where were they intercepted? And lastly, what is the Zimmermann Telegram No. 11?

"The Commander will explore these questions solely from an intelligence exercise perspective, and that's why this is a closed session. A few members of the group are drawn to inconsistencies, and we thought, including Major Dansey, that a quick look at the process is warranted. Last week I discussed the essential importance of knowing context, and although we will not address political policy, we must recognize that the mystery surrounding Zimmermann's telegrams could be a direct consequence of political policy or concerns.

"The first requires an understanding of the imperial intentions of Germany, which is the basis for the war itself. Second, we must understand the desperate situation in Great Britain, and that they need our help. Third, many industrialists and members of intelligence communities, here and in Great Britain, are long frustrated with Wilson's commitment to neutrality. It pains him to declare war, as it should, but perhaps a declaration of war after his reelection would have been reasonable.

"As you know, telegram No. 158 went from Berlin to the German Ambassador's office in Washington, DC. It was then forwarded to the German Ambassador in Mexico City. We now know it was up to him, *"when instructed to do so",* to hand-deliver the fully decrypted message to the President of Mexico."

Was it possible that if a few members of the group, including me, had not questioned inconsistencies of SIS's explanations, that this lecture would not have been arranged? Were the intelligence agencies searching for answers? Or was it members of the training group? A complicated and contentious session was likely.

But I couldn't let this distract me from my mission. Whytock mentioned the concept of double agents during a group discussion on the first day of meetings, and it is reasonable to assume that the enemy spy, if there is one, is being groomed for that role. Our State Department rescinded Bernstorff's passport, and shortly he will be on his way back to Germany. Local Jersey City newspapers published a photo of him arriving in Hoboken. My mind continued to return to Miss Muriel's motives. I want to ask Whytock to have lunch for a few reasons, including why he was at the Cosmos Club Saturday night.

"And another reminder," Van Deman said, "we know that telegrams No. 157 and No. 158 were sent in a single 1000 coded group encrypted telegraph. Last week you proved that they could not have been sent via wireless, as Page was told by Hall."

The Major nodded to Commander McCauley and took his seat.

The Commander looked impressive in his white uniform. Everyone must have thought the same, the "audience" was uncharacteristically subdued. Or they expected a contentious session, too.

I had a good look at the black shoulder marks on Commander McCauley's white jacket. These designated his rank. And the two rows of colorful service ribbons above his right chest pocket, as well as the seven medals that hung from his left pocket, signified his accomplishments. Two of the medals rattled when he walked to the podium, but when he stood, the medals silenced themselves, as did the class. He spoke in a calm voice and was as serious as anyone I've seen.

"Good morning," the Commander opened, then got right into it, "There is one fact about the Zimmermann cypher telegrams that is irrefutable. In the annals of history, they will not be forgotten, of that, I am certain.

"We'll start by connecting the first date on the chart, January 16, with the last date on the chart, March 1. According to Room 40, No. 158 was sent January 16 via wireless to the German Ambassador in DC. And then Bernstorff sent it to the German Ambassador in Mexico City. This was Heinrich von Eckardt, whose formal title was Resident Minister of the German Empire in Mexico City. He is one of Germany's accomplished diplomats.

"Without belaboring the point, Eckardt's office was responsible, when the time came, to hand-deliver messages to the President of Mexico."

Van Deman interjected, "The reason they are hand-delivered is because there was no other way for President Carranza to receive confidential messages."

"Thank you, Major," the Commander acknowledged. "On March 1 the telegram and the story accompanying it were leaked to the press. Astonishingly, it remained in the headlines of every major newspaper throughout the world for weeks on end."

Commander McCauley reached into his pocket and unfolded the front page of the March 1 *Washington Evening Star* and showed everyone its headline. He said nothing as he returned it to his pocket and looked around the room.

"There are strange things about this episode. I was surprised to wake up one morning to find the Brits publicly gave credit to the Office of Naval Intelligence for intercepting and deciphering No. 158."

He looked at Major Dansey standing against the wall. "Claude, any comment?"

Dansey looked up. "I was out of the country, I'm not sure what happened."

"I can assure everyone," the Commander continued, "that the ONI had nothing to do with it. Intercepting and deciphering them was solely the result of the extraordinary espionage efforts of the SIS's Room 40. We can take no credit, but we understand they need to hide sources and processes."

Claude Dansey stepped forward, "We do what every intelligence service does."

Given the strange and legitimate events unfolding, this lecture, the enemy spy in the room, and Emma's fear that she no longer feels safe at the Hamilton Hotel, I began to wonder if our personal safety and national security are linked. But my job was to identify the spy, and repeatedly reminded myself of John's advice: "Observe members of the group when they are preoccupied, focused on an interesting topic, or when commotion is occurring."

"I will not cover, again," the Commander repeated, "what code the telegrams were transmitted in. I do agree with Annie Rose that the German's newer new code was used to transmit the message from Berlin to the German Embassy in DC. Cryptologists deciphered the code, encrypted it into the older German code, and then sent that message to von Eckert in Mexico City. No need to consider wireless."

He looked around the room. Dansey was preparing to speak but held back, gathering his thoughts. What was Commander McCauley leading up to? And why wasn't Yardley in attendance?

Major Van Deman interjected a question. "Claude, any explanation why it took six weeks to let our Ambassador in London know about No. 158?"

"I understand Blinker Hall made that clear in his discussion with

Ambassador Page."

"Yes, I understand the same, but I also understand that when Page pressed him ... Hall answered, 'That's not your concern.'"

"I cannot address that issue. Again, I was out of the country," Dansey emphasized.

This was the second time Dansey asserted that he knew nothing because he was out of the country. I wondered, what country was he referring? Great Britain, the United States, or both?

"Okay, fair enough. Let's look at No. 11," the Commander said.

Dansey took a few steps forward. "What is No. 11? I've never heard of that. Does it even exist?"

"Yes, Claude, it exists. Perhaps you were out of the country."

Everyone laughed, especially Edwards and Whytock. Dansey, uncharacteristically, was also unable to suppress his laughter. But I thought he was brilliant, because his laughter distracted the Commander, and he let it go.

"Understanding *this* Zimmermann Telegram opens questions that may help answer the other questions. Here's a handout of the deciphered text of No. 11. The first important distinction between No. 158 and No. 11 is that No. 11 gives permission to the Ambassador in Mexico City to hand-deliver it to the President of Mexico."

Commander McCauley slowly scanned the room, then reiterated, "No. 11 finally gives permission to give it to President Carranza and Von Eckart hand-delivers it."

Johnston called out, "Are you saying 158 was never delivered?"

"Correct." McCauley said. "We've had agents on the ground in Mexico City for years and have infiltrated the President's office on and off. Let's look at No. 11 that was recently obtained by one of our ONI agents in Mexico City, before it was decrypted."

Dansey, in an understated manner, asked, "Assuming that No. 11 is not a fake, which I suspect it is, what code was it sent in?"

"The copy we obtained is in the usual German code."

"Did I not say that Germany used only one code? And about this No. 11. Did you call Room 40 and ask Hall if he's aware of this telegram?"

"I called this past Saturday, but he said he'd have to get back to me.

This is all very confusing."

Dansey became uncharacteristically defensive, "If it's not confusing, it's not intelligence, and of course, if it isn't confusing, it certainly is not negative intelligence. Commander, Room 40 does use this approach in a conspiracy-like manner."

"Claude," the Commander responded, "your use of the term in this situation as a defense is only an attempt to deflect from the truth and hide underlying motives and methods. We would never use such an approach with Great Britain."

Lt. Edwards broke an awkward silence, "We're allies, but many in the United States support their homeland, Germany. That's understandable. Foreign interference to change perspectives is common. Our own Presidents have done the same thing in other countries."

I thought his statement was one of diplomacy, to be expected from a future leader in the State Department's intelligence service.

*

The class worked together and in less than an hour we completed the task. It was indeed in the old German code. The important text, besides ordering the Ambassador to deliver it, was easy to decipher. It didn't take long to determine No. 11 was slightly different than No. 158. The content was similar, but the context and tone were not. Johnston thought that No. 158 was a draft. I agreed. It was easy to conclude that Room 40's deciphered version of No. 158 misquoted, or omitted sentences. Weller mentioned how desperate Great Britain's citizens were, fearful of being taken over by the Prussians.

"I direct your attention back to the chart on the board," the Commander said. "On February 22 a pivotal meeting took place at Ambassador Walter Page's residence in London. As a reminder, Professor Ewing had been replaced as Head of Room 40 last year by Major Reginald Hall. Hall met with Page, divulged the contents of No. 158 as they had deciphered it, but made no mention of No. 11. On my recent phone call with him, he denied knowing that it existed.

"Hall assured Page that Eddie Bell, Ambassador Page's Third Secretary in our Embassy in London, was involved in deciphering a portion of No. 158. I didn't know Bell was a cryptologist. Nevertheless, Bell did say he helped decrypt it. I will confirm my suspicions when I meet with him in London in three weeks' time.

"And in Mr. Harrison's recent conversation with Ambassador Page … he learned that when Page asked Reginald Hall how Room 40 intercepted the message, Hall replied abruptly, 'That's not for you to know. What you need to do is, please, make sure the United States does something about it'."

Dansey interjected, "That was quite direct, and completely understandable, if you comprehend the context in which this was sent."

Clark raised his hand and asked a rare question, "But Zimmermann recently acknowledged that he *did* send No. 158?"

"Not really, Clark," the Commander said. "He acknowledged sending No. 11." He paused and looked around the room. "Zimmermann had no idea that No. 158 had been intercepted or knew that No. 158 was never delivered to the President of Mexico. He could not have been referring to No. 158. He was referring to No. 11. This is important to understand."

I tapped, *Commander, how did we obtain No. 11?*

"From our agents on the ground in Mexico City." The Commander looked at Dansey.

Dansey looked up. "I never heard of No. 11."

I believed that Dansey was being honest and had not heard of No. 11. Perhaps he was out of the country, but where was he?

As if on cue, General Kuhn walked in and summoned the Commander, Dansey, and Major Van Deman to a meeting on the third floor.

"We'll take a thirty-minute break," Major Van Deman announced.

Mr. Harrison signaled to the Major that he'd stay, but most attendees took a break and left the room. Except me, Lt. Edwards, and Whytock. Edwards and Whytock had developed a good relationship in a short period of time; it was a joy to hear them banter back and forth. Apparently, Mr. Harrison thought the same and pulled up a seat behind us. We turned around and formed a circle.

Mr. Harrison asked me if Emma was enjoying the Sketchers lab, and I raised my eyes. Mr. Harrison surprised me when he openly answered a confidential question by Lt. Edwards. I felt that I was a trusted member of the ONI. Edwards asked his former boss if Eddie Bell had overstepped his bounds at the Embassy.

Mr. Harrison answered vaguely but with a purpose, "If he was instructed to do so by State Department officials then it was okay. But if he did it on his own, that's a problem."

I interpreted his answer as a teaching point for Lt. Edwards.

Whytock asked, "Leland, can we share with Annie what we've found about Miss Muriel?"

Mr. Harrison nodded. "Yes, of course. Annie, I asked Ross to offer an opinion about the journalist from Nova Scotia. And to provide counsel on the obituary that her friend, Dalia, was mentioned in."

"Interesting woman and a more interesting obituary," Whytock said. "Annie, may I talk openly about Nicholas Ball?"

I raised my eyes.

"Nicholas Ball was a patriot, without question. He did much good for Block Island, as well as the United States. For example, he convinced President Grant to fund the building of the Southeast Lighthouse. I checked the minutes of the Lighthouse Board, and they mention the need for a lighthouse at that site, but would not approve the monies. It was too expensive."

I tapped, *Why?*

"Other land-based lighthouses were funded at the $12,000 level. The cost for the Southeast Lighthouse was enormous. Ball asked Grant to sponsor legislation to provide the money, which he did, at the $75,000 level. Grant also visited with Ball again, in 1875, to obtain funding from the State of Rhode Island to fund a submarine cable from the mainland to Block Island. That enabled the Island to have a Weather Station. This was because of the influence of Nicholas Ball."

I never knew the financial aspects of those stories. I know Grant and his family vacationed on the Island in 1869 and he returned again without his family in 1875.

Mr. Harrison asked, "Ross, what about Dalia?"

"I figured out a plausible explanation for Dalia's death. I've covered a lot of murders during my career as a journalist in NYC and in St. Louis, and I do not think it was a nefarious death. We don't have the time to talk now, but I will share more later."

"Ross, do you think she's a real journalist?" Mr. Harrison asked.

"Very possible," Ross thought for a moment. "Did she know Dalia? Probably. From her perspective it happened quickly. Someone must have alerted her that Annie and her sister were staying at the Hamilton."

"Do you think Miss Muriel was surprised Emma was with Annie?" Mr. Harrison asked.

"We're correct to be concerned about Emma and your safety." Ross sat back, worried.

I looked down until Mr. Harrison was about to take his leave.

I tapped quickly, *Mr. Harrison, before you leave, do you agree it's possible that the messages were not sent wirelessly?*

He nodded. "I'm impressed you realized that with such limited information. We have identified the cable that was used to send the messages, but that is top secret. Please, Annie, don't try to figure out which cable!"

We both laughed.

Harrison added, "President Wilson was shocked when Lansing and I informed him of which cable was used!"

Given the SIS hides everything, we should do the same.

"Have you made any progress on the enemy spy in the room?"

I was stunned Mr. Harrison asked the question with Lt. Edwards and Whytock present, but they did not flinch. That let me know that they were in on the concern.

I regained my composure, and tapped, *I have a few possibilities, but cannot narrow it down further.*

"Let's try to figure out what the spy will do tomorrow, and not focus on the past week. When the meeting resumes, ask the Major for permission to go to the firing range tomorrow. He knows you're worried about passing the proficiency test. Especially after your 'fall' on Saturday night."

I tapped, *You know about that.*

"The gentleman by the name of Ross sitting to your right was at the Cosmos having dinner Saturday. Did you not see him?"

I glanced at Mr. Whytock and smiled.

"I heard the noise and looked out the window," Ross said. "By the time I got to the front door you were in your chair. It looked like you were beat up but okay, and I watched from the doorway as Clark pushed you up the street. Crazy he chooses the street, but the walkway was a mess."

I sat back and took a deep breath. It was a relief that they knew.

"How's your arm?" Whytock asked. "And please, call me Ross."

I raised my eyes but said nothing.

Ross tapped slowly, *We're in dis togeter, Annie.*

I tapped right back, *Can't you spell?*

Laughter from everyone stirred interest from the men standing in the hall.

Mr. Harrison turned serious and sat back down. "Lieutenant Edwards, arrive to the Naval Yard before Annie, and talk to the instructor. Let's see who shows up."

We were still alone and able to continue our conversation. Mr. Harrison asked Ross to elaborate on miss Muriel and the dilemma of the obituary.

He pulled his chair closer and spoke in a whisper. Lt. Edwards and I responded using Morse Code, tapping on my armrest.

"It's been a pleasant diversion analyzing Miss M's behavior and actions," Whytock said.

Lt. Edwards asked, *Diversion from what?*

"My beat at the *Evening World* includes the crime stories of NYC. I also spend a lot of time on the docks, on both sides of the Hudson, trying to figure out German sabotage efforts."

Are you working with Guy Gaunt? Edwards tapped.

"Yes. My editor of the *World* and I meet with him regularly."

I thought Gaunt was a Naval Attaché here? Edwards tapped.

"He's been in NYC for the past year and a half," Lt. Gordon whispered.

I tapped, *Who is Gaunt*?

"The Brits Naval Attaché," Ross explained.

I tapped, *A colleague of Major Dansey?*

"Yes," Ross said.

I tapped, *They must have the same sources.*

Edwards tapped, *Meaning?*

I tapped, *The SIS and Room 40.*

"Annie, you connect the dots quickly. What else have you figured out?" Ross asked.

I smiled and tapped, *If you tell me how the editor of the Providence Journal gets his scoops, I'll tell you even more*.

At this point Mr. Harrison interrupted the conversation, "Ross, tell me about your thoughts on the obit."

Ross explained, "There's an explanation for Dalia's death, and to me it doesn't look like a crime. Here's why. In the decade of the 1890s, there was a great deal of discussion in major newspapers, to allow someone to die at the end of their life, if they didn't think they'd live long. If a person wants to die, that's okay. I read through much of the commentary on the subject, and suggest you read through it as well."

"Will do," said Mr. Harrison. "And what about this Miss M?"

"I think she's a journalist or was one. She must know about those columns, but surely doesn't agree with them. Perhaps it brought her to Nicholas Ball's obituary."

"Sounds plausible, Ross, but we still don't know her motives."

The other men started returning to the room and our conversation ended.

41

ANNIE

When the Commander returned to the room, I was still thinking about the conversation with Mr. Harrison. I startled when he asked me a direct question.

"Annie, do you have any comments or questions?"

I tapped at a high rate of speed, *I was thinking about the timeline. Perhaps we should add February 3 to the chart on the blackboard. On February 3 Wilson severed relations with Germany, and two days later on February 5 Zimmermann sends cypher telegram No. 11. I believe it was sent with a Top Secret/High Urgency Prelude. We did NOT see a Prelude on No. 158.*

Thinking about No. 11 it does clarify an important point that would have negated the possibility of any alliance between Germany and Mexico. Apparently, it was not present in No. 158.

"How so?" the Commander asked.

Zimmermann made clear that the alliance between Germany and Mexico could not occur until after a peaceful resolution of the Great European War. That assumes Germany would win. Who would agree to that? I think No. 158 was a draft and was meant as a heads up for the German Ambassador to America and von Eckart in Mexico.

I don't think anyone, including the Commander, expected that analysis and commentary.

The Commander continued. "My agent confirmed with the staff

working in Carranza's office that No. 158 was never delivered. No one remembered such a telegram. And your point about Zimmermann acknowledging he'd sent the telegram, but was referring to No. 11, not No. 158, is reasonable."

Dansey started talking and I realized right away that his sole purpose was to reflect the authority of the SIS, and Room 40. His orchestrated ten-minute discussion confirmed one thing: He was brilliant at creating distractions. When Dansey spoke of hypothetical agents on the ground in Mexico City, I got the impression that he knew the locals so well that I wondered if he'd been there in the not-so-distant past.

While he was talking, I wondered about Yardley. Where was he? Had he left Washington, DC? Had he found the enemy spy? I gazed at Royal Weller. He looked disinterested, and whether or not he was the spy, I could not imagine him long for this business. I preferred not to look at Johnston. But my key observation was that in Barnitz's presence Johnston's behavior was more pleasant. In his absence, which was frequent, he was back to being a henchman for Yardley. I also wondered why Johnston and Weller spoke infrequently.

The Commander returned to the narrative of the telegrams and focused on the sixth puzzling aspect the Major had introduced at the start of the session. The Commander referred to the chart on the board behind him and asked the class, purely as an exercise to understand espionage, why go to the trouble of painting a confusing picture regarding the Zimmermann Telegrams?

Numerous hands went up. Most thought the SIS had every right to do what they did. A few differed. A quick glance at Dansey confirmed he was content with the collective response. But I differed and wanted to make my opinion clear. This was an exercise, wasn't it?

I tapped, *On February 24 Colonel House and our State Department were handed a decrypted No. 158. They did not hand us No. 11. They are concealing sources, shielding the truth, which is good for them, but not us. Perhaps after the war we need to know how and where the messages were intercepted.*

Major Van Deman stood up. "Claude, do you have an answer for Annie Rose?"

Dansey shook his head but did not venture a rebuttal. I noted that he, uncharacteristically, looked at his feet.[9]

I scanned the room. Everyone, except Clark, was attentive. He was staring at me. I realized I'm a novice at reading faces and must develop that skill.

During a pause in the conversation, as instructed, I raised my right hand.

"Yes, Annie."

Tomorrow morning, may I report to the firing range, for practice? I was hoping I did not have to elaborate on my request.

"Are you able to handle a Colt .45?" Major Van Deman asked. He was standing against the side wall.

I tapped, *I was issued a Colt 1908. It's lighter and has magazine cartidges.*

"You spelled cartridges wrong, Annie," Ross blurted out.

Lt. Edwards could not contain his laugh. Everyone else looked on in amusement, assuming, and rightly so, that it was an inside joke.

Van Deman agreed with my request and nodded to the Commander to continue.

42

ANNIE

Dansey sat with me during a late afternoon break.

"You ask good questions, Annie. I'm not sure what's going on in London, but we need the U.S. involved. Or we'll all be Prussians. That's why I'm here, helping the Major."

I know, and I'm learning a lot, Mr. Dansey.

"You handle the arrogant men well. Their behavior hasn't changed but let's hope. It certainly reflects upon their character."

Thank you.

"I want to mention that the SIS, and Room 40 hires women, mostly as decoders. I know Ralph, and the ONI, tried to recruit Mrs. Smith. She would've been a brilliant mentor for you, but she's staying at Riverbank, outside of Chicago."

I nodded and raised my eyes. *Do you know her?*

"I've heard of her," he paused and looked directly at me. "Annie, keep your eye on the prize. A career in espionage, at any level, would be good for you. Focus on what's important and I'm sure you'll succeed."

Thank you. I will try.

Dansey walked up to the Commander, then left the room. He did not appear happy. I went to the telegraph to Morse a message to Geo. It was plugged in, but the time stamp was not accurate. I angled my chair hard against the door of the cabinet, and the pressure against it disengaged the lock. I reached in and pretended to change the roll. This did not attract anyone's attention because everyone knew that Emma and I clean the insides of these old telegraph machines. Well, to be accurate, no one would care, unless ... someone in the room did not want me reading sent messages. The exception was Johnston, but now, thanks to Barnitz, he no longer sent insulting messages about me to the Bomb Squad.

I grabbed two messages. The first had the code for Mexico City.

"Annie, what are you doing?" Byer asked indignantly. "I saw you open that door."

I raised my eyes, *Are you interested or did someone ask you to ask me?*

I did not answer his question, and he did not answer my question.

"What are you reading?"

I reached into the cabinet with my right hand and gave him the message that wasn't sent to Mexico City.

"I can't read this," he said.

I tapped, *You're in the Signal Service and can't read telegraph messages without a manual transmitter?*

"You can?"

I tapped very slowly, *Yes, of course. I've been doing it for years.*

He nodded but said nothing.

I asked again who asked him to talk to me.

"Someone at the table." He walked away and I tapped on the cabinet door loud enough for everyone to hear, *I can teach you if you want.*

Morsing is attitude-neutral unless one can grasp the context of the message. I would have taught Byer that, too, if he had so desired.

Overhearing my tapping brought the Commander to the Telegraph Machine. "We heard that, Annie," the Commander said with a grin. "What did you say to him?"

I smiled, and tapped, *I was being cordial.*

I handed the message sent to Mexico to Commander McCauley. He knew right away where it was sent, and after thirty seconds, handed it back. "This is a nonsense transmission. The person who sent it is now fully aware that you know."

That's helpful, right?

He nodded.

To change the subject I asked, *Germany has agents in Mexico City, too?*

"Yes, and in the same building as the Western Union office."

Who controls that Western Union Office?

"It's owned by Western Union, a U.S. company. But it looks like the British control it. I wouldn't be surprised if someone in this room was there recently."

Whoever it is, he's everywhere.

He nodded, then walked back to the podium to continue his lecture.

"Can you imagine the reaction if the public found out No. 158 was never delivered?" he asked the class. Claude is in the hall talking to General Kuhn, but I wanted to tell him that there's something about No. 11 that makes it much less threatening to the United States than 158."

Major Dansey must have heard his name and walked back into the conference room.

"I asked you before if you called Hall to discuss these findings." Dansey said. "It's possible your spies don't have accurate information."

"As I mentioned to you I called him Friday and asked if he was aware of No. 11. He said he'd get back to me. It's a good reminder that having operatives on the ground is important."

Dansey added, "If it's not confusing, it's not negative intelligence. And you know we use red flag operations in a conspiracy like manner."

An awkward silence was followed.

"Claude, your use of the term 'conspiracy or red flag operation' as a defense is only an attempt to deflect from the truth. And, while I'm at it, the SIS's measured tactics suggest it's the 'others' in the room that spread the falsehoods. That's all well and fine except when used against an ally. The ONI would never use a conspiracy theory retort against allies."

I raised my hand. The Commander nodded.

I tapped at great speed, *Is it true that those who use conspiracy theories project their innermost truths? And they use conspiracy theories to hide their motives?*

Dansey did not respond.

Before the Commander could respond Lt. Edwards spoke, "We're great allies with Great Britain, but we all know that throughout our country there's great support for Germany. Foreign interference changes the public's perceptions, and it is quite common. Our own presidents have used negative intelligence to change public opinion in other countries, too."

43

EMMA

Today's meeting with the Commander was top secret. The fifth floor was off limits, and I could not help my sister with lunch. At the Sketchers lab Mr. Lyle distributed sandwiches, and after I tossed a football with a few officers on the Parade Grounds. Then we played with Fritz. Dogs roamed Block Island, but Fritz was the best dog I've ever known. Big, beautiful, powerful, loving, and smart.

I glanced down the Parade Grounds to Roosevelt Hall and saw Mr. Harrison walk out of the building. I gave him a wave and he signaled me over. I ran as fast as I could and met him at the bottom of the steps.

"I can tell you're enjoying the Sketchers."

"I am Mr. Harrison," I said, trying to catch my breath.

He smiled. "I'm glad I saw you. First, Miss Muriel is no longer at the Hamilton."

"I haven't seen her this week," I acknowledged.

"If you see her, let us know right away. And for your future, I think you should attend college."

That took me by surprise. "I haven't thought I could."

"You can if you want," Mr. Harrison assured me. "If a career with the State Department interests you, graduating from college is a first step."

We spoke until his security guard arrived. They drove off campus and I ran back to my fellow Sketchers.

Ten minutes later, Mrs. Lynch drove up and waved me over. I ran right back across the Parade Grounds, for a third time. She said Annie had another late meeting, and she needed to head back to the War Department. "Can you leave the Sketchers lab early so I can drive you home now?"

I ran back and asked Mr. Lyle for permission, grabbed Maury's book, and ran back across the Parade Grounds for a fifth time.

"Mrs. Lynch," I said, trying to catch my breath, "I saw Mr. Harrison. He said I'd have to go to college if I want to work for State."

"Leland thinks highly of you," Mrs. Lynch said with assurance. "The Foreign Service has many different roles."

"I like being an observer, hidden or not."

There was no traffic, and we were at the War Department in no time. Mrs. Lynch dropped me off before she drove in the garage under the War Department building. I leaned over, gave her a hug, thanked her for the hundredth time for getting me the job at the Sketchers lab, and slid out the passenger door. I walked to the Hamilton from there.

After she disappeared into the garage, I bowed my head and said a David Copperfield prayer. I liked saying my prayers and can't figure out why Annie doesn't say them as much as I do.

I walked the perimeter of the White House grounds. In the front was a demonstration; women arguing for the right to vote. I looked carefully but did not identify any suffragettes from Block Island.

The architecture of the Executive Office building has always caught my attention. I stood staring, and a guard walked over and explained why it was built by President Grant. He suggested I walk through Lafayette Square on my way to the Hamilton. I walked diagonally through the park, and stopped at the statue of its namesake, the great Lafayette. When I emerged from Lafayette Square the Cosmos Club was one street to my right, on the corner of 15th Street and H Street. I stood motionless, staring at the visitor's entrance, trying to visualize what happened to Annie on Saturday night. The mere thought of my sister bloodied and bruised made me uncomfortable, and I ran to the Hamilton.

A bellhop mentioned Miss Sarah was off, and I knew Irving was still in Providence. Knowing that Miss Muriel was no longer at the Hamilton, I went straightaway to her room. The door was unlocked. No one had checked in.

A little after 7:30 PM, Sgt. Lightfoot dropped Annie off, and a bellhop brought her to our room. While she ate dinner, I shared that Mr. Lyle had approved my project, drawing an underwater three-dimensional map of submarine cables in the English Channel. Tracing how the Zimmermann Telegram may have gotten to DC.

Then I told her about Mr. Harrison.

Annie tapped, *What did he say?*

"He said Miss Muriel is no longer at the Hamilton. I checked her room and it's empty."

He's worried that she's not who she says she is.

"If we see her again, he wants to know."

What else?

"He said if I'm interested in the Foreign Service, I must graduate college."

We should both do that.

"Have you narrowed down the men?"

Annie raised her eyes. *Tomorrow morning I'm going to the Naval Yard firing range. More practice with the handgun. One of my suspects will be there, too.*

44

ANNIE

Emma was excited that Mr. Lyle approved her project. Perhaps she's right that a three-dimensional drawing of submarine cables in the English Channel might help conceptualize how messages travel from Berlin to DC. If the Sketchers' motto "visualizing by drawing" is helpful on the battlefield, why not in the war of undersea messages?

While Emma washed up, I reflected on the discussion that occurred just before the end of today's session. Dansey asked if our State Department had revoked Bernstorff's passport. The Major said yes, and that all eyes were on Germany's NYC Consulate, to see if anyone would replace him as Germany's Chief Espionage Officer in North America.

But then, in an abrupt manner, the Commander revisited a conversation from earlier.

"If Room 40 engages in negative intelligence against us, we all need to be aware of the consequences that that may have on our relationship with Great Britain. We know Room 40 tells us *truths*, but to do it selectively, especially if it's part of a strategy, is simply an abuse of our relationship. The ONI is in the business of exposing the truth among allies." He paused, but no one said anything. "I'm sure the director of the MIS feels the same way."

What I thought was a message for Dansey and the Major was really a message for the SIS. Lt. Edwards was right, it's best to look past this episode.

Emma startled me when she jumped in bed. She asked about my

bruises, then the spies. "Let's say the enemy spy is out of NYC. Who would be a prime suspect?"

I tapped, *Johnston was a Captain in the NYPD, and more recently a detective in the Bomb Squad. Barnitz was the second in command of the Bomb Squad. Byer lives in Brooklyn, and he talks about it all the time. Weller grew up and still lives in Manhattan. Clark's parents lived in London and NYC. And Whytock lives in NYC as well, but although he's a journalist, I am learning that he has worked closely with the NYPD for solving crimes on and around the docks of New York Harbor.*

"The same men, and it sounds like Whytock is much more than a journalist and explains why he was invited by Van Deman to join the MIS. But the question that I cannot answer, Annie, is how do the Zimmermann Telegrams relate to the spy?"

The disclosure of his telegrams in the press created angst in Germany. They believe that it was an intelligence success for the United States. Now, they want retaliation, even though they've already performed sabotage after sabotage in our country. That's where the spies come in. If Germany can place a spy or two in the MIS, what a coup that will be for them.

Emma, from the SIS perspective, although the telegrams have outlived their usefulness, they will create multiple distractions to make sure no one discovers how and where they were intercepted.

Emma grabbed her head with both hands. "This is too complicated. All I know is that I'll never forget No. 11 and No. 158."

In my mind, it starts as a three-dimensional puzzle using ideas that are not yet proven facts.

"And when they become facts, you understand everything. Right?"

I nodded.

"Was Yardley rude today?"

Yardley didn't show up. I wonder if he found the spy.

"What's on the agenda for tomorrow?"

I have permission to report to the firing range, and hopefully can narrow down who the spy might be.

"How?"

To see who accompanies me.

"What?" Emma gasped.

45

ANNIE

We found sleep at the same time, but Emma woke first. She nudged my shoulder.

I tapped, *It's 5 AM.*

"I know. I start my project today." Emma was immersed in Maury's book.

I was not amused and pulled the pillow over my head with my right hand.

On the ride to the AWC, Mrs. Lynch was greatly amused to see Emma clutch the reference manual to her chest *and* speak incessantly of underwater maps. At Roosevelt Hall she jumped out of the car and, with a flick of her wrist, waved us a quick goodbye and ran full speed to the Sketcher building.

Everyone on campus, whether they were standing on the granite steps, walking about the Parade Grounds, peering out a window, witnessed my sister running down the center of the Parade Grounds. Fritz was nowhere to be seen, or he'd have followed her.

Lt. Edwards saw Emma as well. He walked to the car to greet us. "What's up with your sister?"

"Mr. Lyle assigned Emma her first project," Mrs. Lynch said proudly.

"It must be one heck of a project, Mrs. Lynch," Lt. Edwards said. "Annie, you're going to the firing range, right?"

I raised my eyes, *Yes.*

"I need practice, too. Mrs. Lynch, mind if I ride with you?" he asked.

Mrs. Lynch agreed, and Edwards jumped in the back seat.

The Latrobe Gate was blocked when we arrived. Having completed the overnight shift, a throng of fifty men delayed our entry through the narrow gate. Once inside the Naval Yard, Lt. Edwards pushed me across the small courtyard and straight to the indoor firing range. The building was thirty feet from the banks of the Anacostia River.

Weller had arrived earlier. He had entered before the workers were dismissed and was talking to today's Officer in Charge, Colonel Sharp. He was not the instructor who had befriended me. He was an officer, a graduate of the Navy School for Small Arms. He waved us in. I was relieved that I did not sense any sign of hostility.

"Good morning, Annie. I've heard a lot about you. And Lieutenant Edwards, I wasn't expecting you."

"Good morning, sir. I'd like to practice on the .45 and the 1908. Would it be okay to share Royal's pistol."

"Of course," Weller said.

"Annie, I have your assigned Colt 1908, and after you attain proficiency, this will be yours," Colonel Sharp explained.

I tapped, *Thank you, Colonel.*

"Colonel Sharp, is it possible for the three of us to take the proficiency test later today?" Lt. Edwards asked.

"Let's see how it goes," he said cautiously.

After a twenty-minute discussion on cleaning handguns, Colonel Sharp demonstrated how to load a magazine into the Colt 1908. He used one hand, and I followed his direction loading it with my right hand. After ten minutes I had mastered it, using the side of the wheelchair for leverage. He looked over my shoulder until I could do it on my own, and quickly. The magazine for this Colt held eight bullets, and I learned to load the magazine as well.

"I'll give you a few extra magazines so you can preload them," Colonel Sharp said. "And I'll screw this to the wheelchair, to store the pistol along with extra magazines."

With three short screws he quickly attached a two-and-a-half-inch metal pocket to the inside right panel of my wheelchair. His helpfulness and to know that he believed I could gain proficiency was all the encouragement I needed.

While I was getting personal attention, Weller and Edwards were firing the Colt .45, but they were also both proficient with the 1908. Until the 1908 jammed.

"What did you do, Weller?" Colonel Sharp asked. "Don't be clumsy with that gun."

The Colonel was not happy. Shaking his head, he took back the pistol and gave Weller a Colt .45 to use from a shoulder holster. He and Lt. Edwards went to an office to fix the 1908 and retrieve a second magazine for my handgun.

"Let Annie shoot, Weller," Sharp said, "And help her to the three-quarters mark."

The firing range was twenty-five yards in length and was an open plan. There were no stalls to separate the shooters, and a pulley system changed the targets.

It had a level, smooth floor and I easily wheeled slowly to the three-quarters mark without help, although Weller offered none. In fact, his conversation was distant, with or without Edwards or Sharp present. It didn't matter. I aimed and slowly fired six shots. I hit the target four times, forgetting I had bruises on the right arm and shoulder.

"Annie, ha, you used all your bullets, and they're wide. You need to improve your aim," Weller scoffed.

I was surprised he commented like that, but then his voice became distant, and added, "Annie, I'm sorry."

Still looking at my target, I heard a shot from behind. It was louder than if I was standing next to him.

"Sorry, Annie," Weller said again, but as if he didn't mean it.

Was he aiming at me? I spun the wheelchair around to see Weller ready to fire a second shot ... at me! I couldn't take chances and pointed my gun at him. I had two more rounds in the magazine. He fired his second and third shot in my direction – but somehow missed both times? Weller looked dumfounded at his gun.

That did it. I steadied my hand, aimed for his chest, and started to pull the trigger. But the Colonel and Lt. Edwards ran out of the office, yelling, "No, Annie! Don't shoot, Annie. No!"

I dropped my arm as I realized Colonel Sharp had handed Weller a gun with blanks. The Officer in Charge and the quiet Lieutenant, who sat to my right at the meetings, were here to protect me. Lt. Edwards clearly was assigned to be with me by Mr. Harrison. I never found out who assigned Colonel Sharp.

Weller was the enemy spy. He looked clammy, like a corpse. I knew he wasn't meant for this business. His handler must have thought the same and put him in an untenable position. When security arrived minutes later, Weller resisted them cuffing him and yelled something about failing to kill his target.

As for me, it happened too fast for fear to surface. And it certainly wasn't anywhere near as traumatic as the day my sister and I almost died. I was surprisingly calm but felt disappointment. The sound of the first shot, its direction, alerted me something was wrong. Why was I slow to fire back? I needed more real-time practice.

Colonel Sharp looked at me with a sense of relief. He nodded in my direction and removed the blanks from the Colt .45.

Naval Security had been alerted, which was why they arrived so fast. They cuffed him and removed him to the stockade.

Lt. Edwards called Mr. Harrison, who stressed that we cannot mention Weller was under surveillance. A senior investigator from the President's Secret Service would arrive to interrogate him. The plan was for the Major to announce he dropped out of the program due to disinterest. Within minutes of Mr. Harrison's call, Commander McCauley alerted Naval Security to curtail their interview with us.

We stayed at the firing range for more practice. We were not in the mood to return to the training group and hoped the Officer in Charge would administer our proficiency tests. During this time, Lt. Edwards opened up, more than ever during training. I learned he had quite the sense of humor.

"Annie, why do Block Islander's annoy so many people?" Lt. Edwards quipped. "Everyone seems to take shots at you – even real shots."

I smiled and tapped, *Very funny, sir. Shall I start annoying you?*

We laughed but drew no one's attention.

Lt. Edwards shook his head in apparent admiration. "Annie, how did you stay calm?"

I think because I instinctually tried to fight back. I'll be faster next time.

"There's a concept that the 'act of fighting back' does help."

I tapped slowly, *Whether it's big, like having a gun shot at you, or something small, fighting back is essential.*

As Lt. Edwards nodded, I realized these were some of the most important words I would say as, hopefully, the soon to be newest and only disabled woman to be a member of the Office of Naval Intelligence.

After a few moments of silence Lt. Edwards asked, "Annie, do you see an analogy between the bullets in Weller's pistol and Zimmermann's telegram No. 158?"

I thought to myself, was this his sense of humor? Or was he drawing an important parallel between the two?

I shrugged my right shoulder and tapped*, Lieutenant, I'm not sure.*

"Both things ... Zimmermann's first telegram No. 158, and the bullets in Weller's pistol ... were never delivered."

Very funny. But wait. That telegram was delivered ... to President Wilson!

We laughed uncontrollably, Lt. Edwards' humor releasing the tension from being shot at.

"Annie, seriously, why do you focus on No. 158?"

To learn how it was transmitted. To understand negative intelligence. To discover where it was intercepted. This may be the only opportunity we have to identify a foreign government's method of spying on us.

"If it's the Brits, they're our ally. You're still fascinated by the puzzle?"

I raised my eyes.

The Officer Sharp returned and was given permission to administer the proficiency test. After a very late lunch, he observed us practicing for half an hour, then opened a back panel to the outside, to increase the distance to the target to twenty-five and fifty yards.

Lt. Edwards went first, and his score was near perfect. I was impressed and said so. "It's nothing, Annie. Using a rifle, I have scored in the top ninety-five percent on outdoor ranges at 200 yards!"

It was my turn and with my right arm pressed against the side of the wheelchair my scores at twenty-five yards were slightly above average. I missed two shots completely at fifty yards bringing my total score to average. But I passed. The Colonel wrote, in the most beautiful handwriting, these comments: "Must strengthen your right arm," and, "With more practice, Annie, you will improve."

We were at the Latrobe Gate waiting to secure a ride back to the

AWC, and I thought about my first day in Washington, when we landed at the Anacostia Airfield. The driver who picked up the mail spotted me and reintroduced himself. Lt. Edwards asked if he would drive us to the AWC and he agreed. He'd be back shortly after a few errands.

We waited in the grassy area near the Latrobe Gate. It was warm for this time of year, mostly because the wind was shielded by the buildings. Lt. Edwards sat in a large bench and I across from him in my wheelchair. He asked me questions. Serious questions.

"I mentioned last week that Mr. Harrison — and the Signal Service cryptologists — had figured out which cable those messages were sent on to DC before they were forwarded to Mexico City."

I tapped, *There were only a handful of cables that were not cut the night Great Britain declared war on Germany. Fewer still that can transmit messages from Berlin to Washington, DC.*

"I heard Harrison and Secretary of State Lansing discussed it with Wilson."

Do they really know which cable? The Commander hinted at it.

"Yes. And they're relying on Room 40 agents in Mexico City to identify who intercepted No. 158 there."

I understand why they are focusing on Mexico City, but why rely on Room 40?

"What do you mean?"

Haven't we learned that statements from Room 40 are fraught with issues.

"SIS thinks they have the person. And you know as well as I that they are a great ally."

Yes, and mean well, too. Of that there's no doubt.

Lt. Edwards frowned. "I don't think you should pursue this any further."

You sound like Major Dansey.

To explain to Lt. Edwards the reason for my persistence, I tapped the longest Morse that I ever did: *We both know on February 22, in London, Ambassador Page was given incomplete information by Hall. Witness the explanation why they waited six weeks to tell us. Here's background you may not know. In January 1917 Reginald Hall officially replaced Professor Ewing as Chief of Room 40. As one of the world's original code breakers,*

Ewing was the first Director of Naval Intelligence for the Royal Navy. A brilliant engineer, he organized Room 40 starting, not in 1909, but earlier in 1903. He contributed immensely to the operations of the Royal Navy. I suspect that working closely with Winston Churchill, Ewing established Britain's nationwide infrastructure for cable communications, and off-loading responsibility for many of these cables to the Royal Post Office cables. And that includes vessels that lay submarine cables. An integral and important part of that system was, and is, a series of relay and intercept stations, for the most part located on the coasts. And although Hall may have masterminded the most famous telegram that was never delivered ... it was Ewing who masterminded the infrastructure of Room 40.

"I understand now, Annie, why they don't want you to pursue this." Lt. Edwards leaned back on the bench. He understood her reasoning but worried that she would seek answers to questions that she wasn't asked to deal with.

What do you mean?

"Annie, on the Western Front, thousands of men are dying. On July 1 last summer, almost 20,000 men died during one day of fighting! German generals are desperate to emulate their country's victories in prior wars and keep pressing for more men and more weapons. The Hindenburg Line of concrete, metal, and trenches has reached 100 miles long."

I know it's bad, but ...

Lt. Edwards interrupted, "The Kaiser's generals will not give up. They're sending large numbers of troops to the front knowing that the day they hit the battlefield they will die."

I did not know how to respond.

"Does it matter, Annie, that there are three Zimmermann Telegrams?" he persisted. "Remember what the Major says, 'that even with negative intelligence sent our way, we can gain positive information'."

There's nothing like being reprimanded by a friend. I tapped, *I agree with you, but I am trying to figure out what that positive information is.*

46

ANNIE

Lt. Edwards and I entered the lobby of Roosevelt Hall at 15:30. We passed General Scott and his assistants as they were leaving the building. Lt. Edwards gave a formal salute, and I raised my right hand as well. In return we received a slight nod. The General looked down and said, "Hello, Annie."

When I entered the Conference room on the fifth floor, my greeting was not as pleasant. Lt. Edwards and I caught the tail end of a conversation Yardley and his sidekicks were having with the Major.

"... and that's why Annie should be excluded from the training. How can we trust her?" Yardley said.

"She had to take the morning off to learn how to use a pistol," Johnston added. "She'll never pass proficiency. Let her work in the office somewhere in DC. It's better for her."

Major Ralph Van Deman's eyes went from the men to me. Then shook his head. He waited for me to respond.

As Lt. Edwards pushed me to my seat, Byer added more venom, "A woman doesn't belong here ... isn't it obvious?"

I reached for my Telegraph Key and tapped, *I passed my proficiency test today. Sorry to disappoint you.*

"How did you do that? You can't even hold a Colt .45!" Yardley was relentless.

I reached into the metal pocket bolted to the inside of my wheelchair and held up my new issue and placed it on the table next to my Telegraph

Key.

It is an automatic Colt 1908. It was issued with two loaded magazines.

"Don't point it at anyone, Annie," the Major cautioned. "Now enough. On day one, I told you that Annie has every right to be here. From what I've seen so far, she will not prove me wrong! Now finish up this project. I've got to answer a call."

Despite the Major's words of encouragement, Lt. Edwards' comments bounced around in my head. If I chose to continue my unrelenting task, now that the enemy spy had been discovered, I suspected it was only a matter of time before they might remove of me from my role in the ONI.

But then Yardley raised the issue of the spy, and I realized that no one, except Lt. Edwards and myself, knew that Weller was the spy.

Thirty minutes had gone by and we realized the Major would not return, Yardley called a meeting. He asserted himself as the training group's de facto leader, by right or not.

"Let's stop deciphering and discuss a concern I've had since late last week."

"About what?" Lt. Gordon asked.

Yardley got to the point, "I'm worried there's a spy in this group."

"How do you know?" Byer asked, surprised. It was obvious Yardley had not shared his concern with his sidekick.

"I've read messages sent from our cipher Telegraph Machine." Yardley pointed to the Telegraph against the wall. "Several messages were sent after hours, and a few during class."

The group was stunned. Everyone waited for Yardley's next statement.

"Before we proceed, it's important that we keep secrecy. No one can find out about this." Yardley took control of the group with his stern approach.

"Why not tell the Major?" Clark Holder asked.

"The Major has three leadership positions open in his new MIS. I understand that they will be filled by the end of training."

Without saying, the group realized that at least one of the positions would go to the person who identified the spy. A leadership role was the prize.

"What message gave it away?" Lt. Gordon asked.

"The messages dispatched to the Mexico City Western Union Telegraph Office. We all know that that place is teeming with foreign agents." Yardley answered the question calmly.

"We discussed Mexico City yesterday. Where were you?" Byer asked in a startingly inquisitive tone.

"I was busy," Yardley said simply. "The third message to Mexico City was a few days ago. It was sent by someone who understands how to use symbols as part of his encrypted message."

Could you decipher them?

I was hopeful that he would have done so, but Yardley ignored me.

"Do you know about symbols, Annie?" Lt. Gordon asked.

The U.S. Weather Bureau transmits weather observations using symbols, but I have not seen other symbols.

"I think a sophisticated Morser sent those messages because symbols were used, and I'm convinced the spy is in this room," Yardley said.

Yardley made an important observation. I knew Weller was not proficient in Morsing. That meant that either he used them and did not understand what he was Morsing, or there was indeed another spy in the training group.

"I've used the Telegraph Machine," Lt. Gordon said.

"I know you have," Yardley interjected.

"I telegrammed colleagues," Lt. Gordon continued. "Maybe there isn't a spy. How would anyone know for sure?"

"If the messages were sent off hours, which is most likely. I doubt it's one of us." Byer seemed confident in his response.

There IS a spy in our group. I know for sure, too.

I surprised everyone in the room, but most shocked was Lt. Edwards. He gasped and sat up straight, but relaxed after he figured that I was playing along.

"You've used the Telegraph Machine, Annie. Who were you trying to contact in New London?" Yardley asked. "Why would anyone contact an area crawling with German intelligence officers?"

My telegraph was not sent to New London. I sent a message to Mrs. Conway, the Head Observer at the U.S. Weather Bureau in Narragansett Pier.

I was pleased Yardley finally figured out there was an enemy spy. I thought I'd ask him a subtle question, meant to be a hint, but would he understand?

Tom, was it you who sent the message to Riverbank last Wednesday?

Captain Johnston blurted out, "Maybe the spy is you, Annie!"

"Do you have proof of that?" Lt. Gordon asked.

"We'll have to uncover proof, won't we?" Yardley said.

Yardley had ignored my question. I wondered if he would contact Riverbank for help.

Clark stood up and gave an impassioned plea in his subtle British accent, "If there's a spy then we need to find out. Everyone should be considered a suspect. Everyone."

I don't think so, Clark.

"We need to look at *everyone*," Clark insisted. "And where are Detective Barnitz and Whytock? They need to be considered, too."

Some took offense at Clark's statement, most noticeably Johnston, but he did not arouse anyone's suspicion, except mine.

Then Byer attacked me in an accusative tone, "And, Annie, what do you do when you're away from the AWC?"

Saturday night, I had dinner with Clark Holder. My sister and I stay at the Hamilton Hotel. It's owned by a distant cousin from Block Island.

"Spies are known to stay at that hotel," Johnston said all knowingly.

I'm aware businessmen and foreign dignitaries stay there.

Lt. Gordon stood. "Would everyone agree to document and show proof where each of us has been after hours?"

"That's a good idea," Yardley said, "but let's keep this to ourselves until we have further proof."

After the impromptu meeting, the men left the room, in pairs. Lt. Edwards stayed back, and whispered, "Do you believe that there's *another* spy?"

I raised my eyes. *It is possible.*

"Should I mention this to Mr. Harrison?"

I nodded, and tapped, *If you wish.*

After he left, I opened the Telegraph looking for new messages. There was one other, but the time stamp was inaccurate. At this point, with Yardley not yet up to snuff, I worried that I would need his help to identify a second spy, if there was one.

I wheeled myself slowly to the elevator and took it to the lobby and found Sgt. Lightfoot sitting behind his desk as usual. I signaled him over and he brought me across the lobby to his desk.

I tapped, *I need help Sergeant Lightfoot.*

He agreed to remain in the building throughout the night and let me know who, if anyone, entered the conference room. I asked about a symbol that I'd seen, and he said he did not know.

At 6:00 PM I was still waiting for Mrs. Lynch and Emma. It turned out Mrs. Lynch was listening to Emma present her idea to the group at the Sketchers lab.

*

A favorite phrase from when I was younger was, "You don't need to know everything to know everything." But a phrase the Major uses is a close second: "Intelligence information that is proven to be a fact is no longer intelligence." The quicker intelligence becomes facts, the more progress can be made.

I couldn't rule out Byer, Clark, or Johnston. And it was inconceivable that Detective Barnitz or another New Yorker, Whytock, the journalist who clearly wore many hats, were enemy spies. And Gordon was highly unlikely, too, although John stressed that anything is possible.

Not sure of what to do, I decided to let things unfold. Lt. Edwards thought that Weller was the only spy. He thought Weller was not happy, whereas I interpreted him as being a Sphinx. In the future I would know the difference.

Regarding the connection between the Zimmermann Telegrams and the spy, I have not changed my opinion.

And although Lt. Edwards does not agree, I believe that the attempt to place a spy in the MIS training may have been a consequence of Germany's embarrassment due to releasing the Telegram to the Press — on that first day of March. And of course Germany blamed the United States; no one seriously thought to blame the Brits. It's payback by the Kaiser, I thought.

My mind kept trying to explain why a New York City journalist was known to Dansey, recruited by Van Deman, and carried a pistol. Emma saw him talking with an officer on the Parade Grounds comparing their respective revolvers, and I noted an empty shoulder holster in his bag. Perhaps it was necessitated by working the high crime docks of New York Harbor. What was even more surprising was why Van Deman trusted him enough to evaluate Miss Muriel. True, she was also a journalist from Canada. But was she a friend of Dalia? Or was she functioning as a part-time German spy? The only thing that I was becoming convinced about was that she was not crazy.

Only clouds above Block Island block the sky, and they rarely stay around for very long. Emma loved a midday blue sky. I loved the cloudless night sky. I'd often tap on the headboard, *Emma, the reason I love the night sky is because it reveals itself. The sky is hidden in daylight and can never reveal itself.*

The night sky opened a greater world. I didn't pray as much as my sister, but when I thought of the celestial, solving a problem was closer than I realized.

47

EMMA

It was the second Wednesday and Annie was already awake when I opened my eyes. She was moving around in bed effortlessly. For the first time since Saturday night I noted that she was no longer in pain. Most of her bruises had faded considerably, although several were still dark yellow.

We took the main elevator to the lobby, expecting to be early, but Mrs. Lynch was sitting on the couch, waiting.

"Emma, I'm assigned to Mr. Harrison this morning. Would you help us carry boxes to a few meetings?"

"Of course! Where are the meetings?" I couldn't contain my excitement.

"On different floors of the War Department," Mrs. Lynch explained.

"That's next to the White House. I must get dressed proper."

I excused myself and ran down the hall and up the back stairway to our room. I put on the only fancy dress I brought from home. When I returned to the lobby they were in the car.

At Roosevelt Hall, Mrs. Lynch waited in the car, and I brought my sister to the fifth floor.

Instead of waiting for the elevator to return to the lobby, I ran down four flights of stairs. I almost ran into Captain Johnston who was walking up the stairs. He smiled, said hello, and moved to the side. Once outside, at the top of the granite steps, I saw Mr. Harrison sitting in the front seat.

I ran down and opened the rear door with a hearty hello.

"Hello, again," he said, and continued his conversation with Mrs.

Lynch. Before we had driven onto the streets of Washington, DC, his warm and friendly personality became evident, and I understood why Lt. Edwards thought highly of him.

"You got here fast, Emma," Mrs. Lynch said.

"I ran down the stairs and bumped into Captain Johnston."

"That man is big. I don't think you could've hurt him," Mr. Harrison said.

"He's from New York City, right?" Mrs. Lynch asked.

"Yes. The Commander recruited Barnitz, and Ralph recruited Johnston, both from Tunney's Bomb Squad," Mr. Harrison explained. "Last year Johnston was instrumental in apprehending six bomb plotters accused of planning to blow up subway stations at Times Square and 59th Street. That group of anarchists were mostly union officials. They had successfully blown up the Lenox Avenue and 110th Street subway station the month before."

"Where did you learn this information, Mr. Harrison?" I asked.

"Emma, I read about it in the *New York Evening World*. It's the best source for crime events and international stories. When the bomb squad solved a case, only Tunney's name would appear in the newspaper. Detectives' names were never released to the public.

"It's also rare that a journalist's name appears in the newspaper articles that they write. That's why Ross's name is rarely in print. And another fascinating thing I learned from the *Evening World's* article on the bomb plot Johnston was involved in was that the NYC DA's office first learned about the situation from reading the front-page article in last year's November 3 edition!"

I was hoping Mr. Harrison would say more about the *Evening World* and its wide-ranging influence, including why journalists were rarely credited with an article, but he left it at that. I was nervous sitting in the backseat and after a few minutes of silence, an awkward comment popped out.

"My sister says that Clark lives in NYC, too, near Grand Central Terminal," I informed them.

"I believe his family has an apartment near or in the New York Yacht Club," Mr. Harrison said.

I then asked another awkward question, "What do you do, Mr. Harrison?"

He answered with grace, "I'm a diplomat at the State Department. I've had assignments all over, including South America and Japan. The challenges are difficult, Emma, but if you enjoy working with people from around the world, you'll enjoy the State Department."

"She says she's thinking of college, now," Mrs. Lynch interjected.

"You have to travel if you're part of the State Department, Emma," Mr. Harrison added.

"Mr. Harrison, did you ever have an assignment in London?" I asked.

"No, but I attended boarding school there for a few years."

"You're the first diplomat I've met."

"There's a diplomat with your last name, Spencer Eddy, who will be here soon. He's very secretive and has been part of the ONI since last year. He's supposed to attend the meetings, next week. Have you heard of him?"

"No, I haven't. I don't think he's part of my extended family."

"Emma has a few questions about Dalia," Mrs. Lynch interjected and changed the topic.

"Mr. Harrison, was one obit more helpful than the others?" I asked.

"You may not know this, Emma, but Ross has been writing about crime stories for a very long time, and he thinks he's figured out the story," Mr. Harrison said. "Except for summers, at the end of his life, Ball preferred living in Newport. And the only 'normal' obit was in the *Newport Daily News*. The obits in the *New York Times*, *Washington Evening Star*, *Providence Herald,* and the *Providence Journal* had intriguing information, but were all very different. The New Zealand article about Dalia, published a month after she died, is interesting, too, but it's not an obit."

"When I first read them, I couldn't help but to think this was a murder-suicide," Mrs. Lynch said.

"Ross is sure this is not a murder. There's another explanation," Mr. Harrison said with confidence.

I jumped in with a pressing question, "I'm sorry to interrupt, but has Ross Whytock figured out if Miss Muriel is really *Miss Muriel*?"

Mr. Harrison waggled his hand. "Yes and No. After reading articles about Block Island published in the early summer of 1896, there's enough information for anyone to create a false identity. And that includes knowing about a green buoy being anchored in June just after the opening of the new channel to the Great Salt Pond. But it is possible that Dalia and Miss Muriel were good friends. I did, however, assign an agent to contact the *Halifax Herald* and the *Toronto Sun*."

"Leland, any response?" Mrs. Lynch asked.

Mr. Harrison nodded. "She worked for both papers, confirming that part of her story. I think she needs to be watched. That's all I can say for now."

"Leland, back to the obits, if it wasn't murder, then how did Dalia die?" Mrs. Lynch asked.

"The obits are consistent for two things. He died of a stroke, or apoplexy as they called it. And every obit ignores reasons for Dalia's death. It's as if no one could figure it out. We know they were close, and the securities found in the closet were substantial. And, if you read the *New York Times* obit carefully, we have a timeline of events."

"Have you ever seen a timeline in an obit?" Mrs. Lynch asked.

Mr. Harrison shook his head, "Never. According to the *New York Times* obit, Ball paid his last visit to Dalia in *her* room at his Ocean View Hotel ... either one or two days before he died. According to the *Providence Journal*, Dalia saw Ball last in *his* room before she died. One day after Dalia died, someone found the bustle filled with securities hanging in her closet. We learned from the Newport paper that his physician from the mainland took the ferry and made a house call at the Ocean View. Ross believes that morphine was almost certainly prescribed. It was readily available at that time."

"I have a question, Mr. Harrison. *The Washington Star's* obit makes no mention of Dalia, or the setting, or the timing, or Dalia's money. Miss Sarah told us the evening my sister and I met Miss Muriel that the publisher of the *Washington Star* and Nicholas Ball were great friends."

"That's true, Emma," he concurred, "and it's no surprise the *Star* doesn't mention the housekeeper. The other Providence newspaper, the *Herald*, makes no mention of Dalia's death at all. More importantly, it prints false information about her past, did not mention of Block Island, and stated that she died in Providence, not on Block Island.

"If Ball was well enough to visit Dalia, that suggests he could walk the steps at that hotel. You don't go visiting after you've had a stroke, especially in a building like the Ocean View with many levels. His stroke must have worsened, or he had another stroke during the last forty-eight hours of his life. Ross read the *Newport Daily News* obit which, as I mentioned, reported that his physician attended to him at the Ocean View. Ross knows full well that during the 1890s morphine was used regularly in those situations."

"So, Mr. Whytock thinks this is not murder?" Mrs. Lynch asked.

"He thinks and I agree ... that it's possible that the cause of Dalia's death may very well be a case of self-murder."

"That means that they decided to die together?" I asked.

"That's not possible to determine," Mr. Harrison said. "As difficult this case is to accept, it's the same in the field of espionage and in crimes, that it is absolutely essential to understand context prior to figuring out motives. Context avoids that easy jump to conclusions."

"Leland, why do you think that?" Mrs. Lynch was clearly upset at the thought of self-murder.

"It's the context of the 1890s. Ross explained that during the 1890s a discussion of self-murder exploded in major newspapers in the United States. Commentary after commentary argued its merits. Ross remembers his parents talking about it as a youngster in St. Louis, and he has read all of that decade's commentary. In certain situations, it was okay to end your life, and morphine the method."

"Leland, you're saying everyone reading the newspapers during the 1890s would have known about this commentary supporting self-murder. And if so, Ball would certainly have been aware of that discussion. I don't like that idea." Mrs. Lynch was firm in her opinion.

"We don't like it, but if it's true it was Dalia's decision, right?" I asked.

"I'll have the librarian show you those commentaries," Mr. Harrison assured me.

By the time Mrs. Lynch parked in the underground garage of the War Department, I put the discussion behind me. I trailed Mrs. Lynch and Mr. Harrison from meeting to meeting. It had only been a few days, but I was proud of being part of the Sketchers lab, and during our walk around the State Department, most enjoyed being introduced by Mr. Harrison as part of that crew.

48

ANNIE

Mrs. Lynch and Mr. Harrison dropped off Emma at the Hamilton at 4:00 PM, and Sergeant Lightfoot drove me back at 7:00 PM. I asked him questions about Native Indian symbols, including the meaning of a word in one transmission to Mexico City.

I tapped, *It's spelled, Patawomeck, and it's repeated twice.*

"That's an Indian tribe who lived along the Potomac River," Sgt. Lightfoot replied. "The telegrapher is using the word to refer to the Potomac River. But it can also mean 'to come and go'."

Both meanings make sense. Something comes and goes in the Potomac River.

The Sergeant flashed a big smile. "Annie, by the way, congratulations on passing your proficiency test at the range."

I gave my hand signal for, *Thank you*, and tapped, *Lieutenant Edwards had a perfect score.*

"I heard that, too. I've known him for a while, but I never knew he was a marksman."

At the hotel, I was surprised that a bellhop met me at the curb. I waved goodbye to Sgt. Lightfoot. He took me right upstairs where I found Emma had eaten both dinners. She apologized and ran to the kitchen while I washed up.

Emma started right in with her questions when she returned with my dinner. "What happened today?"

I cannot share what we did in the morning or early afternoon.

Emma threw up her hands. "Is there anything you can tell me?"

The Major is anticipating that at least two positions will be filled from members of the training group, and the third will be his temporary assistant, Major Dansey.

"What are the other positions?"

As expected, Ross will be assigned as the Chief Intelligence Officer for the Port of New York Harbor and surrounding area. The Chief Liaison Officer will most likely go to Edwards, and the Director of Cryptology will be Yardley.

"What does the liaison officer do?"

He'll interact with Congress, Cabinet members, and bureaus in and out of the Armed Forces. That position requires diplomacy as well as deciphering and investigative skills. Edwards will be assigned to the State Department's U-1 or U-3 secret service.

"Anything else?"

The Major stressed, again and again, the importance of understanding the context in which messages are sent. It may be more important than the message itself. Geo always said understanding nuances is essential, although not easily learned. Different angles to stories reveal themselves when perspectives change.

"In the car with Mrs. Lynch, Mr. Harrison said the same thing, but he was talking about understanding the context of the 1890s and Ball's obits."

How was your ride with him?

"It was good. He and Mr. Whytock have discussed Ball's obits at length and do not believe it was a murder. The context was this. During the entire 1890s, self-murder was discussed in newspapers throughout the country ."

Makes sense, but it is still sad.

Emma said, "To change the subject, Mr. Harrison mentioned Captain Johnston."

Why?

"When I was running down the stairs at Roosevelt Hall, around one of the corners, I ran into Johnston. He smiled and said hello."

What did Mr. Harrison say about him?

"That he was recruited from Tunney's division along with Barnitz."

I lay back on the bed and stared at the ceiling. If Tunney had such high regard for Johnston, there was little chance that he was the enemy spy. I was upset with myself. How did I make that mistake.

Emma must have noticed my glum face. "Annie, what's the matter?"

I gave Emma a hand signal, *Nothing. I'm tired.*

But I wasn't tired. I was upset that I could not determine if there was a second spy in the room. The odds were low and the only thing I was sure of is that if there were two spies, they probably did not know about each other.

A knock on the door brought me out of deep thought.

"Bellhop. I have message for Annie Rose," he said.

Emma opened the door slowly, and he handed her the note.

"Thank you." She closed the door and locked it. "Want me to read it?"

I raised my eyes, *Yes.*

Emma cleared her throat and read: "'Thursday's session cancelled, due to an urgent funding meeting at the War Department. The session will be rescheduled for Saturday morning, at the Naval Yard. It's a live firearm session. Everyone must attend'."

An hour later Miss Sarah delivered another message: "Annie, Clark called the front desk and wants to know if you'll have lunch with him, considering your session has been cancelled. I know they don't want you in the dining room, but that's where you should eat. Let's tell him that, eh?"

Invite him here for lunch. Emma, alert the kitchen staff.

49

ANNIE

Thursday, 11:30 AM. Clark was sitting on the long couch in the lobby. The door to the main elevator opened and Emma and I saw him. I took a long, deep breath and Emma pushed me out and into the lobby. He greeted us in a subdued manner, a far cry from the way he saluted me the night we went to the Cosmos Club.

"Hi. Miss Sarah suggested lunch in the dining room," Emma said, right away.

Clark blinked back his surprise. "Hi, Emma. I didn't know you would be here. Aren't you supposed to be at the Sketchers lab?"

"I'll be on my way soon," Emma said brusquely.

"There's a wonderful restaurant on 16th Street that we could go to, Annie?" Clark proposed.

Emma answered no for me and shook her head for emphasis. She gave Clark a brief wave and took the elevator to our room. While this was going on, I saw a man in the far corner near the kitchen stand up, and then sat just as quickly. It was Whytock. It was the first time I saw him at the Hamilton. He knows how to keep a low profile.

"We can go to a nice restaurant," Clark said, again, as soon as Emma was out of earshot.

I tapped, *This is fine.*

"You said you weren't allowed in the dining room," he pointed out.

The owner is out of town. He is the only one who objects.

"Can we go for a walk after lunch?"

He seemed insistent so I raised my eyes to say, *Yes*.

The section of the dining room we were directed to was filled with light, due to windows overlooking Franklin Park. It had very comfortable oversized chairs set against the wall. Clark helped me sit in one. It was perfect. I could see everything, including the kitchen doors. But I couldn't see Whytock now that he was seated.

I made idle conversation, *Irving said these chairs are from France, as are the chandeliers.*

Clark moved the wheelchair to the side.

I asked Clark who he thought was driving the vehicle last Saturday night.

"Up until recently I had no idea. I was sure it was a drunk. But now I believe that he was aiming for us."

Do you think it was the spy? Yardley hasn't figured out who it is yet.

"I have no idea," Clark gave a shrug. "It could be anyone."

The waiter showed up, and I ordered a New England meal of clam chowder and a lobster tail, a rarity in Washington. A New Englander at heart, Irving Ball always had lobster and chowder on the menu. They were rarely available in Washington, DC, restaurants. Clark said he had never had lobster and was excited to try it. All of a sudden, there was no further talk of going to another restaurant. I explained that Block Island waters have always had an abundance of lobster.

After ordering, Clark asked a question that I usually answered in a casual, matter of fact manner. But today was different. I did not want to talk about death.

"Would you tell me about your accident at sea?"

I'll tell you about my Island.

And that is what I did.

50

EMMA

From the archway leading to the dining hall, I watched a waiter bring Clark and Annie to a table directly in front of a large window. It was on the opposite side of the long dining room from the kitchen. I could see Annie's broad smile when Clark helped her transfer to a plush chair against the wall. Clark moved the wheelchair between two tables and sat facing Annie, affording him a view overlooking Franklin Park.

I hoped Annie and Clark would enjoy themselves and it looked like they were off to a good start. Using the back staircase, I headed back to our room, but as I closed the door to the stairwell, a quick glance back to the lobby startled me. Miss Muriel had entered the Hamilton.

Through a crack in the stairwell door, I watched her walk hesitatingly to the registration desk. She waited patiently until a porter, someone I had not previously seen, walked out of the office and handed her a key. I scurried up to the second floor to lock our door, then returned to the stairwell to observe Miss Muriel's actions and figure out what to do.

Not more than a few minutes had gone by when Miss Muriel left the lobby using the main staircase. I ran back up to the second-floor landing, cracking the door ever so slightly, and was stunned to see her walk onto the second floor. I closed the door quickly. Her footsteps came toward our Room 207, but her key sounded like she opened a door of a room across the hall from our room.

My first thought was that I wished that I had a gun, but what would that have gotten me? I had to contact the Army War College, but I did not have a phone number. And I certainly could not interrupt Annie and Clark.

Not knowing what to do, I returned to the busy kitchen. While I waited to see if my "friend" was around, the kitchen door swung open to the dining area and there sat Mr. Whytock. He was alone at a small round table set a few feet from the kitchen door.

Although we were told not to contact Mr. Whytock, I knew I had to. But I would be discrete. When the door swung open again, I made ever so brief eye contact with him, and he gave me a most subtle nod of recognition, and then looked away.

I grabbed a pencil and paper and wrote a note: *Mr. Whytock, I need help. I just saw Miss Muriel walk in the lobby of the Hamilton and check into a second-floor room. I think she's across from our Room 207. She's not supposed to be at the Hamilton.*

Annie is having lunch with Clark, and I do not want him to take her out of the Hamilton now that Miss Muriel is here. I do not want to hand this note directly to you, so I will bring Annie's wheelchair back to this wall by the kitchen. By bringing Annie's wheelchair close to your table I'm able to deliver this note to you and will take the wheelchair away from Clark — on the chance that he wants to take her for a walk, which Annie would agree to. Perhaps you can hide it somewhere? Until we figure out why Miss Muriel is in a room on the second floor, it will be safer for her to remain in the dining hall.

Can you meet me in the back stairwell, please? No one uses that stairwell. Thank you, Mr. Whytock.

I swung the kitchen door open, walked past his table, and crossed the dining area and came up behind Clark. I startled them when I announced, "I'll take the wheelchair and put it near the kitchen."

Clark, recovered from surprise, said with a smile, "Why? It's okay right here, Emma."

Annie looked confused. She smiled broadly yet said nothing.

"Annie," I said casually, "I ran into Miss Muriel. She says hi."

My comment was an immediate jolt to Annie's sense of well-being. I lied about talking to Miss Muriel to make a point. I wish I could tell her Whytock was in the room, but I dared not.

"Sorry to bother you, Clark," I said with sincerity. With Clark and Annie 'stuck' in the dining room, I knew she would be in good company with Clark.

I pushed the wheelchair toward the kitchen and left it against the wall a few feet from Whytock. My note was folded and tucked in at an angle where he could easily see it. I pointed to it without making eye contact, and he said say softly, "Got it."

I walked into the kitchen and stood by the door, keeping out of everyone's way. My friend was not there. A short time later another waiter walked out and swung the door wide open. Whytock looked up and gave me another imperceptible nod, indicating that he had read my note. I quickly walked to the back stairwell and waited for him. Because I was always in the kitchen, my presence drew little attention.

It was twenty minutes before Whytock joined me in the back stairwell. Much longer than I had anticipated. But there was a reason. After reading my note, he immediately called Major Van Deman at the War College.

"Emma, good job alerting me. I moved your sister's wheelchair into the kitchen, and I placed it behind a curtain by the door that opens to the delivery area."

"Mr. Whytock, you're more than a journalist, aren't you?" I asked, raising my eyes.

"And you, dear Emma, are far more than just a sister. I opened Annie's metal drawer on the wheelchair, but I didn't see her 1908. Does she have it on her person?"

"I don't think so," I said, shaking my head.

"I called Van Deman about Miss Muriel. He was impressed that you thought to remove Annie's wheelchair right away."

"What should we do now?" I asked.

"He gave me instructions. Here's the plan."

Ross Whytock seemed confident, and I assumed it was because he worked closely with NYPD detectives assigned to the crime-ridden docks. And according to Annie, he was familiar with Barnitz, spies, and as a journalist for the *Evening World*, he writes and studies about crime.

I listened to his instructions intently, but no more than thirty seconds went by, and he stopped abruptly.

He looked to the side, then at me. "Emma, I need to call Van Deman again, to clarify something. He is *not* telling me everything, and I need to know what he knows. I'll be back in a few minutes. If you hear anything, don't pursue it and go back into the kitchen."

I had no idea what concerned him, but I trusted his judgement. He bounded up the stairwell to use a phone in his room.

My "worrying" was interrupted by more footsteps, but no voices, coming from the second floor. I was too scared to take a peek, and instead, said a prayer. But it wasn't my usual David Copperfield prayer. It was full of fear.

Whytock returned in twenty minutes.

"Emma, you're quite right, Miss Muriel is indeed back in the hotel," Whytock said, appearing only slightly winded.

"I heard someone on the second floor," I said, "but I was afraid to see who it was."

"I'll check it out, Emma," he said in a comforting manner. "This time I spoke to Major Dansey. He choose his words carefully, but I got the impression that both he and Van Deman think that although Miss Muriel might be crazy, it's more likely that she's acting."

"If that's true, then they've changed their opinion since we spoke to Mr. Harrison."

"They? Meaning?"

"The Major, Mr. Harrison, and perhaps the Commander," I said.

"That does make sense from what Dansey told me, Emma. I'm reading between the lines, and apparently, they have interrogated someone, and now know who she really is. With Annie stuck at her table, the Major and Dansey asked if you could do two things right away."

"If I can, I will," I said. "What did they find out?"

"They did not tell me specifics, but they want you and your sister out of the Hamilton, but it is essential that Miss Muriel thinks that you two are still in Room 207." Whytock looked to see my response.

"Sure. What do I do?" I remained composed.

"Dansey suggests a ruse that one of the Navy's agents can help with. This porter will pretend to overhear you on the phone with your mother, that you and your sister will be at the hotel for another week. And we'll let Muriel stay in her room."

"Okay, that is fine with me," I said calmly, "but Annie and I will leave, soon, I hope."

"Yes, but not before we convince Muriel that you are still in your room."

"How are we going to do that?" I asked.

"I'll tell you in a moment. You can pretend to call your mom or call her using the phone in the manager's office. Miss Sarah is on duty and will assist you."

"I'll call her. Block Island has a party line system, and the operator can reach her anywhere on the Island, unless she's on the ferry."

"The Major has alerted Detective Barnitz to help with this. He wants you to bring the wheelchair up to the room and talk to an empty chair as if your sister is still in it. Hopefully, Muriel will hear you talking. After putting the wheelchair in the room, you'll take your leave and exit down the main staircase, and back to the kitchen."

"Where will Annie be?"

"She'll be in the kitchen, after Clark takes his leave."

"When you see Detective Barnitz, do not say hello. He'll be dressed as a worker."

"What will he do?" I asked.

"He'll help convince Muriel who surely will be listening, that you two are still in the room."

I hid my apprehension as best I could. "Why is she back at the hotel? I don't want to be in the room anymore."

"Don't worry, Emma, Van Deman found another place for you and Annie to stay."

"How is Miss Muriel going to know that I made the call to my mother?"

"When you're finished with the call, sit on the couch in the lobby and wait for Muriel to show up."

"Okay, but who's going to alert Muriel that I spoke to my mother?"

"It will be a porter, who knows Miss Sarah."

"Oh, yes, Miss Sarah's boyfriend is in the ONI."

"How did you know that, Emma?"

I shrugged. "Please clarify for me that the porter will tell Miss Muriel that he heard me say to my mother that we will be at the hotel for at least another week." I wanted confirmation.

"Correct, Emma. While you're doing that, I'll make sure the

wheelchair is unavailable until Clark takes his leave. Then you come get the wheelchair and bring it to Room 207."

"What about Annie?" I asked.

"After Clark leaves, I will walk her to the kitchen and sit her in a chair in the back of the kitchen. We will retrieve her wheelchair and your belongings from the room tomorrow."

"Okay. Should I go to the lobby to make the phone call now?"

"Yes, Miss Sarah will be there, waiting. I'll see you in the kitchen after you are done."

"Miss Sarah, I need to use Irving's phone to call my mother on Block Island."

"Sure," she said, opening the door to the manager's office.

Once inside and after closing the door, I asked, "I understand that there's a porter nearby?"

"Yes. He'll sit at the registration desk. And I'll be in here with you. You might as well talk to your mom, if you can get through," Miss Sarah said, handing me the phone.

"I'll get through. Lillie is the Postmistress on Block Island, and the operator always knows where she is."

As usual, Gladys was working the switchboard at Block Island's Bell Telephone Exchange and answered right away. She asked about Annie's training at the National Weather Bureau before connecting me to Lillie at the Post Office.

"Hi, Mom. Yes, Annie's here, but she's having lunch with a friend in the dining room. She says hi, too. What? We missed a major Nor'easter. Any damage? Really. Glad we were here but we've had our 'storms' to deal with as well. What? Yes, I am working. At a place that teaches perspective drawing skills and maps. What's that? It's a drawing lab. Yes, I love it. Annie's training is going well. We don't know where she'll be assigned. She has a few more weeks of training."

When I got off the phone, Miss Sarah confirmed that Miss Muriel had indeed checked into a room on the second floor.

"May I ask who's making noise outside the door, trying to listen to our conversation?" I asked.

"That's Seamus, the porter. He's with us."

We opened the door and Seamus made a beeline for the lobby stairs and bounded up to the second floor. I assumed that Miss Sarah trusted Seamus. I sat on the couch in the lobby and waited for Clark to leave the hotel. That would be my signal that to retrieve the wheelchair and return it to Room 207.

Shortly after I sat on the couch, Miss Muriel walked out of the main stairs from the upper floors. Apparently, she avoided the hotel elevators.

"Emma, good to see you?" she asked. "Did you and your sister find more information about Dalia?" Her tone was such that I am sure she wasn't expecting anything new.

"I spoke to my mother, and do not have any news. Sorry," I said.

"May I sit with you?" Miss Muriel asked. She did not appear nervous and sat a few feet from me.

She rested her hands in her lap and didn't move them for the duration of our short conversation. She was Dansey-like in her *lack* of expressions, a stoic. I figured that wasn't a good sign, but I'm not sure what it all meant. All I knew for certain that by early evening Annie and I would no longer be here. Little did I know that Miss Muriel had the same thoughts.

After a few brief moments of staring, she thanked me and excused herself, "I need to take a walk outside."

She left the Hamilton and walked toward Franklin Park.

Not wanting to appear that I was in a rush to go anywhere, I lingered on the couch and waited for Clark to leave the Hamilton. I thought, even marveled, that Mr. Whytock and I were working together, and that our "office" was the back stairwell near the kitchen. Later, when I mentioned this to Mr. Whytock, he said, "Emma, when you're in the field you choose any safe place, but not before identifying an escape route. If we're ever together in New York City, I'll show you the docks and a few of the temporary "offices" that I've used to gather information."

After an hour had passed, Clark left the hotel and walked out of the building with a big smile, not a grin, but a smile from ear to ear. I waited fifteen minutes and then returned to the kitchen using the back stairwell. Mr. Whytock was in the kitchen talking to my 'friend' on the far side of the kitchen. I walked over to report my impressions of Miss Muriel when I stopped in my tracks. My sister's wheelchair was being cleaned of a thick coat of Italian gravy!

"What happened?" I asked, interrupting their conversation.

"How did it go?" Whytock asked. At this point our friend laughed and walked away leaving us to ourselves.

"When I placed the wheelchair in the kitchen, I assumed Clark might come looking for it, so I asked our friend to pour something on it to prevent Annie from using it."

"It looks like a gallon of tomato sauce," I said and raised my eyes in approval. "That was quick thinking. Who made the sauce? It smells great."

"They have a new Italian cook, and she makes this every day. Takes her four hours."

"Clark has left the hotel, so we can clean it up and I can bring it up to the room. Is Detective Barnitz here yet?" I asked.

"Yes. He'll be right back. Did you see Muriel?"

"Yes, for a few moments, after my call. Miss Muriel is an enigma. I can't figure her out," I said in all honesty.

"We don't have to figure her out. We just have to stay out of her way."

"What's that mean?" I asked. I looked Whytock in the eye and waited for his response.

"We need to step outside."

Whytock opened the far back kitchen door which opened to the driveway in the rear of the Hamilton Hotel. There were two trucks parked, but what he wanted to show me was placed against the side of the outdoor shed. It was a battery-operated motor-scooter.

"Have you ever seen one of these?" he asked.

"I've seen photos of them. They're made in Long Island City, in Queens."

"So you're not surprised?" Whytock was impressed. "Do they have them on Block Island?"

"No. But my Uncle Geo has friends in Brooklyn that have them. They're called Auto-Peds," I explained.

"The NYPD uses them from time to time."

"How did it get here?" I asked.

"This belongs to Detective Barnitz. He brought it with him when he reported to the AWC."

"Where is he?" I asked again.

"He's upstairs in my room. Let's walk away from the building," he whispered. "We have one more task to accomplish."

51

ANNIE

I very much enjoyed lunch with Clark. It was more relaxed than our dinner at the Cosmos Club and filled with laughter. We never spoke about the training sessions. When Clark insisted on a walk around the neighborhood, despite it being brisk outside, I readily agreed.

We had finished dessert when Miss Sarah peered into the dining room. I waved her over with my right hand.

"Hi, how was your lunch?" Miss Sarah asked.

"We had a great time," Clark offered right away.

I raised my eyes and smiled broadly in agreement.

"Where's Emma?" Miss Sarah asked, as she looked around the dining hall. "I thought she was with you two."

I hand signaled, *Upstairs. Emma brought the wheelchair to the kitchen.*

"I went to the kitchen to bring it back," Clark offered, "but a waiter dropped food on it. What a mess."

"I'll look for it," Miss Sarah said, as she turned to walk toward the kitchen.

Clark and I were laughing about the mess on my wheelchair when Miss Sarah returned. "It's still covered in thick, dried tomato sauce. We'll have to find Emma."

Miss Sarah suggested sitting in the lobby, but Clark said that he wanted to walk back to his barracks. I thanked Clark for a wonderful lunch, and after saying goodbye and kissing me on the cheek, that is what he did.

Miss Sarah sat in his chair and together we waited for the wheelchair to be cleaned.

"You enjoyed lunch, Annie, I can tell." Miss Sarah said with a smile.

I nodded and raised my eyes, twice.

Ten minutes later Emma entered the dining hall from the kitchen and walked slowly across the long dining room pushing my wheelchair. She looked tired. Except for a few late lunch reservations, we were the only ones in the room. Miss Sarah noted the wheelchair looked great. "The kitchen got it cleaned before it could smell." She got up and left when Emma started Morsing on the table.

Annie, there is a change in plans.

Emma looked serious, not fatigued. *What are you talking about?*

Emma tapped, *Much has happened since you and Clark sat for lunch. Miss Muriel checked into the hotel and is on the second floor. And Detective Barnitz is here, sent by the Major.*

Did she really say hi to me?

"No." Emma shook her head.

Who saw her?

"I did, so did Miss Sarah, and a porter that Miss Sarah brought in also saw Muriel. And Whytock is aware."

Where is Miss Muriel?

"She checked into a room on the second floor."

Really?

"Yes, but there is a plan," I whispered.

Why is Barnitz here? And what plan?

Emma tapped slowly, *He is here to monitor Miss Muriel, and he arrived using his Auto-Ped. You wouldn't believe it, but he has an Auto-Ped."*

Barnitz rode a scooter here. No!

Emma whispered, "He brought it down from New York City."

I raised my eyes, then tapped, *Emma, what is the plan?*

It has been arranged that you leave the Hamilton right away. I'll follow later this evening. Major Van Deman found a place for us at the AWC.

Why am I leaving so quickly?

Emma spoke in a barely audible whisper. "That new porter I mentioned."

I raised my eyes, *Yes*.

"The one that knows Miss Sarah, well, he saw a handgun with a silencer in Muriel's bag."

I gave my hand signal for, *A silencer! I understand now.*

"You will leave in shortly, through the back kitchen door. A truck will take you to the Army War College. I think Sergeant Lightfoot is driving you, and Mrs. Lynch will retrieve our clothes and wheelchair tomorrow morning."

Oh, that's why tomato sauce was dumped on the wheelchair. Who thought of that?

Emma laughed and tapped, *No one knows.*

That was good thinking.

"I have to be honest, Annie, I was scared when I spotted Miss Muriel in the Hamilton. But when Whytock told me that Barnitz was on his way, I felt better."

We are in good hands with the Deputy Director of the NYPD Bomb Squad present. Emma, walk me to the kitchen.

"Yes, let's go. I'll support your left side, and you move your right leg. Let me know if you need a rest."

My sister supported my left side, and I slowly put my right foot ahead, one very slow step at a time. It helped that the dining hall was almost empty.

I couldn't help but think that something big had happened for Major Van Deman to send Detective Barnitz to the hotel the moment Miss Muriel showed up. I'd figure it out in due time, but little did I know that Emma had already figured out the reason.

I tapped on Emma's arm, *Where exactly is our new temporary home?*

"My instructor's house. He and his wife live on the Army War College campus."

I raised my eyes. I rested in an oversized chair in the back of the kitchen, while Emma looked for Whytock.

With the porter seeing Miss Muriel's silencer and the Bomb Squad's best detective assigned to the Miss Muriel case, I was sure a murder was anticipated. But who was the target? Most likely me, but could it be my sister? Perhaps both of us. It was comforting that the leadership at the AWC and ONI were taking no chances. Detective Barnitz is now a senior officer in the ONI, and that means the Commander was also involved in the decision to send him to the Hamilton. Or did the order come from elsewhere? I do wonder what the *Providence Journal* will say in the morning – the *ProJo*'s editor always has the scoop. And the editor of the *Evening World* will know something soon enough.

I waited patiently for Emma to return, and dwelled on the fact that we would never spend another night in Room 207. But someone else would.

52

EMMA and Third Person

At 8 PM someone tapped lightly on the door of Room 207. I answered the door and Barnitz walked in. He closed the door and whispered for me to talk normally as if Annie was in the room. He scouted the room while I had an imaginary conversation with my sister.

The cleaned wheelchair was in the room, and he moved it to be adjacent to Annie's side of bed. He removed the lightbulbs from the ceiling and table lamps, and after deciding where he would sit, he settled down on the bed.

"Emma, when I fall asleep, take your leave and quietly take the main elevator to the lobby. Don't lock the door. Then go to the kitchen where Mrs. Lynch and Ross should be waiting."

He explained to me that before I entered Room 207, Miss Sarah had returned the wheelchair to the room, acting as if Annie was in the wheelchair, keeping a constant conversation with, well, nobody. She placed clothing under the bedsheets, to mimic two bodies asleep.

It didn't take long for Detective Barnitz to be prepared for Miss Muriel to make an entrance.

I took my leave around 9:30 PM.

*

At 03:15 Miss Muriel quietly left her room and curiously walked up the main staircase to the top floor. Barnitz heard her door open and her footsteps. He rightly assumed that she would descend to the second floor using the back stairwell. And that is what she did.

Detective Barnitz was waiting, sitting in a chair behind the bathroom door. He intentionally left the door to the room partially unlocked and when she slipped a thin piece of metal into the lock mechanism, the door popped right open. She looked around the room, and then closed the door. Seeing what she thought were bodies asleep under blankets, she took aim with the pistol with a long silencer attached.

In a split second, Barnitz could not help admiring her German silencer. He waited until she fired one shot. "Drop it. Now, Muriel!" he commanded. He noted in his report that she fired at where Emma would be sleeping.

She startled and turned her gun toward him; but he was too quick and fired at her hand. The gun flew to the far corner of the room, as blood gushed from her wrist. He pushed her onto the bed and subdued her. After she was cuffed and he wrapped bleeding her wrist in a pillowcase, he opened the door and knocked three times. Out of an adjoining room came two Washington Metro DC detectives.

It was fast and quiet. Not one guest heard the shots or Muriel's groans. She refused to answer any questions, and the only behavior she exhibited following the gunshot to her hand was an occasional grimace. She was a stoic in real life, and a German spy for sure.

Although Whytock was stationed on the second floor, he did not participate in the arrest process, nor did he consider writing an article due to the sensitive nature of this operation. The arrest itself was handled by the detectives from the Washington Metro Police Department. Detective Barnitz was referred to as a member of the NYPD Bomb Squad. There was no mention of the ONI. Two detectives walked Muriel down the back staircase and out an emergency exit to the front of the hotel and a waiting squad car.

Bernitz and Whytock watched as the patrol cars drove off. She was brought to the police section of the old Providence Hospital in SW Washington, DC. Not the new Providence Hospital near the War College.

Before Barnitz took off on his scooter for his temporary home — the barracks recently built in the shadow of the Washington Monument — Whytock asked why he so readily turned Muriel over to the Metro Police and did not interrogate her.

Without clarification, Barnitz said, "No need. Someone else was interrogated and we know who she is."

53

ANNIE

Sgt. Lightfoot waited for dark before he drove into the Hamilton Hotel's driveway to pick me up. He was wearing civilian clothes. Within minutes Emma was in the back of the small truck and on her way to the AWC. When he drove me several hours ago, it felt odd not having my wheelchair, but the importance of using it as a prop in Room 207 was not debatable.

The small delivery truck was black and had no print or logos painted on the sides. Unlike most trucks it had a substantial opening between the front seat and the back of the truck. Once on the AWC campus, Lightfoot drove in the opposite direction of Roosevelt Hall, on a narrow road that was more like a path. Emma recognized the series of small, two-story brick homes to Mr. and Mrs. Lyle's home, but Lightfoot knew very well where the Lyle's lived. Located between the Parade Grounds and the Potomac River, the small home was fifty feet from the river. It wasn't until the next morning when Emma realized she could see the house from the Sketchers lab.

The Lyle's greeted Emma in a more subdued manner than they greeted me. Both times I noticed that Sgt. Lightfoot addressed Mr. Lyle as General. I was surprised because Emma always referred to Mr. Lyle as Mr. Lyle, but in fact he was a Brigadier General.

"See you in the morning, girls," Sgt. Lightfoot said, as he bid farewell to the General and his wife for the second time.

Mrs. Lyle showed Emma to our bedroom. It was on the first floor of their very small home. It had two narrow beds which were pushed together.

The four of us spoke for about thirty minutes, and then we retired to our bedrooms. We were safe, and Emma and I fell asleep faster than we thought possible.

We also woke up faster than we thought.

General Lyle woke us at 6 AM. It was Friday morning, the last day of my second week of training. But this was different. Major Van Deman was in the kitchen!

"Annie and Emma, it's 06:00 on Friday morning. The Major wants to talk to you two," Mr. Lyle said in a loud voice from the living room.

"We'll be right there Mr. Lyle," Emma said through the door after a few seconds.

General Lyle walked slowly toward our bedroom, "And, Annie, your wheelchair was delivered to the front door early this morning."

I tapped on the bedroom wall, *Thank you.*

"You're welcome."

Once we were settled in the living room, I in my wheelchair and Emma on the couch, the Major explained that Barnitz was successful in his mission, but offered few details.

"And Miss Miss Muriel is safely locked up in a police ward in the old Providence Hospital."

I tapped, *So, we have another answer to the puzzle.*

"Yes, we do, Annie," the Major said, "You two were remarkable, especially you, Emma. You knew something was wrong and sought help right away."

"Thank you," Emma said with a fair amount of pride.

"One other thing. Please refrain from telling anyone that you were removed from the Hamilton. Eventually people will find out on their own and no explanation will be required or necessary."

The Major took his leave and Mrs. Lyle offered breakfast. "Girls, I can assure you that there is not a safer place in Washington. And Emma, you are most welcome to sit in on today's lecture."

After a breakfast of cornmeal and canned ham, Emma thought about attending the lecture, but decided her "home" was with Mr. Lyle and she walked to the Sketchers lab with General Lyle. Mrs. Lyle pushed me in my wheelchair to the base of Roosevelt Hall. It was the first time she had seen such a wheelchair and took a keen interest in my disability. I should not have been surprised that she could Morse, and I answered as many of her questions as I could.

At the base of the granite steps, we waited for a fellow trainee to take me to the fifth floor. Lt. Gordon showed up first, and I Morsed a thank you and a goodbye to Mrs. Lyle.

*

On the board were a few announcements: **Tomorrow, Saturday, is a mandatory session at the Washington Naval Yard. Don't be late. Next Tuesday we will begin the third week of training.**

"Good morning, Annie. Where's Emma?" Major Van Deman asked.

I tapped, *Emma reported to the Sketchers Lab.*

"I mentioned that she could stay for this lecture. If she comes up here, please remind her that she's welcome."

I noticed that for some reason the Major was disappointed that Emma wasn't here.

Emma feels she belongs with the Sketchers. It's her new home.

The Major smiled, and said softly, "Literally and figuratively."

I smiled, also, my broad smile. It was not lost on me that two weeks ago my sister, because she was not eligible for clearance, was not allowed to attend any session, and now the Major was extending an invite. She was becoming part of the training group without becoming part of the training group.

"Annie," the Major continued, "Parker Hitt and his wife are here to present their experiences deciphering encrypted messages during General Pershing's involvement in the war with Mexico. The Commander and I tried to recruit Parker, but he favors General Pershing. He'll soon sail with him to Europe. Hitt is the best cryptologist in the army."

Last week I saw Yardley with the cryptology manual Hitt wrote.

"I did want Emma to sit in on Colonel Hitt's lecture as well as Mr. Harrison's lecture."

What is Mr. Harrison lecturing about?

"The importance of understanding context, and will use Dalia as one an example."

Will Hitt discuss his training manual?

"Yes, and the difficulties in code breaking. His wife, Genevieve, is also a codebreaker."

I want to meet her, too.

"Genevieve knows you're here and will say hello."

Ten minutes later, Colonel Hitt and his wife were escorted into the room by General Kuhn. The three sat together at the end of the table. Mrs. Hitt made eye contact with me immediately.

I tapped on the telegraph key, *Hi, Mrs. Hitt. Welcome to our group.*

She waved at me and said, "Thank you. Good to meet you, Annie."

On my side of the table the seating had not changed. Lt. Gordon sat on my left, Lt. Edwards on my right, then Whytock, and finally Johnston. At the end of the table sat the Hitts to either side of General Kuhn. On the other side Byer and Yardley sat together in their usual positions. Clark sat directly across from me. Barnitz, looking rather tired, had moved to Weller's chair. Barnitz's presence brought a level of professionalism to that side of the table that had been sorely lacking. Unfortunately, I did not get the chance to meet Spencer Eddy, the diplomat turned ONI spy. He was in attendance when I was at the Naval Yard's firing range and sat in my spot.

The Major walked to the podium. "Welcome everyone. Thank you, General, for bringing the Hitts up to the fifth floor. I've asked Colonel Hitt to provide a brief history of his involvement with making and breaking codes for the Army. He's been a member of the Signal Corp as well as being an accomplished infantry commander. In addition to publishing a book last year called *The Manual for the Solution of Military Ciphers*, he has also created a cylindrical device for coding and deciphering codes in the field.

"He and his wife, Genevieve, have been active in breaking codes for several years. I have asked him to focus on his role in General Pershing's 1916 Expedition to Mexico to capture Pancho Villa, and to provide an overview of what led to publishing his book.

"I'll start by asking Mr. Whytock to provide background for the article he wrote in mid-1915 for the *Evening World*, about the lost briefcase of German spy, Heinrich Albert. The briefcase was 'removed' from the subway by Frank Burke, one of our Secret Service agents detailed to NYC."

Ross Whytock stood up and introduced himself to General Kuhn and the Hitts, then said, "It's a pleasure to meet you, Colonel. A few in this room are aware that my newspaper has a good relationship with members of the Secret Service, the NYPD Bomb Squad, and a colleague of Mr. Dansey's, Guy Gaunt. Our editor takes credit for the article I wrote about the information contained in the spy's briefcase.

"It was indeed snatched by Mr. Burke off a subway seat. Albert fell asleep, was momentarily distracted, and jumped off the subway without his life's work. His briefcase was loaded with incriminating information about the enormous monies Germany was spending on sabotage and misinformation in the United States. It was mid-1915 and we now had all the information the President needed to fully understand the true motives of Germany. Wilson was informed of every detail by Flynn, his director of the Secret Service.

"A few documents were in German code, and they were sent to Colonel Hitt for deciphering. That's how I found out about you, sir. It's a pleasure to meet you, and your wife."

Whytock sat, then Colonel Hitt and his wife walked to the front of the room. Genevieve took a seat in the large chair. Throughout her husband's lecture she interjected information, including her thoughts on why certain transmissions were impossible to decipher.

Parker Hitt lectured by telling stories and spoke for an hour and a half before taking questions. Parker Hitt was a military celebrity, but not as famous as Lawrence Sperry. He recounted, "Time seems to go very fast when we are very busy. It seems like yesterday, but it was March 9 of last year, a little over a year ago, when Pancho Villa attacked and burned a small town in New Mexico called Columbus. It was two miles from the border with Mexico. There were a few reasons for Villa's violent attack on this town. Some say it was President Wilson changing his support in 1915 from Villa to supporting Carranza. Or, it may have been the burning of twenty Mexican men, alive, in El Paso two days before. But whatever the reason, the 600 troops stationed at Columbus, New Mexico fought Villa's 400 troops back into Mexico for at least several miles.

"That set the stage for General Pershing's Punitive Expedition. During the several-month battle, mostly on Mexican land, I was assigned to an infantry. But every night I would decipher telegrams sent by radio — you may call it wireless — or intercepted from cables. It was a very good, but humbling, learning experience."

Mrs. Hitt raised her hand, then spoke when her husband acknowledged her. "It's painstaking to decipher messages. It wears on you, day in and day out. We need large numbers of soldiers or civilians working as a team. Colonel, tell them about the British telegram that was sent your way deep in Mexican territory."

Colonel Hitt resumed, "One night, after a long battle with Villa's calvary, we were handed a transmission taken from a Western Union cable. I could not decipher the code, but it wasn't a Mexican code. Turned out it was a British Naval message. I forwarded it to our intelligence crew in Texas the next morning. I still do not know what it said.

"I want to turn back to the German messages found in that briefcase on the subway that Mr. Whytock referred to. That was two years ago. If we had a permanent espionage division in our military, as Major Van Deman has long sought to establish, we could've been able to develop the manpower required for a deciphering program. But two years after that episode, we still have very little. Only Germany, Great Britain, and France have well-developed programs. I'm disappointed that I couldn't do more, but my wife and I can only do so much. Codebreaking requires a lot of people working together to the same end.

"Thank you, Major Van Deman," Colonel Hitt concluded his lecture, "and all those assisting, for doing as much as you have."

After the question-and-answer session ended, Mrs. Hitt moved to Lt. Gordon's seat. We spoke for fifteen minutes. She wasn't the least bit bothered that I was disabled and made eye contact throughout our conversation. I was impressed that she can Morse as fast as any soldier in the Army. How I wished she would stay in Washington, DC, after her husband set sail for Europe with General Pershing and the AEF. Unfortunately, she anticipated returning to Texas. If only the Lyle's had a fourth bedroom.

I was surprised that food was served in the conference room. Mr. Harrison's lecture began during the meal, and Emma did not return for lunch. But I was not surprised that Colonel Hitt and his wife remained, or that General Kuhn returned to his office.

Mr. Harrison started his lecture as soon as he walked to the podium. "I need to discuss a topic mentioned repeatedly. And that is the importance of understanding context. As you can imagine, it has been an essential skill for diplomats for centuries. But it's important in the intelligence community, as well. Why? The fields of diplomacy and intelligence struggle to understand foreign intentions and motives. Recognizing the context is basic to that effort."

He paused and appeared to look at his notes. It was his way of highlighting his next comment. "Context is complex and nuanced, not easy to understand, even when it's handed to us on a platter of gold. It's as if this concept must be discovered, because it doesn't fall into our laps.

"For example, I argue that my boss, Bob Lansing, became Secretary of State after it was clear his predecessor, William Jennings Bryan, could not understand context. Remember the Lusitania? It was May 7, 1915. A U-boat sank it, killing over 100 Americans.

"At the time, Lansing, the second in command at the State Department, urged Wilson to respond aggressively. Lansing argued that 'German absolutism' is a great menace to democracy and encouraged Wilson to respond. But Secretary of State Bryan did not encourage a response, claiming that it wasn't 'becoming' of a neutral power. Shortly thereafter, his resignation was tendered, and six days later Lansing and Wilson sent off the first of three memos to the Kaiser admonishing Germany for such a ruthless act."

Lt. Gordon raised his hand. "Secretary Lansing become Secretary of State without a political background?"

Mr. Harrison replied, "Lansing's background is in International Law. But he's married to the daughter of John Watson Foster, a former Secretary of State. He learned a great deal from his father-in-law. The point is ... even when events are looking at us in the eye ... we often cannot recognize true intentions. And if it's difficult when people are talking to one another, it's far more difficult to figure it out from encrypted messages."

Yardley raised his hand. "Especially when many are misinformation messages."

"Exactly," Mr. Harrison replied emphatically. "I agree with the Hitts.

We need infrastructure to manage communications, and that requires manpower and funding. Without funding, from the private sector or from Federal monies, messages will never find their way to our ears."

He continued to comment on our military and Foreign Service, European spy networks, and spent an inordinate amount of time discussing the many roles of the United States Army Signal Service. I had no idea of the breath of its responsibility.

Mr. Harrison's next example answered the question why Emma was invited for the lectures. To my surprise, and without mentioning her name, Mr. Harrison shared the story of Miss Muriel and Dalia.

"My next story is about context," Mr. Harrison said ominously. "Mrs. Lynch, Ross, and I were asked to review a situation from twenty years ago. I'm discussing this because the answer becomes clear only after understanding the context in which the events happened. I am referring to the decade of the 1890s.

"Ross Whytock, the well-read journalist that he is, understood right away. Mrs. Lynch and I had to dwell on it for a while before the context changed our thinking. Mrs. Lynch still has doubts about the conclusion drawn.

"The story goes like this ..." Mr. Harrison did a dramatic pause. "A very prominent and famous elderly man owns a large hotel in New England. On two different occasions, his fame was substantial enough to convince President Grant – once with his family – to visit his hotel and tour the Island. The event I will discuss requires an understanding of context, occurs during early August of 1896; he has a sudden onset of a stroke. He's quickly attended by his physician, despite the two-hour boat ride to reach his Island hotel. As is the usual protocol, he is prescribed a medication, morphine. A few days later he dies of apoplexy, an old term for stroke.

"Then comes not one, but a series of obituaries, published in most large American newspapers. All slightly different, but not one addresses the context of the 1890s. Being quite prominent, the *New York Times* publishes a not-at-all 'normal' obituary. It includes a timeline of his death and, at the end, a paragraph about a housekeeper at his hotel. According to the *New York Times*, he visits her in her room, on a lower level, to say goodbye. She dies the next day. He dies one and a half to two days after that. The day after she dies, one day before he dies, another housekeeper at the hotel is cleaning out the deceased housekeeper's room and finds a substantial sum of money hidden in her closet. In the form of securities. Enough to buy *two* hotels on this Island."

Murmurs of surprise swept the room.

Mr. Harrison held up a hand to call for silence. "But there's more. Without known relatives, her body is quickly removed from the Island cemetery to a city forty miles away, and she is forgotten. But she was not forgotten at the famous hotel that for decades employed her during the summer months. By the way, during the rest of the year she worked at another famous hotel, the Hamilton in Washington, DC."

Another pause as Mr. Harrison's eyes surveyed his audience. "One might think that the owner was murdered, given it appeared to be a mild stroke. After all, he walked down three levels to see the housekeeper. Or ... one might think that he *helped* the housekeeper die." It was like the air left the room. Mr. Harrison went on, "But *if* he had a hand in her death, he somehow forgot to take the bundle of money from the closet. Were these two natural deaths, or a murder-suicide perhaps? Or are we confronted with *two* murders, and if so, by whom? More likely this is the story of a natural death and a self-murder."

Mr. Harrison let that sit for a moment, then said, "Before we speculate further, let's look at what was happening in the 1890s. What were folks reading? As uncomfortable as it may seem, a man by the name of Robert Ingersol was writing for the entire decade about the acceptance of what we call 'self-murder at the end of life'. Ingersol's commentaries were published almost weekly for years.

"Does it make more sense that this was a case of a self-murder pact? During that decade, morphine was readily available to anyone. With respect to Dalia, does it make sense that she may have decided Ingersol was correct? If so, then in the context of the 1890s, if they read Ingersol over several years, this suggests Dalia's actions may correlate with intentionality."

Lt. Edwards raised his hand. "Who was Ingersol, and who wrote responses to his commentary? And why was this in the papers for so many years?"

Mr. Harrison replied, "He was a lawyer and a well-known free thinker by the early 1870s. He brought back the writings of Thomas Paine to the American consciousness. An agnostic, he wrote about everything, and in the early 1890s he focused on the utility of self-murder as a method to end one's life. Incidentally, he was obese and died in 1899 from congestive heart failure."

Mr. Harrison pulled a large envelope from a briefcase and emptied the contents on the table. "The first article is about how readily available morphine was in the 1890s. The next few are Robert Ingersol's articles from different newspapers. From what Ross was able to determine, Ingersol's earliest commentary on self-murder was published in 1893. The newspaper includes rebuttals to his assertion, that it is acceptable to end your life if one see's no easy path to death."

"What exactly is self-murder?" Johnston asked.

"The term, as Ingersol uses it, means suicide at the end of one's life."

"Did the owner of that hotel know Ingersol?" Johnston asked.

"It's possible. Ingersol's position is understandable – if one is in pain and survival appears futile."

"Mr. Harrison, if they had a pact to kill themselves, did he provide the morphine? Was it coercion?" Johnston postulated.

"That question could be addressed by interviewing friends or family."

"But there were no family," Johnston pointed out, "and it was uncertain if friends were contacted."

The room quieted.

I tapped my thoughts, *This suggests that neither death was nefarious. But I worry that one can take advantage of someone else and yourself at the very same time. This points to the importance of intentionality.*

The Major joined Mr. Harrison at the podium and the two of them answered questions pertaining to this unique discussion of context. After a short break, Major Van Deman returned to the podium to discuss future assignments.

"I have a few brief announcements about who will be assigned to what posts after the training ends."

I wondered right away what he would say about Weller. Only a very few knew about his arrest, most took it on face value that he'd resigned voluntarily. It didn't take long to find out.

"Our friend Royal," the Major explained, "has decided to return to Manhattan to practice law. I expect to one day utilize his legal services. I will recruit others to his intended role of translation services for the MIS."

The Major's approach to Weller was a special learning experience.

After he had given everyone's assignments, at the end everyone realized that I was not on the list, and a few noted my disappointment.

Lt. Gordon leaned over and said he'd overheard talk of sending me to Illinois to work with Mrs. Smith at Riverbank; or perhaps Texas to work with Mrs. Hitt. For the first time since the middle of the first week, I wondered if I'd be assigned anywhere.

At 4:45 PM Emma came up to the conference room and sat with me for a few moments. Congratulations among the men continued as they filed out of the room. After they left, I asked Emma to stay back with me, not wanting to be the brunt of ridicule anymore. She waited with me as I checked the messages on the Telegraph Machine, then we took the elevator downstairs.

Once in the lobby, we saw Mrs. Lynch standing with Sgt. Lightfoot. She waved us over.

"Hi, Annie and Emma," the Sergeant said, then noted my sad face. "Is that a tired face or a sad face, Annie?"

I shrugged my shoulder and managed a weak smile.

"Saturday's training starts at 9:30 AM, Annie," Mrs. Lynch interjected. "Emma, I spoke to General Lyle, and he agrees you can spend the day with me, at my office in the Latrobe Gate. I'd like you to meet my family and have lunch at my house."

"Thank you!" Emma was enthusiastic about the invitation.

"Tomorrow morning at 9:00, I'll pick you and Annie up behind Mr. Lyle's house. No need to walk to Roosevelt Hall."

We said goodbye, negotiated the granite steps of Roosevelt Hall and then negotiated the length of the Parade Grounds to the Lyle's Army War College home. They'd been living there for almost two years. We anticipated we'd stay with his family until the end of the third week of meetings, and perhaps longer. But it wasn't to be.

54

ANNIE

That night we had dinner with Mrs. Lyle and her 27-year-old son. He entertained us with stories of training to be a Naval aviator. He knew Lawrence Sperry and was aware of his crash on Block Island. After General Lyle returned from the Sketchers lab, we washed up, climbed into bed, and found sleep, despite being enamored with their son. We skipped our nightly ritual of Morsing on the headboard. We were too tired, but also because we felt safe. A home was more comfortable than a hotel. And we did not have to worry about Miss Muriel anymore, she was now the Washington Police detective's concern.

I woke early, rested only to find Emma asleep. I closed my eyes and dozed again, but then she awoke and leaned over.

"Your sleeping smile tells me you're happy. I think it's because of the attention that Clark has bestowed upon you. If not, why are you so happy?" Emma asked.

I tapped, *I did have a very good time with Clark.*

"I thought so, but you are not worried?"

There is nothing to worry about.

Emma became silent. I couldn't figure out why. But soon the conversation took a direction I never expected. It was sister-to-sister bantering that would have occurred on Block Island, not at an Army War College.

"When am I going to meet someone? You're older and I'm aware of the 'natural law' of sisterhood."

What's that? I knew what she was referring to. Lillie and her younger sister, Nellie, lived through that situation decades ago, as did my cousins.

"It's when the older sister must find a mate before the younger siblings," Emma said. "And all hell breaks out if it's the other way around."

It is not the only law of sisterhood. The important one is that we love each other.

"What's love got to do with it? I don't want to be left alone."

Emma's sadness was confirmed by watery eyes. I felt my love bounce from my heart to hers. I said nothing for a few minutes.

Emma, we're lucky, aren't we?

She looked to the floor and raised her eyes at the same time.

Emma, would you find my green puffy dress in our luggage?

"You want to wear that dress to the Naval Yard?"

Yes, and please find my leather jacket.

"You're wearing the green dress *under* your leather jacket? It's too small for the puffy dress."

Emma, yes. It's cold out.

The coat was a tight fit, but Emma was able to button the buttons.

And put my 1908 in the inside pocket of the jacket.

"But you have that metal pocket in your wheelchair."

Within 30 minutes we were dressed. In the kitchen her spirits picked up. Mr. Lyle's son was preparing breakfast. I wondered if Emma had a crush on the future aviator of the Lyle family.

Spies weren't required to carry handguns, but it was required to pass the proficiency test. Although I passed, I looked forward to increasing my score, an option at the end of the session. I wondered how I would feel when I entered the firing range and visualized Weller firing at me.

In addition to the 1908, they'd experimented with a new Garrote, developed by mechanics in the ONI machine shop. It was a fallback weapon to use in the field. It required the use of two hands and was ruled out for me.

As we were leaving the Lyle's home Mrs. Lynch knocked on the front door.

"You're late, girls," she said with a smile. She looked at the new aviator and was introduced by Emma, then Emma started complaining about my insistence to wear the jacket over my fancy dress.

"I struggled to get Annie's coat over her dress."

"That's the reason you're late. I never heard of a 'coat excuse' before."

Mrs. Lynch smiled and looked at me. "It's a tight fit, Annie."

"I told her, but she wouldn't listen," Emma said, emphatically.

Emma handed me my metal file with its long locking bar, and I placed it inside the left side of the wheelchair.

We all waved goodbye to the Lyle's, and I noticed Mr. Lyle trying to contain his joy at witnessing Emma and I banter back and forth.

"Mrs. Lynch, will Fritz be at the Naval Yard?"

"If he's at the Yard, you can bring him into the office."

*

From Emma's perspective the morning went well. She played with Fritz on the grounds as well as in the upstairs office in the Latrobe Gate.

Around 11:30 AM, they drove over the Anacostia bridge to Mrs. Lynch her home. Along the way, she pointed out Frederick Douglas's estate, Cedar Hill. Emma noted that Mrs. Lynch's home, and every other house in Anacostia, was dwarfed by Frederick Douglas's mansion and grounds.

"We moved to Anacostia because of Frederick Douglas."

"Did you know Mr. Douglas?" Emma asked.

"Everyone did. I've mentioned that my ancestors were slaves, didn't I?"

"Yes," Emma said.

"Some men in our families, especially my husband's family, were murdered. By lynching."

"Who murdered them?" Emma asked.

"White folk, not happy with them, for one reason or another."

Conversations with Mrs. Lynch were often uncomfortable, but she was always honest. We treasured our time with her, and Emma was looking forward to lunch with her husband and two of her three children.

As soon as they entered their home, Mr. Lynch walked right up to Emma, introduced himself with a hearty smile and then walked her to a framed newspaper clipping of Frederick Douglas that was hanging on the wall. It was at the foot of the stairs leading to the bedrooms. Mr. Lynch spoke as if Douglas was still alive.

After lunch Emma played with her children until Mr. Lynch called Emma back to the kitchen table to revisit the Ingersol commentaries.

"Harriet, such a topic for Emma to hear. Does everyone at the AWC talk about death so freely?"

"Honey, Mr. Harrison and Ross Whytock explained the importance of the commentary of Ingersol."

"What newspaper would publish that?"

"Many of them, but most were in the *New York Herald.*"

"That doesn't mean everyone did it, Harriet." Mr. Lynch raised his eyes. "I don't think Emma needs to know about that. Can we talk about Frederick Douglas?"

Mrs. Lynch agreed. "Emma, did you know what Nicholas Ball and Frederick Douglas had in common?"

Emma shook her head.

"Nicholas Ball invited President Grant to his hotel on Block Island and President Grant invited Frederick Douglas to the White House," Mr. Lynch said. "I wonder if they ever met."

On the ride back to the Navy Yard, Mrs. Lynch circled the perimeter of Cedar Hill and its acres of tall cedar trees. His land was like a countryside, miles from our nation's capital, rolling hills, deep glens, and a natural flowing spring. "I find it difficult to believe," Mrs. Lynch said, "that Cedar Hill is only ten minutes from the Naval Yard."

The ride back was free of all talk of death, until they drove through the Latrobe Gate.

55

ANNIE and Third Person

(Due to the confusion and ramifications of events that unfolded before Mrs. Lynch and Emma returned to the Naval Yard, and because details were not known until weeks later, what follows is a composite narrative of events that occurred on Saturday, the last day of the second week of training. I am not privy to details, and for security reasons, should not be.)

Early Saturday morning Mrs. Lynch drove through the Latrobe Gate and dropped me off at the security building where our group was congregating. The liveliness among the officers was remarkable. No petty comments or looks of distain were sent my way.

"Everyone's chatting and cheerful," Emma observed.

"Probably because there's only one more week of meetings. And they're freed from the confines of the conference room," Mrs. Lynch said.

Emma retrieved the wheelchair from the boot and that was all she had to do. Clark and Peter pushed everyone aside, and although I transferred myself to the wheelchair, I let Clark push me to the building.

I gave a quick wave to Emma. She was looking forward to spending the day with Mrs. Lynch and walking the Yard with Fritz. Mrs. Lynch used an office on the second floor of the Latrobe Gate. It had two windows that looked onto the Naval Yard and one window that looked onto M Street. Surprisingly, little traffic entered the gate this Saturday morning, and many of the industrial buildings were quiet.

The first session was a review of "Close Combat Weapons for

Bombers." It dealt with hand grenades and pistols. Before Sperry, the term "bombers" referred to infantry trained to throw grenades. After Sperry, the term gradually took on a new meaning.

The next session introduced the new Naval Garotte. The original Garotte received poor reviews, and many argued it should be withdrawn from service. It was designed as an accessory weapon for close fighting situations. Johnston was the best at using it. Demonstrating his skills on a padded pole, a stand-in for an enemy's neck, he could rip anyone's head right off. Under his breath we heard him say, "Could've used this in NYC."

At 11:30 AM a second officer, the instructor I met at the firing range during my first week of training, was on duty. He nodded approval when he saw me. The group split into two and we entered the firing range. My group consisted of Clark, Peter, Tom Yardley, and Byer. Barnitz was excused.

Right away, there was a misfire of a Colt .45 and Byer was burned on the wrist.

Then, before I used my own Colt 1908, I used the instructor's Colt .45. The gun recoiled and the wheelchair moved back. The bullet went awry.

"It's a good thing this it's a Saturday and no one saw that," Yardley yelled out. "Stick with your little handgun, Annie." Clark and Byer couldn't stop laughing. And I must admit that I couldn't contain a laugh, either.

"Best to use your own pistol, Annie. No need to shoot that heavy pistol," the instructor said. "They're a rough crowd."

With my 1908 I hit target after target from my seated position in the wheelchair. I held steady the wheelchair with my right foot. I had improved since Tuesday, which impressed the instructor. He opened the back wall and gave me an informal proficiency test. I passed, this time with an average score, not below average. No laughter from the crowd this time.

But then Lt. Gordon used the original Colt .45 to take the proficiency test, and it misfired, too. The instructor promptly ended the session, to figure out what went wrong.

"Holder and Yardley, you'll have to return to take the test," the instructor yelled over his shoulder.

I think everyone had tired of our small group, especially with Yardley's condescending remarks. They were not only directed toward me. After ten minutes of listening to Yardley, Clark announced he'd had enough and walked out of the firing range. I was left with Yardley, Byer, and the instructor.

"Maybe someone deliberately sabotaged the training session," Yardley thought out loud.

"Not possible, these guns are locked up," the instructor said.

I didn't offer an opinion and was grateful I had my own pistol. Could the guns have been sabotaged?

After a while, Clark came back and pushed me outside.

"Yardley is stifling," Clark said. "He doesn't like me or you."

He was difficult with everyone today, not only me.

"And he dresses so tidy, never carelessly, and that bald head of his. He's full of himself, and he thinks he's the future of the MIS."

I was amused at the extent of his antagonism.

"The *Boothbay's* back from a run. I wonder what Naval Yard got her last shipment of long guns. Do you want to see it?"

I raised my eyes to say, *Yes*.

The SS *Boothbay* was docked at the same location on the bulkhead as the day we flew in from New York City.

"Were their portholes in this boat?" he asked.

Very few. It was built as a cargo vessel.

Clark continued to push me along the bulkhead, to a spot near a sandy beach. Located behind several buildings it was secluded and quiet. So quiet that I could not believe we were still in the Naval Yard.

"There are several of these small, sandy, and secluded beaches upriver."

We walked further until we arrived at a longer 30-foot-long narrow beach directly behind two of the longest buildings in the Naval Yard.

"I like this place. I come here on weekends. It drops off quickly and gets deep. There's another small beach further upriver, too," Clark said.

Annie looked to her right. *Long guns are manufactured in these buildings.*

"I know," Clark said. "I've been inside."

They are off limits, Clark!

"You want to see inside? It's fascinating."

I looked sideways, *No. Why should we do that?*

Clark sat in front of the wheelchair and stared out to the Potomac River where it meets the Anacostia River. He didn't respond to my answer and seemed preoccupied. Like Emma was this morning.

We sat for ten minutes, and he turned to me.

"You look beautiful in that dress, Annie," Clark said, softly.

I smiled and wondered what he was going to say or do next. His eyes darted about, mostly toward the Navy Yard. All the while I looked out at the confluence of the two rivers. I was trying to read his mind.

Today, the front of the Naval Yard was quiet, and back here more so. The only sounds came from inside a few buildings, and they were muffled. Almost no one was walking about this morning.

Clark wanted to show me his favorite beach, near where his barracks were located. We walked along the bulkhead to another beach that was behind yet another group of buildings that I had not seen.

Suddenly Clark, assured that no one was looking, bent down and gave me a kiss.

I did not want to return the kiss, but I did. This wasn't the passionate kiss from our date last week, perhaps because of the cold breeze off the river.

Something was wrong and I was afraid he might "out" himself before my very eyes. I started to shiver, even though I was warm, my leather jacket buttoned to the top. Clark removed his winter coat and laid it over me.

He blocked my view of the river, but when he moved to the side, I saw what I thought was a periscope in the Potomac River, at the mouth of the Anacostia.

Is that a U-boat? *Can't be.*

I waited for a response from Clark, who turned to look out to the Potomac. He became unsettled before my eyes.

"Ah, right on time."

To buy time, I tapped slowly and watched his every move, *What's that low profile boat doing out there? It looks like a German U-boat. Like the one I saw off Block Island.*

Although I long suspected he was the spy and his affection more or less contrived, I hoped for the opposite. I fell for him, but I didn't fall for him. Or was I simply naïve? I had to act calm, and why not? There was no indication that he would hurt me.

"That's how I've been instructed to escape," Clark said.

I needed to protect myself. I continued to tap slowly, *Escape? Really. You're running from something?*

"I'm the spy, Annie. Big surprise, huh? And after I dispose of you, I'll row out and climb aboard the boat."

I tapped more slowly, *Were these new orders that you were given, Clark? Do you think you can escape?*

"I will escape. I was asked to eliminate you, of all people, a crippled, lovesick girl. But you're a threat to a lot of people, including German intelligence. They know about your involvement on Block Island. If it wasn't for you that man would still be alive.

"Sorry to break your heart, Annie. From day one I wanted to frame you, but didn't have to because of the unexpected help from a few of the group. But you contributed a lot and outfoxed them. Now everyone respects you. But it's over for you now."

I realized he was going to kill me. Otherwise, there was no need for him to have an escape plan. He glanced around the Naval Yard, expecting to see men coming toward them, but saw no one. Clark had chosen the most secluded section of the Naval Yard. Large amounts of vegetation in the shallow areas of the Anacostia River created privacy. Few boats were on the Potomac during this time of year. The multitude of working and secure buildings blocked this small beach. If I yelled, or fired my 1908, it would unlikely gain attention of anyone. Clark had chosen the best spot to kill me.

I figured out a way to escape and continued to tap slowly to gain time. *My heart is fine, Clark. I really liked you. Even though, you were a suspect. But I needed to prove it before I exposed you.*

Ensign Clark Holder looked upset, "How did you know?" Instead of killing her on the spot, he took the time to hear the explanation.

My first clue were the messages sent from the training room's telegraph to Mexico City. No one should have known to telegraph messages to that Western Union office.

"Why?" Clark asked.

You don't know? It was my clue that someone in our group was communicating to someone in the German Embassy in DC – via Mexico City!

"You're smart, Annie," Clark said. "How did you figure that out?"

I was glad he paused to ask questions. Slowly, almost imperceptibly, I moved toward end of the beach near the bulkhead. I stopped shaking when I remembered that to fight back is perhaps the best way to address fear.

After I deciphered the reference to a "U-boat" ... I asked Sergeant Lightfoot to help me understand what the symbols meant. That was crafty of your handler, Clark. Using a U-boat to leave DC was very clever.

I was hoping he would change his mind and not kill me. But it was to no avail. I ended my lengthy Morsed messages and focused on moving closer to the water's edge.

Suddenly, Clark became agitated, eye's wide open and darting from side to side. In front of my eyes, he became wild and frantic, and was no longer the Clark that I had dinner or lunch with.

"You're not getting the chance to prove I'm the spy, Annie. You're going to die."

He pulled out his Naval Garrote, and I started wheeling away, but in a direction he *did not* expect. I sought the safety of the river. Deep water has always been my salvation.

Clark initially backed up, thinking I'd wheel toward the front of the Naval Yard. But when he saw where I was going, he caught himself, jumped back up and got behind my wheelchair.

With my right hand I grabbed the metal file and blocked a punch that he threw with his right hand. His clenched fist bounced off the locking bar and the file went flying. It gave me a few seconds to reach the top of the bulkhead where it ended on the beach. I did not have time to reach for my 1908.

He wrapped the Garrote around my neck, and I thought of Johnston ripping the "head" off the pole. If Johnston was the spy, there would be no possibility to maneuver around him and I'd be dead in seconds. With all my might I yanked the right wheel hard, to run over Clark's foot, and wheeled into the river.

The weight of the wheelchair, and the angle that it hit his foot, caused such pain that Clark dropped the Garrote and yelled out. He picked up the Garotte and advanced toward me, again, keeping an eye on my right hand. He was ready to place the wire around my neck, and hesitated when I started breathing heavy, a technique that I hoped would give me a few more seconds. He hesitated and probably figured I had panicked and wouldn't fight anymore.

To his complete shock, after taking the deep breaths, I used the strength in my right hand and pitched myself out of the wheelchair. I landed on the top of the bulkhead and rolled directly into the safety of the river. I quickly sank and swam with my right hand and leg. The murky water provided all the cover I needed. Within seconds I disappeared from his view and knew a limiting factor was my need to surface to breathe.

I heard Clark yell, but did not hear splashing and I assumed he'd tripped over my wheelchair. I had never mentioned to him that I love to swim, and I hoped he thought I was drowning. I couldn't see my outstretched right hand and I knew there was no way Clark could see me.

The Potomac had lower visibility than Block Island waters, but the temperature was warmer, even in winter. I surfaced twenty feet from the bulkhead, treaded water, and took as many deep breaths as I could. And then I took more. I wished for the safety of pilings that I could swim around, but I felt comfortable in any body of water. I watched his every move and continued to take deep breaths.

Then I saw the skiff and thought I'd swim to it. But Clark saw me looking at the small boat and called out, "It was dropped off last night. It's for me."

I dove under again but came back up after thirty seconds to see what his next move was. Clark stood still, perhaps unsure of his next move. He looked with vacant eyes at his mission. He needed to kill me, and I dove back under when I saw him drop his Naval Garotte and remove a small Luger from his ankle holster.

I dove deep when I saw the gun. But when I didn't hear the gun go off, I realized I made a mistake. I surfaced with only my mouth and took as many breaths as I could, to prepare for a deep dive. When I was ready,

I surfaced and drew his attention, and he aimed his gun at me.

I was about forty feet from where I rolled off the bulkhead.

"Goodbye, Annie." He took aim and fired his first shot. "It was great knowing you."

I heard him fire a second shot, and I dove deeper. Then I surfaced and, out of the corner of my eye, I caught the site of Fritz running at full speed. I was back under several feet when I heard the third gunshot. It missed its mark, too. I surfaced again. I knew Fritz had exceptional hearing, but worried that no one else could hear the gunshots.

The moment after Clark fired his third shot, Fritz jumped on him. When I surfaced again for a quick breath, I saw Clark struggling to get up from the edge of the bulkhead. I didn't see his gun anywhere and thought it must have gone flying out of his hand and into the river. I was relieved Fritz kept barking, but realized that he might kill Fritz, too.

I could hear Fritz barking underwater. When I heard him stop, I was worried and surfaced again. But he was okay and had taken chunk out of Clark's right hand. Fritz then jumped into the Potomac and swam to me.

Clark jumped right in and followed Fritz, holding his Garrote. He'd have to drown me, but Fritz got to me first. He grabbed the sleeve of my thick leather coat sleeve, his teeth piercing the leather. I started kicking with my good leg and we both swam along the bulkhead to the other beach.

We reached the embankment before Clark. Had I made a tactical error, or did he? He should have stayed on land, but I should have stayed in the water.

But it was too late, and I pulled myself up onto the beach, a few feet from the edge of the bulkhead. Fritz pulled as hard as he could on my sleeve, and slowly backed up and I was almost out of the water.

But then Clark reached us and thought he would kill me for sure. I had given it a gallant fight and Fritz helped, too. When he grabbed my ankle and pulled me back into the river, I kicked with my good foot and took several deep breaths. I could stay underwater and was not worried if he pulled me deep.

But I forgot he had his Garrote, and then realized it was my tactical error. I should have stayed in the water!

Fritz continued to bark ferociously and only stopped when he dove into the water to bite Clark, this time on the left hand that was wrapped around my ankle. I saw Fritz's teeth sink deep into Clark's wrist and he let go only when blood began pouring into the murky water.

Clark screamed in pain and released his grip on my ankle. He then reached for the Garrote to complete his mission.

I was getting tired, but Fritz and I repeated what we'd just done moments before and together got back to the small beach. But Clark reached us within seconds, more determined than ever to kill me, and Fritz.

He dropped the Garrote and took out a knife with a four-inch blade and lunged at Fritz first. But Fritz's reflexes were too good, and he missed his mark. Fritz continued to bark as a dog possessed.

Two armed guards had recognized the bark of Fritz and raced toward us. The first guard to reach us grabbed Fritz to calm him, and the second guard approached Clark, now standing in a foot of water, his knife hidden.

Unfortunately, the guards did not understand Morse Code. I pointed at Clark with my right hand.

"No, Annie's the real German spy!" Clark yelled immediately. The guards had no idea about a spy.

I shook my head pointing out to the middle of the Potomac River. I kept pointing until one of the guards recognized what we thought was a U-boat periscope. And then I pointed to the Garotte. I tapped, *It's the murder weapon* but neither guard understood. And finally, to the skiff, *Escape boat*.

The first guard said, "She's right. Is that a damn U-boat? What's that doing there?"

The other guard drew his gun and trained it on Clark. "She could swim to it, but it's a long way."

The first guard said, "I can't believe that the Germans brought a small U-boat up the Potomac. It's not deep enough to come in this close without being seen."

By then I had caught my breath and pointed to the skiff.

"Of course, of course. The skiff. She can't row a skiff herself."

To Clark's astonishment, the first guard let go of Fritz, knowing he would jump at Clark with more vengeance than before.

The first guard convinced that Clark, if not a spy, did not belong in the Navy Yard, drew his gun. "Make any move of any kind and I'll shoot, so help me God!"

But a moment later Clark reached for his knife and lunged at me, but the second guard ran up to him and pointed his gun at his face. Clark dropped the knife. He stood standing in a foot of water.

I crawled back to the water's edge and leaned against the bulkhead, while both guards stared at Clark in total disbelief.

I tapped on the bulkhead, not to the guards, but to my colleagues who were approaching, *He wears an ankle holster with a Luger. He's the other spy.*

The guard tried to figure out what I was trying to say, but at that point Yardley, Gordon, and Edwards were there. Capt. Johnston was not far behind.

Yardley understood. "You found another spy? Where's his Luger?"

In the river. He used his Garrote, too.

Yardley saw the bloody bruise on the left side of my face. He took a good look at it and walked over to Clark and wanted to punch his face. The guard kept his gun drawn, and warned Yardley, "Don't do it, Sergeant, don't do it."

Yardley nodded compliance, turned, as if to walk away, but then I saw him spin back around, take two steps, plant his feet, and punch Clark Holder in the face, snapping his head back and knocking him back into the water. Clark yelled out and brought his arms up to his face to protect against another blow.

The guard pushed Yardley away. But Johnston was right there to take his place. Astonished at what had just happened, he walked into the water's edge and punched him right back into the water.

"Enough, now stop. We'll take him." The guards cuffed Clark and searched him for more weapons.

Ignoring the pain inflicted on his right hand from landing that punch, Yardley walked over and lifted me off the ground. He placed me in the wheelchair that Peter had retrieved.

Nice hook, Tom.

"You must be freezing, Annie," he said, and then added, "We should've never doubted you."

I smiled and raised my eyes.

"But of course, it would be *you* who figured out Clark was the other spy," he said, shaking his head.

I realized then that he too was aware of Weller being in a stockade and not a law office in Manhattan. I gave Yardley my one-handed signal for, *Thank you*. He took his coat off and placed it over me and the wheelchair.

Lt. Edwards and Capt. Johnston kept their eye on the U-boat.

"They saw what happened. It's heading downriver," Capt. Johnston yelled.

"There it goes," Peter confirmed.

Capt. Johnston walked over, "I'm sorry, Annie. I'm very sorry."

I tapped, *You're the good New Yorker!* I vowed then to always trust Capt. Johnston and look past behavior that might be considered brute-like. I would work with him any day.

Lt. Gordon smiled, gave me a hug, and wiped water from my head. Lt. Edwards accompanied the two guards as they took Holder away, his arms cuffed behind him. Clark didn't notice the Lieutenant as he looked over his right shoulder and yelled to me, "Do you want to know who the driver was?"

I heard his comment, later confirmed. But this part of the story, the night at the Cosmos Club, is still missing. Who was the driver?

I reflected on this day for years to come. I had helped identify the German spy on Block Island, and two spies in the first series of meetings at the Army War College. I was grateful that my colleagues worked behind the scenes to place blanks in the gun Weller used at the Naval Yard firing range. And that I was able, with Fritz's help, to survive an attack by Clark in the waters of the Potomac.

Remarkably, I did not feel sad that Clark followed through on his orders to kill me, it simply is part of the profession. Back inside the security office, the boys, and yes, I referred to them as the boys, took turns drying the murky water off me. Until Lt. Gordon said, "Let's clean her wounds." During that process, Yardley announced that whenever he saw me on campus, he'd push me to wherever I need to go.

56

ANNIE

The objective to kill me played out on two narrow sandy beaches separated by a bulkhead. By the time Emma and Mrs. Lynch returned from lunch the Naval Yard was quiet. Fritz had stopped his wild, unrelenting barking and the boys had dealt the final blow to Clark. When Mrs. Lynch and my sister walked to the Latrobe Gate's second floor office, they had no idea Clark tried to kill me.

Until the phone rang.

"Good morning, sir," Mrs. Lynch said. It was Commander McCauley's assistant.

"The Commander is on his way," the assistant said. "There's been a disturbance at the bulkhead."

Mrs. Lynch's jaw dropped. "Her sister and I ... we were at my house, having lunch. Got back a few minutes ago. I had no idea. What happened? ... Oh, no! Okay, we'll walk there now."

She hung up and looked at Emma in disbelief.

"The Commander is on his way in."

"What happened?" Emma asked.

"Your sister was attacked."

"What?"

"The spy tried to kill her. But she's okay."

"Not again!" Emma turned pale and leaned on Mrs. Lynch.

"Emma, she'll be okay. Let's go."

At the security building the officers were standing outside.

"Emma," Lt. Edwards called out, "your sister's okay. She's in the back room."

"Go ahead, she's with the Major and Yardley," Johnston said.

"Thank you," Emma said, rubbing away tears. "Is that Annie coughing?"

Emma was shaking but settled down when she saw that I was having a heart-to-heart with Yardley. I was in my wheelchair, my hair wet and filled with sand and dried blood all over. Under the muck of the Potomac, she saw my bruised face. I kept coughing up dirty Potomac water.

"You must have aspirated a lot of water, Annie," Emma said.

To add to Emma's distress, the Major kept muttering, "What did I miss, how did I miss this?"

I tapped to Emma, *We're waiting for the Commander. Is Mrs. Lynch outside?*

"Yes. The Commander hasn't arrived," Emma said, her face became paler after registering the shock of seeing me.

"Your sister's tough, Emma," Sgt. Yardley said, cleaning the grime from my hair.

Emma nodded and came closer, wiping her tears. "What happened? You're beaten bad. Where does it hurt?"

Everywhere, but I'm okay.

Emma leaned over and hugged me and whispered, "Why is Yardley here?"

"Emma, your sister is the bravest person I've met in a long time."

"What happened to her?" Emma looked up from her crouched position at Yardley.

"It's what she accomplished," Yardley said.

Clark is the spy.

"Clark?" Emma exclaimed. "Did he try to drown you?"

"Yes, Clark, did," Yardley said, somewhat subdued. "He's been taken away."

Emma couldn't know, but the Major was aware that Weller, and very recently, Clark, were both German spies. Yardley admitted that he stopped focusing on finding a spy after Weller was arrested. But no one, including me, expected Clark to be given an order to kill me.

In my mind there were several factors. Miss Muriel became frustrated after Weller's arrest. Add that to the loss of a spy on Block Island and she wanted revenge. I suspect that this is when Clark's spy status changed from sleeper to active.

Security had summoned two nurses to attend to me. They washed my face and rinsed the dried blook from my hair. They brought enough bandages to cover my wounds. My cough brought out their stethoscopes and they listened to my lungs. My breath sounds were noisy, the nurses said. And I agreed that I aspirated a small portion of the river. It was painful when they scrubbed my wounds, but it kept my mind off Clark. Thirty minutes later they said goodbye, leaving bandages to take back to the Lyles.

I relived the past week – where I was on target and where I wasn't. I thought about the importance of avoiding the wrath of Miss Muriel, yet somehow, I initiated the order for Clark to kill me.

"I feel awful, Annie," Yardley said, after the nurses left.

You said I might be the spy. Why?

"I don't know."

I know why. I'm a young woman, from a little-known island in the Atlantic.

"I've never been to Block Island." Yardley said, avoiding comment on my assessment.

Don't worry, we do not think Herman Melville visited either.

"Annie, it must've been harrowing to be attacked. That's never happened to me."

If the water was deeper, with pilings, it would've been easier to escape him.

Yardley looked under my bandages. "Your face is swelling. If need be, we'll find a physician."

"Your face looks bad. Much worse than your hip," Emma said.

Yardley walked to the front room to ask the Major for medical attention, and to allow time for me to talk with Emma.

"After the second day of training you said something that I'll never forget," Emma said.

What did I say?

"... that you alone would have to change Yardley's mind to make him believe that you belong in the ONI. And now you are allies and will never have to prove him, or anyone else, wrong again."

I smiled.

"Aren't you in pain?"

I tapped on my portable telegraph key; *I feel beat up. I fought back and completed my mission to identify Clark as a spy.*

Yardley heard my tapping, “Emma, your sister was right, again”.

While Yardley and I spoke, Emma scrubbed more dried blood that the nurses missed. Several lacerations were exposed and the red line around my neck became more prominent. The Garotte got more of me than I thought.

Emma saw bite marks on the sleeves of my leather coat. “Fritz helped, too?”

“You should’ve heard Fritz barking,” Yardley said. “All of DC heard him.”

“Did Fritz get Clark?” Emma asked.

I raised my eyes three times and gave a hand signal that I’d share more later.

Major Van Deman was called out of the building when the Commander arrived. They both spoke to the group to ask their perspective on the morning’s events.

“The Major admitted,” Yardley said, “that he figured Clark was a second spy two days ago. But couldn’t believe he acted so soon.”

Well, we know what their conversation will be.

“We all stopped thinking about a spy after Weller was put away. But you didn’t give up.”

It was my assigned mission.

At that point I needed to ask Yardley questions that I could not answer. It was a long shot, but he was privy to my mission, and I thought it would be safe to ask. I wasn’t wrong, he kept my questions and his answers confidential.

Tom, I need your knowledge and advice.

Yardley looked surprised. “There’s more to your mission?”

I tapped on the key at my fastest speed, that only Yardley could understand. Even Emma was flabbergasted at my speed, realized I needed privacy and walked to the front room.

I have four questions.

“I’ll answer honestly, or not at all.”

When you were absent from the Commander’s presentation, 1) Had you identified the spy? 2) Did you know about the Zimmermann Telegrams before March 1? 3) Do you think Eddie Bell is too cozy with Room 40? Mr. Harrison or someone else at State figured out that the Zimmermann messages were sent on our own State Department’s Atlantic Submarine

Cable. 4) My question is, does that make you suspicious Room 40 intercepted it? 5) And if so, do you think it was intercepted at the Brits' coastal sites, or in the basement of Whitehall?

"That's five questions, Annie! I'll answer the first three. You're on your own with the other two."

I raised my eyes.

"I couldn't figure out who the spy was, but I knew it wasn't you. Spies are well-trained, and you were eager to learn everything about intelligence. Plus, you're from Block Island."

Why weren't you at the Commander's presentation?

"I knew the Commander wanted to make a point about Room 40, to Dansey, along the lines of the questions I will not answer."

Your answer to my second question, please.

"My first assignment at the Signal Service was the State Department, about nine years ago. They gave me a desk on the third-floor balcony in the library. I deciphered transmissions before Leland Harrison was called up from his diplomatic responsibilities to head up State's intelligence bureau. And yes, I was summoned the day after Ambassador Page and Eddie Bell learned about the telegram. I believe, as does the Commander, that despite the Brits being our closest ally, we need some separation from them. I spoke to Eddie Bell before I deciphered the portion of the telegram that they gave me ..."

What?

"To answer your third question, Bell agrees with everything that comes out of Room 40, and claims to have deciphered part of the Zimmermann Telegram before March 1 ... but I know he's not capable of decrypting anything. Even with a German code handbook by his side."

What did you think after you deciphered the telegram?

"I was presented with only a small section of the telegram, and it was in the old German code. We know from our exercises last week that the Germans use the new code for top secret transmissions."

The only thing that makes sense to me is that Room 40 intercepted and deciphered the telegram in the newer German code. They then re-wrote it in the old German code and gave it to State.

"You're on the right path, including the idea of three Zimmermann Telegrams."

Thank you. Is it possible the two spies are related to the Zimmermann Telegrams?

"Possible. The Germans are embarrassed about their stupid idea and want payback. In the end, perhaps you were the easiest target."

Are my thoughts about Room 40's ruse, and knowing about Professor Ewing's design for the Brits' cable network, puts me in the eyesight of Dansey?

"You are in everyone's eyesight. We know Ewing, with Churchill's support, masterminded the communication strategy for the UK. He's central to the success of Room 40. Dansey likes you, but we're not supposed to acknowledge his attachment to the SIS. I only worried when you suggested that Dansey may have been in Mexico City dealing with the Telegrams. He's everywhere for sure.

"We're also never to discuss what Whytock knows, that House, Guy Gaunt, and others in the SIS NYC office are in contact with our Secret Service. I've made my feelings about Eddie to Harrison. And now the SIS knows how I feel."

Mr. Harrison appears independent.

"Yes, he is, and that's why he's one of our most important diplomats. I think that he's tolerated by Room 40 because he attended a boarding school outside of London."

This is more than jealous inter-office arguing. Personal and personnel relationships are important, aren't they?

"Annie, yes! And, one other things, I had no idea that it was you who raised that issue last October, when you weren't even in the ONI."

Emma came into the room and let us know that the Commander and Major were walking in. Before she left, Emma asked Yardley one question: "Was Clark acting?"

"He genuinely liked Annie. You could see it in his eyes."

"Then why would he want to kill my sister?"

"His handler instructed him to carry out his mission after an event happened to create an urgency. That event was Weller, but you are not supposed to know that, Emma."

57

ANNIE

The Commander and Major Van Deman entered the room as Emma and Yardley walked out.

"I can't believe you didn't act yesterday," the Commander said, irritated. "She was almost killed."

"I know. I never thought a sleeper spy would be given an order to kill, and Annie at that. And, at the bulkhead."

"The training could've been postponed, giving time to figure it out, and arrest him."

"I know. Both Weller and Holder were recruited from outside the military," the Major said. "I'll never recruit so hastily again."

It wasn't lost on me that the two highest-ranking intelligence officers in the United States positioned seats around my wheelchair as they finished their conversation.

"Ralph, who tipped Clark off, or was it purely a Miss Muriel decision?" the Commander asked.

But before the Major could answer, the Commander looked at me. "Annie, you should have said something sooner."

I looked down and said nothing. The Commander spoke only after I looked up.

"You knew Leland and I, as well as the Major, were available to you."

I raised my eyes, twice.

"What are your thoughts, now."

Miss Muriel must have changed Clark's mission after Weller was arrested, and after he, I presume, outed Miss Muriel. I don't think anyone tipped him off. The U-boat in the Potomac suggests it was planned.

"Annie, it wasn't a U-boat. It's a boat with a low gunwale equipped with what may have been a periscope," the Commander said. "From the description I think it was a Hickman Sea Sled. Very fast, and beautiful."

"Only Germany has money enough for those boats," the Major added.

That makes more sense than a U-boat.

"Annie, I'm sorry I gave you the okay to have dinner at the Cosmos with Clark. It was a mistake," the Major said.

I was able to spend time with him, to figure him out.

"I'm glad you think that. And we must thank your sister, because her information led to Joe identifying Weller at the German Embassy. Annie, when you, Mr. Harrison, and I met at the library, you mentioned the possibility of two spies."

I tapped, *Three spies, if you include Miss Muriel. But it wasn't a mistake for me to have dinner with Clark. If there was a mistake, it was Miss Muriel showing up at the Hamilton! But I wonder if she acted alone, in that Bernstorff was on his way back to Germany.*

"I would think Bernstorff left a plan after he sailed for Germany. Poor Miss Muriel. How was she to know that she'd run up against the sisters from Block Island?" the Commander added. "I'll call John next week and explain everything."

At that point I thought the conversation was over.

But it had only begun. It started innocently, but over the next thirty minutes I realized that not only was I being admonished, but my "suggested" vacation seemed more like a suspension. It didn't make sense. I had done so much.

"Lieutenant Edwards mentioned that you're aware the Zimmermann Telegrams were transmitted from Germany to Bernstorff on our diplomatic Atlantic Submarine Cable. He says that you also know where it was intercepted."

Yes.

"Could you explain?"

We all know that in 1914 the ships of the Royal Post Office cut the

English Channel Submarine Cables the very night Britain declared war on Germany. They did not cut our State Department's diplomatic cable. And, because President Wilson adhered to a neutrality policy, he gave permission to the Germans to utilize our Atlantic Diplomatic Submarine Cable to contact the German Embassy.

"You must not repeat what you know. Do you believe Room 40 of Britain's Secret Intelligence Service is hiding information from us? You are aware that they have been helpful to us since 1914 by identifying sabotage and influence missions the Germans have undertaken."

I am aware that Mr. Dansey represents the SIS and have learned that Guy Gaunt also represents the SIS and they have been helpful to the United States.

"Annie," the Major interjected, "in 1915 the SIS identified Franz von Rintelen as a German spy. He was trying to recruit the old president of Mexico, Huerta, with large sums of money, if he agreed to fight our Calvary, at the Mexican border. Room 40 intercepted another telegram from Berlin that summoned von Rintelen back home. He was arrested by the Brits and interrogated by the head of Room 40. He's now locked up."

Of course they helped us, but Room 40 must have intercepted those telegrams the same way they intercepted Zimmermann's telegrams. In one of their relay stations.

"Annie, another example was last year when the SIS helped us identify another spy, von Papen. He tried to blow up a train bridge in Maine, crossing to Canada."

I read about the bridge explosion. Are you concerned I know the SIS has two senior agents in the U.S., Dansey and Gaunt? Is that the problem?

"Annie, the Brits have been helpful in many ways and it's important to recognize that. Don't look for answers to questions that we don't ask."

The Commander and the Major were unified in their admonishment.

I'm interested in missions involving foreign negative intelligence and would like to pursue that in the ONI.

"We know you are. But you must remain silent about what you learn."

"A final question," the Major said, "how do you think Room 40 developed the capacity to intercept messages so readily?"

Their system is the brainchild of Professor Ewing. One day he'll be recognized as the man who saved the British Empire. If my ideas interest no one, then he'll never gain recognition for his accomplishments.

When our conversation ended, I wasn't sure what happened. Was I correct when I worried my future in the ONI was in doubt? Unbeknownst to me, after they left, they asked the training group to stay with me and Emma and drive us back to the Lyle's home.

I wheeled myself to the small lavatory and closed the door. I reflected on the reprimand and wondered how different the experience of training would've been if Miss Smith or Mrs. Hitt were in attendance. It would have been easier, and a lot more comfortable than being the only woman in attendance. That thought did not prevent me from resting my head in my right hand and sob.

A few minutes later, aware someone was outside the door, I stopped sobbing, washed up, and opened the door.

It was Yardley. "I marvel you're not in pain."

I'm sore. I wanted to mention that the reprimand was more painful than being beaten up.

You're right. I must watch what I say ... what I think.

"Yes, you do, Annie."

They want me to take a long vacation. Tom, a spy protects methods and sources without fail.

Yardley raised his eyes, and tapped at lightning speed, *Can you imagine Room 40 acknowledging how and where they intercepted the Zimmermann Telegram? It's like imagining a day without a yesterday. Both inconceivable events.*

I looked down and tapped, *You're right, and even if I'm right, I'll never be right.*

Yardley Morsed faster than me and understood context and intentions embedded in telegrams better than anybody. That skill would serve him well. Would I enjoy working with him? I would prefer Parker Hitt and his wife, not only because he is a pioneer of American military code-making and breaking. But because Hitt is such a pleasant man. I would also favor Miss Smith but she lives in a different part of the United States.

I thought that with Sergeant Yardley, Parker Hitt, along with Miss Smith's husband to be, and Colonel Moorman, the United States has a great group of budding cryptologists. Could they rival Room 40?

"Annie, Annie. Stop dwelling," Yardley admonished. "Let's go outside, with the rest of the group."

Once outside, Johnston called out my first and last name, then threw a ball he was tossing to Fritz in my direction. Fritz came running, ignored the ball, and jumped in my lap.

Byer yelled, "You look like a coughing mummy." I was covered in bandages; his comment drew the biggest laugh. Emma sat against a tree where Byer, Edwards, and Gordon were throwing the football. She had tripped in her dress while playing with the officers and was tending to her wounded ego.

And then Barnitz showed up with Spencer Eddy! They came over to say hello. Spencer looked erudite, confirming he wasn't from my family, and was quite the gentleman, as was Detective Barnitz. After ten minutes of conversation they left for a meeting with the Commander.

"Come on, let's head to the bulkhead. Let's figure out how Annie avoided being killed," Johnston said.

"Annie, the Commander wants you to walk us through what happened," Lt. Gordon said. "On land, not in the water."

I was reluctant to relive the experience and started shaking. Lt. Edwards came right over. "Pretend we're the Calvary. You've gotta get back in the saddle, Annie."

Realizing he was right, but not knowing how to respond, I tapped, *Remember, Lieutenant Edwards, I only work for the Weather Bureau.*

The group laughed and did not stop until we reached the bulkhead. Along the way Lt. Gordon suggested my code name should be, "Bulkhead". I tapped that I prefer pilings, but Bulkhead it was. I explained that the word "bulkhead" has two meanings, but they didn't care.

Fighting back, of course, was important, but so too, was the need to be with everyone. Another lesson confirmed, that in the future, at another time and place, it would be someone else who would bear the brunt of war.

58

ANNIE

Cumbersome bandages over bruises and lacerations, a worsening cough, and my aching disabled body made it difficult to fall sleep Saturday night. Unexpected were the waves of burning in a line around my neck, a sinister reminder of Clark using his Garotte. It wrapped tight as I spun away.

Despite my reprimand, I felt accomplished. I completed my mission, but did not report Clark soon enough, but am thankful both spies were locked up at the Indian Head Proving Grounds, many miles south of Washington, DC. Also, that Miss Muriel, thanks to Mr. Harrison's borrowed agent, was identified as a journalist-turned-spy. Given her diplomatic immunity, would she try to make her presence known to me, or my sister again? I wondered if she was the driver at the Cosmos Club.

Yardley pushed me to the narrow beach near the bulkhead. There the men gathered around my wheelchair, a few stood, some sat on the bulkhead, others on the ground. Question after question they asked. How did I manage to escape the Garotte, and the gun, and then the knife. They marveled at the way I zigged and zagged and spun my wheelchair. How I held my breath and lunged for the comfort and safety of the Potomac River. Then Fritz came and he sat in front of me, while the men asked more questions than I can remember.

Lt. Edwards ran back to the Latrobe Gate and returned within minutes with an announcement. He had located an unmarked Naval truck, large enough to fit us all, plus a wheelchair. We piled in, drove through the

Latrobe Gate, and no one complained that he took his time driving the long way back to the Army War College.

When we approached the White House, someone reminded Lt. Edwards that Emma and I were staying with the Lyles. Without missing a beat, he slowly circled back to the other side of Washington, DC. I was certain that he did that on purpose to prolong the time we would spend together. The discussion at the bulkhead and in the truck was as important to the group as it was to me.

They eagerly wanted to see Mr. Lyle's home and our temporary bedroom, then we all settled in the living room. Mrs. Lyle was gracious. One look at me and she thought something bad had happened, but knew better than to ask.

Huddled in the living room, Yardley and Byer leaned against the windowsill, Edwards and Gordon on the floor, Emma sat cross-legged on the bed, and Johnston in the oversized cushioned chair. Whytock and Barnitz eventually joined us. We discussed issues in the training that had confounded us, but I did not mention my wish to train with Mrs. Hitt or Miss Smith.

The group was unrelenting to dear Emma, about her refusal to acknowledge to Lillie the bulkhead episode or the near-miss accident outside the Cosmos Club.

The sense of cohesiveness of the group was comforting and I hoped it would last. But why did they continue to stay with us, at the Lyles? I began to suspect that Yardley had mentioned that I would have a forced vacation. Instead of the group being happy, as they would have been ten days ago, they realized they might miss my sister and me.

Yardley wondered out loud that if it were not for my presence, would Weller and Holder have gone undetected. Until a later time, or not at all? No one ventured an answer.

During a lengthy discussion of our need to develop a sophisticated intelligence service on par with Room 40, Johnston explained what he, Barnitz, and Whytock had done at the Hamilton the night Emma and I moved to the Lyles' home. I did not know that Johnton was also at the Hamilton that night!

"Whytock was our point man. He hung out in the dining room,

pretending to drink. I was in the room next door, and my boss was hiding inside Room 207. Guess who showed up?" Johnston said.

"No, she didn't?" Lt. Edwards said.

"Yup. She had a card that she slipped into the doorframe and wedged the lock until the door opened. Muriel looked up and was greeted with a loaded Colt .45."

"Damn, that was close," Yardley exclaimed. "That would have been four near-misses for Annie."

"Yes! Whytock had alerted the Metro Police, and they assigned two detectives who waited in the kitchen. When she took the elevator to the second floor, Whytock alerted them, and they moved up to the second floor in the back stairwell. I waved them in. Then, the three of us left the hotel and left everything in their hands."

I thanked Capt. Johnston and asked him about the NYC bomb squad. At this point, the entire Lyle family had joined in.

Were you recruited?

"I wanted to investigate the anarchist bombings and demonstrations that were filling the headlines in the newspapers every day. If it wasn't the anarchists, it was the striking union workers. NYC was a mess. Many demonstrations occurred around Union Square on 14th Street."

"Is Union Square named after the unions?" Emma asked.

"No, it's called Union Square because it is the location of the 'union of many streets'. I think nine or ten streets enter the square," Johnston said.

"Did you witness Black Tom?" Lt. Edwards asked.

"Yes, while on a middle-of-the-night investigation near the Hudson River docks, I heard Black Tom explode."

"We read that it was wild, destroying everything in sight, including the top section of the Statue of Liberty," Emma interjected.

"Yes," Johnston said, "every barge laden with munitions destined for, we think, Russia was destroyed."

"Was it loud?" Yardley asked.

"It rocked the entire city and New Jersey. Eventually the island, which was really a massive, wide pier, disappeared into the New York Harbor."

"Why did it damage the Stature of Liberty?" Mrs. Lyle asked.

"The Black Tom pier was two-hundred yards from the Statue of

Liberty. Shrapnel destroyed much of the torch."

Yardley asked, "What about the Lyndhurst, New Jersey munitions explosions from this past January?"

"I can't discuss it." No one asked why.

Finally, Lt. Edwards asked, "How did we get duped, by two spies in the group?"

The answers did not come easy. Johnston said he has difficulty expressing himself and would prefer not to answer.

"Oh, come on, Johnston," Yardley implored but he remained quiet.

I was clearly wrong about Johnston, to think that he was an enemy spy because he was quiet and at times rude. Or that he ignored me. The face one gives to the outside world is not a way to evaluate capacity for empathy or kindness.

Byer responded that he liked Weller, "because he didn't show Annie much attention, and I didn't like Holder because he lavished attention on you."

He said he was sorry five times after the explanation.

The living room quieted but then Emma threw a book at him, "You be nice to my sister!" The laughter that followed was cathartic.

It's a good thing she did not throw a Dickens novel!

Things calmed down and Yardley became serious. "The Major and Leland have met with Dansey to establish criteria when recruiting to the MIS, ONI, MIS, or U-1. I'm assuming they'll use SIS protocols."

"How do you know?" Lt. Gordon asked.

"Remember Dansey's lectures with armed guards at the doors? He'll share administrative and organizational information next week in another lecture."

Our informal meeting wound down and gradually everyone thanked the Lyles and left. Except Johnston. He continued his conversation with Mr. Lyle and asked Emma about the accident at sea.

"You're the first person with a disability that we've met," Johnston said.

I acknowledged with a nod and waited for a question.

"On the Bomb Squad, Annie, I learned that being involved in often-dangerous activities requires a quiet life. It's lonely at times. Do you feel that way with your disability?"

Yes, at times, but I have Emma.

"The Bomb Squad almost requires we lead a secret life, like the ONI and MIS. It leads to problems in my family and with friends."

Johnston explained that life events have an impact on how spies are born but also how they self-destruct — like Clark and Weller. He offered to always be available to me, if need be, to listen. I returned the favor and hoped he would follow up with me if the need arises.

I fell asleep that night with Johnston's offer on my mind. Two weeks ago, I worried about the men. And now, what helped most? The men in my training group, yes, the group of men that had been antagonistic of my mere presence. And it didn't hurt that Emma said one of her sweet David Copperfield prayers to end the evening.

Monday's session, the beginning of our third week, was cancelled. I spent most of the day at the Sketchers with Emma.

On Tuesday we were called to a meeting in a windowless oak paneled conference room on the third floor of the War Department. The official name of the building is the State, War, and Navy Building and is across from the West Wing of the White House.

I anticipated the Major would announce assignments following completion of the third week of training. I was surprised when Major Van Deman began his discussion with the bombing of the munitions plant in Lyndhurst this past January. The explosion wasn't as massive as Black Tom, but Johnston admitted no one was allowed to discuss it.

That didn't stop the Commander who stood up. "We all know that this was another act of German sabotage. Those of us in intelligence find it worrisome President Wilson has forbidden our security agencies and the Bomb Squad from telling the truth. At this point, Wilson makes all decisions regarding our intelligence findings."

"That's not the way it is in the SIS, as Claude has reviewed with us," the Major interjected. "More than one person in the Admiralty and Parliament discuss events like this. Sabotage would never be tolerated in Great Britain."

The conversation then went in the direction I fully expected, but not the outcome I had hoped.

Van Deman discussed industrial security. "As you know this was Clark Holder's future assignment. Captain Johnston has agreed to assume this position in the ONI, and in doing so, will work closely with his old boss, Detective Barnitz. They'll also work with Spencer Eddy in New York."

He then handed out assignments sealed in AWC envelopes. Even Emma was handed a small envelope.

But my envelope was empty, and my heart sank. Emma's said envelope contained a short note that she would be *considered* for a job at the Sketchers lab. There was no mention of attending college or working toward a position in the State Department.

The Commander saw my head drop when I opened my envelope and said a few kind words. "After Weller revealed himself at the firing range, you alone, Annie, focused on Clark as a second spy. And because of that, you were prepared and fought back as best you could. Your quick thinking saved your life a third time. Annie, we think, you need to take a vacation. When I return from Europe, I'll determine an appropriate assignment."

Two days later, Emma and I said goodbye to the Lyles. Emma thanked them for taking us in. It was upsetting that Mrs. Lynch was busy at the War Department and could not drive us to Washington Union Station. We boarded a train to New York's Penn Station, and there planned on transferring to a train to Providence, Rhode Island.

Emma sensed what I knew, that this was not a voluntary vacation. I had proved myself, over and over, and yet my future was in jeopardy. And so too was it for poor Emma.

59

ANNIE

Changing trains at New York Penn Station was far more difficult than we imagined. Stairs everywhere. Emma helped me up the twenty steps from Platform Three to the cavernous waiting area, then ran down to retrieve the wheelchair and luggage. We had two hours to wait before the train to Providence departed from Platform Seven. Besides the beautiful and massive interior of Penn Station, I will never forget the hundreds of men dressed in suits scurrying to meet trains.

Penn Station is the largest public space in New York City, and it felt like it. The main lobby, if you can call it a lobby, is 150 feet from floor to ceiling, as high as Block Island's Mohegan's bluffs. Emma and I were mesmerized by the dozens of steel columns that held up a roof of glass. But it was the numerous sculptures and the fancy shops that kept my mind off the "vacation" I did not want.

"Does this mean I can't work with the Sketchers?"

Not if they don't ask me back.

"Did they say you can't come back?"

It was implied. The Commander isn't scheduled to return to the States for at least two months.

"I don't want to go back home," Emma lamented.

Neither do I. Call Mrs. Conway and ask if we can visit with her.

Emma located the main office at Pennsylvania Station. Geo's older brother and sister were telegraphers for the competing New York Central

Railroad, and they taught us how to access telephones in large railroad stations. Emma walked in the main office and, after a quick introduction that mentioned Geo's siblings, a word about me working for the Army War College, without asking any questions the clerk dialed the U.S. Weather Bureau Station at Narragansett Pier. Mrs. Conway picked up and, after Emma's short explanation, readily agreed to meet us at the Providence train station in four and a half hours.

She was waiting on the platform when the train pulled into the station. It was a long drive from Providence to Narragansett Pier and impossible to hide my sullen mood. When we arrived at Narragansett Pier, she drove past the Weather Bureau to the end of the road that overlooked the mouth of Narragansett Bay and Atlantic Ocean beyond. She turned to me right away and asked what was wrong.

I tapped a vague explanation that I was asked to take a vacation, and was not given an assignment after the training had concluded.

Mrs. Conway listened but did not ask me to expand.

Emma interjected, "I want to work with the Sketchers on campus. I prayed for that job, and love it, but now we may not be asked back."

Maybe I did not do a good job in training.

"You did a great job, Annie!" Emma said with authority.

"Well, let's see what happens. When do you think they will call you back?" Mrs. Conway asked.

A few weeks, perhaps. I am not sure.

At dinner Mrs. Conway's husband offered no opinion of my dilemma and focused on Emma's work at the drawing lab. I knew he worked for the U.S. Army Signal Service, but did not know in what capacity. He took a keen interest as Emma explained about her two-dimensional drawings of submarine cables under the English Channel.

"Interesting, Emma. You drew an undersea map of the submarine cables that were *not* cut by the Admiralty the evening the war started or shortly thereafter," Mr. Conway said. "Great idea."

"It was in 1914. How did you know?" Emma asked.

"Emma, I work for the Army's Signal Service."

Mrs. Conway and I laughed.

"Oh, sorry, I forgot. Mr. Lyle liked my project, too, and asked a draftsman to redraw my underwater map and distribute it."

"Why are they important?" Mrs. Conway asked.

"To help my sister solve a dilemma," Emma said.

"I don't understand," Mrs. Conway said.

"I don't think Annie Rose should answer that question, my dear!"

We all laughed because Mrs. Conway of all people understood the need for secrecy.

We stayed for another day until Lillie asked us to return home. Mr. Conway found an agreeable captain to take us to the Old Harbor on Block Island, and our short respite was over. Early the next morning we boarded a fishing smack out of Point Judith's Harbor of Refuge. It was an uneventful crossing, and we arrived late morning at Old Harbor. The crew lifted me and the wheelchair onto the ferry dock, and Emma carried the luggage. We thanked the crew and waved goodbye as Emma assured the captain he'd have great luck fishing Georgia's Bank.

Emma would have pushed me up the hill to Old Harbor Village were it not for a classmate that spotted us on the dock. He was driving the truck owned by Island Grocery & Market and offered us a ride. It was a small truck with room in the front seat for only the driver. It had an open back that was only five feet in length, the only one of its kind on the Island. He helped me up to the flat bed and Emma swung the wheelchair and luggage up. Emma sat holding me tight.

Without asking, he knew we were on our way to see our mother at the Block Island Post Office. He carried me from the truck to the wheelchair that Emma had placed on the front porch of the Post Office. Immediately Lillie walked out of the front door and hugged us as if we were one. If she noticed our sullen moods she did not let on. Until Emma ran to the Island Grocery & Market to find milk and muffins.

Once inside the post office and after two customers finished their transactions, Lillie asked, "What happened? I know something is wrong."

I held back the tears for as long as I could but started to cry, for myself and Emma.

I tapped, *I failed.*

"You what?" Lillie looked instantly worried.

I cannot explain. I looked down and did not look up without prodding.

Mom, I did the best I could. I completed a dangerous mission, won over the men who didn't want me there. But they sent me home.

"I don't know what to say. I'm sorry. Emma is upset, too."

Emma was offered a job at a drawing studio the Army uses to teach perspective, to estimate distances on a battlefield. She felt at home, and they paid her, too.

"Did they say you couldn't come back?"

No one else was sent home, and I am the only person to not get an assignment after the training concluded.

We sat in silence until Emma returned. We let Lillie get back to work and Emma and I sat outside on the porch and ate lunch. We were content to watch Islanders moving about in Old Harbor Village, many of whom waved hello. This we did until Lillie came outside, again.

"I forgot to mention that yesterday a short man mailed a postcard to his parents, and he asked about you, Annie. He said he heard about a smart disabled young woman in a wheelchair, and did I know of her."

"Who was it?" Emma asked. "Did he mention Annie by name?"

"Not by name but said he was aware of young woman in a wheelchair. He's staying at the Narragansett."

A man in civies staying at the Narragansett?

"He's visiting from the Newport Naval Yard."

I tapped loudly on my chair, *What did he look like?*

"He wore round glasses."

Thanks, Mom.

"Shall we get a ride in that truck again?"

Emma and I were thinking the same thing.

I raised my eyes, and Emma ran back to the Island Grocery & Market.

I will tell Mom to pick us up after she finishes work.

My classmate drove us to New Harbor and let us off in front of the Narragansett Hotel. Without explanation, Emma jumped out and ran up the short hill to the hotel's side porch. Near the entrance to the attached dining room, a man sat bundled in wool blankets. Emma recognized the back of his head and ran back to the truck.

"Thanks for driving us," Emma said with sincere appreciation. "Our mother will pick us up after work."

"Who is it?" he asked politely.

"Annie's teacher, from the mainland."

I raised my eyes to agree. Satisfied, he waved and continued with his deliveries.

The man was indeed a teacher that she met on the mainland.

"Hi," Emma called out, as she pushed me up the hill in front of the hotel.

Dansey turned his head, smiled and waited for us to get closer.

"How did you get here?" Emma asked in a quieter tone.

He responded in a whisper. "General Kuhn and I were in Newport at the Navy War College. I took the ferry to the Island yesterday."

I tapped, *We are surprised and happy to see you.*

"Welcome to Block Island," Emma said.

"Thank you. When we're not at work please call me Uncle Claude."

For the rest of our lives that is how we referred to him.

"Now I can say I've been on Block Island. Oh, I forgot, I have a short novel for you two."

Dansey reached into his satchel and handed Emma a thin book.

Emma read the title, *"The Thirty-Nine Steps.* By John Buchan."

"It's read by our soldiers on the front lines. The novel teaches how to escape and evasion using the land as cover."

I tapped, *Who is the author?*

"Buchan is a friend of mine. If you come to London, I will introduce you."

We should give you a tour of the Island and show you our "land".

Remarkably, I was no longer upset, and neither was Emma. It did not matter what he had to say.

"I trust the weather is a wee warmer in the Summer?" Uncle Claude asked.

"Yes, it's like Bermuda."

"Let's get inside by the fire. The staff at the Narragansett was told that I'm an aide to General Kuhn. Call me Captain Sherman if anyone is around us."

We entered through the side porch and sat off to the left of the fireplace. The fire was loud and drowned out the back-and-forth Morsing. Only in a building controlled by the military would three adults converse naturally in Morse Code — and not be noticed. Uncle Claude got right to the point and within the first few minutes made it clear why Emma was included in the conversation. But first came the admonishment.

Dansey: *Annie, until you have a higher rank, do not pursue answers to questions that aren't asked. You too, Emma.*

Emma: *Yes, sir. I understand.*

Dansey: *Those of us in espionage have a responsibility to keep secrets. But so does everyone else.*

Emma: *I understand.*

Dansey: *Emma, did you enjoy your interactions with Whytock?*

Emma: *Yes. And I promise not to draw any more underwater submarine maps of English Channel cables, Uncle Claude.*

He laughed, enamored with my sister's naïve sweetness.

Dansey: *Annie, the Commander wants you to return to the AWC in two weeks' time. Emma, you'll continue at the drawing lab, but you should graduate from college, if you want the challenge of working at State.*

Annie: *Where will I be assigned?*

Dansey: *If I were in charge, I'd assign you wherever you want. But I have an idea.*

Annie: *I tried so hard at the training and am grateful for your confidence.*

Dansey: *You have two options, Annie. I have recommended to the Commander and the Major that both of you could be assigned to the Port Control Officer for New York Harbor. The Port Control Officer will report to Major Van Deman in the MIS and I anticipate that it will be Ross Whytock. Other ONI and MIS officers will be assigned to New York City in a variety of capacities.*

Annie: *Why the Port Control Office?*

Dansey: *It's an important role for an intelligence officer. I established the Port Control Officer system for Great Britain, from 1914 until the end of last year.*

Emma: *What was your role?*

Dansey: *To create and manage a system that identified and prevented foreign spies from entering any port in Great Britain. Ultimately, Great Britain has not had any episode of sabotage. Unfortunately the United States has had dozens. That needs to stop.*

Emma: *What is the other option?*

Dansey nodded, then tapped: *I'm leaving the United States in the second week of July. When I return to Great Britain, I'll find positions for both of you as assistants to a Port Control Officer in one of Great Britain's harbors. If you decide to return to New York, you will be assigned to Whytock.*

"Really!" Emma blurted out.

Dansey: *I expect that your training will take a few months. Emma, you must not only accompany your sister but be an active trainee as well.*

Emma nodded and raised her eyes, surprised.

Dansey: *You will also have the option of being assigned to the Telegraph Office at the Central Post Office in London. This may be more interesting going forward during the war.*

Annie: *To work with the Postal Service Inspectors, as part of the Red Line?*

Dansey: *Yes, and you will both be employed in the same building, although in different departments.*

Emma smiled, again: *I understand.*

Dansey: *But, please, say nothing to anyone.*

I raised my eyes, twice.

Dansey: *One other item.*

I looked up.

Dansey: *You must promise that you will never tell Lillie that Germany is bombing London.*

Emma said out loud, "I'll go to my grave before I mention that!"

Annie: *You will be in your grave if you mention that.*

We spoke for a few more minutes before Dansey asked an officer to borrow a car.

"Can we borrow a Model T," Emma interjected, "to show Officer Sherman the 'End of the World'?"

The officer scratched his head but returned with permission. "You can use the car for an hour," he said.

And for an hour we showed Uncle Claude our Island. We drove north, stopping at Crescent Beach, then the North Lighthouse. We circled back to the New Harbor, driving past the Weather House and the burned out remains of the Hygeia Hotel. Down past the Hog Penn and up the winding West Side Road, stopping briefly at the Island Cemetery.

As we continued driving south along West Side Road, Dansey expressed puzzlement why there was so little vegetation on the Island, and why there were so many livestock roaming about. We explained that Islanders had over 1,000 heads of cattle, cows, goats, mules, and horses. These animals grazed the fields and consequently, little brush was left.

At one point, Emma asked him to slow down and turn into a barely perceptible dirt lane. The car slid on horse manure at the base of a small hill, but gradually it climbed the narrow, hidden entrance to what we call Lewis Farm Road. We kept driving until a few homes, several barns, and a lot of cattle appeared. We explained that we were now near the southwest point, close to the bluffs.

All first-time visitors to this part of Block Island are mesmerized. The pastures separated by low stone walls, the view of the Atlantic Ocean, Block Island Sound, Connecticut coastline, and Long Island's Montauk Point. He wanted to stop the car, but we told him to keep going, down a hill and up over a crest, toward the old salvage road that led to the base of the bluffs.

He stopped the car again as soon his eyes had an undisturbed view of the Atlantic Ocean. He looked west right away and saw Montauk Light at the tip of Long Island.

"Where are we?"

"This land is the Lewis Farm and that's Black Rock Point. Dickens Point is off to the right."

"I feel like I'm at the end of the world. Who lives in that house at the edge of the cliff, way over to the right? And am I seeing things or is that house held down by chains?"

"Four chains to be exact," Emma said. "It's a summer house. It gets windy out here, Uncle Claude, and those chains are necessary."

I tapped, *It is the Ultima Thule.*

"Not only for Block Island, but perhaps for all of the United States," Dansey added, clearly in awe.

It is perfect here, isn't it.

"I've been everywhere in the world, and this is mint, simply brilliant," Dansey said in his British accent, struggling to look for words to describe what he was seeing. "The house, the barns, the expansive land of this plateau, perfect for cattle grazing. And the sea beyond, and on three sides!"

"Everyone gets mesmerized, and no one can explain the feeling. It's just felt," Emma said. "The south and southwestern border is the Atlantic, to the west is Block Island Sound, where the land gradually meets the sound."

"Emma, is there a way to get to the base of the bluffs?" Dansey asked.

"Yes, horse carriages can wind their way down to the beach using a path," Emma explained. "Years ago it was created by the owner, to salvage wrecks at sea and to reach the fishing camps."

Livermore, the Island historian, wrote about this land, here, at the edge of the bluffs. I can quote him, 'This is where nature made one supreme and final attempt to achieve perfection. The land and sea and sky always appearing its best, in all her varied moods'.

"Who is this Livermore?"

"I'll get you the latest edition of his book," Emma promised.

Before returning to the Narragansett, we drove by Wallace's bungalow. Dansey squinted his eyes and read the inscription inside the porthole. "That's a porthole I will never forget."

At the Southeast Lighthouse, with no one around, we walked the grounds.

"Commander McCauley tells me Nicholas Ball played a big role getting this lighthouse funded, against the wishes of the Lighthouse Board. Is that true?"

"I don't know what the Lighthouse Board is," Emma said. "But the Commander must know."

President Grant visited Block Island twice. I understand that one or two years after he first visited the Island, he wrote a bill that funded it.

"I'm sure he bypassed the Lighthouse Board," Dansey said. "How many times did Grant visit the Island?"

"Twice," Emma said.

We sat mostly in silence on the drive back to the New Harbor, except for one question that I asked him about our training.

What's the most important thing about negative intelligence that I should know?

"More generally, Annie, it's important to remember, that security is the reward for unceasing vigilance, regardless of the type of mission."[10 11]

He parked in front of the Narragansett Hotel and an Ensign ran up to the car.

"Sir, a high-speed patrol boat has arrived. It's at the end of the Ferry Dock, waiting to take you to New London. General Kuhn will meet you there."

We got out of the car, and I stood supported by the car and Emma, who stepped away as I reached out to hug the British Naval intelligence officer. I tapped on his arm, *Thank you.*

"You are most welcome," he said in a quiet voice.

I then tapped, *I am as tall as you!*

I never explained to Emma why he broke out in a hearty laugh.

We waved goodbye as he walked to the end of the pier. A few minutes later we heard the roar of the engines as the Naval Patrol boat pulled away from the dock. At full throttle it left a large wake as it set a course for the Cut out of the Great Salt Pond. Soon they were in Block Island Sound on a course NWbW-bound for New London, Connecticut.

That evening, before we went upstairs to bed, Emma flipped a coin. Emma lost, and I wheeled myself into the Old Harbor Village to be as far from Lillie as possible. It was a pleasant night, without a winter wind or pounding surf to interfere with the idle conversation of Islanders in Old Harbor Village. So, it wasn't surprising that everyone could hear a woman's anguished scream and her lament: "You are not going to London! The Germans are *bombing* it!"

60

Emma and I returned to Washington, DC three weeks after Van Deman's meetings had concluded. Once on the AWC campus, before taking the long walk to Mr. Lyle's home, I said to my sister that I wanted to climb the granite steps of Roosevelt Hall.

"What? No way."

I tapped, *Hold me on my left side. One granite step at a time.*

Soon one officer after another offered to help us, but Emma declined their generous offers. Until she tired, and then she let them take over and ran down to retrieve the wheelchair. By the time she had brought the wheelchair to the top of the steps, Sgt. Lightfoot had heard the commotion and was outside waiting to greet us.

"Annie," Sgt. Lightfoot said, "there's a small group upstairs. They said to send you up if I saw you."

Emma pointed to my wheelchair, and I obediently took my seat. On the elevator ride, on every floor everyone smiled as I entered and invariably someone mentioned seeing me walk up the steps. These were pleasant welcomes of recognition, much different from those I experienced when I entered Roosevelt Hall during the early part of my training.

Emma knocked on the conference room door. Voices were heard but we could not distinguish them. The door opened easily, and we found three men. Major Dansey, Mr. Whytock, and General Kuhn. The General waved us in.

"Good to see both of you," Dansey said.

"I heard you entertained Major Dansey on Block Island," General

Kuhn said. "Welcome back."

"We arrived at Union Station an hour ago and came right here. And we are glad to be back," Emma said, smiling from ear to ear. She then turned to Major Dansey. "Mr. Dansey, here's a recent edition of Livermore's 'History of Block Island' that I promised."

"Thank you very much. Grateful." Dansey was sincere and immediately leafed through an updated history of Block Island.

Major Dansey summarized to the General and Whytock the tour we gave him on Block Island. "You have to see it to believe it, General," he said, finishing his story. He then turned to my sister.

"Emma, I'd like Annie to listen to the conversation we're having with Mr. Whytock, but it's top secret."

"Yes, of course," Emma said, getting up to leave the room.

"We'll meet you in the library, on the third floor. After that, you can report to the lab."

"Okay."

"Annie, before I forget, I set sail across the Atlantic on July 11th."

Usually when I raise my eyes it's to say, *Yes*. But this time I acknowledged a timeline to be aware of. The General read between the lines, too.

"That's a 'Block Island secret'," General Kuhn said, grinning. Whytock must have been in on the secret because he smiled and nodded in agreement.

After Emma had walked out and closed the door, I listened to Ross's new job description. I had known that his work as journalist for the *Evening World* brought him to every nook and cranny of the entire NYC and New Jersey waterfront. He probably knew more about the docks than anyone else in NYC. His title: New York Harbor's Port Control Intelligence Officer, assigned to Van Deman's MIS, not the ONI. His jurisdiction included the New Jersey waterfront, Arthur Kill — the waterway behind Staten Island, and parts of Long Island. He was to monitor all passenger and cargo ships entering and leaving the harbor. He was to work hand in hand with the Bomb Squad. Before we arrived back to the AWC, Whytock had readily agreed to take me and Emma under his wing.

"Annie, in many ways, last October, you and Geo functioned as Port Control Officers for Block Island," Dansey said.

I smiled. *But we only had three spies to worry about! You had an entire country!*

"But it was your concern that brought John to Block Island," General Kuhn added.

Mr. Whytock's responsibilities would be modeled after Major Dansey's for the past two years.[12] He was Head of E Branch and had the added responsibility of organizing Great Britain's Port Control program. One of his title's was, 'Inspector of Port Intelligence'. He was assigned both positions in August of 1915. Port security requires different kinds of professionals, at each and every port. Emma and I could fit in that section. Dansey opened visa offices in every neutral country, as well as allies, to prevent sabotage efforts. As he explained to us on Block Island, his program was a resounding success because England had no port sabotage.

"Compare that to the long list of sabotage efforts of the German Embassy in the United States," Dansey said, in a very quiet modest tone.

During the conversation I was stunned when Ross Whytock mentioned his interactions with Gaunt and Weisman last fall, and then spoke of familiarity with London. I was puzzled because I did not realize local NYC journalists travel to England.

I tapped, *Were you in London recently, Ross?*

"The eleventh of December. It was colder than NYC."

"You mean the twelfth of never," Dansey interjected abruptly, changing the subject.

Had Dansey and Whytock made each other's acquaintance in the past, through the British Intelligence Office in NYC? Or, last December when Whytock was in London?

I took mental notes of the conversation and Dansey's organizational skills. There's little doubt in my mind that in the four months Dansey will be stationed at the Army War College, he will be able to create a foundation for Van Deman's entire intelligence organization. And, most importantly, one that interacts with other services, including, of course, Britain's SIS.

General Kuhn ended our meeting by announcing that Tunney would report for duty to serve in the MIS in a few days' time. At that point Ross

Whytock and General Kuhn took their leave.

Major Dansey remained seated, and I fully expected another round of reprimands. I held my head high. But he remained in a chatty mood, asked a few more questions about Block Island, and then recounted at length his rough ride on the Naval Patrol boat when he left the New Harbor for New London, Connecticut.

"Everything was okay until we cleared the Cut. Oh my, was Block Island Sound rough. But the worst was when we passed the Race Rock Lighthouse and entered Long Island Sound. It was awful."

He talked about the wind, the waves, the sudden reduced visibility, and the extreme difficulty docking the boat at the submarine base dock in New London. During the telling of his story, I tried to contain a laugh but could not. But what I learned was that he was personable and kind man; I looked forward working with him if that was in my future.

On the third floor we found Emma sitting at the table in front of the couches. I observed the manner Major Dansey interacted with Emma and wondered how often he was indeed this relaxed. The fact that he included Emma in my plans was revealing. After meeting him on Block Island, I think affection is a proper term to describe how I feel toward him. I wonder if other of his colleagues in Great Britain feel the same way.

In the library Dansey repeated his version of the "rough waters of Block Island Sound" to Emma. But she gave him no quarter. "Rough? Would you like to hear about our accident at sea?"

He smiled, shook his head, and asked to see the headlines Emma had been reading. We were amazed at the bold headlines in the *Evening World*.

"Mr. Dansey, every headline is about union strikes, the war, New York City anarchists, or bombings."

"It's the world right now, Emma. It's the world right now."

"I don't understand the anarchists, Mr. Dansey," Emma said.

"Neither do I, but they are quite common, here and elsewhere in the world."

The three of us left Roosevelt Hall together. Dansey's armed guard met him in the lobby, and at the foot of the granite steps, Emma and I waved goodbye as Dansey's car drove him to the British Embassy. We would have one more encounter with him before his departure for London on the 11th of July, at which time instructions for us to board an ocean liner bound for Scotland was handed to me in a sealed envelope, in code.

Emma pushed the wheelchair to our second temporary home on the far side of campus. We were delighted that Mr. and Mrs. Lyle were still willing to 'house' Emma and me. They were also pleased their son returned for dinner more frequently.

That afternoon, when Emma showed up at the Sketchers lab, a notebook with a new assignment was in her locker. But there was no sign of her previous project. And when I reported to the ONI's main office in the Naval Building, I was no longer assigned to the negative intelligence section run by Capt. Taylor's secretive MI 3C.

The Navy Building I was assigned to was on an isolated section of New York Avenue. Few know of this section of New York Avenue, between 17th and 18th Streets. It was located near the War Department and walking distance to the West Wing of the White House. The building is a grand old structure, with high ceilings, marble floors, and walls lined with portraits of Naval heroes.

My sole responsibility was to learn coding with Sergeant Yardley, soon to be appointed by Congress as the Director of the Code and Cipher Bureau (MI-8) on June 10, 1917. My second assignment had been cancelled: I had looked forward to studying the German Embassy's efforts – from 1914 until this past February when Bernstorff was escorted out of our country – to support Wilson's neutrality policy. I wanted to discover how the German Ambassador functioned as Germany's chief spy for North America, to understand how he used negative intelligence to that end. I found it unconscionable that while Bernstorff tried to convince citizens to support Wilson's neutrality policy, he also directed German sabotage activities. I wondered if that pattern would repeat itself in our democracy. But I would no longer be able to do so. In its place I was handed a top-secret file to study; I was only allowed to read the document in the private library of a senior naval officer on the fourth floor. It was the final report written by Dansey of his accomplishments as SIS's Port Control Officer for Great Britain.

I never discussed with anyone my concern that Room 40 intercepted and deciphered messages off of our State Department cable, and where those messages were intercepted. My thought was it had to be at Whitehall, rather than a relay station on the coast. Why? I reasoned that only employees of the SIS's Room 40 could be trusted to intercept secret messages off our dedicated diplomatic cable. After all we were the best of allies.

I fully understood that the techniques and deviousness of Germany's negative intelligence efforts were far worse than the brilliant cunning of Room 40. The Brits influenced our country *to help our country*. Germany influenced our country – with sabotage, murder, and theft – *to help their country*.

The day before Dansey left Washington for New York City, he handed me an envelope in the presence of Major Van Deman.

"Annie, the Commander and I have read the contents of the note," Major Van Deman said. "It's up to you."

The note was not signed. 'You have impressed for many reasons. You understand the value of espionage and the influence it can have on the course of history. In a democracy, the influence is beneficial because it is dedicated to help the entire country. In dictatorships, espionage appears to primarily benefit the leadership, to keep them in power, and not the citizens. Countries without an intelligence service are manipulated by those with them. The British Secret Intelligence Service has and will always support England's sovereignty to prevent wars and keep the peace. I would like to see you learn from the best. As discussed, when you are on your way, the ONI will contact us, and an agent will meet you at the dock. You can rest assured that if the bombing of Central London continues, we will assign you to a port of entry well north of the city.'

To be continued ...

Notes

The theme of *Annie Rose* explores various aspects of disability culture and 'sisterhood', while the plot focuses on the emerging American intelligence community of 1916-17. The subplot of the Zimmermann Telegrams represents an unusual and rare example of foreign negative intelligence. Rare because it was executed by our closest ally.

Annie's conclusion is reasonable: if President Wilson had abandoned his commitment to neutrality, particularly after Bernstorff's widespread sabotage and misinformation campaign came to light, the British Secret Intelligence Service/Room 40 would not have exaggerated the significance of the telegrams. After all, why would they jeopardize one of their most closely guarded secrets? Wilson argued against isolationism, yet favored appeasement, and clung to neutrality despite that being the position of isolationists. A confusing contradiction.

She also wondered why Wilson did not *value* an active, comprehensive intelligence community, and she was not surprised when, at the end of the war, Wilson had Secretary of State Lansing write a memo stating the U.S. did not need a permanent intelligence presence. Were they not aware that an active intelligence community can uncover secret motives and intentionality of foreign governments? A global world view requires an understanding of all nations, and an active intelligence agency would support this objective. Is it possible that Wilson believed intelligence agencies would circumvent democracy?

By the early 1900s, Winston Churchill, Professor Ewing, and others in the Admiralty had learned the importance of a permanent, highly-secret intelligence community, and vigorously supported its operations. This view would have helped President Wilson achieve his vision of a United States with a global reach, a country that he believed was destined to be a world leader among peaceful nations. This fit perfectly with Alexis de Tocqueville's vision of a Pax Americana, primarily because of America's unique experiment called democracy.

The Historical Notes section can serve as a quick reference to characters in the novel, as well as individuals and events in the WW1 era.

Note: Some entries are spoilers.

Historical Notes

Including organizational meeting/training attendees
Roosevelt Hall, Army War College, Early 1917

Coordinators of organizational meetings/training sessions:

Major Ralph Van Deman, Director MIS, and later the MID

Rear Admiral Ed McCauley, acting director ONI; reporting to Roger Welles, Chief of the Office of Naval Intelligence

Participants/invitees Representing Office of Naval Intelligence:

Annie Rose, 22 years old — initially recruited to the MIS Code section. Neither the MIS nor ONI have cypher sections early in war, therefore she is considered for Capt. Taylor's secretive MI 3C, as she appears to have a talent for negative intelligence. She is eventually accompanied by her 19-year-old sister, Emma. Interactions between themselves and the men are a window into various aspects of the culture of disability.

Mrs. Harriet Lynch, War College staff member, assigned to Annie.

George Barnitz, Former Deputy to Tunney at the NYPD Bomb Squad[13] — late arrival.

Elizebeth Smith, Riverbank. *Heavily recruited* by Van Deman and the ONI, but she declines.[14]

Representing Van Deman's new Military Intelligence Service:

Capt. Harry Taylor, one of twenty-three former NYPD Bomb Squad members recruited to the ONI, or MIS (later called MID). He creates MI 3C for guard duties and counterintelligence activities. Office at 310 E Street, NW, DC is *highly* secretive. Arrives in third and final week of meetings.

Sgt. Lightfoot, Roosevelt Hall guard, friend of Mrs. Lynch.

Anna Keichline, invited but delayed; assigned to Capt. Taylor.

Capt. Johnston, NYPD Bomb Squad. Sends telegram to his buddies at the Bomb Squad mocking Annie's disability. She intercepts said telegram.

Royal Weller, lawyer, recruited to develop language section for Van Deman.

ENS Clark Holder, recruited to develop industrial safety/prevent plant sabotage.

Bill Byer, friend of Yardley from the Signal Corp, but not State.

Capt. Barnitz, NYPD Bomb Squad.

Roslyn (Ross) Whytock, specifically recruited by Van Deman to be head of NYC's Port Control section in the MID. He stays at the same hotel as Annie.

2LT Peter Gordon and Lt. Edwards, previously assigned to Roosevelt Hall, Army War College.

SFC Tom Yardley, assigned to the U.S. Army Signal Service/State Department.

Professor John Manly, University of Chicago, invited, delayed. Becomes deputy to Yardley. (Manly made short order of invalidating Riverbank's bizarre Shakespeare/Bacon Theory.)

Guest speakers and observers:

Claude Dansey, the only agent assigned to the Army War College to work with Van Deman. He is part of British Secret Intelligence Service,[15] Whitehall, and is the third high-ranking agent from Britain's SIS assigned to the U.S. (The first is Guy Gaunt, the second is William Wiseman.) How does (then) Colonel Dansey find himself at the War College in the first place? Dansey, is chosen to accompany Lord Arthur Belfour, the British Foreign Secretary, to sail to Washington, DC, along with a large contingent of British Officials.[16] Dansey is listed as a member of the War Department. This ship arrives after the U.S. enters the war. Ultimately SIS/MI6 sends ten officers to the British Intelligence office in Washington, and seven officers to the New York City British Intelligence office which is under the direction of Wiseman. Before WW1 ends, under Cumming/Vernon Kell, Dansey heads up the MI6 sections on military and political affairs; shortly after he is reassigned to the MI5 to work directly with Vernon Kell. It is unknown how closely the ten agents assigned to the Washington office work with Major Van Deman, Leland Harrison, the ONI, or the Secret Service, if at all. As usual, he keeps a low profile. Few are aware of his mission, and fewer still of his association with the SIS. Before Balfour dines at the White House with President Wilson and Colonel House, Dansey has already introduced himself to General Kuhn and Major Van Deman at the Army War College.[17] The question of his involvement in the Zimmermann Telegrams episode remains unknown.

Major Van Deman must create a comprehensive organizational structure for the MIS. Major Dansey walked up the granite steps of Roosevelt Hall at the right time. He is known as an excellent administrator, extremely knowledgeable about German propaganda and sabotage, and essentially aware of everything in the world. Dansey fit the role perfectly and Van Deman a good student. His advice was never recorded by design, but it impressed General Kuhn who was present for his top-secret lectures. Kuhn and Dansey develop a good relationship and perhaps it is fortuitous that Kuhn oversaw the Army War College. For Van Deman's trainees Dansey brought German intercepts that were initially decrypted by SIS's Room 40 cryptologists. In one very top-secret lecture, with multiple armed guards at the doors, Dansey encourages Van Deman to embed intelligence agents in American corporations that have overseas branches. But the most important secret lecture, also with armed guards at the doors, concerned the organization of the SIS. Never had the inside the Admiralty been exposed to outsiders. (In the novel, only a few trainees were invited to attend allowed in that lecture.) Van Deman followed that system as best he could. And lastly, but not least, Dansey stressed the importance of passport control; he helps Van Deman choose Ross Whytock as the Port Control Officer for NY Harbor and surrounding regions. (How British Intel infiltrate NYC's passport office will not be discovered until 1918.)

Leland Harrison, experienced, highly-intelligent diplomat. Becomes ad hoc supervisor of Annie Rose. Director of the State Department's small intelligence unit, the Bureau of Secret Intelligence, later U-1 and U-3. Secret Service agent Joe Nye is the first agent Mr. Harrison hires, after Nye's successful mission at the German Embassy. Mr. Harrison runs U-1 as an 'interagency coordinator of intelligence', the first of its kind.[18] *Note: The Bureau of Investigation, Justice Department, becomes active in negative intelligence months after the passage of the Espionage Act of 1917. The novel ends before it is operational.*

Parker Hitt, "Father of American Military Cryptology". Lectures to the training group, with his wife, Genevieve. He is heavily recruited by Van Deman, but ultimately sails with General Pershing to France. Considered the foremost American cryptologist for years, until William Friedman took that honor.

In 1916, **Spencer Eddy**, Former State Department Diplomat, and former Secretary to John Hay, a towering figure in American politics. Eddy is recruited by FDR to create the ONI's NYC branch office. A Harvard grad, he is the first of the Ivy League university graduates recruited by FDR and Roger Welles. (FDR created the Naval Reserve Force.) Many of these Ivy League recruits were part of the inner circle of Welles. Eddy actively recruited individuals to FDR's Naval Reserve Force, and for Plant Protection. Eddy was assigned the responsibility of the General Electric plant Schenectady, NY, and as well as Elmer Sperry's Plant. He is a late arrival to Van Deman's meetings because he'd been active in the ONI for a year. Reported his frustration with management at the GE plant; it takes a while but eventually he works well with Elmer Sperry.[19] Spencer Eddy also develops close working relationships with NYPD Bomb Squad detectives, those that enlisted in the ONI and MID and those that remain on the Bomb Squad. His photo is included in Tunney's *Throttled,* the summary of the Bomb Squad's accomplishments.

Characters with mentions who had overwhelming impact on WW1-era events:

President Wilson; his unofficial foreign policy advisor, **Edward House**, NYC; **Walter Hines Page**, Ambassador to Great Britain; **FDR**, Asst Sec of Navy, DC; **Winston Churchill**; **Arthur Balfour**, British Foreign Secretary; **Professor Ewing and Reginald Hall,**[20] British Secret Intelligence Service/

Room 40; **Guy Gaunt**, SIS, of extreme import, was present in Mexico City to facilitate the resending of the Zimmermann Telegram text back north to our State Department[3], works closely with Wilson's Secret Service and the NYPD Bomb Squad, and is a "friend" to the newspapermen, **John Rathom**, editor of the *Providence Journal* and **Frank Cobb**, editor of Joseph Pulitzer's *Evening World*; Bomb Squad also works closely with Wilson's Secret Service; **Charles Apgar**, in early 1914, is the first to record Morse Code onto Edison's wax cylinders (father of Virginia Apgar). This is extraordinarily important for Annie Rose, for obvious reasons. We cannot leave out: **Admiral Sims**; the Great **General Pershing**; the not-so-great German Ambassador to the U.S. **Johann von Bernstorff**; the German Kaiser **Friedrich Wilhelm Viktor Albert**; and of course, the German Foreign Minister **Arthur Zimmermann**.

Characters with brief appearances, and a few for historical interest:

Lillie Rose, Annie and Emma's mother.

Miss Sarah, maid, Hamilton Hotel; functions as an agent on the ground, as many maids have done through the years.

George (Geo) Washington Eddey, Major, U.S. Army Signal Service and Chief of the Weather Service on Block Island. Uncle to Annie and Emma; no relation to Spencer Eddy.

John, ONI supervisor for Annie; he recruits her to the ONI after working with her on Block Island in October 1916. Before he is reassigned to the Caribbean theater, John sails from Block Island to Maine to evaluate a site for ONI's new powerful radio receiver. This is a superlative example of a public/private partnership, common during the WW1 era. When the ONI adds a powerful transmitter a few miles distant to the receiving station, Otter Cliff becomes the most powerful and secretive wireless transmission installation in the world. Of note: direct communication from Otter Cliff to the White House is by private cable.

The Chief of the Army War College, **Brigadier-General Kuhn**, (Van Deman's supervisor prior to reorganization under the General Staff of the Army) is highly regarded by Claude Dansey, and vice versa. Kuhn had been appointed to the AWC in January 1917, after returning from Germany where he was an Army attaché (a spy) assigned to our Berlin Embassy. He supports Major Dansey's contributions to the organization of the MIS, soon to be named MID. Did Dansey know of Kuhn before meeting him at the AWC?

Lawrence Sperry: The sisters first meet the son of the industrialist, Elmer Sperry, on Block Island's New Harbor Dock in October 1916, the day after he crashed on Block Island. He introduces Annie to the concept of the "Air Scout". They continue to fawn over him.

Mrs. Conway, Head Weather Observer, Narragansett Pier, RI. The only woman in the United States Weather Bureau awarded forecasting privileges. She encourages Annie Rose to use telegraphy to communicate complex thoughts.

Lieutenant Cole. An experienced Navy radio operator assigned to the Otter Cliff receiving and transmitting tower on Mount Desert Island. He accompanies John and the sisters from the Hog Penn to Governors Island in New York Harbor.

Irving Ball, owner of the Hamilton Hotel, Washington, DC, where Annie, Emma, and Whytock stay. Irving is a direct descendant of Nicholas Ball, known as the 'King of Block Island' by the *New York Times*, and a distant uncle to the sisters. The Hamilton Hotel is approximately equidistant between the White House and the German Embassy, which Bomb Squad detectives call, "the Embassy of Destruction".

William Wiseman was assigned to the NYC office of British Intelligence in the fall of 1915. Because there is no documentation that he interacted with Van Deman to help establish the MIS division at the Army War College, Wiseman is not included as a character in the novel. His contribution primarily evolved into a diplomatic role rather than an intelligence role. At this time, Dansey was masterminding Great Britain's Port Control system, which prevented any incidents of sabotage during WW1.

Guy Gaunt, from an accomplished Australian family, is a British Naval Attaché assigned to DC in early 1914.[21] A mishap in the Royal Navy lands him his first job as an agent for the SIS.[22] His boss when he starts is possibly Professor Ewing, then Cumming, and after that, perhaps Admiral Hall. He understands the extent of German CI, and develops an astonishing relationship with fellow Australian, John Rathom, Editor-in-Chief of the *Providence Journal,* since 1912. Gaunt's efforts represent an early success to counteract clandestine German sabotage and their misinformation campaign. Soon after, Gaunt develops a close relationship with another newspaper, this time through President Wilson's Secret Service detail, as well as with the contacts of the SIS. Gaunt and Dansey both represent the British Secret Intelligence Service, but they have vastly different roles, and their interaction is elusive. He remains in close contact with Wilson's Secret Service until the day he leaves the United States.

In early July 1915, Mansfield Smith Cumming, director of the newly-created Foreign Intelligence section of the British Secret Intelligence Service (eventually called MI6), sends a memo to Guy Gaunt with explicit intelligence data that the Germans are well into a sabotage campaign against American trade. He is directed to meet with NYPD Commissioner Wood (Tunney's boss) and Franklin Polk of our State Department. *It is important to emphasize that this is before either of the MIS/MID and U–1 is created.* There is no evidence of contact with the ONI. It is unknown if Bell is involved in this episode. Polk is a friend of Wilson. After the meeting in NYC, Polk reports directly to the President. If Wilson was unaware of German sabotage prior to this, which is unlikely, he knows now. But his appeasement of Germany continues unabated. Fortunately, the industrialists in the United States are planning for an eventual war.

In January 1916, Mansfield Smith Cumming realizes a need for a full-fledged, secret office in New York City. He recruits Weisman, then Capt. Norman Thwaites, a complete novice, recently returned from the front with a non-life-threatening injury.

But Cumming knows full well that Thwaites, as an intelligence officer, has a long-standing relationship with the publisher of *Evening World*, Joseph Pulitzer, and its editor-in-chief. Pulitzer is highly respected but so too is one of his journalists, Roslyn (Ross) Whytock, who knows everything there is to know about shipping and passenger movements in and out of New York Harbor, and reports on it regularly. His name rarely appears, anywhere. Gaunt interacts with them, also, and at this point is living in NYC. It has been reported that at the end of the war, before Gaunt leaves America, the Bomb Squad and members of Wilson's Secret Service give him a hearty series of goodbyes at various NYC bar and restaurant venues.

Gaunt has the editor's ears at two newspapers to which he provides war related information: The *Providence Journal* and the *Evening World*. It is important to note that when a major NYC public relations firm is contacted by German propaganda officials ... those German officials wish to counteract truths that originate from and published in ... *these two newspapers.* And it becomes a certainty that 1) information provided by British intel is accurate, and 2) the German Embassy funds both propaganda and sabotage efforts. Where did that intel originate? And how did they obtain it? Unknown, because these are stories that by their very nature are resistant to the telling.

In 1916, the NYPD Bomb Squad under Tunney's direction is the best we had to uncover German sabotage and it is not surprising that Van Deman recruits Bomb Squad members to his MIS. But the Bomb Squad never had legal authority to investigate sabotage, they were detectives who entered the fray after explosions. Therefore, they were unable stop or even identify the German saboteurs of Black Tom in July 1916. They knew it was Germany but could not prove it. They also could not predict the sabotage of the Kingsland Plant in January 1917, which turned out to be the last major sabotage of the Germans in the U.S.

There are few remaining records of the *Evening World's* Roslyn Whytock, and those that remain may not be accurate. We know he was a true patriot. When Ross asks to enlist in the American Expeditionary Forces, to join his younger brother, Lt. Norman Whytock who is scheduled to sail to France, the War Department says, "No." When he asks why, they respond, "You are exactly where we want you to be, in NYC at the *Evening World*, where we can use you to our best advantage." Soon, Whytock is ordered to report to Major Van Deman at the Army War College. (Whytock's father, a physician, is often asked why he named one of his sons, Roslyn: it's a town outside Edinburgh, Scotland.)

What's a code? An example from early 1917 from *Colonel Z*: If one uses the second letter in every word ... the embedded code for, "Pershing sails from N.Y. June 1" ... can be found in this sentence: "A**p**parently, n**e**utrals p**r**otest i**s** s**h**arply d**i**scounted a**n**d i**g**nored. I**s**man h**a**rd h**i**t. B**l**ockade i**s**sue e**f**fects p**r**etext f**o**r e**m**bargo o**n** b**y**products e**j**ecting s**u**ets a**n**d v**e**getable o**i**ls."

An original source regarding Dansey sailing to the U.S. with Arthur Balfour, the British Foreign Secretary, and arriving in the United States on April 21, 1917: Charles H. Towne, ed., *The Balfour Visit: How America Received her Distinguished Guest; and the Significance of the Conferences in the United States in 1917*. This large mission deals with joint war measures, not aspects of other issues Balfour is known for. (New York: George H. Doran Co., 1917, 15-24). Data of Dansey in Mexico City during the time of the Zimmermann Telegram has not been found. A delegation from France, headed by René Viviani, a former premier, and Marshal Joseph Joffre, arrived two days after Balfour's contingent. Their influence has not been recorded.

Not for distribution/Publisher's notes

While in Paris, after the war, I spoke to Annie Rose about her experience at the ONI. This is what I recollect from our long conversation:

Major Van Deman supported General Pershing's effort to expand the network of field intelligence officers that collected and analyzed information from the front lines, and when the Great War ended in November of 1918, the Major played an outsized role maintaining security for Americans at the Armistice meetings.

Annie Rose considered John her first mentor, the Major her second, and Dansey her third. The Major was involved with Military Intelligence Division until 1929. After that he collected information on domestic and foreign individuals, privately, with unknown funding. Was he trying to emulate Z company? The day after Van Deman died in 1952, Hoover sent agents to his home to remove all files. Although Van Deman supported industrial security, most efforts during the war years were assigned to the Office of Naval Intelligence. The ONI continued to place Naval Attachés in various countries worldwide, but industrial security fell by the wayside, and they focused on protecting harbors, because they alone had the ships.

Regarding Black Tom (Pier) Island and New York Harbor: It has been written that the ONI sent a memo to the Chief of the Army War College warning about an impending explosion on Black Tom Pier. If so, why didn't the ONI protect the man-made pier that was used as a storage depot for munitions? A lot of munitions? Dansey told Annie that Black Tom was an operation of Section P of the German Military Intelligence group.

What's one difference between Churchill and Wilson: Their opinions concerning the need for intelligence services. Churchill knew the value;

Wilson shunned it. Leadership in political and military ranks matter, and they chose different approaches. Wilson ignored danger; Churchill confronted it whenever, and as early as, possible.

Toward the end of the war, Rear Admiral Roger Welles, Director of Naval Intelligence, wrote: "Our National Government encounters Germans in sixteen different ways, through fourteen bureaus in our State, Treasury, Post Office, Interior, Agriculture, Commerce, and Labor. It is well known in this country that the Germans established a "wonderful" spy system. It is probable that there is not a manufacturing establishment in the U.S. that does not have at least one paid agent of the German Government." Did anybody listen to his plea? President Wilson ignored it.

In 1917 the success of Britain's Secret Intelligence Service was due, in part, to vigilant oversight by Churchill and others in the Admiralty and Parliament. Another reason for its success: Extreme secrecy. Churchill's interest in espionage was long standing and continued until the day he died. Yet, Professor Ewing, often overlooked, must not be ignored. The signals intelligence infrastructure to monitor espionage in Great Britain was a direct result of his contributions. He had the technical knowledge to establish a comprehensive wireless and cable network in Britain, which became the domain of the SIS, with a small part 'operated' by the Royal Post office. Ewing included 'intercepting stations' scattered on the coasts and, of course, in the basement of Whitehall. *How many times did Churchill say that Ewing saved the British Empire?*

Annie Rose was fascinated with 'mistakes' and how they might reverberate through time. In 1919 she thought a most tragic episode occurred regarding the Office of Naval Intelligence. Hundreds of ONI personnel struggled to solve the mysteries of espionage. Never in her waking life did she believe she would hear that a Vice-Admiral would say, "There was no need for an ONI." But that is what Albert Niblack, Welles replacement, wrote in 1919. The ONI had lost its way, and, unfortunately, 1919 was also the beginning of the decline of the MID. And President Wilson set the tone for such decisions.

Gary E. Eddey, New York City
See: Eddey.com

Endnotes

1. https://www.history.navy.mil/research/publications/documentary-histories/wwi/may-1917/rear-admiral-william.html and https://www.history.navy.mil/content/history/nhhc/research/publications/documentary-histories/wwi/may-1917/rear-admiral-sir-dud-0.html.
2. Attendees at the meetings and training sessions can be found under Historical Notes, most of whom Annie meets. Embedded in the list are Annie's antagonists, her friends, the antagonists that become friends, and her friends that become antagonists. It also includes important historical figures of WW1.
3. Lowenthal, M. *Vigilance Is Not Enough.* Chapter 5. Yale University Press, 2025.
4. During the meetings Annie identifies several falsehoods of the Zimmermann Telegrams, but the one she was reprimanded for would ultimately be kept secret for twenty years. Besides this novel, the best reference is: David Sherman (2020), *Barbara Tuchman's The Zimmermann Telegram: secrecy, memory, and history*, Journal of Intelligence History, 19:2, 125-148; and Mark Lowenthal, *Vigilance is Not Enough*, 2025.
5. For an introduction on the culture of disability: Eddey, G. and Robey, K., *Considering the Culture of Disability in Cultural Competence Education*, Academic Medicine, Vol. 80, 706-712 (2005).
6. Smoot, Betsy Rohaly (2017), *Impermanent alliances: cryptologic cooperation between the United States, Britain, and France on the Western Front, 1917 – 1918*, Intelligence and National Security, 32:3, 365-377.
7. Smoot, Betsy Rohaly. *Parker Hitt*. University of Kentucky Press, 2022.

8. Stout, M. (2017) World War 1 and the birth of American intelligence culture, Intelligence and National Security, 32:3, 378-394.

9. In retrospect, this was the moment when Dansey became worried about my reasoning ability, to arrange pieces of a puzzle that no one else appeared able, or interested, to do.

10. Did Dansey have anything to do with the "messages" to and from Mexico City, where a man with similar features was seen?

11. Andrew, Christopher. *Defend the Realm. The Authorized History of MI5*. Alfred Knopf, 2009.

12. Northcott, Chris. *MI 5 at War 1909-18*. Tattered Flad Press, Chevron Pub., 2015.

13. Tunney, T and Hollister, P. Throttled. *Detection of German and Anarchist Bomb Plotters*. Small, Maynard & Comp, 1919.

14. Fagone, J. *The Woman Who Smashed Codes.* Dey St, William Morrow (2017).

15. Read, A. and Fisher, D. Colonel Z. *The Life of a Master of Spies*. Hodder and Stoughton, 1984.

16. Charles H. Towne, ed. *The Balfour Visit: How America Received her Distinguished Guest; and the Significance of the Conferences in the United States in 1917*. George H. Doran Co., 1917.

17. Although the French also sent a contingent to visit Wilson, there is no evidence that an intelligence official met Van Deman at the Army War College. But, Viviani and Joffre were awarded honorary doctorates at Columbia University.

18. Mark Stout (2017), World War I and the birth of American intelligence culture, Intelligence and National Security, 32:3, 378-394, pg. 380.

19. Dorwart, JM. *The Office of Naval Intelligence. The Birth of America's first Intelligence Agency, 1865–1918*. Naval Institute Press, 1979.

20. Friedman, W and Mendelsohn, C. *The Zimmermann Telegram*, War Department; Chief Signal Officer, USG Printing Office (1928) pg. 24.

21. Arsenault, M. *The Imposter's War*. Pegasus Books, 2022.

22. Delano, A. *Guy Gaunt.* Arcadia Publishing, 2016.

About the Author

Annie Rose is the second novel by Gary E. Eddey. His first, *The Weather House*, introduced the protagonists, Annie Rose, her sister Emma, and Block Island, their Island home. *Annie Rose* was inspired by multiple true stories. This adventure focuses on the intelligence community *before* the United States enters WW1.

With the two sisters as protagonists, Eddey merges an in-depth knowledge of the culture of disability with a story of our fledgling intelligence services before the United States enters the Great European War.

Eddey lives and works in Manhattan.

Acknowledgements

Many thanks to my editors Cliff Carle and Sharon Zinc. My readers and longtime supporters, Sandra Saunders, Jo Ellen Rust, Pamela Sumler, Annmaria Mazzini, Tim Strelitz, Tom Pichi, and Grayson Eddey. To the artist, Maria Krasinski, who drew the cover and artwork, thank you! The Block Islanders: Martha Ball, George Mott, Bob Downie, GS, Carder Starr, James Murray, and his parents, Bill and Marie. And of course the late Samuel Truesdale Livermore. Rhode Island Booksellers extraordinaire: Bob Ryan, Sue Martin, Susan Bush. To those who know history matters more than anything: Cedric Leighton, Military Analyst, 8th Air Force, 70th Wing, and so much more; his palpable interest in history and his world view contributed greatly to the direction of the novel; Rob Simpson, National Cryptologic Museum, the most enthusiastic Librarian/Archivist I've ever met; Mark Stout, PhD, for sharing his expertise about American Intelligence during WW1, including references; Dave Sherman, PhD, who wrote the definitive paper on the Zimmermann Telegrams and provided guidance on historical details not otherwise available; Deirdre E. O'Regan, an old friend, the editor of Sea History; Nadine Thompson, the gold standard in caring for individuals with complex disabilities; Rashanna Lynch, MD, a role model who inspired a character in the novel; D. Thomas, whose historical anecdotes are scattered throughout the novel; Pam and Ian Lyle, distant first cousins, who introduced me to John Buchan and the importance of his novel. To the most gracious and helpful Danita Norville, Cornell Libraries. The staff at the Milstein Research Library at NYPL. Professors Larry Epstein, PhD and Todd Collins for their encouragement.

To the late Fritz, a loving, loyal, powerful, and cherished Cão de Água and his mom, D. Bustamante, who shared his kind spirit. To Dr. Ken Robey, my collaborator. Most importantly I am grateful to my patients and their parents who taught me all there is to know about disability culture. To my family, including those-who-wagered-I'd-never-finish-the-manuscript: John, Rachel, Annie, Jim, Emily, Eric, Wynn, Roy, and Joel. Finally, Annie Rose is dedicated to my seven grandchildren, for whom I added the twenty-two references.

About *Annie Rose*, a novel

Set on Block Island, Rhode Island, the island home of Annie Rose and her younger sister Emma, and Washington, DC, Annie Rose is equal parts mystery, adventure, WW1 historical fiction, and international espionage. The novel was inspired by multiple true stories. It is a classic American tale of rugged individualism at a time of unflinching sense of purpose and ability, and where the line blurs between villain and hero.

It's early 1917. On the Army War College campus in Washington, DC, Major Ralph Van Deman struggles to develop his Military Intelligence Service (MIS). In total secret, a British Room 40 agent, is invited to the Army War College by General Kuhn to help the Major organize his new service. Under armed guard, this agent provides a structure for Van Deman to follow.

On Block Island, an unlikely candidate waits for an offer to serve with the Office of Naval Intelligence. Against all odds, Annie Rose, our 22-year-old protagonist with a significant acquired physical disability, is determined to contribute to the war effort, but if selected, will she overcome obstacles her disability presents?

Annie Rose, an acute observer of everything, explores issues encountered by America's fledgling 1917 intelligence community: learning coding, identifying spies in the ranks, understanding the true story of the Zimmermann Telegrams, and of course witnessing the unrecognized influences of Britain's Secret Intelligence Service.

Through the actions and behaviors of Annie, her younger sister Emma, and the men at the Army War College, the novel reveals various aspects of disability culture, the importance of 'sisterhood' and demonstrates that although navigating the intrigues of espionage is difficult, the challenges faced by our female protagonist at the Army War College are as formidable, if not more so.

www.ingramcontent.com/pod-product-compliance
Lightning Source LLC
LaVergne TN
LVHW051023080826
845145LV00009B/2783